STEROID BLUES

Other books by Richard La Plante

Mantis
Leopard

Hog Fever

RICHARD LA PLANTE

STEROID BLUES

FORGE

A TOM DOHERTY ASSOCIATES BOOK ■ NEW YORK

This is a work of fiction. All the characters and events portrayed in this novel are either fictitious or are used fictitiously.

STEROID BLUES

Copyright © 1995 by Richard La Plante

All rights reserved, including the right to reproduce this book, or portions thereof, in any form.

This book is printed on acid-free paper.

A Forge Book
Published by Tom Doherty Associates, Inc.
175 Fifth Avenue
New York, N.Y. 10010

Forge® is a registered trademark of Tom Doherty Associates, Inc.

Library of Congress Cataloging-in-Publication Data

La Plante, Richard.
Steroid blues / Richard La Plante.
p.   cm.
"A Tom Doherty Associates book."
ISBN 0-312-85810-8
I. Title.
PR6062.A66S74   1995   95-2067
823'.914—dc20   CIP

First edition: May 1995

Printed in the United States of America

0 9 8 7 6 5 4 3 2 1

For Paul C. Mims, my teacher

ACKNOWLEDGMENTS

Lt. Martin Taylor
of the Philadelphia Police
Department

Doctor Stephen Renzin

Doctor Simon Holmes

Mr. Peter Gordon

Terry O'Neill

Terry O'Neill's Fighting
Arts International

Dave Hazard

Betina Soto Acebal

Bernie Price

Better Bodies Gymnasium

Ollie Odebunmi

Nigel Foster

Liz Thorburne

Those who look too often in the mirror will see the devil behind them.

Anonymous

STEROID BLUES

PROLOGUE

It is one o'clock on a Friday afternoon. It has been snowing, but the temperature has risen and now the four inches of clean white powder have turned to one half-inch of slush. A perfect color match for the Delaware River which sits like a strip of dull silver less than three hundred yards from the red brick house on Front Street.

The house is tiny, less than twenty feet wide, and known as a "Trinity" because of its three-storey configuration—father, son, and holy ghost. Constructed in the middle of the nineteenth century, when the Southwark area of Philadelphia was the hub of shipbuilding and commerce, it is one of three buildings on Front Street that have not been restored. The other two are condemned, but the Trinity is a preserved property of historical interest. It will be renovated, as soon as the City Redevelopment Authority allocates the necessary funds.

In the meantime, the Trinity has a solitary occupant.

Jack Dunne.

Jack lives behind curtained windows and triple locked doors. Most of his time is spent in the basement, a square, windowless room with a distinct odor: a pungent mix of mildew and human sweat. The mildew is caused by the nearby river while the other smell, the human smell, is Jack's, the result of hundreds of hours invested in the creation of his body. His creation, however, required more than time, effort, and sweat: it required racks, benches, and iron weights to exercise his muscles; anabolic steroids to increase their mass; recovery time; and strength. Plus, a "body bag"—the type that boxers use—four feet high and stuffed with dense cotton fiber, to relieve his frustration, and a full-length mirror, with two naked light bulbs overhead, to view his accomplishment.

Other than the mirror, Jack requires no visual stimulus.

No television, no books or newspapers. He has a telephone, but he has not answered it in two years.

Jack has just finished his morning workout, and eaten the second of the six meals that he eats every day; this one began with a serving spoon of amino acid powder placed beneath his tongue. The powder smells and tastes like rotten eggs, but Jack is used to it. In fact, he believes the more horrible the taste, the bigger the rush of nitrogen to his muscles. Following the powder, he ate a dozen cooked egg whites, and half a skinned chicken, all grade "A" protein.

Now, he sits in his kitchen, in a red, vinyl-covered chair in front of a Formica-topped table. There is a cheap, battery-operated tape recorder on the table.

"Hello, my name is Jack. My name is Jack Dunne." He speaks into the recorder. His vocal cords are thick and fibrous, and his voice is a low tenor.

He repeats these two lines many times, stopping after every three or four takes, to rewind and listen, increasing the volume of his voice as he warms up, forcing it higher and higher. By his tenth repetition he is shouting into the recorder, shouting at the top of his lungs, until each word feels like a shred of glass, tearing the lining of his throat, causing his vocal cords to rip and his voice to break, rising from tenor to soprano. Then, he sounds like a woman. Almost.

At this point Jack changes his name to Jacqueline, so that he is screaming, "Hello, my name is Jacqueline. My name is Jacqueline Dunne!!!" Over and over again, the scream evolving to become a shriek, and the statement, a plea, "Help me!! Help me!! For Christ's sake will somebody help me!!" He continues until he is exhausted, physically and emotionally. Then he presses the "stop" button, and stares at the recorder. He appears frozen, his entire body locked and rigid. Sometimes he remains like this a few seconds, at other times it can be minutes, even hours. He is hallucinating; dancing devils with long, shining hands, moving towards him, touching, probing, tearing, their steel fingers forcing inwards, against his flesh. His muscles seize as he locks his thighs, protecting his groin, trying to keep them out. Hunching forward in the vinyl chair, arms crossed in front of him. From far away, as if in another realm of consciousness, he hears music. An orchestra is playing; a pounding bass drum, and crescendoing violins, joined in great, powerful swells of sound. The sound of music and the sensation of pain fuse in blood-stained harmony. He sinks lower in the chair, squeezing his eyes shut. He feels cold hands on his body, prodding and pushing. "Dead?" A hissing voice enquires. "Dead?" Yes, he is dead. His personality has fragmented. "Dead?" Yes. His will has dissolved. He is a corpse by the time they bundle him into a metal coffin. The highway is a distant rumble beneath him. It drolls on and on. Finally, the coffin is opened and, for a moment, he can breath. Then, he is lifted up, and dropped into a sea of rotted flesh; the stink swallows his remains.

The explosion comes as a relief, a blinding fire and a deafening roar, blasting the polarity of his inner vision, turning all colors then to stark black and white, dissolving his memory. Even the pain, that feels like a fat needle pushing through the socket above his right eye, dulls with the quieting pulse of his heart.

Another space of time and Jack Dunne begins to move, tentative at first, as if to ensure that his bones and muscles still function, rotating his shoulders, twisting his neck, massaging the knuckles of his hands. At last, he pushes the "rewind" button on the recorder, turning the volume knob all the way up before pressing "play."

It takes a moment for his ears to adjust to the frenzied noise, to recognize the voice. Finally, he stands and looks down at the recorder. The voice sounds shrill and far away. Flat and tinny, as if it is coming from another dimension. It is Jacqueline's voice. Terrified. Shrieking for help. For rescue.

"Help me! Help me!!"

Jacqueline's pleas continue as Jack Dunne lurches to the far end of the small kitchen, pulling open the door which leads to his basement. He runs down the steps, propelled by the screams behind him.

His body bag hangs from the ceiling, waiting for him. In the darkness and shadows the bag has many faces. Jack Dunne hates each of them. He begins pounding with his right hand, working the weight of his enormous frustration and anger into each blow, his arm cocked and fist thrown from the shoulder, smacking into the tough hide strongly enough to make the stuffing fly from the top. He grunts and shouts as he explodes into each punch, cursing the faces he sees staring at him from the smooth surface of the leather; using both hands now, changing the angle of his attack by bending down and uppercutting, the force of his blows causing the chain to go momentarily slack as the hundred-pound bag lifts upwards. By the time he stops, Jacqueline is no longer screaming.

Jack returns to the kitchen, then climbs the stairs to the top of the Trinity. There is a single bed in the room, a chair like the chairs in the kitchen and a wooden night table, on top of which a carved crucifix sits perched beside a reading lamp with a dull white shade. There is a bottle containing one-hundred tablets of Valium, ten milligrams per tablet, beside the crucifix. Next to the Valium is a small, self-sealing plastic bag containing ten grams of crystal methamphetamine.

Jack Dunne walks to the bed, pulls back the red woollen blanket and top sheet, sits down, unties the laces of his training shoes, slips out of them, then slides his sweating body beneath the sheet and blanket. Just to be sure of a good rest he grabs the bottle from the night table, uncaps it, and shakes two Valium into the palm of his hand, then swallows them without water.

Jack Dunne sleeps in constant motion. Even with the muscle relaxant his body twitches defensively against the hard mattress. But at least he is unconscious.

Four hours later he is seated on the edge of the bed; his head feels thick and his thoughts are not clear. *Is it time?* He takes a quick look out the single window in his small, rectangular bedroom. "Dusk," probably about five o'clock in the afternoon. He bends over the table and pours a three-inch line of the tiny white crystals onto the smooth, dark wood, chopping them with the razor blade that he keeps inside the bag, then drops his head down, over the powder. He holds his left nostril with his index finger and inhales through his right. The meth goes up in a single snort; that's the advantage of his new, splayed nostrils, just one of the side-effects of the anabolic steroids that he's been using, continually, for two and a half years.

The meth burns as it hits the back of his sinus cavities and his head clears instantly. He licks his middle finger and touches the finger to the remaining powder, rubbing the finger against the vein beneath his tongue.

Then, Jack puts his training shoes on and returns to the basement, walking straight to his medicine cabinet. He opens the metal door and removes an Upjohn pharmaceutical bottle, containing one hundred 10 ml. tablets; the tablets are halotestin, a steroid developed in 1957 to stimulate the growth of the penis in underdeveloped, adolescent males. Strength and aggression are a side-effect of the drug. Jack places three of them underneath his tongue and a handful more in the pocket of his training pants before returning to the upstairs of the Trinity.

He showers with cold water, towels dry, then pulls on a pair of tight jeans, a T-shirt, and lizard-skin cowboy boots. Everything is black, including the long overcoat that looks more like a cape than a topcoat. He takes the tablets of halotestin from his training pants, wraps them in Kleenex, and puts them into the pocket of his jeans. Looking at himself in the mirror, he combs his hair using his fingers, and rubs his right hand over his moustache and beard, making them lie down, silky against the thick, tawny skin of his face. Finally, Jack picks up a pair of deerskin gloves, the regulation riding gloves that motorcycle policemen wear. Soft and pliable, they will allow his hands a full range of movement.

The methadrine really kicks in as he closes and locks the door of his house. His heart is beating like a trip hammer and his senses are heightened. He walks into the cold wind, and has a rush of paranoia. Is he being followed? He turns several times and searches the darkness. Nothing. He continues to walk.

By the time he hits Head House Square, with its beautifully restored shops, restaurants, and ice-cream parlors, he is surrounded by people: shoppers, diners, folks out for a stroll. He can feel the heat from their bodies as they pass; but now, his paranoia is under control, and he is reciting something that sounds like a line from a Clint Eastwood film, not so much in content, as in tone. He repeats it over and over again, deadpan.

"Hello, my name is Jack, I'm a friend of the Horse, he said you might be able to help me." He keeps his voice low as he speaks.

A few people glance at him as they pass; he is very striking. Six feet tall and two hundred and twenty pounds, extremely broad at the shoulder and disproportionately narrow at the hips, dressed entirely in black and wearing what appears to be a cape, with flowing blond hair, and a tightly cropped beard, emphasizing the heart-shaped line of his jaw. Mumbling as he walks, eyes dark, pupils dilated, and staring straight ahead. A man with a singular purpose. He'd be handsome if it weren't for a particular quality to his demeanor, a kind of "craziness" that distorts the features of his face and creates a distinct aura around him. That, and his mumbling, cause the other pedestrians to give him a wide berth.

"Hello, my name is Jack, I'm a friend of the Horse, he said you might be able to help me."

BONES

Every bone in this man's body appears to have been broken." Doctor Josef Tanaka's voice was a thin whisper, "I'm talking literally, every bone. Look at his feet, even the phalanges of his toes have been crushed." He spoke as he peeled the sheer stocking down and over the swollen right knee, lifting the victim's calf slightly as he rolled the silk along the jagged bones of the instep and off, away from the foot, "the stockings are perfectly intact, almost certainly put on after the incurrence of the injuries."

Captain Bill Fogarty listened and stared. "Ugly feet, yellowed with callous and blotched with red, fat and splayed, short ringlets of black hair growing in clusters on the toes and along their tops. Everything flattened, as if the feet had been hammered or stepped on with great force. The terrible wounds made more perverse by the fact that they had been encased in delicate silk stockings." His eyes trailed up. "Ugly feet to match ugly hands" . . . Thumbs that were out of proportion . . . too long, almost the same length as the index fingers . . . and each finger bent and broken, some ripped at the base, severing the webbing between them . . . others forced backwards, left hanging only by tendons and ligaments. . . . This had been a cruel death. Cruel and ugly, but then violent death always emphasized the ugliness of the human body. Every imperfection seemed to glare.

Fogarty felt something akin to pity for the man in the chair. Pity and shame for this final indignity; of having a team of people examining his nakedness, recording it, analyzing it. The captain lowered his head and, just for a moment, closed his eyes, breathing inwards, exhaling slowly. As if he was performing some secret incantation that would separate him from this inhumanity. When he opened them, he had regained his "third-party" perspective. Clinical, detached, as if he was watching a movie. Participating in it and watching it at the same time. His "survival" perspective.

In the background, several feet from the chalked perimeter surrounding the dead man, a photographer, assigned to the mobile crime unit, was operating a hand-held videocamera, using the zoom lens to record details of the body in relation to the desk, two chairs, filing cabinet, examining table, and bookcase in the medium-sized room. The electric motor which operated the zoom made a quiet whir as it slid into focus on the frozen eyes bulging from the slits in the leather hood which covered the victim's head. Beneath the eyes, two further openings in the leather revealed a cartilaginous mass which had once been a nose and a mouth full of broken teeth, pieces of which were scattered, along with a dozen tufts of coal black hair, within the chalked perimeter. A dark leather, silver-studded dog harness was fixed around the man's neck and the adjoining leash, with its nickel-plated chain and hard, rubber hand grip, trailed down his back and on to the parquet floor. Below the harness, down from the broken sternum of his hairless chest, beneath his navel and shaved pubis, his penis was dark and contracted; there was a visible tear in the skin beneath the glans, and a small pool of dried blood on the swollen and distended scrotum.

"Make sure you go from the wound on the genitalia to the gold ring below the chair," Tanaka instructed, drawing the photographer's attention to the piece of jewelry lying on the floor.

The zoom lens moved forward, obeying the doctor's orders.

"The guy was wearing a cockring, and whoever did this tore it out," Tanaka whispered to the captain.

"Christ." Fogarty spat out the word. He was already figuring this one as some kind of cult murder. The stockings, the mask, the dog harness; he'd seen it all before. Cross dressing, sadomasochism. And sometimes it got out of hand. Way out of hand.

"You look like a spare prick at a wedding," he said, turning his attention to the young detective who was standing on the outside of the chalked perimeter. The captain's tone was meant to sound buoyant, but inside, he was descending rapidly into a deep depression. *I'm not gonna be able to just pick up my marbles and leave. There just had to be one more. One more to get through.* Fogarty was thinking of his retirement, of Santa Fe, New Mexico, of Diane Genero. Of everything that would put some distance between himself and the greyness of this city and the greyness of the last ten years. *There just had to be one more.*

The detective looked up. His name was Dave Roach and he was twenty-six years old. His red hair was already going at the crown and he had a nervous twitch which caused his left eye to open and shut as the subcutaneous muscles convulsed in spasm beneath the socket.

"Don't want to disturb anything, Sir," he answered, winking four times at the captain while purposely avoiding the corpse in the chair.

"Good thinking," Fogarty answered, winking back once.

The preliminary phase of the video recording was complete and the photographer, female, black, and young—everybody seemed young to Fogarty, he was at that time of life where anyone below forty looked like a teenager—had placed her camcorder in its metal box and was getting her Nikon ready to reproduce the crime scene in stills.

The uniformed "beat" officer who had discovered the body, by virtue of a hysterical Filipino cleaning lady, babbling something about the "Antichrist" and pointing towards the red brick, two-storey Delancey Street townhouse, which was the home and registered office of John Winston Flint, M.D., was securing the crime scene by way of standing on the front steps and turning away the few people claiming to have appointments and discouraging others, passersby, drawn by the police cars and ambulance.

Two more men, attached to the mortuary, were preparing the body bag in the far corner of the twenty-by-twenty-five-foot room.

Josef Tanaka was concentrating hard. In the three years that he had been assistant to Bob Moyer, the city's medical examiner, this was the first time he had handled a scene-of-crime investigation on his own. But today, there had been no alternative. Bob Moyer was on his back in a hospital bed recovering from amoebic dysentary, leaving Josef Tanaka in charge and a younger man, one year out of medical school, assisting him.

Tanaka had already estimated the time of death to be between eight P.M. and midnight, which made the corpse, at best, eight hours old.

Eight hours. A lot can happen to a human body in that time. Heat production ceases at the moment of death, leaving the body at a continuous, measurable rate. Causing everything to contract, every organ. Particularly the largest organ, the human skin.

Which meant that the one area on which they may have discovered the killer's identity, through fingerprints, was the most unreliable surface to powder and test. Too much distortion or actual disappearance of finger prints on the human flesh.

Which was a pity, because, by the nature of the victim's injuries, Josef Tanaka reckoned that the killer's prints would be all over him.

Fogarty was standing at the far end of the room, studying the single-entrance door. There was no sign of forced entry. *Had to be somebody he knew. A friend, a patient—*

"Bill . . ." Tanaka's voice sliced into his thoughts.

Fogarty turned.

"I'm ready to remove the hood from his head and cut him loose from the chair."

"Okay," Fogarty answered, then, glancing toward one of the mobile crime unit officers, "why don't you lift the prints from the desk and dust the restraints, harness, and hood; there's bound to be something on the hood."

The man nodded, lifted his print pad and walked toward the body, leaving Dave Roach standing alone by the mahogany desk.

Fogarty stepped closer to Roach. Out of earshot from the rest of the people in the room.

"I believe this is your first murder investigation, detective?"

Roach looked up as the flash from the Nikon backlit Fogarty's head, adding shadow to the scarred side of his face. *He killed his wife and daughter in a car accident*, he thought. Everybody on the force knew that about Captain William T. Fogarty. That's where the scars came from. God, what would it feel like to have that on your conscience?

He met Fogarty's eyes. Forcing himself to hold the contact, trying to keep his mind and eyes from the scars.

"Yes, sir. My f . . . f," Roach stammered, inhaled, then pursed his lips and expelled a quick little blast of air, followed by the word, "first." Roach had learned the technique in speech therapy; the breathing exercise was intended to calm him but, when he was particularly nervous, the out-breath sounded like a whistle.

Fogarty dug deep into his drying well of compassion.

"Well, you're starting at the top. 'Cause you won't see many worse. . . . Now," Fogarty's voice became more practical, matter of fact, "I need good people on this one. No slackers . . . do you understand me?"

The flash exploded again and the scarred side of Fogarty's face appeared to turn from yellow to stark white.

He waited.

If Roach wavered Fogarty was prepared to drop him from the case, then and there. If Roach was weak, he was gone.

"I'm going to be fine, Sir."

"Good . . . then why don't you go and take a look at the other parts of the house, bathrooms, bedrooms—"

Roach nodded again and walked towards the door connecting the office to the living space.

Behind them, Josef Tanaka had slipped into a pair of latex

gloves and was squatting down, between the legs of the man in the chair, lifting the gold cock ring with a pair of tweezers and placing it into a small plastic bag. He stood up and stepped back, allowing the mobile crime officer to dust the hood.

BANDAGES

Not far away, in terms of city blocks and traffic lights, Doctor Rachel Saunders was seated in front of what appeared to be a mummy. She was unwrapping the mummy's facial bindings.

"How long am I going to look like a chipmunk?" the mummy asked.

Rachel Saunders smiled, a very warm but very professional smile. It was the kind of smile developed after being asked the same question, or a variation of the same question, over two hundred times in the past twelve months.

"Mearl," Rachel spoke the mummy's name as if she were a schoolteacher reasoning with a small child, "it's been five days. You're an exceptionally fast healer. And you don't look like a chipmunk."

"Well I feel like a chipmunk," Mearl Glinger complained.

"C'mon, you're going to look beautiful."

"When?"

Rachel unfurled the last of the long bandages and examined the hard swelling beneath her patient's chin, then moved her fingers gently up along the bridge of Mearl Glinger's nose.

The fifty-six-year-old interior designer had admitted to having had one previous "lift," and one "nose job," but, judging by the scar tissue that Rachel had uncovered; she'd estimated the number of Mrs. Glinger's previous procedures to have been closer to four.

"Ten days for the discoloration around your eyes, three weeks for the initial swelling, then, four to five months for everything to return to absolutely normal."

"Five months?! I can't stay locked up in my house for five months."

"You won't need to. In fact, put on a pair of dark glasses

and you can be back at work on Monday." Doctor Saunders's voice grew more authoritative.

"Five months, it's never taken five months before."

"That's just my point, Mearl," Rachel continued, examining the razor-thin, pink scar tissue directly behind her left ear. "I've had to go over a lot of rough work. Where did you say that you had this done?"

"Once in L.A. and once in London," Mearl admitted, leaving out the first "lift" in Atlanta.

"Well, whoever worked on you last should reconsider their career."

"It never looked any different. I kept saying that to my husband. All the way to England for what? You know, trying to be discreet. Like I was on 'holiday.' And nobody ever noticed any difference. I never looked any different."

"Well, you're going to look great now."

"George, my husband, said if I had it done again I'd end up with a beard."

Rachel nodded as she eased the last stitch free from the closed incision beneath her patient's left eye and replaced the tough thread with a butterfly bandage.

"Ouch! You know what he meant, don't you?"

Rachel was concentrating so she didn't answer.

"That I'd be wearing my pubic hair on my chin," Mearl Glinger explained.

Rachel laughed lightly.

"All these stitches can come out at the end of next week," she said. "In the meantime, get a nice pair of dark glasses."

"I've got 'em with me. Armani tortoise shells. George gets them wholesale in L.A. when he's out there on business. Which is very frequent recently. I keep wondering if he's got some young toosh out there? And I've been through all this—"

"Mearl," again the voice of the schoolteacher, "after this heals, George isn't even going to 'look' at any young 'toosh'."

"I notice you don't use your married name, Doctor," Mrs. Glinger commented. "Very wise in this day and age. Stay as independent as possible. I'll bet you make more money than your husband anyway."

Rachel smiled and clipped the bandage into position.

About twenty times the amount to be exact, she thought, wondering what Josef's early morning call had been about. "A homicide," that's all he'd told her.

After Mearl Glinger, wrapped in her artificial leopard-skin coat, wearing her white turban, and hidden behind her wholesale Armanis, exited Rachel Saunders's office, the doctor poked her head out of the examining room.

There were five patients waiting, in various states of bandaging: three looked like Egyptian mummies, the recent recipients of full "lifts"; one was wearing a tape-covered splint across the bridge of his nose; and another, a woman, was in dark glasses, an "eye job." Two more patients waited in the two other examination rooms adjacent to the one that Rachel had used for Mrs. Glinger. A full house.

Her secretary, Marge Yates, turned round.

"Josef called yet?" Rachel asked. They were supposed to have dinner tonight. She, Josef, and Bill Fogarty. At Bookbinders.

Marge looked disturbed.

"No. Nothing from Josef, but I had another of those calls. That makes two this week."

Rachel walked to Marge's desk. "From the breather?" she whispered.

"I don't like it," Marge Yates insisted.

Rachel nodded her head.

"I'll mention it to Bill Fogarty tonight; Josef and I are seeing him for dinner."

Marge nodded and looked up at her boss.

"Is he kicking?"

Rachel pressed a palm, inwards, against her belly.

"We don't know if it's a 'he.' I'm not letting them tell me. But it's kicking."

"I'll bet Josef wants a son," Marge said.

"He does," Rachel answered, smiling. Then she straightened, pulling the fabric tight across her stomach.

She was five months pregnant and it was just beginning to show. She reckoned she could work till the last month, seeing patients anyway, then start again a few weeks after the delivery.

"Okay, what have I got," she asked, turning and looking towards the closest examination suite.

"Murray Shosput," Marge confirmed, then whispered, "formerly, Murray the 'Shnoz'."

Rachel laughed.

"Watch out, now that he's been de-beaked, he thinks he's irresistible."

Margery Yates watched as her boss disappeared through the lime green door. She truly admired Rachel Saunders; the blue eyed, honey-blonde doctor seemed to be everything that she, the plump, mousy-haired secretary, was not. And Rachel Saunders had a man, a "man and a half," Margery was fond of saying when referring to Josef Tanaka. And here the doctor was, at thirty-seven, carrying her first child, and working as usual.

The reason Marge's admiration had never turned to outright jealously was that she had seen the price of Rachel's life. Known the trauma she had endured. Living with the "man and a half" had incurred its own karmic debt. Rachel had been involved in two of Josef's cases, neither by her own choice. She'd suffered a stress disorder as a result of the first, and had been forced to shoot a man to death at the conclusion of the second.

That which does not kill us, serves only to make us stronger. Margery Yates had memorized Nietzsche's line in college, for an exam. Then, the words had made little sense to her. Now they did. Rachel Saunders was one strong woman. Marge truly admired her guts and her determination, but she would not have traded places with her employer; the price of strength was too high.

The office phone was ringing again, all three lines. Marge

pressed the button on the first as she lifted the handset to her ear.

"Hello. Dr. Saunders's office."

Nothing. Just a vacant hollow. Not even the sound of breathing. But someone listening. She was certain someone was listening. The feeling sent a chill up her spine. She disconnected the caller, trying to force the feeling away.

DISTORTION

There's a few prints here, Captain, but I'm afraid there's a lot of distortion," the mobile crime unit officer announced, using his rubber lifter pad to remove an impression of the fingerprints from the back of the leather hood.

"Get what you can, take them across town and get 'em run through the computer. Maybe we'll be lucky."

The man did as he was told, and made a fast exit from the premises.

Now it was Tanaka's turn.

"It would be better to record this with the videocamera, you can do the stills afterwards," he said, positioning himself to the side of the body.

The lens whirred and Tanaka used a long-bladed scalpel to slice through the leather strap, several inches back from the buckle. He spoke to the camera as he worked.

"I am now removing the harness, leaving what appears to be a nickel-plated buckle intact, as I believe the buckle may be the cause of strangulation, although as the harness is removed it becomes apparent that the victim's neck is minimally bruised and only slightly furrowed."

Tanaka ran his fingers gently across the flesh to the front of the corpse's throat.

"It is also apparent, after a superficial examination, that cartilages of the trachea are intact, although examination of the hyoid bone will require internal examination. This does not rule out strangulation but," Tanaka leaned forward and carefully, with the aid of a set of tweezers, lifted the left eyelid of the hooded head, "the conjunctival surface of the inner eyelids and the eyeballs reveal no bloodspots, indicative of hemorrhaging. This would indicate that death was not caused by strangulation leading to asphyxiation."

Fogarty listened, jotting down notes, and making his own

pencil sketch of the crime scene. Video and stills were one thing but, sometimes, a detailed pencil sketch contained a different kind of clue. Something subjective, something the mind noted at a subconscious level that caused the hand to enlarge it in perspective.

"I am now cutting away the hood which covers the victim's head; it is made of a coarse-grained black leather and contains a single zipper in the rear." Tanaka continued, looking up at the photographer, "Concentrate on the head region."

The zoom extended and the leather hood fell away. The head tilted slightly forward, held rigid by the muscles of the neck, already in the middle phases of rigor mortis. The region to the front of his head, forming the hairline, was covered in small, scabbed wounds.

"The victim was, at one time, the recipient of a hair transplant, and the plugs have been pulled from the anterior region of his head and dropped to the floor," Tanaka noted.

Then he bent down and studied the blackened, grotesquely swollen features of the face, superficially examining the fractured eye sockets, crushed cheek bones, torn ears, and half-open mouth. Finally he ran his fingers across the depressed sternum in the center of the shaved chest.

"I may have a cause of death."

Fogarty stopped drawing and took a step closer to the corpse.

"Tell me."

"This man has been bludgeoned or punched so hard in the sternum that I believe his xiphoid has punctured his heart."

"Speak English, Josef," Fogarty said.

Tanaka turned towards the video recordist.

"You can shut that thing off and do some stills." Then, towards his assistant, "You keep taking notes."

The young man said, "Yes, Sir," and continued to record Tanaka's words in short hand.

"Okay," Tanaka said, focusing again on the police captain, "the sternum is this flat narrow bone, approximately six-inches long, sitting between the pectoral muscles in the front of the thorax." He traced the area as he spoke. It was radically depressed, like an extremely sunken chest.

"This upper region is called the manubrium, the middle is the gladiolus, and this lower tip, which should be approximately here, below my hand, is called the xiphoid. The manubrium and the gladiolus form an attachment for the first seven ribs and act like a bit of armor plating for the heart. The bottom piece, the xiphoid, is unattached. Are you with me?"

"Go ahead," Fogarty urged.

"Well, the xiphoid is made of hard cartilage and shaped like the downwardly projecting blade of a knife."

The flash exploded capturing Tanaka's latex finger in line with the fatal injury.

Fogarty was beginning to get the drift.

"If it is struck properly, that is, with a sharp, penetrating blow, directed upward at about a forty-five-degree angle, it will detach from the rest of the sternum and puncture the heart."

"Are you wearing your doctor's hat now or your *gi*?" Fogarty questioned, referring to Tanaka's fifth-degree black belt in Shotokan Karate.

Tanaka straightened, pulling back his broad shoulders. His body, beneath the white disposable gown, was muscular, but in an athletic sense, and very functional. Fogarty could testify to that; he'd seen Tanaka defend himself, on the floor of the *dojo* and in the street. Like trying to stop a freight train, he had surmised. Plus Josef was big, six-feet-two-inches tall and just over two hundred pounds. Huge for a Japanese man. But then Tanaka was only half Japanese, his father's half. His mother was from Boston.

"It's a hard target area, Bill. If there is any movement it's almost impossible to hit in a combat situation. But this guy wasn't moving; he was strapped to a chair."

"What are you saying?"

"It took a very strong man to do this degree of damage.

With or without a weapon, and the more I look at the victim, the more I'm inclined to think it was done with the empty hands. It's the imprint of the bruising. These are thumb and fingerprints," he explained, drawing Fogarty's attention to the blue-black marks which lined the length of the dead man's arms and legs, marking a trail of dislocated joints and broken bones.

The flash lit the discolored flesh, adding red and purple to the spectrum of injured tissue.

"Empty hands," Tanaka repeated.

Fogarty met Tanaka's eyes, picking up the flicker of certainty from inside the wash of brown.

"The killer wanted a lot of contact with his victim," Tanaka added.

"It looks like a sex crime," Fogarty acknowledged. The type of wounding, particularly the disfigurement of the face and genitals, was typical of a homosexual crime. They were often the most brutal, spurred by intense feelings of passion and jealousy.

Tanaka turned back to his assistant, "Cause of death on preliminary examination appears to be a puncture wound caused by the xiphoid cartilage detaching from the sternum and penetrating the victim's heart."

Fifteen minutes later, and the body was zipped into a plastic bag and headed for the mortuary, to be prepped for Tanaka's postmortem.

The doctor stayed behind, working with Fogarty, the photographer, and the remaining officers. By the time they were finished they had bagged tufts of hair, fragments of teeth, a gold Rolex Oyster wristwatch, and several threads of fabric, potentially from the clothes of the killer. An appointment diary lay beside the phone on the desk, and four scrapbooks of family snapshots and several framed, eight-by-tens of a dark-haired, ruggedly featured man in his middle forties— hair plugs in place—had been recovered from the adjoining rooms of the three-storied house. The man was Doctor John

Winston Flint, the registered owner of the home and residential office. Currently deceased.

According to his wall-mounted certificates, the late doctor held a medical degree from the University of Rochester, New York, with a specialty in endocrinology.

Fogarty had to ask Tanaka the meaning of the word.

"It's the study of glands, Bill, and their relation to the human body, the hormones they release and the effect of the hormones."

"So what type of patients would Doctor Flint have been seeing?" Fogarty asked, opening the diary to Friday, February 18, and checking the last entry of the day.

"Endocrinology is a very specialized field. Ten-to-one he ran a general practice out of here and acted as a consultant at one of the big hospitals."

"Right," Fogarty answered, still unsatisfied but now concentrating on the name allotted to the twelve o'clock slot in the doctor's diary: *Kimberly Loggins, problems with menstrual cycle, 648–9900, Clomid.* Beneath Kimberly Loggins's name, in appointment slots, the diary contained a series of letters, numbers, and, possibly, initials: *T.C., IOML, IO. H.N., T.E. IO, IO'S W.B., CLOMID, HCG, J.B., CBC. H.N.*

"Josef?"

Tanaka turned.

"What's Clomid?"

"It's a fertility drug. Stimulates ovulation in women."

"T.E.?"

Tanaka shook his head. Fogarty took another look at the diary, flipping through the pages. There were similar entries, penciled throughout. There was something tentative about them, something out of context with the more formal appointment entries, written clearly in ink. He bagged the diary and pocketed it.

In the far corner of the room, a detective was removing a pile of brown, manilla folders from a restored Victorian cabinet.

"Make sure you get them all," Fogarty instructed.

Tanaka was concentrating on the examination table, positioned behind a folding screen. A fresh sheet had been stretched across the padded surface, and there were three starchy looking stains on the linen.

"Bag the sheet," he said.

Something didn't quite make sense about the table. It was very modern, built in sections, with the elevation of each section electronically controlled by a set of buttons on the side console. It was also equipped with straps and stirrups. More a setup for a gynecologist than a G.P., Tanaka thought. Tanaka looked across the room and caught Fogarty's eye.

"It's a strange table for a G.P. to have."

"What's wrong with it?"

"Nothing wrong, just a very sophisticated piece of equipment. Usually in an office like this, you'd expect a more basic setup."

Fogarty nodded, then motioned to the photographer.

"Get me another set of shots of the table. From different angles, close up on the stirrups, and straps."

Tanaka made a mental note to check into John Winston Flint's medical practice. Then, walking over to Fogarty, "I'm just about there. What do you want to do?" He knew that, on occasion, Fogarty watched Bob Moyer perform the autopsy; that being present often triggered something that words and written reports left out.

"I'll wait for you on this one, Josef. Right now I want to follow up on a couple of names in this diary." He held up the Filofax. "Then I'm going to see who was around here last night. Somebody saw something. I know it."

TEARS

Jack Dunne is seated on a bench overlooking the Schuylkill River, four miles from the doctor's house on Delancey Street. He can see the Philadelphia Museum of Art, rising like a grey monolith, two-hundred yards beyond the last in the row of wooden boathouses which line the middle of the east bank of the river. Across from him, along West River Drive, and the expressway running above it, a steady stream of cars form a metal bridge between the suburbs and the city.

Jack is transfixed by the rhythm of it all: the incessant flow of the automobiles, the light wind through the trees, the way the branches bend and sway, the snow which falls in flurries, the water in front of him, the way it swells and rolls, lapping against the concrete retaining wall, moving, constantly moving. He has become a witness to this rhythm of life, but he is no longer part of it, more a shadow figure, moving outside the boundaries of time and reality.

He cried as the sun rose, hidden behind a wall of cloud, turning grey to silver, but bringing no hope to Jack Dunne. Even his tears were somehow disconnected, as if they were being cried by someone else. They burned his eyes and stung the flesh of his face. Acid tears. Punishing him.

He studies the brown water of the Schuylkill, wondering how deep it is and what his body would look like if it were to be found floating after several hours, or days. Swollen and bloated, fingers like plums, lips stretched to bursting, flesh a grey-blue. Lying naked on a cold metal table, beneath a surgeon's scalpel. Lying naked. No. He can not permit anyone that much intimacy with him. Never again. Not even in death.

Then he thinks of Jacqueline. She seems distant to him now, more distant than ever, after what he has done. He pitches forward, hands raised, palms digging into his eye sockets, as if he can block his thoughts. He retches.

"Sir. Sir." A voice breaks into his consciousness.

Jack sits up, turns and sees a man on a horse looking down on him. The man is wearing the uniform of a policeman.

"Are you all right?"

Jack stares. At first he is lost for words, as if he is being pulled back through time.

"Hello, my name is Jack," he answers.

The policeman does not appear to understand him. He begins to dismount. Jack stands up; eye-to-eye with the young man. He is recovering his composure quickly, his survival depends on it.

"Sorry, Officer," he says, controlling his voice and using the term "officer"; he knows that young policemen appreciate being treated with respect, "I wasn't feeling well. I sat down to clear my head." He trains his eyes on the suspicious face, fighting to keep his thoughts in order.

The policeman steps back and looks Jack over. His clothes seem clean and reasonably well-kept. Definitely not a street person. Then he notices Jack's right hand.

"Have you injured your hand, Sir?"

Jack follows the policeman's eyes. The knuckles of his right hand are swollen and one, the knuckle above his index finger, is bleeding.

"Yes," he laughs, feigning confidence, "I slipped." Pointing to a patch of ice on the sidewalk.

Ironically, it is the truth. The only time Jack removed his gloves was to press the digits on the telephone.

"If the ice gets any worse, I'll bet they'll call your horses in," he adds.

The young cop smiles and nods his head. Then, he adjusts his helmet and remounts his horse, never even glancing back as he rides slowly away. Jack watches until the man and his horse are a hundred yards from him, then he begins to walk in the opposite direction, towards the city.

EVIL

Birth records showed John Winston Flint to be forty-seven years old. An only child. Both his parents were alive and living in the rich suburb of Bryn Mawr and his ex-wife and two daughters had moved to New York City.

His mother and father were currently on a cruise ship, bound for China, and his ex-wife refused to make the hundred-mile journey from New York for the purpose of identifying his body.

"John was a very sick man," was all she was initially willing to say to Captain Bill Fogarty on the telephone.

"Are you talking about a physical illness?"

No reply.

"Listen, maybe if I come up there and see you—"

"You try coming anywhere near me and my kids and my lawyers—"

"Hold on, hold on. I'm not intending to cause you or your children any further hardship, but surely, at some time you must have loved your ex-husband. Believe me," Fogarty hesitated, lowering the tone of his voice, setting the bait, trying for sympathy but settling for curiosity, "no matter what problem you may have had, no one deserves to end up the way he did. Believe me. No one."

He stopped speaking and listened through the silence on the line. Waiting.

Thirty years in law enforcement had taught him one thing. Human nature was basically perverse. Even though Karen Elms, formerly Karen Flint, professed to hate her ex-husband, the captain expected her, at the very least, to be curious as to the circumstances of his death.

"Mr. Fogarty," the throaty voice began.

Fogarty listened, notebook ready, pencil in hand.

"This may sound corny or melodramatic to you and I don't

personally give a shit, but if evil had a face, a human face, it would look like John Winston Flint. However he died, I hope it was painful and slow. Now anything else you need to know, you can find out through my attorney. Good-bye." The line clicked and the connection was broken.

Fogarty made a mental note to look into Karen Elms; she obviously hated the victim. Then he placed the phone back in its cradle and looked down at the empty page of his notebook. Almost empty. Below the name of John Winston Flint, the captain had drawn a passable rendition of a death's head.

He put his pencil down and gazed out the window of his new office. New since he had been made captain, nine months ago. Now he was on the east-facing side of the Roundhouse, the city's police administration building, looking out onto Vine Street and the Ben Franklin Bridge. Across was New Jersey and the Jersey shore; the last place that he had been with Sarah and Ann, his wife and daughter, before he'd got stinking drunk at a barbecue party and had driven head-on into an oil tanker, out there on Route 70, along those desolate miles of pine trees and sand. He had been thrown free, left lying by the side of the road, looking at his wife and child through the shattered windshield of the overturned automobile. He remembered their faces, their eyes, calling to him, before the car exploded.

Fogarty felt a chill; he looked down, again, at his drawing of the death's head, then closed his eyes. Outside the window, a new snow was falling, and he could hear the distant hiss of tires as their heat turned the powder to slush against the asphalt. He had an empty, far away feeling, a dark melancholia, mixing loss with despair.

He thought of Diane Genero. He had fantasized about moving to New Mexico, to be near her, after his retirement. He needed her energy, her enthusiasm for living. He was dry. But before he was permitted this final chance at salvation, he had to get through one more bad trip on his own, one more homicide, one more bit of ugly death. That was his entrance fee.

John Winston Flint. Who was he? Fogarty wondered. *Beyond the expensive house on Delancey Street and the diplomas on his wall, who was he?*

Fogarty was about to pick up the phone to dial Josef Tanaka when his intercom buzzed.

"Yes?"

"Ah, Captain F . . . Fogarty?"

He recognized the stammer.

"That's right."

"This is Detective Roach, Sir, w . . . w . . ." Roach stopped speaking and Fogarty could hear the hollow whistle on the other end of the line. "We have something down here we think you should see," Roach said.

"What's that?"

"A videotape. It looks pretty, ah, serious."

"I'll be right down." Fogarty answered.

The audiovisual communications center of the Roundhouse is in the basement of the building. It is a three-roomed unit containing state-of-the-art audio recording equipment, a wall of television receivers, each tuned to a separate news channel, that record any data relevant to United States law enforcement, and a playback room, which contains a twenty-seven-inch square Mitsubishi television set. At any given time, one of the four police technicians who operate the equipment is available to investigating officers.

Fogarty took the elevator to the basement of the building, turned left and walked along the grey-painted corridor towards the solid metal door.

He was certain he could feel the sliver of carbon fiber, which took the place of a cruciate ligament in his right knee. The winter weather always caused it to play up and, at this time of year, the basement of the Roundhouse felt cold and damp. He imagined the implanted fibers to be rubbing together, grating, ready to tear and cripple him. He stopped, and in a much practiced movement, lifted his foot from the floor and straightened his leg. Something clicked: a bone, a ligament, a carbon fiber? And he was "together" again. Then he adjusted the lapels of his Brooks Brothers tweed and examined his blue-and-grey-striped tie for coffee stains.

"Christ, I'll be glad to get out of here," he groaned between clenched teeth as he opened the door. Inside were three detectives, one female and two males, who looked too young to be policemen, and a technician who was closer to Fogarty in years. Everyone appeared in a mild state of shock. Dave Roach's twitching eye was moving in four-four time.

"I found them in a suitcase in the closet of Doctor Flint's bedroom," Roach said, his voice stretched tight.

Fogarty looked in the direction of Roach's eyes and saw an evidence bin sitting on the table. Then Fogarty looked at Sharon Gilbey, an African-American woman in her early twenties. Her hair was cropped short and she was wearing a blue pinstripe suit and flat shoes. Like Roach, she was four years out of the police academy, and this was her first homicide.

"I've had the mobile unit go over them for prints, Captain, entered them in the records and tagged them," she said. She met Fogarty's eyes. Hers were brown and honest.

Fogarty walked to the bin and looked inside. There were half-a-dozen video cassettes.

"At first we thought they might be home movies, or something like that, so we played a couple. Just to gauge the importance of them. Before we called you in," Roach added.

"So what is it, Detective?" Fogarty was impatient.

"Well, sir, the first couple are pretty short, maybe eight, ten minutes in length. I mean the guy, the deceased, the deceased victim, was into some pretty strange stuff, you know, perverted."

"What exactly are you talking about, Detective?" Fogarty asked, walking up to Roach.

Roach took a step backward.

"I mean homosexuality, Sir, or some type of masochistic

homosexuality. It appears the deceased was involved with a number of, ah, m . . . muscle men. Letting them rough him up, throw him around," Roach hesitated, "tie him to his chair, urinate on him, even—"

"Right. I've got the picture. Can you see faces on the tapes?"

"They're all in masks, Sir."

"Well, that's not too good, is it?"

"Except the last tape, Captain. It's different than the others. It gets a lot rougher—"

"Play it," Fogarty ordered, taking a seat in the closest chair, straightening and clicking his leg once more as the lights went down and the Mitsubishi lit up.

Fogarty recognized the doctor's office immediately, the mahogany desk, the blue-green walls, and the single window with its white curtains and closed venetian blinds.

The doctor, or a man that Fogarty presumed to be the doctor, was seated behind the desk, his diplomas visible on the wall behind him. He was dressed in white examining robes and wearing what appeared to be the same Rolex Oyster that had been found on the floor beside Flint's desk; he was staring straight into the camera, his dark eyes made hollow by the shadow of a full-faced leather mask. Below, his nose appeared pink and bulbous while his mouth was not much more than a slit behind the slit in the leather. Then it began. Music. Like a crescendoing wave.

"That's from *Space Odyssey*, the Kubrick film." Roach's voice disturbed the concentration of the room.

"Thanks, Detective, I was just trying to place it," Fogarty answered sarcastically.

The doctor stood from his desk, squared his shoulders, and walked to the door of his office. Pulling it open and stepping back, all his movements precise, as if he was performing in time with the music that bellowed from the hidden speakers.

A large man filled the door frame, dressed in black trousers and a red shirt. Wearing the same type of leather mask as the doctor. The man entered, dragging another person behind him.

At first Fogarty thought the third person, hooded and wearing a denim shirt, jeans, and a dog collar and lead, was part of the game, a willing participant—a submissive—but the more he watched the more he began thinking in terms of a prisoner.

"Remove the clothing." The doctor's voice was a hard whisper against the waves of music.

Fogarty noted the steel cuffs which secured the captive's hands. *Standard police issue.* Then the white of a bra as the denim shirt was torn open. *A woman, it's a woman!* the thought shocked him, as if he had, subconsciously, predetermined the person's sex as male.

The shirt was ripped from her body. Next her bra, freeing her breasts. She stood straight and rigid, reeking terror, like an animal on the executioner's block. A few seconds later she began to shiver and shake, then spun so quickly that, for an instant, her captor lost control, almost dropping the lead. He recovered by wrenching the harness inward against her neck. She slumped forward, knees to the floor as her cowboy boots, blue jeans, and remaining undergarments were torn from her body. Then she was dragged to her feet, standing alone in the eye of the camera. Even then she retained a presence; she was statuesque, with wide shoulders, jutting breasts, and a long slender waist. Her skin was copper in color and her pubic hair rose like a golden crown from between her legs. The camera took her slowly, probing and examining, nipples to navel, nothing held sacred. She was muscular, but the muscles enhanced her body like a tailored suit of clothes, their definition adding a third dimension, something functional to her beauty.

Fogarty had never seen a body like hers. He stared at the screen. *Like a wild animal. Magnificent.* The fact that he found her attractive embarrassed him. The music stopped, and he was left with the silence of his guilt.

"This is as far as we got with it before I called you," Roach whispered nervously. Fogarty nodded his head, keeping his eyes on the screen.

The doctor took the dog lead and pulled the woman towards his examination table. She began to swing her manacled hands. Fighting hard, until the bigger of the men stepped forward and punched her once, dropping her to the floor. Then, together, the two men dragged her to the table, lifting her into position against the white sheet.

Fogarty's guilt had turned to outrage. He was seething, using every ounce of reserve to stay objective, to pick up details, gather data. He reckoned the woman to be between five-ten and six feet in height and probably one hundred and fifty to one hundred and sixty pounds in bodyweight. In spite of her size, he was amazed at how easily the big man handled her; like a rag doll. He also wondered why she wasn't screaming, until the heavy white hood lifted enough to reveal the surgical tape which held her lips shut.

The doctor unlocked her cuffs, then strapped her hands to the sides of the table, securing her feet in the stirrups as he pushed one of the buttons on the console. Her legs separated.

Now the camera concentrated on the big man; he was removing his clothes. First his wide, leather walking shoes and socks, then his shirt and trousers. Beneath, he wore a black jockstrap. Keeping it on as he posed, his body tanned and shaved, he flexed his biceps, pumping the veins until they seemed ready to burst through his flesh. Then he lowered his arms and pressed his fists into the sides of his body, inhaling as he spread the muscles of his back, his latisimus dorsals fanned outwards, wide and flat beneath his armpits, tapering into his waist.

He looked, to Fogarty, like a cartoonist's version of a warrior god, something that flashed in neon on the back panel of a pinball machine. Too huge, and too perfect in proportion to be actual flesh and blood.

A quick but noticeable splice in the tape and the doctor reappeared. Uncapping a bottle of baby oil, pouring the liquid into the palm of his hand, he applied it to the freak body, massaging worshipfully.

Fogarty noted the doctor's hands, the abnormally long thumbs. The same hands and the same man he had pitied hours ago.

The muscle god preened, moving his arms up. Allowing his anointer the freedom of his flesh as, gradually, the doctor worked his way down the glistening torso, fingers hedging toward the elastic top of the jock strap, darting in and out. Until he was on his knees, teasing the strap down and over the erect penis.

"Jesus Christ, the son of a bitch has got no balls," Jimmy Stark, the third detective, uttered from the corner of the room.

Fogarty ignored the remark and stared at the screen.

"Maybe he's a eunuch," Roach offered.

"Be quiet." Fogarty ordered, but what they said was apparently true. The giant had no visible testicles and his scrotal sack seemed to have withdrawn into his body.

The doctor stroked the man's penis, squeezing and kneading its swollen head, then abruptly stopped, stood, and stepped back towards the examination table. He pressed another button on the console and the entire configuration of the table changed, the upper portion of the woman's body dropping while her pelvis was repositioned down and forward. Easy access for the muscle god. Yet he was unable to enter her. He pushed and prodded, struck her once in the face. When he stepped back, his penis had wilted.

There followed a snapping sound off-camera, above the swelling strains of music, like rubber against skin, and when the doctor reappeared he had removed his watch and was wearing latex gloves and carrying a long metal tube. He took his place at the foot of the examination table and attempted to insert the tube into the woman's vagina, peering down the end as he worked.

"Some sort of optical device," Roach said, as if by speaking he could relieve the horrible vacuum of the room.

"It's a speculum, a gynecological instrument," Sharon Gilbey confirmed.

The doctor was forcing the speculum and his prisoner was resisting, perhaps by some involuntary contraction. And the hooded doctor was becoming increasingly brutal.

"I can't watch anymore of this." It was Stark's voice, from the side of the room.

"Stop it there," Fogarty said.

The technician hit the "freeze frame" button, halting the tape on a close-up of the doctor, bending forward, putting his full weight behind the speculum.

"Oh, man, this is makin' me sick," Stark rasped.

"Turn it off!" Fogarty snapped. The screen went black.

"Get me some light."

Stark, nearest the exit door, turned on the overheads.

"Listen," Fogarty began, keeping his voice soft and controlled, looking from young face to young face, "you people are all new to homicide. Well I'm going to tell you something, plain and simple. It's one of the ugliest areas of law enforcement. You are forced to see the human species at its lowest. Human beings doing things to each other that no other animal on this planet would ever do. If you allow yourself to identify with any of what you see, or are obliged to witness, you will lose your belief in man, in religion, in authority, even in yourself. The kind of sickness on this video cassette is exactly the kind of thing I'm talking about. Man at his lowest, sickest. I know it's ugly, I've seen the same kind of ugliness before, believe me, I've seen it. And it still makes me feel the same way you're feeling now. Makes me ask the same questions. About the types of people out there. About why I do what I do. About God." Fogarty was into it now, a lot deeper than he had intended when he shut off the tape. And each of the young police officers was listening. No laughs, no snickers, no embarrassment. Listening. "It gives me the same sick hollow in my gut, makes me angry, indignant. Makes me want revenge. Makes me think that that sick bastard in the doctor's uniform, waltzing around on that videotape, that same sick bastard we found tied to a chair and broken to pieces, got exactly what he deserved. That's how it makes you feel, doesn't it?"

Again, Fogarty searched from face to face.

Roach and Gilbey remained stone still. Stark was nodding his head in agreement.

Fogarty held his eyes on Stark.

"Well, if you can't control that feeling, put it way back in your mind, or your heart, or wherever feelings go, then you'd better get the fuck out of this job." *Which is exactly why I'm getting out*, he thought, adding it like a mental postscript to his own soliloquy.

There was a moment of silence.

"Now, Mr. Stark, I'm not keeping you on this case anyway, so there's no need for you to stay—"

"But, Sir—"

"I don't need you, Mr. Stark. As simple as that. I'll see that you're reassigned."

Jimmy Stark nodded silently. His round face looked a mixture of defeat, relief, and uncertainty. Mostly uncertainty.

"This isn't a demotion, son, I just have too many first-timers on this case already," Fogarty lied, then waited for Stark to leave the room before turning to Sharon Gilbey.

"I'd like to stay attached, Sir," she said.

"So would I, Captain," Dave Roach added.

"Then let's finish watching this thing," Fogarty said, settling back in the chair.

Fogarty had lied to all the young detectives.

He had never actually dealt with anything as upsetting as the video cassette found in John Winston Flint's suitcase.

In the past, he had seen the results of torture and perversion, victims twisted and mutilated, organs removed and bodies dismembered; he had seen photographic stills, not scene-of-crime stills, but photographs taken for or by the perpetrator, for the purpose of pleasure or blackmail, or both. But these were all "after the fact." He had never, until this instance, seen such a graphic "moving picture" of the crime in progress.

He got back to his office, closed the door, and phoned Josef Tanaka.

"I have a positive I.D. on the body," Tanaka said, recognizing his friend's voice.

"That's a relief," Fogarty answered.

"Fingerprints, blood type, dental records. It *is* John Winston Flint."

"That's better than I could do. His ex-wife refused to make the trip down from New York City for the I.D.. Her only comment was that however he died she hoped it was slow and painful."

"Well, from the results of the postmortem, I'd say she got her wish."

Good, Fogarty thought, remaining silent.

"By the looks of the bruising and contusions surrounding the fractures," Tanaka continued, "I'd say that the blow to the sternum or, more accurately, the series of blows, were about the last of his injuries. I'm sticking with that as the cause of death. They occurred maybe two or three hours after the initial breaks to his toes and fingers. There was no sexual interference. Nothing came up on the swabs, no semen. But it sure as hell looks like this fellow suffered."

"Good." This time he said it out loud.

"What's up, Bill?"

"I've just finished watching a videotape, Joey. A tape that shows John Flint participating in rape and probable homicide. That son of a bitch was sick. He deserved to suffer."

"What tape?"

"One of the detectives found a suitcase full of them in Flint's bedroom. It seems the doctor was into muscle men. Oiling them up, rolling around with them naked, a little spanking, bondage—"

Tanaka waited.

"There's a woman on one of the tapes," Fogarty continued as he felt his anger building, "with probably the most beautiful body I've ever seen. At least it's beautiful to begin with. After about twenty minutes she's not so beautiful anymore. She's been tortured, raped, defecated on, and from what I can tell, strangled to death by what looks like the same dog harness and leash that was wrapped around Flint's neck."

"Can you I.D. the people on the tape?" Tanaka asked.

"Everybody's masked, even the victim, I can only tell it's Flint by the odd shape of his hands," Fogarty stopped a moment, "and, by the way, you were right."

"About what, Bill?"

"The table. Flint's examination table. It was a very sophisticated piece of equipment. Lots of uses. It features in most of his home movies."

"What about the names listed in his diary?" Tanaka asked, pulling Fogarty back on course.

"I'm about to start a check on them now. I've already got two detectives rounding up any eyewitnesses to people going in or out of the house from noon onwards. The only problem is—" Fogarty stalled.

Tanaka waited.

"When I find whoever did this to Flint, I'm not going to feel like arresting them, but more like giving them some kind of award for public service."

REQUIEM

Johnny Rocka was alone in his darkroom, running a series of black and whites through the developing fluid, exposing images of two extremely muscular naked men indulged in the act of mutual masturbation. Pretty mild stuff for the South Street photographer. Bread and butter stuff, the kind of thing he sold to the syndicated gay trade journals. He was about to hang the first of the prints on his drying line when he noticed the red light flashing above his door. That meant there was someone downstairs, ringing his entrance buzzer.

He had been living alone in the house, since Rick had died of AIDS a year ago and Bob, Rick's boyfriend, had moved back to San Francisco. *Probably one of Bob's friends, one of the muscle boys who doesn't know he's gone*, Rocka surmised, and continued to hang the prints. But the flashing persisted and it began to irritate him. Besides, he'd advertised the "house to share" in the local paper, even posted a three-by-five card, with the address and details, on the bulletin board in the laundromat on Bainbridge. He couldn't afford to keep the place on his own, so maybe the flashing red light was good news. He hurried the last print from the tray, washed it, and hung it by a single clothespin from the nylon line that stretched the length of the room.

"Hold on! I'm coming!" he shouted, leaving his darkroom to hobble down the narrow steps from the top of the house. He was wearing an old pair of Converse basketball shoes, the black-and-white high tops, with an interchangeable sponge lift in the left shoe. The sponge kept shifting position and his short leg was playing hell with his lower back; he clung tight to the banister to keep from falling and by the time he got to the bottom he was heaving so badly that he had to stop, bend over with both hands on his thighs, and gulp oxygen in huge mouthfuls. The bell was still ringing over and over again. Whoever was outside sounded manic.

"I'm coming," Rocka repeated, mostly to himself. Then he stood, running his fingers through his few remaining strands of hair, straightened the bib of his Mexican wedding shirt, and limped towards the door.

Another series of rings. The old broken bell grated against his eardrums.

"God damnit, I'm coming!"

He unchained the door, disengaged the bolt lock, turned the key, pulled it open, and stood eyeball to belt buckle with the man outside. *A muscle man*. Not good news.

Rocka looked up. There was something vaguely familiar about this muscle man. He tried to place the face.

"If you're looking for Bob, he split last month, San Francisco; he's gone."

Jack Dunne stood very still. He had now been awake for twenty-six hours, most of them spent walking or sitting in the freezing snow and cold, and the combination of sleep deprivation and methadrine had altered his reality. Everything had a thin, glassy veneer. Johnny Rocka appeared one dimensional and very brittle.

Jack cleared his throat. The last of the halotestin tablets had just dissolved, and his mouth was dry and tasted like chalk.

"I'm a friend of Doctor Flint. He said you might be able to help me." The words felt stuck together.

Johnny Rocka began to close the door.

Jack placed his palm against the old wood and pushed, stepping inside. Rocka backed away, hands extended.

"Sorry, man, I didn't mean to offend you," he spoke carefully, trying to stay calm, "it's just that I haven't heard that name for a couple of years an' it kind of took me by surprise."

Jack Dunne looked at the little man and nodded his head.

Rocka faked a smile and attempted to lighten his tone. "Do we know each other?" He was rummaging his mind. Trying to place the face, the voice.

"Indirectly," Jack Dunne answered, closing the door behind him. The click of the lock sounded dead and final.

"So what can I do for you?" Rocka was frightened. *Was this the Horse?* Rocka had never seen the Horse without the hood. *Has Flint sent the Horse? But why? I never talked. Never said a word. Nothing.*

Jack Dunne held him steady in his sight, heightening the tension between them. The little man looked like he was about to splinter.

Finally Jack Dunne spoke. "I need some pictures."

The photographer's laugh sounded like a hiccup. Suddenly, he was animated, "Pictures! Pictures! That's cool! That's what I do!"

"I need them as soon as possible."

"Right," Johnny Rocka answered, smiling. Moving. Walking towards his visitor, "I'm in the middle of some work at the moment, but if ya' tell me what kind a' stuff you had in mind, we can make an appointment—"

"Doctor Flint said you would take care of me right away," Jack insisted, "I've got cash on me."

This time Johnny Rocka detected the hint of a plea in the man's voice. He bit his lower lip and reappraised his prospective client. Maybe the vibes he'd felt weren't bad, maybe the guy was simply nervous.

"What kind of thing are you looking for?"

"I'd like some body shots. Naked."

Rocka nodded. "My session fee is three-hundred bucks."

"That's fine."

Rocka hesitated and Jack Dunne slipped his gloved hand into his overcoat and brought out a handful of folded fifties. He handed the wad over. Rocka took the money, counted off six of the ten bills, and handed back the rest.

"Let's do it then," he said, loosening up some more. "My studio's on the second floor; there's a dressing room up there, baby oil, sun tint, even a couple sets of dumbbells if you want to pump up."

"Are we alone in here?" Dunne asked.

Rocka looked at him again, hesitating.

"The stuff I want is fairly intimate. I don't want any-body—"

Rocka raised his hand. "Don't worry, man, it's completely cool. There's nobody here but me and I'm not expecting visitors."

Jack Dunne followed the photographer up the stairs and into the biggest room on the second floor.

"Dressing room's over there, next to the back drop," Rocka said.

Jack Dunne walked into the room and closed the door.

Inside, there was a collapsible card chair, a table strewn with tubes of Quick Tan, K-Y jelly, and a half-empty bottle of baby oil with strands of body hair, brown and black, stuck to its cap. There were also two hair brushes clogged with remnants of past users, a box of Kleenex, and a pink-and-white plastic blow-dryer. Two terrycloth dressing gowns were hung by a hook on the top panel of the door, both stained with oil and instant tan. A cracked mirror hung on the wall, above the table.

The mirror. Jack Dunne had a thing about mirrors, a compulsion. He bent down and stared at his face. The crack in the glass ran at a slant, starting in the upper-left corner and trailing down, across the tarnished silver, to the lower right, cleanly bisecting his reflected image.

The resemblance is there. In the lower half of the reflection. In the lines of the jaw and the formation of the lips. Jacqueline.

A terrible sadness comes with this recognition, deep and unrelenting, like feeling the presence of a ghost. Of someone loved and gone forever. He looks again and meets his own eyes. His pupils are so dilated from the methadrine that they form a brown wash against the surface of the iris, tears beginning to well. Jack Dunne breaks away from his reflection, removes his gloves, then takes off his shirt, folding it meticulously.

"What kind of music do you dig?" Rocka called from beyond the door.

"I prefer classical," Dunne answered, unbuttoning the front of his black jeans.

"I don't have much a' that, how 'bout some vintage Zeppelin or Clearwater Revival?"

" 'Thus Spake Zarathustra' ? "

"What . . . ?"

"By Strauss." Dunne said, removing his underpants, then slipping his gloves back on before reaching for the cleanest looking of the grey-white robes. As he turns, gown in hand, he sees a reflection of the coarse hair that has sprouted along the tops of his shoulders, like an ugly hedge, growing in clumps and tufts. It is darker by several shades than the beard which trails from his cheeks, down his neck, to encircle his throat like a fur necklace. Jack is getting hairier. Like an animal.

"Come on, man, give me a break." The photographer's voice draws him back through the looking glass.

Jack Dunne opened the door, "It's the theme from the film, *2001: A Space Odyssey*."

"I don't like that kind of music," Rocka answered.

"This isn't your session," Jack said, stepping from the dressing room.

The first thing that Johnny Rocka noticed was that his client was still wearing his gloves, the second was how his body stretched the seams of the robe. He was a very big boy.

"Have you got it? The *Space Odyssey* record," Dunne repeated.

"Yeah, I've got it on tape somewhere," Rocka replied.

"Would you please put it on." This time a little edge beneath the hoarse tone.

"It's your session, man," Rocka agreed, walking to the cassette rack. He found the tape quickly; he had actually known that it was in the same place he had put it after the last time he'd played it. On that night.

He switched on his amp, pushed the cassette into the deck, and pressed "play." Music filled the room. It made him feel uneasy, like a bad premonition. He turned, stood up, and lifted his Polaroid from the stool.

"Your gloves, man?"

"I keep them on," Jack answered.

"That's cool."

Jack Dunne nodded.

"If you want to stand over there against the backdrop, I'll take some practice stills, and get the lighting together."

Jack walked to the far end of the twenty-foot room, about a foot from the high black curtain that blocked the light from the room's two windows. Then he turned to face Johnny Rocka.

The photographer stared at the thick-muscled calves that protruded from the frayed bottom of the robe.

"Do you compete?" The photographer spoke loudly above the music. It was one of his standard lines. The muscle boys all loved to be asked if they "competed."

Jack Dunne shook his head.

"You look big enough," Rocka continued, loading the Polaroid.

When the photographer looked up again, Jack Dunne was untying the belt of the robe.

The music crescendoed and Johnny Rocka stepped on the footswitch, activating his twin strobes.

They flashed and Jack Dunne exploded in light.

He opened the robe.

Another flash as the robe slipped from Jack Dunne's shoulders, disappearing in black as it fell to the floor.

A third flash, and the moment froze.

"Jesus Fucking Christ—"

Jack Dunne could hear the photographer gasp from behind the wall of light as he hurtled forward.

"Jesus—"

SYNCHRONICITY

Less than five blocks from Johnny Rocka's house, Rachel Saunders sat in a softly upholstered burgundy leather chair in front of a mahogany wraparound desk.

Jay Berg sat behind the desk. He looked ecstatic, his recent hair weave freshly washed and set, and his rust-tinted contact lenses a perfect match for his Armani three-piecer. His smile revealed twenty thousand dollars worth of capped implants.

"Well Dr. Saunders," the accountant said, using Rachel's professional name, "you're showing three hundred thousand dollars for the last quarter of last year. That includes your investment in the clinic in Bryn Mawr, which," Berg looked down and checked his paperwork, "is just beginning to show a profit. It's going to put you over the million mark." Then Berg sat back, rested both manicured hands on his desk and beamed, as if he had just earned the million.

This time Rachel shared his smile. A million dollars, that was really some going for a Philadelphia surgeon, even if she was in "plastics." Maybe up in New York, where they ran them through on a conveyor belt, altering noses, eyes, chins, and cheekbones as if they were serving up Big Macs, but for Philadelphia, the "City of Brotherly Love" and conservative tastes, Rachel Saunders was making big bucks.

She finished her business, agreeing to spend more money from her clothing allowance, maybe even buy a new car to replace last year's Mercedes 500 SL, anything to prevent being robbed by the tax man.

As she left Berg's office, walking along the busy sidewalk towards the car park, she decided to buy Josef a new Harley Davidson to make up for the one he'd sold when he had decided to return to his native Japanese origins, during last year's identity crisis. She knew he'd regretted it ever since, but with the baby coming, and his chauvinistic nature—it was hard enough for him to swallow the fact that his wife out-earned him—Tanaka had accepted the loss with his standard stoicism, he never mentioned it. The giveaway was in his eyes, every time a Harley roared by the window of their car or passed them on the street, he looked like he was about to cry.

A Softail, that was the model of his last bike. Rachel remembered because Josef often patted her on the backside and referred to her by the same name. She may have out-earned him, but he was still the king of macho.

That's one of the nice things about making a million, she told herself as she rounded the corner of Pine Street and Fifth, I can buy anything I want, including a Harley Softail. She didn't feel guilty about her income; she still worked the emergency room at the hospital, still attended to crash victims, burn victims, and a host of birth abnormalities. She loved what she was able to do with her hands, sculpting the human body, improving its features, correcting cosmetic injuries, as if the body were a piece of clay. Cosmetic surgery was Rachel Saunders's art.

She was walking quickly now, her low-heeled Louis Jourdans light against the pavement. Feeling good, confident, happy to be carrying Tanaka's baby. She had it all: her health, her career, her man, and pretty soon, his child.

A chill wind caught her as she turned the corner into the outdoor parking lot, lifting the bottom of her coat. She pulled the cashmere tight around her neck, looked down, stepping to avoid the puddles of melting ice that pitted the macadam. When she looked up a man was walking towards her, a tall man in a long coat, almost a cape. A blond-headed man with a beard and hard, glazed eyes. She froze. A familiar, sinking feeling in her belly. *No. This isn't going to happen. I'm through with those feelings. Finished with them.* But this wasn't the same, nothing like the trauma that had accompanied her stress disorder. This was something else. Some other form of recognition. She looked up as the man approached, finding his eyes. There was something about his eyes, something she knew, understood.

The man stopped, caught like a fox in the glare of the torch.

"He . . . hel . . . hel . . . ," he tried to speak but his words stalled, unformed, and Rachel assumed he was deaf and mute, perhaps begging. She reached towards her purse, but, before she could open it he'd pushed by, and begun to run. Fast and desperate, like a wounded animal.

TESTOSTERONE

How are you doing with Flint's diary?" Tanaka's voice sounded insistent over the phone.

Fogarty settled back in his chair and fingered the pages of the Filofax marked "T."

"We're almost through and, so far, businesswise, the guy's as clean as a whistle. His patients, the ones we've been able to contact, can't stop singing his praises. I'll tell you, Joey, I've talked to these people, and I've seen the tape, and had his ex-wife tell me he was the devil himself, and it's like the guy lived two completely separate lives, with no spillover from one to the other. The only thing that's still got me beat are the initials, and the numbers, all through the diary, initials and numbers—"

"Well, I might have something for you."

Fogarty squeezed the telephone tighter and sat forward.

"C'mon, Josef, make an old man happy."

"It was something you said to me a couple of hours ago, after you'd seen the videotape. About the other guy on the tape, the bodybuilder—"

"Biggest motherfucker I've ever seen."

"Right. Well, during the postmortum, I'd noted that Flint had small tumorous growths beneath the nipples of both breasts. They were benign, but unusual—"

"Josef, you're driving me crazy, will you please come to the point."

"John Flint was suffering from gynecomastia. Which means, that unless you're twelve to sixteen years old and going through your heaviest spurt of puberty, you are probably taking some form of testosterone-based hormone. So much of it that the testosterone aromatises, which means it converts to estrogen, which is the basic female hormone, and you start to grow tits. A lot of bodybuilders suffer from gynecomastia, since testosterone is the basis for most of the anabolic steroids."

Fogarty was listening, and thinking of the collection of videos in the evidence bin; they had all featured bodybuilders.

"So I got on to your men at the chem lab and asked them to run a specific test on Flint's blood sample," Tanaka continued. "The result was that Flint's testosterone levels were about fifteen times what they should have been for a man of his age."

"He didn't exactly look like a competitive athlete to me, Josef."

"There can be side-effects to these hormones."

"Like?"

"Priapism."

"What's that?"

"A sustained erection."

"From what's on the video, that makes sense."

"It also makes his degree in endocrinology relevant," Tanaka added.

"Explain that to me."

"The guy would have been an expert on the administration and effects of the steroids, and since they were classed as Schedule-111 drugs a few years ago, putting them in the same league as narcotics, which made pharmaceutical quality stuff almost impossible to get, a crooked doctor would have been a very valuable man."

"Keep going."

"If I wanted to put someone on steroids, Bill, all I'd have to do is order up a blood test, interpret the red blood cell count on the CBC part of the test as low, diagnose them as anemic, and prescribe the drugs—"

"Hold on a second, Joey," Fogarty interrupted, starting to turn the pages of Flint's diary. "The initials CBC are scattered all through his diary."

"Right. Now read me a few more."

"T.C.?"

"Testosterone cypionate."

"HCG?"

"Human chorianic gonadotrophin. It's purified from the urine of pregnant women. In men, it stimulates the function of the testicles, producing more testosterone."

"How the hell do you know all this?"

"I'm a doctor, Bill. I'm also an athlete. Performance enhancers have always fascinated me. I've got reference books on them. I should have put the connection together right away, with Flint's degree in endocrinology, but I was slow."

"Where do I go with it?" Fogarty asked.

"Check Flint's medical supplies, and his prescription records. I'll bet the doctor treated a lot of pernicious anemia. All the blood test results would be classified as private; they couldn't even be subpoenaed by a prosecutor. You told me that Flint had a thing for muscle men. Add that to the fact that he was pumped full of testosterone, plus the endocrinology degree, and maybe we've got something."

"Maybe we do," Fogarty agreed. "Joey, one more thing, a favor. It's not very pleasant but I'd appreciate it if you would take a look at the Flint video. You've got an eye for detail, and there might be something on it I missed."

"Give me a couple of hours."

"See you." And Fogarty put down the phone.

Sure enough, Fogarty found that Flint's records confirmed a dozen cases of pernicious anemia in the last eighteen months, all male. Prescriptions ranged from 30 ml. multiple-dose vials of cyanocobalamin, vitamin B12, to 10 ml. vials of testosterone cypionate. The problem was the names, all of them were abbreviated to first and last initials. The initials H.N. appeared throughout the diary, right up until the day of Flint's murder.

Tanaka and Fogarty sat silently as the Flint video rolled; it was the fifth time that the captain had seen the tape and it didn't get any easier with repetition. They had come to the part where Flint snapped into his rubber gloves.

"Stop it there," Tanaka said.

The technician froze the frame.

"Look at the watch, Bill."

Fogarty could just see the gold Oyster sitting on Flint's desk, to the far side of the frame.

"Yeah, I see it."

"It's the same Rolex the mobile unit took from the crime scene."

"Probably."

"It's got a calendar on it, tells the day and the date."

An hour later Fogarty was on the phone to Police Commissioner Dan McMullon.

"Dan, I need you to make a call to Quantico for me, to your friends in the crime lab."

"What's up, Bill?"

"Maybe a break in the Flint case."

"Go ahead."

"We found a videotape in his bedroom; I think it could give a motive for his homicide."

Fogarty could feel McMullon about to speak. He spoke first; it was too soon to answer questions.

"In a couple of the frames, towards the middle of the tape, Flint removed his wristwatch and laid it on his desk. I think the watch may have a calendar on it, a month and a day. I need those dates, but the fellows downstairs can't enlarge the frame and keep the focus clean enough to pull them. I'm wondering if the F.B.I. lab could do it?

McMullon wanted more, but he sensed it was the wrong time to push.

"I'll make the call," he answered.

Jack Dunne is walking quickly and grinding his teeth. Too much methadrine always makes him grind his teeth; it is the overload to his nervous system. His stomach feels like a hollow fist and his mind is beginning to fragment, the veneer of reality giving way to scrambled messages from his subconscious. Voices, like the voices on a radio. He is trying to hold it all together, concentrating on his footsteps, willing his legs to carry him the last three city blocks to the safety of his home. But the voices have discovered his frequency and the messages are bombarding him: *We've got a probable homicide at Third and Delancey. You copy. Fire rescue and backup unit required. You copy. Fire rescue and backup unit.*

Then the sound of a siren and Jack Dunne freezes in mid-step. A fire engine races along Delaware Avenue. He watches it pass, listens to the whine fade in the distance, and continues. Two more blocks, one thousand and four hundred steps, he knows. He used to count his footsteps when he walked the city streets. He had it down, he knew how many steps it took to get from City Hall to South Street, from Delaware Avenue to Washington Square. He knew.

White male, approximate age, forty to fifty. Probable homicide. Officer! Don't touch that! It might have prints. Leave everything where it is. What's the matter with you? First case. First case? Secure the outside of the building. Go head.

"Yes, Sir. Yes, Sir. Yes, Sir." Jack Dunne answers the voice.

A group of children hear Jack talking to himself and laugh. Jack lifts his head; he stares at them, taking all four in with a sweeping glance, checking for weapons; even a twelve-year-old with a razor blade is dangerous. They look clean. He locks onto the tallest of the group, a coffee-skinned boy with sharp brown eyes and a leering smile that dies as Jack targets him.

"You kids all right, no problem?" Jack's voice cracks like a gunshot against the cold air.

"Yes, Sir," the coffee boy answers as he shepherds the others in a wide arc around Jack. A moment later they are all running. The children in one direction, Jack in the other. He knows he's losing it and he needs to get inside. By the time he arrives at his front door he is hyperventilating, but once he is in the house he regains a low threshold of control. Up the stairs, into his bedroom. His body is tired beyond exhaustion and every joint aches, as if there is no longer any cartilage or lubricant between the bones: elbows, hands, knees, feet, every movement is painful. Without medication, he could remain awake for another twelve hours. By then the voices will be swarming inside his mind, and the headaches will begin. He picks up his bottle of Valium and tips six tablets into his hand. That should be enough to make him lose consciousness, which is all Jack Dunne yearns for right now. No more voices, no more mind flashes. His mouth is so dry that even with a glass of water the last three tablets remain lodged in his throat. He coughs and drinks another glass, then lays down on his bed. He tries not to, but he can't help but listen to the voices. They sound like thin, tinny echoes inside a cave. Their messages are scrambled: male voices, barking orders and urgent bulletins. Radio signals crackle, and a woman screams, then there is a smell. Not in the room, but a smell inside Jack Dunne's head, an olfactory hallucination. It is the stink of rotted cabbage, dead flowers, rancid meat, and excrement. Jack Dunne raises his arms above his head, protecting his face from the weight of the garbage that he imagines is burying him; he tenses every muscle in his body and enters a spasmed rigidity.

"Help me. For God's sake will somebody help me!" he screams.

Help me! Help me! His mind continues to scream even after he muffles his mouth with a pillow, and mercifully the Valium numbs his brain.

BLESSED

Rachel Saunders loved to have sex in the morning. She loved it in the evening, too, but morning, specifically, at five or six o'clock, was her preferred time. There was something in the quiet of the city and stillness of the air that made the act itself one of awakening and renewal.

It was exactly 5:45 when her eyes opened; she had that feeling. Sort of half an energy, the other half lay beside her. She slipped out of her silk nightdress and slid closer to Josef; he was sleeping on his side, his hips facing her. Three, even two months ago, she could have nestled right into him, burrowed tight, her thighs against his thighs, her pubis against his hips, her breasts against his back, warm and soft and secure. But now the baby was there, really showing, and her stomach was round and hard and her breasts were sensitive. And they were getting big, for the first time in proportion to her long, thick nipples, their porcelain skin stretched tight and smooth, with only the faintest hint of the blue veins beneath. She loved her swelling breasts and often stood naked, examining her body in the full mirror of her wardrobe. Pregnancy had changed her, made her skin glow and her body swell and, even though she was thirty-seven years old and a medical doctor, there was something in the miracle of creating new life that caused her to feel young and strangely innocent; and blessed.

"Are you awake?" she whispered, reaching forward with her right foot and rubbing softly against the outside of his calf. She knew he wasn't.

Rachel moved a little closer to him, placing her left hand down, between her own legs, touching lightly, resting her palm in the full, soft spread of pubic hair while gently caressing herself.

Masturbating, I'm masturbating. I haven't done this since I was in college, she thought and nearly giggled. *My estrogen levels must be soaring.* Then, as her arousal grew, she reached for his hips with her other hand, feeling their heat, and began inching down slowly, moving her hand in small, delicate circles, barely touching him.

"Are you awake?" she repeated.

He answered by opening his legs, just enough to allow her hand to slip between his hips, stopping to cup his scrotum before moving to the hardness of his cock. She found the head and rolled it between her fingertips until a single drop of pre-seminal fluid gave the velvet skin an oiled smoothness. She released him and they rolled over at the same time, reversing their positions in the bed, so that he was on his side, behind her. She was very wet and he entered her easily, gripping her shoulders with his hands, wanting her breasts but knowing they would be tender to his touch. They remained like that a full minute, without motion, just the pulsing of his cock inside her. Then she began to push her hips softly inwards, signalling his movement. He bit lightly into the skin above her shoulders, tasting her as he pushed his hips forwards, entering her more deeply. They had been lovers for two years before they had married and they had known from their first night together that, physically, they were a perfect partnership. It was a mixture of feeling and mechanics; like two dancers with a sympathetic sense of rhythm, whose bodies aligned, creating a single flow of energy. And now, with the pregnancy, Tanaka had become more gentle, touching her only lightly with his hands and keeping the movement of his pelvis smooth and controlled, adding a delicacy to their lovemaking. Often, when he climaxed, he would lay his hands across her belly, sending the warmth from his palms inwards, as if to fuse the three of them. He was there now, arms wrapped around Rachel's body, his palms against her stomach. No feeling of animal passion, no hard fucking, simply love.

The telephone rang. It was a sound that broke in upon them, grating and unnatural. Because of their professions, both their minds were tuned for emergencies. Josef was closest; he withdrew from her slowly and rolled to the side of the bed, reaching out. He caught it on the fourth ring, one before the answering service cut in.

"Hello?"

A hollow silence.

"Hello?"

Then a sound, like a word forming, but trapped.

"Who is this?" Josef asked.

Rachel was sitting up in the bed, leaning towards him. "Let me have it," she whispered.

He handed her the phone.

"Why are you calling me?" She spoke calmly and clearly, as if she knew the caller.

"Why?" She repeated.

Sobbing on the other end of the line. She motioned for Josef to come closer and pulled the phone back from her ear, allowing him to listen. The sobbing continued another few seconds and then the line went dead. Rachel put down the phone.

"Press 'star,' then 'six,' then, 'nine,' " Josef said, "it will automatically redial the caller's number."

Rachel pushed *69, then listened as the phone rang on the other end. No one answered.

She handed it to Josef. Still, nothing.

"That's the first time she's called me at home."

"I don't understand, who is 'she'?" Josef asked, placing the phone down.

Rachel shook her head. "I don't know. I was going to mention it to you and Bill last night, at dinner, but then you guys got that new case, and we never got to dinner and—"

"Well I'm here now, so mention it." Tanaka's voice hardened.

"Three weeks ago Marge started getting calls at the office, just a couple at first, maybe two or three calls in five days. She'd answer and the caller would listen for a while, then hang up. We didn't think anything about it, then, in the middle of last week, we got a couple of them in a single day. This time Marge could hear somebody breathing, but not like heavy breathing, you know, not like somebody trying to frighten us, more like a hyperventilation, like somebody trying to catch their breath, then the sobbing. High pitched, we figured it was a woman."

"How come you haven't called the telephone company, got them to put a check on the calls?"

"I was going to ask Bill about it, Josef. Believe me. Until now, they've only been coming in to the office."

"Well, we're going to get everything recorded, beginning today."

"Fine. That's fine with me," Rachel replied, pulling back from him.

Then, as quickly as he had hardened, Tanaka turned toward her, shook his head, and smiled.

"I'm sorry, Rachel, but you know how I am about this kind of thing."

She reached towards him, finding his hand, pulling it towards her belly, laying it there.

"I understand," she answered.

Josef smiled, but still, he looked unsettled.

"I'll get Marge to call the phone company first thing," Rachel reaffirmed.

"Good."

She studied his profile, his neat, almost pretty features, shadowed beneath a fringe of black, rumpled hair. She knew his moods, could almost read his thoughts by the formation of his full lips, and the set of his jaw when his eyes narrowed. She sensed his anxiety.

"What's going on Josef?"

He shook his head.

"What have you and Bill been doing?"

"It's a real mess," he answered.

"Come on, as much as you can tell me, you need to talk."

Josef looked at her face in the half light of the morning.

Her blue eyes were soft but demanding. She was right; he did need to talk. The Flint tape had upset him. It had reminded him of the ugliness that lay waiting outside their curtained windows. It made him feel vulnerable and protective.

"We've got a homicide victim who deserved to be a homicide victim," he answered.

"I don't follow you."

"The man we took to the morgue yesterday."

"I still don't understand."

"You would if you'd have seen the video collection that one of the detectives found in his bedroom. This guy was an animal, into every kink you can imagine. Three years ago his wife took him to court, claimed he was attempting to involve their two daughters in his sex games. The case was ugly and the child abuse allocations were never proved; there was a little bit of press on it, but he must have had enough legal clout to stop it. His ex-wife and daughters moved to New York. She refused to come down and identify his body." Josef managed his explanation without mentioning the specific tape, the one Fogarty referred to as the Flint video. That tape was classified, and Rachel didn't need to know.

"Who was this guy?"

"He was a doctor," Tanaka answered.

"A doctor? What was his name?"

Josef hesitated.

"Come on, Josef, you're not telling me anything that isn't going to be in the morning papers."

"His name was John Winston Flint."

Rachel shook her head. "Never heard of him."

"He ran a general practice, with a specialty in endocrinology."

"Has Bill got any suspects?"

"Nothing real. A couple of ideas, but as of ten o'clock last night, nothing specific."

"How involved are you going to get?"

"Until Bob Moyer comes back I've got my hands full, and Bill's got a real good forensics unit—"

"But he likes having you around."

"Bill Fogarty's an old-time cop, he works on trust, and it takes him a long time to trust people. He trusts me, and I trust him. Besides, it was me who discovered that Flint had 'bitch tits'."

"Bitch tits?"

"That's what the bodybuilders call gynecomastia. Flint was overloaded on testosterone, no doubt to help him get it up for his home movies. After I discovered the gynecomastia, the forensics unit ran tests on every chemical in Flints medicine cabinet. He had the biggest stash of steroids this side of Muscle Beach and I doubt if he was using them to treat anemia," Tanaka said. "That, and the fact that most of his partners in his home movies were bodybuilders, adds up to something."

"You think one of them killed him?"

"It looks that way. Flint was into some very rough sex. Most likely, one of them got carried away and went too far. Broke every bone in Flint's body. Each of his fingers had been broken so many times they'd virtually splintered. The metacarpal bone at the base of his thumb looked like sawdust when we opened the joint."

"And you're telling me he deserved it, because he was into rough sex?"

"John Winston Flint got some of his own medicine, pure and simple."

"That's the first time I've ever heard you talk like that."

"Flint was a bad man."

"And Bill? How does he feel?"

"Same way."

"Isn't that going to bias the investigation?"

"We won't let it."

Rachel arrived at her office at nine o'clock in the morning. Marge had beaten her by five minutes and was already seated, scanning her computer screen for the days appointments.

"You've got twelve people to see today, eight follow-ups and four new ones. There's an R. Larson here, coming in for a consultation on breast implants," Marge said, smiling.

"I hope you told Ms. Larson that I'm not in favor of them, not even with the nonseep bags."

"I tried to tell him."

"Him?"

"R. Larson is Rick Larson, the TV sportscaster. He actually wants 'pec' implants, to make him look more athletic. Since his football career ended he's gone a little soft. I said you'd speak to him."

"What's the problem with these guys, Marge? Yesterday it was Danny Resnick, you know the singing diamond merchant, the one who does all those weird radio ads; he was looking for an engorgement."

"A what?"

"He'd heard some guy on the Howard Stern show talking about having fatty fluid injected into his penis, claimed it gave him an extra inch in diameter."

Marge started laughing.

"He had his pants half down by the time I told him I didn't do 'engorgements.' Then he got furious. Told me I wasn't being politically correct."

Marge was roaring.

"He said if I did breast augmentation I should be doing engorgements—"

"Don't tell me, I know what comes next. You sent him to Merve Phipps, master of liposuction—"

The two woman were both laughing now.

"I did. I figure if Phippsy likes taking it out so much, he can slip a little back in where it counts; he'll probably sue me for the referral."

Then Rachel glanced at the phone and stopped laughing.

"Marge, before I forget, you know those calls we've been getting, the breather?"

"Yes."

"Well, today, would you call the Bell Telephone office and get a trace put on the star sixty-nines?"

"I'll do it right now," Marge said, picking up the phone.

MEL

"The police drawing looks like Mel Gibson with blond hair," Fogarty growled, balancing the phone between his ear and his shoulder while he spread his copy of the drawing out on his desk.

"Who I.D.'d the suspect?" Tanaka asked.

"Her name is Ligeya Antonio, she's Filipino, works across the street from Flint's office. She said she saw this guy enter and exit Flint's place, but she can't get the time together at all, somewhere between seven o'clock and midnight, right on the hour."

"How did she know it was on the hour?"

"Because she prays hourly, twelve times a day. Her prayer seat looks out the upper-bedroom window, directly opposite Flint's. She's a religious maniac. She's also an illegal alien, but I had to let her slide on that one. Anything to get her to cooperate."

Tanaka laughed.

"She doesn't speak much English," Fogarty continued, "and she couldn't understand why we were showing pictures of dead criminals to her. Trying to get a nose off one and a set of ears off another, all she kept saying was Mel Geebsone. So Arty Pearce draws a picture of Mel Gibson, straight off one of those *Lethal Weapon* posters, and she starts whooping, saying Hail Marys, then she gets Arty to add a stubble of beard, color the hair blond and lengthen it. By then she was talking about the Antichrist, saying the guy was dressed entirely in black, boots, a cape, black gloves, which according to Miss Antonio is the color of death, on top of which he was the size of a *caballo*.

"A what?"

"A horse, Josef, a horse," Fogarty explained. "Add that to

Flint's predilection for muscle men, and I reckon it's time to hit the power gyms."

"Who have you got on this?" Tanaka asked.

"A couple of kids who don't know their assholes from a hole in the ground. I'm going to bury 'em in paperwork till I make my investigation. Besides, they look like cops. Twenty-five or -six years old and they already look like cops."

"And you don't?" Tanaka questioned.

Fogarty lifted his left hand to the scarred side of his face and stroked the coarse flesh.

"I don't exactly know what I look like anymore, but I do know that I've risen above the laws of vanity. Or sunk beneath them."

Tanaka laughed again. He knew what he wanted to do. He could feel it.

"Listen, Bill, Bob Moyer's back in here now, a little lighter in the body, and swearing he'll never touch another Mexican hamburger, but he's back. Let me have a word with him about helping you out. I can talk the steroid talk—"

"You're a fucking adrenaline junkie, Josef."

"I know that."

"How's 'the Juice Pit' sound?" Fogarty asked, scanning down his list of health clubs and power gyms.

"Like my kind of place," Josef answered.

"Right. I'm coming over," Fogarty said, then put down the phone.

While Dave Roach circulated the police drawing and Sharon Gilbey combed the last two years of police and mortuary records for missing persons and "dead on arrivals," Bill Fogarty grabbed his white, police-issued Chrysler and headed west, toward the medical building. He circumnavigated the center city traffic and drove down Chestnut, making the three-mile journey to University City in under ten minutes.

"Nice suntan, Bob, you look like a dried fig," he said as he walked into Moyer's office. It was the first time that he'd seen the chief medical examiner in a month. And it was the first time in ten years that he had seen Moyer with a tan.

Bob Moyer lowered his reading glasses and looked up from his papers.

"Thanks, Bill, that's very kind of you."

Fogarty extended his hand. "What was it, horse meat?"

Moyer shook and smiled, "The hospital's running the tests now, I figure if I can find the secret ingredient, I'll corner the market in weight reduction. How's eleven pounds in three days sound?"

"Plus a suntan?"

"And an I.V. electrolyte drip, to balance the dehydration factor. Jesus, Bill, I thought I was going to die, it was coming out of both ends, at the same time. I collapsed in the lavatory of the airplane; they had to carry me off. I've never been so embarrassed in my life. My own kids pretended not to know me. Paramedics brought me through customs on a stretcher."

Fogarty imagined the scene. Moyer, prim and proper, with his wire rims and natty red goatee, dressed in his blue seersucker jacket, strapped to a stretcher while his wife, Norma, and their two sons watched, red-faced, from the sidelines.

"It must have been a killer," Fogarty agreed, trying to keep a straight face, but cracking at the seams.

"You think it's funny, you son of a bitch," Moyer said, smiling as he stood up. "And now, after laughing at my distress, you want me to loan you my assistant?"

Fogarty raised both hands in mock surrender. "It's Josef's idea, Bob, I swear it."

"Well, I've seen the postmortem reports and I took Dr. Flint out of the refrigerator and checked him over," Moyer said. "Looks like he was hit by a truck."

"Or by a powerlifter with a roid rage."

"Yes, I know, I've spoken to Josef," Moyer confirmed.

"Can you spare him?" the lieutenant asked.

"For what and for how long?"

"All right, here's what we've got," Fogarty said, pulling the

Mel "Geebsone" print out of his pocket and handing it to Moyer.

Moyer examined the drawing silently.

"That drawing and a bunch of video cassettes showing Flint performing sexual acts with a series of bodybuilders and one tape of rape and possible murder. Then Josef discovered an abnormally high testosterone level in Flint's blood and we lifted a load of steroids from his medical supplies. It doesn't take a rocket scientist to put it together."

"Flint was trading drugs for sex," Moyer stated.

"Looks that way."

Moyer nodded his head and handed the copy of the drawing back to Fogarty.

"Listen, Bob, the steroid connection was Josef's call, but I'm sure I've got somebody somewhere who's familiar with those kinds of drugs—"

"I don't mind if you borrow him, just tell me, how long?"

"I figure, with this," Fogarty said, holding up the picture, "and with the drugs connection, it's not going to take a lot of time."

"Josef's in the morgue," Moyer said.

The morgue was in the basement of the Philadelphia Department of Health's medical building. There were four, high windows in the off-white room, opening into wells, leading to the sidewalk at the back of the building. Five examination tables and three metal trolleys were positioned inside, and a bank of walk-in freezers, each capable of storing twenty corpses, lined the far wall. The smell of death hung frozen in the recycled air.

Fogarty looked through the rectangular window in the swing door. He could see a woman, naked, and spread-eagled on the tiled floor, positioned so that the police photographer could get a clean photograph of the tire marks which crisscrossed her legs. Her face was a broken mask, one eye open the other shut; a young attendant, wearing his green apron, rearranged her by lifting her right foot, moving it to the side, and placing it down again, causing the jagged bone of her upper thigh to shift below her pelvis, forcing the skin upwards. Her toenails were painted red.

Fogarty remembered his wife's feet, long toes and red painted nails. Graceful feet. After the accident, she had been taken to a similar place, a similar room; so had his daughter.

He forced his eyes away from the woman on the floor and looked to the other side of the room. He saw a child's body on a trolley. An attendant was washing the small boy down; water gushed from the end of a brown hose, and mud, leaves, and diluted blood ran through the purpose-built holes in the metal trolley, trickling to the floor, down, and into the drains.

"Josef." Fogarty spoke the name, as if it could save him from the feeling that his own time was near, when his crime against his family would be exhumed. Then his body would be examined, his flaws exposed, and his stained soul washed away with the cold water from the rubber hose through the rusted metal grates and into the city's sewer.

"Josef?" He spoke louder, through the open door.

Tanaka slid the storage unit shut, turned and saw Fogarty staring at him. He could detect the discomfort in the policeman's blue-grey eyes, and knew him well enough to understand why it was there.

"Give me five minutes, Bill, I'll meet you upstairs, five minutes."

Fogarty backed up, allowing the door to his nightmare to close, turned and walked to the elevator.

He took a seat in the waiting room next to Bob Moyer's office, then spent the next few minutes rearranging his mental filing cabinet, pushing back the spill of memories stirred by the scene downstairs, and concentrated on the business at hand.

He took the copy of the artist's drawing from his pocket and studied the charcoaled features of the face. It was not an unnattractive face, in fact it was nearly handsome, just a shade too broad in the nose and slightly swollen, particularly around the cheekbones and eyes, as if the bones were forcing the flesh outward.

"Is that the suspect, Bill?" Tanaka's voice hit Fogarty from the side, causing him to sit bolt upright in the chair.

"Jesus, Joey, I wish you wouldn't sneak up on me like that!"

"Sorry," Tanaka said, smiling. Fogarty was always accusing him of "sneaking up."

"Yeah, this is what we've got so far, from the Filipino woman," the lieutenant continued. "It was dark, and I don't know what she actually saw. This looks more like a portrait of Jesus—"

"Looks like Willem Dafoe."

"Who?"

"The actor."

"The Filipino woman said Mel Gibson."

"No. Different bone structure, the features are too refined for Mel Gibson."

"And the chances are it isn't either of them anyway, so why don't we take a ride?"

"Has Bob given me the all clear?"

"Can't wait to get rid of you," Fogarty said, standing. He was feeling better now, back on the job, making distance between himself and the room downstairs.

"I've got half a dozen places I want to check out. There are a few clubs with interesting names and a few hardcore power gyms that some of the district cops use. You know anything about bodybuilding, Josef?"

Tanaka shrugged his shoulders, "I've worked a bit with the *chikaraishi*."

"That's a big help," Fogarty answered sarcastically.

Tanaka's use of Japanese, Okinawan, or Chinese had initially been a source of irritation to Fogarty, four years ago, when they had combed Philadelphia's martial arts' clubs, working their first case. When they were in Japan, Tanaka rarely condescended to speak English; it had nearly driven the policeman crazy. Now it was part of their rapport, part of their patter, a gentle needle between them.

"All right. What the fuck's a *chiarishi*?"

They were walking now, towards the door. That good old energy was flowing between them, the kind of energy that got things done.

"Chi-kar-aishi, Bill, *chikaraishi*."

"Right. Got it. What is it?"

"A one-foot-long wooden pole with a ten-pound block of cement on the end of it. Kind of like a barbell, but Okinawan style," he explained, "used to develop the arms, chest, and abdomen. Haven't you ever noticed my pecs?"

JUICE

The Juice Pit was located on Walnut Street, midway between Broad Street and the Schuylkill River. It was a two-storey building with a glass front and chrome-framed doors.

Fogarty and Tanaka stopped in front of the glass and looked inside. Beyond the double glazing they could hear the grind of treadmills and the pneumatic rhythm of the stair machines. Behind that they heard Madonna, belting out "Like a Virgin." A lineup of female flesh in leotards and high-cut lycra workout suits wobbled in various stages of muscular atrophy and development on the six Stairmasters closest to the window. One balding fat man in Michael Jordan training shoes, knee-high socks, short shorts, and a sweatshirt with HARLEY DAVIDSON, VENICE, CALIFORNIA printed on the back, was stationed on the nearest treadmill, his eyes aimed at the firmest of the female gluteous maximi, as he marched stalwartly, like a mouse on a wheel, towards the cheese.

"Dirty old bastard," Fogarty commented, honing in on the object of the fat man's inspiration.

Inside, a bleached blonde in a spandex bodysuit worked the reception desk, and behind him, along the near wall, there was an elaborate juice bar which advertised Enzyme Enhanced Smart Drinks at fifteen dollars a pint and a full selection of protein and yogurt cocktails, plus Amino Freezes. Two women sat at the bar, sharing a blender full of what looked like crushed bananas.

"Wrong kind of juice," Tanaka said as they approached the reception desk.

"May I help you?" the spandex blonde asked, looking straight at Tanaka. The man wore a name tag that read EMILIO.

"Have you got free weights?" Josef inquired.

"Sure thing," Emilio answered, with a lisp, eyes aglow, "would you care for a complimentary workout?"

"Could we take a look at the weight room?" Fogarty interjected.

Emilio kept his eyes on Tanaka and pressed a button on his intercom.

"Francois, we've got a party down here who'd like to have a look at the free weights," then, to Josef, "what's your name?"

"Josef Tanaka."

"Francois, his name is Josef."

The fey voice and coy glances were too much for Fogarty, besides, he didn't like being ignored.

"And I'm Captain Fogarty."

Emilio stiffened up, "You mean as in police captain?"

"Exactly," Fogarty answered.

"Is there a problem?" Suddenly Emilio's voice was as tight as his spandex.

"Not necessarily, but we would like a look at your facilities."

"You got it," Emilio assured, pressing the button of the intercom again. "Francois, would you please hurry up."

Francois was small, dark, and pretending to be French. Fogarty waited until he'd walked to the reception desk before he brought the police drawing from his pocket.

"Cute, but I don't know 'eem," Francois said.

"Is he dangerous?" Emilio sounded hopeful.

Fogarty smiled, refolded the drawing, then asked, "How 'bout a look upstairs?"

Francois led Fogarty and Tanaka up the single flight of steps to the free weights section of the Juice Pit. It was a large-mirrored room with signed pictures of physique champions on the walls, a full array of dumbbells, Olympic weights, racks, benches, pulleys, and barbells. There were several people working out, but one was conspicuous. Sitting on an incline bench, beside the three-tiered rack of gradiented chromed dumbbells, she was grossly overweight and in her middle years, crammed into a cotton training suit, and performing a loose rendition of a bicep curl with a dumbbell that looked like a quartered broomstick. She was chewing gum ferociously and groaning, between chews, as if she was in mid-orgasm, while an instructor, with a body that looked as if it had been carved from black marble, hovered above her. "Come on Doris, two more reps, two more reps, they're the ones that make you grow. Two more reps."

Doris stopped mid-groan, chewed three times, and met his eyes, "I don't want to 'grow' Ollie, I don't want to look like that." She motioned with her head to a photo of a female bodybuilder which hung above the dumbbell rack.

"That's Bernie Price, Doris, Miss World, I don't really think you have anything to worry about," he explained.

"All right, but just two more. I've got three nicotine patches on my left hip and they're starting to itch. And my nicotine gum's getting dry."

"All right, Doris, two more," the marble gladiator said softly, then, looking towards Fogarty and Tanaka, his eyes lit up.

"Sensei!"

Tanaka did a double take. "Oliver, how are you?"

"Voila, you are friends," Francois chimed in.

"He's my teacher," the Jamaican answered, leaving Doris to finish her orgasm solo. "Francois, could you take Miss Walove through her chest routine, just flys with the five-pound dumbbells and flat-bench presses with the Olympic bar, no weight."

Francois wrinkled his nose and walked towards the sound of smacking lips.

"Good to see you, Sensei," Oliver beamed.

It wasn't the first time that a student or member of the Philadelphia Karate Club had spotted Tanaka in the street, or in a restaurant, and Fogarty was always impressed with the amount of respect that his friend commanded. He watched as the six-foot-four-inch bodybuilder bowed to Josef Tanaka.

"Come on Oliver, this isn't the *dojo*," Tanaka said, extending his hand, "in fact, I should be bowing to you in this place. How's it going?"

Oliver glanced in the direction of Doris Walove and smiled. "Driving me nuts, but it keeps me in protein powder." Then he looked from Tanaka to Fogarty, "Are you planning to join?"

"No. We're here on official business," Tanaka replied. "Oliver, this is Captain William Fogarty, from the police department."

Fogarty extended his hand. Oliver shook and Fogarty felt as if his hand had been engulfed in hard leather.

"Would it be possible to speak to you in private?" Tanaka asked.

"No problem," Oliver assured him. He looked towards the lamp-tanned Francois and added, "I'm going to take my break now, I'll be downstairs, in the juice bar."

"Yeah, okay, see ya' later." And suddenly Francois was just plain Frank.

They chose a table to the side of the juice bar, away from the spillover from the twelve o'clock aerobics class. Oliver ordered a blender of Strawberry Smoothie and three glasses.

"Seventeen grams of protein and only one gram of fat," he said as Fogarty sipped the pink drink.

"Just what I needed," the policeman commented.

"Now, what can I do for you?" Oliver asked.

Tanaka looked toward the captain.

Fogarty sipped the strawberry drink once more and licked his upper lip. "What we've got, Oliver, is a homicide that may be connected to the sale or distribution of anabolic steroids." He watched the Jamaican's face tighten as his left pectoralis muscle twitched beneath the front of his T-shirt, like an exaggerated heartbeat.

"I'm completely natural," Oliver answered.

"Relax, Oliver," Fogarty said, "I couldn't care less about whatever you're taking. Believe me, I don't give a shit."

Oliver looked at Tanaka.

"Trust him, Oliver."

Oliver relaxed.

"What is it you need to know?"

"It looks like we've got a medical doctor who was supplying steroid drugs to the bodybuilding community."

Oliver smiled. "Out in L.A., half the bigtime guys have doctors on the payroll; they take them with them to all the major shows."

"This isn't L.A.," Fogarty answered, "and the doctor in question may have had motives other than money. It probably cost him his life."

"I don't understand."

"Sex. Sex for drugs. Does that ring any bells?"

Oliver sat quietly, shaking his head slowly.

"How about gay bodybuilders? Have you got any gay bodybuilders in here?"

"Aside from Emilio and Francois, if you can even call them bodybuilders, I don't know. A couple, I guess, but, really, this place is pretty tame. You want gay bodybuilders you should try *Stallion*, or *Swinging D's*."

Fogarty jotted the two names down in his notebook.

"Where are they?" he asked.

"They're not clubs, they're contact magazines. Full of gay bodybuilders, some of them local."

Fogarty nodded his head and slipped the police drawing from his pocket.

"Do you know him?"

Oliver studied the drawing, shook his head. "Hey, I like the women, man. That gay shit's not for me."

"How about steroids. Where would I go to get steroids?" Fogarty asked, taking back the drawing.

"Try one of the power gyms, Animals or Gladiators, that's where the boneheads hang out."

Fogarty took the list from his pocket and looked it over; Gladiators was on the list.

"What was the name of the other place, not Gladiators, the other one?" he asked.

"Animals. It's way up on North Broad," Oliver replied.

Fogarty wrote the name down as Oliver looked at Tanaka. "I don't mean to be disrespectful, Sensei, but you'll save yourself a lot of hassle by letting the captain go in there alone, or with another police officer."

"Why's that?" Tanaka asked.

"Because the German guy who owns the place is a psycho. A few years back, when I entered the Mr. Northeastern and I needed," he glanced quickly at Fogarty, "a more serious place to train, I tried going in there. The bastard nearly broke my neck."

"I don't understand," Tanaka said.

"I'm not Aryan. He's got a whole Third Reich thing going. White people only."

"In an all-black neighborhood?" Fogarty asked.

"That's all part of his power trip. You train at Animals, you're protected. Even the drug gangs steer clear. Plus the rent's cheap enough that he can operate an entire compound, weight room, offices, parking area."

"What's this guy's name?" the captain asked, still taking notes.

"Horst Nickles. They call him 'the Horse.'"

Fogarty grinned and looked at Tanaka, "H.N., Horst Nickles. Do you think we just got lucky?"

COCONUT

The second floor of the Trinity is also comprised of a single room. But this room is different from any of the other rooms in the house, in both content and feeling. This room is a shrine. Its single, blue-curtained window casts a sliver of cold light along the quilted cover of a double width, canopied bed. Beside the bed, a trunk contains a wardrobe of women's clothing—shoes and stockings, underwear, blouses, skirts, and dresses. All are cleaned, pressed, and neatly folded. More clothing, suits and a uniform, hang in the closet to the left of the trunk. A bright kilim rug, orange, gold, and blue, is at the foot of the bed, and an antique dresser is positioned against the wall nearest the entrance door. There is a vanity mirror mounted on the walnut top of the dresser.

Jack Dunne looks down at the tabletop, at the pots of skin lotion, nail varnish, files, scissors—scissors? There should be scissors, where are the scissors? His mind slips a moment, then returns to a passive observation of the cut-glass perfume bottles, hand-blown and graceful, and three pictures in silver frames. Pictures of a young woman. One is a high school graduation picture, the other a college graduation picture, and the last depicts the woman in uniform.

Jack Dunne shuts the door and stands in the center of the room. He can smell the faint aroma of perfume in the air, like honeysuckle. He inhales, as if the fragrance itself contains the means to center his mind and give resolve to his actions. He looks around slowly, checking the bed covers and floor for any sign of dust or disarray, careful not to allow his eyes to linger too long on the framed pictures on top of the dresser. He doesn't want to be drawn to them, to be compelled to touch them, to lift them from the dresser and carry them to the bed, to sit and study the face in the picture for hours, even days.

He opens the wardrobe closet and stands, studying himself in the full-length mirror which is attached to the door; his body is changing every day. With the amount of drugs he is consuming, the amount of protein he is ingesting, and the amount of exercise he is performing, the changes are inevitable. Still, they are miraculous.

He is wearing a pair of red, soft leather, spike-heeled shoes, silk stockings, white, frilly panties and a lacy garter belt. He tried to put on the bra, but the strap was twelve inches short of joining at the back. Jacqueline's chest was forty inches around, Jack's is over fifty. Still, wearing her clothes gives him a strange sensation of being very close to her and, in fact, it is the man he sees in front of him now, reflected in the mirror, who is the stranger; the muscular man in the woman's underclothes, coarse and hairy. Yet, if he ignores the man's face and body and centers his attention on his eyes; he knows who he is. He can "feel" who he is, as if he is aligning himself to "her" soul.

"There's nothing to be ashamed of, be proud of your size, being tall can be very attractive." It is the voice of Albert Dunne, their father.

They are standing on the back porch of their farmhouse in Lancaster, Pennsylvania. Looking out onto fields of yellow, orange, and green; it is harvest season and it is Jacqueline's sixteenth birthday. She is already five-feet-ten-inches tall and self-conscious about being the tallest girl in her class at school. Taller than most of the boys. "Yes, Jacqui, you're tall, but so am I, and so is your mother. Nothing wrong with being tall. Stand straight and be proud, like God made you." Albert Dunne looks into their eyes as he speaks, his voice echoing, filling the gap between then and now.

Like God made you. Jack straightens up, flexing the bulky quadriceps muscles that hang to the front of his thighs. The entire bulk jumps to life beneath the sheer fabric of the stockings, shifting upward from the kneecap. Then Jack arcs his upper body forward, holding the flex in his thighs, while he bends both arms in front of him, bringing his clenched

fists together in line with his navel, flexing his pectoralis muscles until they cramp. He looks like a crab, his torso the
armored shell and his arms and fists the legs and claws. He
holds this pose a few seconds, watching the blood being
pumped to his chest, causing a network of veins to stand like
thin, blue-grey ribbons above his flesh. He then straightens
up, relaxing, standing "at ease," his feet apart, his arms down,
and hands to his sides.

This posture draws his eyes to the center of his pubis. As
hairy as Jack is, particularly in this region, his sexual organ
seems also to be metamorphosing, developing. It has fallen
out of the side of Jacqueline's panties. He examines it. Visu-
ally. He *never* touches *it*. That part is off limits to Jack Dunne
and to anybody else who might have ideas; he would rather
die than be touched. Still, he is hanging lower, the head and
wrinkled shaft of his organ dropping several inches below
the frilly white cotton. Like a brown, oversized earthworm.
It repulses him. He turns his head and glimpses another
reflection in the mirror; one of the framed pictures of Jacqueline. She is wearing her police blues, and she is smiling at
him. He knows what she wants.

Horst Nickles opened his refrigerator and removed a box
from the lower shelf; it was the type and size of box which
could have contained a birthday cake. It was shiny-white cardboard, wrapped with brown twine and tied with a bow. The
box and its contents weighed four pounds and had been
delivered earlier that afternoon. A similar box was delivered
to Horst Nickles each week, at the cost of one hundred and
fifty dollars. Some contained local product. Others were
shipped from Harrisburg, Pittsburgh, or Allentown, or any
place which tested hair or beauty products on laboratory
animals.

First, Horst placed the box on the top of his desk. He then
walked quickly to the steel-reinforced door of his office and
made certain the door was locked. This was a particularly
sacred moment for Horst Nickles, and he did not want to be

disturbed by either his staff or any member of his club. Satisfied, he walked back to his desk and untied the twine, pulling open the flaps of the box to reveal a round object, covered in plastic bubble-wrap and packed in ice. The object was about the size of a bowling ball. Decent size, Horst thought, recalling that he had warned his supplier against any more preadolescent specimens. He placed both his hands around the hard globe and lifted it clear of the packed ice. He returned it to his desk and picked up a Stanley knife to cut away the surgical tape that held the wrap in place. It was then that his warning buzzer went off, a dull continuous buzz, like an old-time dentist's drill. It was a sound that could mean only one thing; trouble in the gym. Probably a fight between two freaks so wired on dexedrine, and pumped on testosterone, that they were willing to go to war over who used the squat racks first. Sometimes things got bloody at Animals. Members went berserk, and the trainers couldn't contain them. That's when the real animal stepped in. Usually just the sight of Horst Nickles stopped the action: six-feet-eight and three hundred pounds, with twenty-three-inch arms, a twenty-four-inch neck, and a sixty-inch chest. All this was supported by legs that resembled tree trunks. He had a face that looked like a Viking god of war, chiseled and cruel, with steel blue eyes and a mane of golden hair that cascaded below trapezius muscles so thick that they fused his neck and shoulders with no visible join. Most of the time that was enough. On the occasions that it wasn't, Horst had another surprise. He could actually fight. Unlike most of the steroid blowfish, who couldn't do much other than rant and shove, Horst Nickles had been an Olympic wrestling champion, a heavyweight. Once he got his hands on the offenders the show was over.

He picked up his cold, plastic-wrapped parcel and placed it carefully back in the refrigerator.

Horst Nickles was hungry, and very pissed off, when he opened the door to the main gym.

There were six people training in the sixty-foot-square

space, four men and two women. The men were powerlifters, more concerned with raw strength than cosmetics, and the women were a lesbian team from west Philly who barked orders and encouragement at each other like rabid dogs. There was a lot of growling and shouting going on, but it was all positive, inspirational stuff.

"Vhat's happening?" Horst yelled above the theme from *The Terminator* which vibrated the wall-mounted Tannoys.

"We got a cop at the door," Jim Pinion shouted back, standing by the intercom and staring at Fogarty's distorted image as it flickered on the security screen.

Nobody else even looked up. That was part of the program at Animals: don't ever be too curious. Horst Nickles would just as soon kill his members as collect their dues. They knew that. They also knew that Animals had the best steroids of any of the five gyms that had any at all. They were the real goods, not the contaminated crap that featured particles of dirt floating around in the oil base of the injectibles or the oral methandrostenolene, better known as dianobol, that turned out to be caffeine. No, Horst Nickles got his stuff straight from Ensenada, Mexico. It was reproduced to American standards, and even the packaging was photographed and duplicated to the letter. That was the stuff he sold. His private stock was on prescription, American-made, and the best.

"Have they got a warrant?" Nickles's voice was calm. He had a few cops who trained at Animals and bought his product. He could pull some strings inside the force if he had to; he'd done it before.

"Have they?"

Pinion was a short man, but his mouse-brown hair was shoulder length, like that of his mentor's. He was extremely broad across the back and bowed in the legs. He'd always blamed his "bad genetics" for his inability to win the "short man's" category in the state competitions.

"I don't know," Pinion answered.

"Fuck them then," Nickles growled, turning to go back to his lunch.

"They won't go away," Pinion insisted.

Horst Nickles marched forward, his jaw set and his eyes narrowing. He didn't give a shit that the men outside his door were cops. Inside his grey-stone fortress, he was the law.

"Get out of the fucking vay," he hissed, pronouncing his "w" like a "v." Sometimes, when the Horse was angry, his old teutonic accent re-emerged.

He elbowed past Pinion and slid the metal bolt of the inside door.

"Lock it behind me," he ordered, turning to look at Pinion. "I'll be back." He used his *Terminator* line, the only redeeming feature, he felt, aside from the sound track, of any of Schwarzenegger's films. "Arnold sold out; he's a Nazi who sold out," was a favorite Nickles proclamation.

The Horse stood in the four-foot-wide space between the inside door to Animals and the metal security door that led to Broad Street. He composed himself, breathing deep, powerful breaths, centering his enormous anger behind the wall of muscle in his lower abdomen. There was absolutely nothing he would have rather done than pull open the door and attack. He loved to attack; it was the explosion, the letting go, that moment when every nerve, muscle, and emotion linked in furious harmony. It had begun when he was a child, chained to the end of his bed by his aunt Gertrude, beaten with the "hose," a section of hard rubber which burly, six-foot-tall Aunty Gerta called her "discipline stick." He was beaten across the back so often that Horst, the orphaned bedwetter, could not sit against the hard, wooden chairs of the desks at school. Not for ten years. He was beaten like a mad dog, until he could no longer feel the pain of the beatings, only the rage, pumping him with hate, ready to explode.

Animals occupied the entire corner of a city block. At one

time it had been a warehouse, constructed of cinderblock with iron-girdered window frames. Now it was painted a gloss grey, giving the stone the look of steel, and the windows had been blackened.

The base of the reinforced door ground against the paving stone as he swung it open.

"Vhat you vant?" Horst Nickles challenged, his eyes fixed on Josef Tanaka. Above Nickles's head, a metal sign had been riveted to the cinderblock; the sign read: ALL NONMEMBERS ENTERING THESE PREMISES WILL BE KILLED. It was repeated in Spanish.

Tanaka took a half step backwards, making distance between himself and Nickles. Bill Fogarty remained to the side of the door, an arm's length away, staring at the layers of muscle beneath the red-cotton T-shirt and tight training pants, like an armored plating. Horst Nickles was the biggest man the policeman had ever seen.

Every nerve in Fogarty's body tingled. It was the same feeling that he'd had when he watched the Flint video, a mixture of intimidation and outright revulsion. That's him. The muscle god from the videotape. Fogarty knew it. Inside, he was trying hard to make the face in front of him fit the face on the police drawing. The hair matched, and the stubble of beard could have been shaved. He held his hand forward, his wallet opened to display his shield.

"We'd like to come in and take a look at your premises."

"Vhy? You had complaints?" Nickles questioned, his eyes on Tanaka, a thin smile playing on his lips.

"No, no complaints. We're investigating a homicide," Fogarty replied.

Nickles stepped forward. This time Tanaka didn't budge.

"Homicide? You saying someone vas murdered in my gymnasium?"

"Doctor John Winston Flint," Fogarty said, then waited for Nickles to react. Nothing, not even a twitch.

"Who's he?"

"The man who has been murdered," Fogarty answered.

"He vas not a member here. I have never heard of him."

"We'd still like to take a look inside," Fogarty said.

Nickles sneered at the captain, "You got no probable cause. That means you cannot come in. Besides," Nickles answered, turning towards Tanaka, "I don't let yellow men inside my gymnasium."

Tanaka stepped forward and Nickles squared up, barring his way. "I said no." Then, to Fogarty, "You got no varrant, you got no business here, now take your little yellow pet and go away."

Tanaka stared deep into the steel eyes. *I'd have to go all the way with this guy; I'd have to kill him*, he sensed.

Nickles remained focused on Tanaka. "Hey, you know how easy I could break your back?" He smiled.

Tanaka tasted the adrenaline on the roof of his mouth as Fogarty slid his hand inside his jacket, over the butt of his thirty-eight. He could draw his weapon, claim his tipoff from Oliver at the Juice Pit was "probable cause," and force his way inside, then contain the premises till a search warrant and a mobile unit arrived. If the papers were processed through his contact at the municipal court, the warrant would take about four hours. During that time, he'd be locked inside a stone bunker, on a dodgy probable cause, with a monster. Anything could happen. He could even blow the case.

"Josef, let's go."

Tanaka and Horst Nickles stood facing one another, eye-to-eye, like two prize fighters before the bell.

"I said, let's go." Fogarty's voice was sharp.

Horst Nickles smiled. "Your keeper has given you a command, now go away. The stink of your fear is ruining the air that I breathe."

Tanaka backed off, holding the German's eyes.

"See you later, Mr. Nickles," Fogarty promised.

The Horse closed the door of Animals, threw the deadbolt into place and turned toward the room.

"Okay, everybody, listen up!"

The clank of iron weights being returned to racks preceded the quiet.

"All of you people who are carrying gear in your gym bags, vials, syringes, anything with a medical label; I want you to collect your belongings and leave the premises immediately. No shower, no changing clothes, just go."

Fifteen minutes later Animals was clear of members. Jim Pinion and Randy Dornt were scouring the floor for spent needles, cleaning and vacuuming, tying the heavy-duty garbage bags, preparing for a fast trip to the dump. Horst Nickles was unloading his wall safe, removing fifty thousand dollars worth of pharmaceutical drugs, repacking them in his two impact-proof carrying cases and hustling them to the back of his pristine 1943 Mercedes sedan, the only car in North Philadelphia that was never burgled.

He slammed the trunk of the black Merc shut, rubbed the top of his left arm above the triceps muscle, which was bruised and swollen from his morning shot of Sustanon 250. Then he marched back to his office where he double-locked the door before opening his refrigerator. He removed the chilled bundle and laid it on his desk, tearing through the bubble wrap to reveal the freshly amputated head of a male monkey. He lifted the head, then lowered it sharply on the edge of his desk, cracking the skull like a coconut, separating it as he lifted it to his mouth.

"Dr. John, here's to you," he said, sucking the hormone-rich hypothalamus fluid from the center of the skull.

Tanaka sat silently as Fogarty turned the Chrysler around and drove back towards town. The policeman could feel the tension, like raw electricity.

"I'd lay odds on that freak being the hooded man on the videotape," he said, trying to get Tanaka to talk, looking for equilibrium. "I mean, it's a stretch, but it could be him in the drawing, same hair. H.N., Horst Nickles."

Tanaka remained silent.

"Although, I've got to say, he didn't look a hell of a lot like Mel Gibson." Fogarty tried for a laugh.

Tanaka clenched his fist and stared at his knuckles.

"Come on, Josef, it's part of the job, a little humiliation," Fogarty lightened his voice.

"Not part of my job, Bill."

"Yeah, I know, I know, but you've been around long enough to take it. It's not important, believe me."

"When are you going back there?" Tanaka asked, looking across at the policeman.

Fogarty caught the glint in the hard, brown eyes. "Not today, if that's what you're thinking. I'll give it a few days to settle, give Mr. Nickles enough time to get careless." Then Fogarty picked up his car phone and called homicide.

"Put me on to Dave Roach."

"Yes, C . . . Captain."

"What have you got for me?" Fogarty asked.

"Another possible I.D. on the suspect, a mounted officer by the name of Roy Graves, on East River Drive. He thought he recognized the police drawing. Said the f . . . fella was sitting on a park bench at about six-thirty on the morning following the Flint homicide. He said the guy was big, like a bodybuilder. He didn't report it, or take the guy's name or anything, but he said the guy was real n . . . nervous."

"Right, Dave. Now I want you to do two things. I want you to bring the mounted officer back in so I can talk to him, and I want you to go out and pick me up a couple of magazines. One of them is called *Stallion* and the other is *Swinging D's*, you got that?"

"*Stallion* and *Shining D . . . d . . . D's*?"

"No, *Swinging D's*, Dave, *Swinging D's*," Fogarty corrected, waiting as Roach wrote the names down.

"Over and out," Fogarty added, then put down the phone. He was grinning.

"That poor fuck," Tanaka said.

"It was either that or send you to Emilio's house, after hours," Fogarty replied, finally getting a smile out of Josef.

SWINGING D'S

Fogarty dropped Tanaka at the medical examiner's building, then returned to the Roundhouse. Roy Graves, the mounted police officer, was waiting.

"It's the guy's eyes that stuck with me, Sir. They were pale blue. Seemed to look right through me. Really piercing eyes. Aside from that, his most distinguishing feature was his size. I'd say he was a football player, or a bodybuilder. One of those Mike Tyson necks."

"How about his voice?" Fogarty asked. "Was there anything unusual about his voice?" He wanted to hear there was a trace of accent. A trace of Horst Nickles.

"It was a husky voice, kind of low. But he didn't say that much. Just a low voice."

Afterwards, Fogarty took the officer downstairs. There, with the help of the police artist, they sharpened up the drawing of the suspect. It could have been Nickles, but it was still a stretch.

Fogarty was seated at his desk, his door open, studying the latest drawing, when Dave Roach walked into homicide. Roach's face was beet red and he was clutching a brown bag, holding it so tightly that his fingers had ripped the cheap paper. He appeared nervous, eyes darting, like a thief.

"You got the magazines?" Fogarty asked.

Roach nodded and laid the brown bag on Fogarty's desk.

"Have a hard time finding them?"

"Yes, Sir, a very h . . . hard time," Roach answered, his right eye twitching. Fogarty wondered how he ever passed the medical to get on the force.

"Had to go to one of those adult bookshops on Arch Street, the kind of place that sells sexual appliances. It was one of the most embarrassing experiences of my l . . . life."

Fogarty looked at Roach and smiled. "Jesus, Dave, I'm sorry you had to go through all that. Right. Now close the door and let's see what we've got."

Fogarty took the artist's drawing from his jacket and laid it out on his desk as Dave Roach clicked the door shut. The drawing had been modified, with some help from Officer Graves.

"The guy running the shop thought I was a q . . . queer."

"You didn't tell him you were straight, did you?"

"No."

"Good. Think of it as your first assignment undercover. Would you please sit down? You're making me nervous."

Roach sat in the chair facing the desk as Fogarty slid the magazines from the envelope and opened *Swinging D's*.

"Jesus, Long Dong Silver's carrying a hosepipe. You'd have to wear that thing in a holster."

"It gets worse, wait till you see the advertisements," Dave Roach said.

Fogarty looked up, "You mean you've already looked these over?"

"Just a quick glance in the shop, to make sure I had the right magazines. A quick glance."

Fogarty nodded and continued to thumb the pages.

" 'Nineteen-inch arms, Fifty-one-inch chest, Ten inches, uncut, Top who likes to give it rough. Call Desmond at 555-BOSS,' " Fogarty read out loud.

"What's an uncut top?" Roach asked.

"Big Des isn't circumcised and he prefers to be the fucker, not the fuckee," Fogarty answered without looking up.

Roach was about to voice his disgust, then he remembered the Flint videotape, thought of Jimmy Stark, sitting in the next room, without a case, and kept quiet.

Fogarty scanned the ads:

MUSCLE MEN WANTED
PREFERABLY HUNG. BIG $ BUCKS.
IF YOU'VE GOT THE BODY, I'VE GOT THE CAMERA;

PHOTOS ONLY, NO KINKS, STRAIGHT BUSINESS.
Send Snaps, Polaroids, and Contact Number To: *Philly Photo Man,
P.O. Box 99, 10th and Dickenson.*

The ad was repeated four times in the classified section. Fogarty leafed back through the pages of naked men. Most of the pictures of bodybuilders were credited to the Philly Photo Man.

"Let me take a look at that magazine, Dave," Fogarty asked.

Roach handed *Stallions* across the desk and Fogarty flicked through the pages, noting that several of the men who appeared in *Swinging D's* were also featured in *Stallion*, with the same photographic credit. A couple of the featured faces came about as close as Horst Nickles to resembling the police drawing of the suspect. Fogarty turned to the classifieds and found the same Muscle-Men-Wanted ad repeated five times.

"Okay, Dave, I want you to take these magazines down to Thirtieth Street station, to the postal service there. I want you to present this ad, your shield, and explain that you've got probable cause to believe that the South Philly P.O. box is being used for the handling of pornographic literature. Get me the name and address of the person who rents the box."

"Yes, Sir," Dave Roach said, taking the magazines from Fogarty, stuffing them back in the brown bag, and getting up to leave.

"Dave," Fogarty said.

Roach met the captain's eyes.

"It's either this or we send a couple of Polaroids of you to the Philly Photo Man. You got anything sexy?"

Roach looked stunned. His eye appeared to freeze mid-twitch. Then Fogarty grinned and the young detective laughed, a high, bursting laugh. "Jesus, Captain, for a second, I thought you were being serious."

Fogarty winked and Roach was gone. Next came Sharon Gilbey.

She arrived at Fogarty's office with a thirty-page computer printout of "missing persons," and "dead on arrivals" from the medical examiner's office, plus "casualty admittances" from the three main Philadelphia hospitals.

"This is from January to June, nineteen-ninety. I'm down to the *D*s in the d.o.a. section. We've got six John Does and two Jane Does. So far there's no one with a physical description that corresponds to the woman on the tape."

"In five days, I may be able to give you some help. I've got the Flint video down in Quantico, with the F.B.I. They're doing some enlargements on individual frames and there's a chance they're going to get a date off the wristwatch that Flint was wearing."

"That would be great, Captain."

"In the meantime, keep on checking the records. I know it's a drag, but that's the way it is sometimes."

Fogarty was still at his desk when the call came from Dave Roach.

"C . . . c—"

"What have you got, Dave?"

"John Roccoletti. That's the guy's name, sir. The Philly Photo man is named John Roccoletti."

"Excellent. Have you got an address?"

"Number six-eighteen South Third Street, right off South, near Bainbridge."

"Dave, you did good," Fogarty said, writing down the details.

Fogarty walked out of his office and into the main room at homicide. There were four officers there, three seated at their desks, one checking files.

"John Roccoletti! The Philly Photo Man. Ring any bells?" Fogarty called out, as he headed for the computer. Everyone looked up, no one answered.

Fogarty sat down in front of the screen, switched the computer on, and punched in Roccoletti's name. He wasn't expecting much; it was more a formality. What he got felt like Christmas.

Twenty-six years ago, when South Street was the hub of

Philadelphia's hippiedom, Johnny Roccoletti was the "main man." Whenever there was action, Johnny Roccoletti was on the scene, in his uniform of torn jeans with paisley patches, his well-worn embroidered "wedding" shirt from Oaxaca, Mexico, and his black suede "Beatle boots" from Carnaby Street in London and, of course, his Pentax camera. Flashing away, shouldering his camera like the M-16 he would never have to carry in Vietnam, because of his short leg and lower back problems. But that was all right in 1967. Nobody ever really noticed that Johnny Roccoletti was actually five-feet-one-inch in height and wore a three-inch lift in his left Beatle boot, or that his nose was a shade longer and somewhat more beaked than that of the singer, Tiny Tim. In the sixties' haze of smoke and acid, Johnny Roccoletti was one of South Street's "Beautiful People."

The turning point of his career came as the mastermind behind *Paint It Black*, an avant-garde movie in the Warhol tradition, filmed entirely on location during South Street's "Carnival of Love." Roccoletti's contribution—aside from operating one of the two handheld super-eight cameras—was the conception, creation, and installation of the "Sperm Bank," a seven-foot-high wall of sheetrock with six holes cut in the material, about three-feet above the base and a foot apart. The Bank was painted black with SPERM BANK, DONATIONS PLEASE printed at the top of the DONORS side. On the other, six barstools were positioned to accommodate the "cashiers." Donations were accepted either manually or orally.

A fourteen-year-old girl named Jane from the suburban town of Ardmore, plied with a thousand micrograms of L.S.D., became the sole cashier, and Johnny Roccoletti was the principle donor, although the height of the "donor's hole" forced him to spend a majority of the afternoon standing on the toes of the foot attached to his longest leg.

The Sperm Bank was a great success until the police and the paramedics arrived, sedated the cashier, arrested the donor, and closed the bank.

John Roccoletti's—a.k.a. Johnny Rocka—rap sheet started there, in 1967, with the Sperm Bank bust: procuring an underage female for the purpose of prostitution and pornography. It continued with an arrest for drug trafficking in 1973 and peaked in 1982 with eighteen months in an upstate prison for the sale and distribution of pornographic films involving minors. Fogarty was buzzing by the time he printed out the sheet, trailing it in his hand as he pushed through the door leading from homicide and into the elevator and up to Records.

And there was Roccoletti, in all his glory, swarthy-skinned with flowing hair; the mug shot was dated 1967. By 1982, the Philly Photo Man looked like a balding pelican. The name of his last arresting officer was given as Al Harris, retired in 1988. Fogarty located Harris's home phone number and placed the call.

Harris had a voice that sounded like a Whisky Sour. "Yeah, sure I remember that little motherfucker," he growled, "I had him in court five times between that bust in eighty-three and when I left the force in eighty-eight."

"What for?" Fogarty asked.

"Always the same thing," Harris answered, "pornographic films. Faggots, bodybuilders, little kids—"

"Horst Nickles?"

"What?"

"Horst Nickles," Fogarty repeated, "he's a German body-builder, was he involved in the films?"

"I've never heard the name. But that shouldn't mean much. Roccoletti was careful, everybody wore a hood. His only mistake was the music, the son-of-a-bitch always used the same music. It must have been some kind of ego thing with him."

"What do you mean?"

"Like a trademark, that theme from the old sci-fi movie—"

"*A Space Oddysey?*"

"That's it, real grand and glorious."

"Oh yeah," Fogarty whispered.

Harris could feel the excitement down the line.

"Have you got something on Rocka?"

"Maybe."

"I'd come out of retirement to see that little prick go down."

"Why couldn't you get him back in eighty-eight?" Fogarty asked.

"He had connections, sick friends in high places. People who couldn't afford to get caught up in a bad scene. People who hired the kind of lawyers that proved all my evidence was circumstantial."

"John Winston Flint?" Fogarty asked.

"I read about him in yesterday's paper. The answer is, I don't know. I'd never heard of Flint till yesterday. Are Flint and Rocka connected?"

"I'm not sure," Fogarty answered. "How about the films? Where are the confiscated films?"

"They got lost."

"What?"

"Whoever was working for Rocka had a lot more at stake than just saving that midget's ass. The tapes were lost, probably destroyed. It ended my career. I lost faith in what I was doing after that; that fucking case broke me."

"Well I'm about to open it right back up," Fogarty promised.

"God bless you, Captain."

CHALLENGE

Josef Tanaka stood on the polished pinewood floor, in front of the class, directly below the portrait of Gichin Funokoshi, the Okinawan-born master who is universally acknowledged as the father of modern karate. Above Funokoshi's portrait were two crossed flags, one Japanese, the other American.

The class was comprised of eighteen people, eleven men and seven women, all black belts, ranked between first and forth *dan*, or degree. Oliver Hall, from the Juice Pit, was in the front line, his popeye forearms just visible below the sleeves of his *gi*. His first-degree black belt was still shiny after six months; in a year or so, depending on how much he practiced, the silk thread would wear and split, revealing the white cotton beneath. Oliver Hall, like all the other people in this advanced class, kept his eyes locked on Josef Tanaka.

"Tonight we will practice *bassai*," Tanaka announced. "Translated loosely, *bassai-sho* means storming the fortress and capturing the enemy. The form has forty-five movements and is particularly effective when defending against a long stick, or," he hesitated, always trying to make the forms, or *katas*, relevant to modern-day use, "in some cases, a baseball bat."

A few members of the class smiled but most remained stern-faced, as if Tanaka were preaching the gospel.

"*Bassai-sho* is a very dynamic *kata*. There is a great deal of body shifting, from back stance to front stance, from straddle-legged stance into cat stance, continual movement. The psychological key to this *kata* is mental resolve, maintaining the attitude that the fall of the fortress is inevitable. Concentrate as you perform the techniques. Never allow the thought of your enemy to leave your mind. When you block, break his legs and his arms, when you attack, attack *through* his body. Your mind will destroy his mind and your body will destroy his body. The *kata* is a structured fight. To master a *kata* you must find the freedom within the structure; you must give your own individual expression to each technique, visualizing its intent and purpose as you perform."

They began *Bassai-sho*, at first slowly, moving the right foot to the left and placing the edge of the left open hand on top of the thumb of the right open hand, then, swinging both arms back to the left side and lifting the right foot. The class surged forward, landing in back stance, concentrating on balance and the correct execution of the individual technique. It was like dancing by numbers, Tanaka calling the tune. Twenty minutes later, he brought them to attention and instructed them to perform the *kata* in their own time, to their own rhythm and, to search for their own meaning and application for each of the techniques within the form, but, most important, "imagine that you are fighting an enemy."

Tanaka gave himself space and practiced alongside his class; his enemy was Horst Nickles. In the minute and forty seconds that it took Tanaka to complete *Bassai-sho*, Tanaka broke the German's nose, sternum, and right knee, leaving the Horse helpless at his feet.

It had been a long time since Tanaka had been challenged. He had grown used to being the Sensei, the teacher, acknowledged within his sphere as a fighting master. To have someone treat him with blatant disrespect was intolerable. The German's cold blue eyes and leering voice had invaded his domain. "I don't let yellow men inside my gymnasium"— from that moment, Josef Tanaka had been preparing for battle.

"Oh, come on, you're letting your ego get to you," Rachel said, watching Tanaka down the last of a bottle of Chateau Figeac Saint-Emilion, his favorite red wine.

"Nothing to do with ego," Tanaka answered, placing the glass down next to his empty plate. "The guy challenged me. It's a matter of honor."

"So, this is a duel at sunrise situation? The German War Horse versus the Last Samurai?" Rachel suggested.

Tanaka looked across their round, mahogany dining table and met her eyes. She wasn't laughing, not even smiling, but there was a certain glimmer; she had a way of making him see the other side of himself, of turning his moods around. She lifted her glass of mountain spring water, and took a swallow.

"And while the Last Samurai does battle his pregnant wife remains pure from head to toe, no alcohol, no caffeine, and no red meat." She raised her eyelids and pursed her lips. "How very fucking boring."

Tanaka held steady a few seconds before he laughed, asking finally, "And what has the Last Samurai's wife been doing all day?"

"Just the usual nip and tuck," Rachel answered, happy to change the subject. Even though she sometimes joked about Josef's obsession with violence, or "the control of violence," as he termed it, his sheer commitment to *bushido*, the way of the warrior, frightened her. Rachel knew her husband would die before allowing himself to be dishonored.

She held his eyes and kept it light. "I mean what do you say to a fifty-three-year-old ex–professional linebacker who wants you to stick two silicone pie plates under his breasts so it looks like he still has a body?"

"You're kidding me?"

"He was deadly serious, claimed he couldn't wear his shirts unbuttoned anymore. He's obviously still very much into the Vegas gold medallion look."

"Who is he?"

"Sorry, that would comprimise the confidentiality of my profession. But if I told you that he was your favorite WPOV sportscaster—"

"Rick Larson?"

"Honestly, it makes me wonder why I do what I do for a living. He's my second menopausal male in a week."

"Are you going to give him the pecs?"

Rachel shook her head.

"Why not?" Josef was grinning.

"Because he needs to go on a diet and do some exercise. The problem with these ex-jocks is that once their competitive days are over they immediately stop exercising and continue to eat everything they could get away with when they were nineteen and active. By fifty it's not a pretty sight."

"And you told him you wouldn't do it?"

"Yes, and he told me I may have just cost him his career in television."

"Why don't you give him a break."

"I'd sooner enroll him for a year in a gymnasium. Six months of bench presses and Rick Larson would be ready for his first training bra," she said, knowing she'd made a mistake the moment she'd mentioned gymnasiums.

Tanaka laughed again, but his eyes had gone hard and his mind was back on the ugly German.

Horst Nickles stood, staring through the sliding-glass window of his penthouse and out over the Delaware River. "I live on top of the mayor." That had been one of his favorite lines when he'd bought the seven-room apartment in Society Hill Towers. Now *that* mayor was out of office and living in Miami and Nickles was remortgaging his penthouse for the second time. The steroid business had never recovered from the ruling which made it a felony to possess the same hormones that the human body naturally produced. Even though Horst Nickles had been quick to get into the nonsteroid performance enhancers such as the Russian plant extracts and Clenbuterol, a nonsteroidal asthma medication known for its anabolic properties, the Horse would never be the "Mail-Order Muscle Guru" again. That was bad. John Winston Flint's death was worse. Flint had been Nickles's last proper medical source. Nickles had fed the bent doctor a constant stream of aspiring physique champions. Guys who didn't mind a little rough stuff in order to get their backsides pumped with pharmaceutical-quality testosterone. And, sometimes, when he was in the mood, the Horse himself would participate in Flint's follies. Although in the last two years their relationship had soured, brought on by Flint's children. Horst Nickles was not a pedophile, and Flint's insistence on involving his seven-year-old daughter in sex games repelled him.

Now, the question was, which of Horst Nickle's Aryan Army, as he liked to call his inner circle of beefcake, had been repelled enough to annihilate the "source." Horst Nickles wanted to find out before the police did; he wanted to administer his own justice.

He turned from the window, and adjusted the dimmer switch on the wall beside him. Eight overhead tracklights beamed down on a wall full of framed photographs; each of the twenty-four pictures featured a current or past member of Nickles's army. Most had come and gone, trained with the Horse for a couple of years and moved on; the serious ones to California, the ones without the heart or the natural genetics required for professional competition drifting away in search of life beyond the "iron grapevine." Horst had made money on all of them, selling their bodies, or pictures of their bodies, and organizing them into a solid distribution network for his anabolic steroids. He repaid them with promises of the big time and an introduction to Dr. John, holding on to them by drugs, force, and intimidation. Horst Nickles was a pimp. A pimp who had almost been a champion.

In 1978, Horst Nickles was imported from East Germany to Venice Beach, California. He was twenty years old and sponsored by Reggie Lane and *Pumped* magazine, the most influential names in bodybuilding. Reggie touted him as the new Arnold, the German supergod.

It all went wrong when, in his postadolescent furor, Horst announced that, in Germany, he had been a staunch neo-

Nazi and went on to expound, in several newspaper articles and magazines, that he believed in white supremacy and the natural inferiority of the black, Semitic, and yellow man. After Horst's revelations, Reggie Lane and *Pumped* disowned him. His sponsorship, which included an increasing bulk of performance-enhancing drugs, was revoked, and Horst Nickles found himself the pariah of the bodybuilding circuit, alone and unloved in the land of dreams. At first, the young German treated his dismissal with arrogance and scorn, but soon realized that he would either have to rescind his stance on the master race or find a new career.

He drifted to San Francisco and found employment as a bouncer in a North Beach strip club, working part-time as a trainer in a local gym, while continuing to use steroids. The cost of the drugs was high, so he began to sell them. Within a year, steroid distribution was his sole source of income. The work suited him, he thrived on the drugs, and he knew how to collect the money from his clients, but competition was fierce and Horst looked East for greener pastures, often flying his Californian product into New York or Philadelphia.

In 1981, Philadelphia looked very green, and Horst was treated like a muscular messiah. The lease on the Broad Street warehouse came cheap and, at that time, the neighborhood was poor but racially mixed. Horst Nickles hauled the first Olympic barbell set into Animals in June 1982. Within weeks the news of the big German from the West Coast and his hardcore power gym had pulled in fifty members. All white.

Horst Nickles worked hard, both in the gym and on the medical circuit, rounding up a team of doctors who would prescribe anabolic steroids for cosmetic and performance use. The practice, among medical doctors, was frowned upon but still legal and John Winston Flint was on the team. Within two years Horst Nickles had established himself as the Mail-Order Muscle Guru, shipping his power courses, steroid handbook, and drugs all over America. He had also formed the first of his Aryan Armies, hand-picked and personally trained to distribute his product locally.

Then, in 1988, the sky fell in. Senator Joe Biden, incensed by steroid use by teenage boys, pushed a bill through Congress making it illegal for a medical doctor to prescribe the drugs for cosmetic or performance enhancement. Everybody jumped ship, except John Winston Flint, who had reasons, other than money, for staying with the Horse. But one doctor, alone, could never prescribe enough drugs to supply Nickle's market. So, while Flint looked after the elite Aryan Army, Horst Nickles imported counterfeit steroids and searched for other avenues to support his upper-middle-class lifestyle. What he needed was a champion, an Olympia or Universe; someone to figurehead his bodybuilding empire, to endorse his legal products, and to front the franchise of Animals gymnasiums that he intended to open. A champion that Nickles would forge with his knowledge and build with Flint's drugs. But champions, in the world of bodybuilding, are born, not made. They must have perfect bone structure, perfect genetics, an inherited characteristic that separates the competitors from the greats. It involves the skeleton, the size of the bones, their symmetry and proportion: the head to the shoulders, the length of the arms compared to the torso, the breadth of hip and distance between the pelvis and the knee, the knee and the foot, the size of the hands and feet; and no amount of physical training, of food or dietary supplements, will alter the genetics of the mature human body.

In the case of Jacqueline Angel, her genetics were perfect.

GARBAGE

Fogarty was at the wheel of his Chrysler, with Sharon Gilbey beside him and Dave Roach in the backseat. The warrant had come through an hour ago, and Fogarty spoke quickly as he drove cross town towards South Street.

"Okay, here's the situation, the little creep we're going to visit makes his living at pornography. There's a good chance he shot the Flint video. He's been arrested before and done time, so he's going to know the score. That means we treat him with kid gloves. I don't want him clamming up on us. I'm carrying a warrant and we'll use it when the time is right, but first, I want to go easy with him, see how much he'll give us on his own. As soon as anyone mentions homicide, whether it's Flint's or the woman on the tape, Mr. Roccoletti is going to lock his jaw and double-time it to his lawyer."

"Sir, are you saying that we shouldn't even tell him we're from h . . . homicide?" Roach asked.

"I'm saying that you follow my lead with the questions. Go easy," Fogarty replied, swinging a left off Broad and heading east down South Street.

"In fact, don't say anything at all unless you feel it's absolutely necessary and, even then, take me aside and run it by me first. If we spook this guy, it's going to cost us time, and right now, time is precious."

Fogarty drove as far as the corner of Third and South, then pulled the Chrysler to the curb, and shut off the engine.

Sharon Gilbey could smell the Kouros cologne, spilling from the collar of Dave Roach's corduroy jacket, hitting her in a sweet wave, as he opened the passenger's door and stepped onto the sidewalk. Six hundred and eighteen South Third Street, the address listed on the warrant, was halfway down the block.

The two young detectives walked behind Fogarty, then

stood silent as he rang the entry buzzer. After the third unan-
swered ring the captain used the back of his fist against the
faded red door. Finally he pushed inward against the mail
slot, bent down, and tried to look inside the house.

"It's dark in there and my eyes are shot," he said, turning
to Roach.

Roach stepped forward, taking Fogarty's place at the slot.

"A load of unopened m . . . ail lying on the floor," he
reported, pressing harder, wedging his nose over the steel
frame, trying to see into the shadowed hallway, "and something stinks, maybe the guy went away and forgot to take
out his g . . . g . . . garbage."

Fogarty was halfway back to the car by the time Dave Roach
withdrew from the opening. Roach and Gilbey watched him
open the Chrysler's passenger-side door, reach inside the
glove compartment, and pull something out, pocketing it,
before continuing to the rear of the car. There, he removed
a flat-ended tire iron from the trunk. By then, a middle-aged
woman, wearing bell-bottom trousers, a denim jacket, and
trailing a toy poodle, had rounded the corner.

"Pardon me, ma'm, but do you live in the neighborhood?"

A look of mild indignance crossed the dogwalker's brow.
She depressed the button on the poodles automatic lead and
reigned the animal in.

"I'm a police officer," Fogarty added.

"I live above Second Seasons Health Foods on South," she
replied, "and I do carry a pooper scooper."

Fogarty nodded his approval, then asked, "Are you familiar with the man who lives in that house?" He pointed to
618.

The dogwalker relaxed her grip on the dog's lead. "I see
him come in and go out, if that's what you mean, usually
when I walk my dog," she answered, as her pet inched closer
and sniffed Fogarty's shoe.

"Can you remember the last time you saw him?" Fogarty
continued.

The woman looked beyond Gilbey and Roach and at the

door of Roccoletti's, while the poodle sniffed twice more before mounting Fogarty's leg. Fogarty raised his foot and shook it, but the dog clung on. Dave Roach caught his laugh mid-throat, turning it into a cough, while Sharon Gilbey stared.

"I haven't seen him in the past week, not for three or four days anyway," the woman said. "He's some kind of photographer, isn't he? Always carries a camera." Then she looked down.

"I'm sorry, Officer," she blurted, bending to grab the dog, then struggling to hoist him clear. Fogarty helped with a short kick.

"Obviously, Officer, you don't have a pet," she frowned.

"No. I don't," Fogarty answered, turning to walk to the house.

"His neighbors haven't seen Mr. Roccoletti for a week; they're concerned for his welfare. We call that probable cause," he said to Roach and Gilbey, wedging the flat end of the iron between the frame and the door and pulling it towards him. The old Yale lock held firm as the wood splintered on either side. Fogarty completed the job with his shoulder. The reek of rotted meat met them from the hallway, and Fogarty lifted the small tube of Vaseline from his pocket.

"Put a touch of this on your index finger, then dab it on the inside of your nose; it'll make the smell a little sweeter."

He followed his own instructions before passing the tube to Gilbey.

"Sharon, you take the downstairs of the house, that includes the kitchen and the basement. Dave, you go to the second floor, I'll go to the top. Draw your weapons, be ready." Fogarty was ninety-nine percent sure that the fragrance wasn't last night's dinner. He switched on the hall light, then closed the shattered door behind them.

Even through the Vaseline, the stink was everywhere, stronger as Sharon Gilbey moved down the corridor towards the room at the end. She held her back tight to the wall and her weapon downwards. Another few feet and she could hear it, quiet at first, but alive, aware of her presence and listening. She stopped and the noise continued, a sharp, grinding noise, then the sound of something being dragged across the floor. Gilbey felt the moisture of her palms against the wooden grip of her thirty-eight. The noise stopped. He can hear me. He's waiting for me down there, listening, getting ready. For a moment, she considered retreat, backing up the corridor to call for assistance. Then the strange grinding, shuffling sound began again and Detective Gilbey raised her firearm, steadied her breathing, and inched forward.

Fogarty and Roach parted company on the landing of the second floor. Fogarty motioned with his head, indicating that Roach should investigate the second floor of the house while he continued to the top. Roach whispered, "Yes, Sir," and watched as the captain climbed the stairs upwards.

The first thing that caught Roach's attention was that the smell of rotted meat increased as he entered the darkened room. A step later and he tripped down onto one knee with his thirty-eight pressed into his right foot. "Jesus!" he hissed, closing his eyes, visualizing what would have happened if the Smith and Wesson had discharged. He looked to see what had caught him. It was a thick black electrical cord, leading from the nearest wall socket, and in through the door of an adjoining room. He stood and walked to the door. It was pitch black beyond. He transfered his thirty-eight to his left hand and used his right to search the wall to the side of the door. Nothing, no light switch. He took another step, felt something hard beneath his shoe. Too late, he had already shifted his bodyweight, pressing downward against the foot switch. The strobe ignited and, for a flash, Dave Roach was eye to eye with Johnny Roccoletti.

Fogarty was staring at a photograph of a man's arm, buried to the elbow in another man's rectum, when he heard the call from below.

"Captain! C . . . aptain!"

Fogarty turned to the sound of a gun firing. He took the steps two at a time, catching up with Roach on the landing.

"The shot came from downstairs. There's a man back there, dead," Roach said, pointing to the studio while allowing Fogarty to lead the way down the steps. They found Sharon Gilbey standing in the entrance to the kitchen, still holding her firearm in the ready position, aiming into the room.

"Easy, Officer, easy," Fogarty said quietly, "we're coming up behind you."

"It came right at me, Captain, I didn't have a choice," Gilbey whispered.

Fogarty looked in the direction of the policewoman's thirty-eight.

"It came right at me," she repeated.

"Jesus, it's the size of a cat," Fogarty acknowledged, staring at the grey rat which lay three feet in front of Sharon Gilbey's polished shoes, half its head missing.

"It was gnawing on a bone when I walked in, didn't run or anything, just turned on me. It could have had rabies or something; I didn't want to kick it. I didn't want to touch it."

"Hey, Officer Gilbey," Fogarty reassured, "I wouldn't have touched it either, you did fine."

"First time I ever fired my weapon in the line of duty, and I shoot a rat, oh man, I shot a rat," she continued, lowering her weapon, unwinding.

"Under the sink, Sir, under the sink." Roach was standing to Fogarty's left, staring at an elongated mass of chewed flesh. A single joint was visible in the middle of the flesh, the bone licked white and smooth.

"That's what it was chewing on," Gilbey explained.

"It belongs upstairs," Roach said.

"What are you talking about?" Fogarty asked.

"The man upstairs is missing his right arm."

Johnny Roccoletti stared at them. He was naked, mounted on his tripod, the camera brace jammed up his posterior, his right arm torn from his body at the shoulder, and his left hand covering his genitals, as if, even in death, he could protect a smattering of dignity. His body was forced erect by an electrical cord, tied round his neck and plugged into a ceiling socket. Roccoletti's cheekbones had been highlighted with a white powder base, his flesh tinted with mascara, and his lips painted crimson red. His eyelids had been removed.

"Nobody touch a thing," Fogarty ordered. "Sharon, you stay here with the body. Dave, I want you on the street, securing the premises. I'm going down to the car and phone for a mobile crime unit. The important thing is that nothing on this crime scene is disturbed, do you understand?"

"Yes, Sir," Sharon Gilbey replied, "I understand, Sir."

There was a quiver in her voice that made Fogarty hesitate.

"Dave, you go ahead," he said, then waited for the detective to leave the room. "Something bothering you, Sharon?" Under the circumstances the question sounded ludicrous.

"The way the face is made up, Captain," she answered, stepping closer to Roccoletti.

"I don't follow you."

"It's beautiful."

Fogarty looked concerned, maybe Gilbey was losing it.

"I've been using makeup for ten years and I couldn't have done a job like that. Look, even the lips have been shaped, then outlined," she added.

Fogarty looked at Roccoletti's mouth, his lips had been elongated to form a thin grimace. Then, into his eyes: they resembled solid glass, enlarged by the missing lids, brown and vacant. The little man's face reminded Fogarty of a Japanese mask; one of those worn by the Noh theater players he had seen in Tokyo, with expressions of emotion painted on. Roccoletti's expression was sheer pain.

"You'll be all right if I leave you here a few minutes?" he asked, lightly gripping Gilbey's arm. This was Fogarty's sixty-third homicide, and Gilbey's first. He felt responsible.

Sharon Gilbey turned to him. "I've had a thing about rats since I was a little girl. I probably needed to shoot one. People don't bother me. I'm fine."

Fogarty smiled, "I'll be right back."

Dave Roach was hovering on the sidewalk, in front of the door to 618.

"All clear, Captain, no response to the pistol shot, all clear."

"Thanks, Dave, I can see that." Fogarty tried not to sound condescending. He knew how the two detectives felt; he could remember his first homicide. He'd rushed onto the crime scene, slid in a pool of fresh blood, landed on his ass, and discharged a slug through the ceiling of the victim's residence. It took him nine months and another case to live it down.

Five minutes after Fogarty's phone call a uniformed officer arrived to relieve Roach from guard duty, and the mobile crime unit was en route. Fogarty had instructed them to bring a set of bolt cutters and a hack saw. Next he called the medical building.

"Hello, Bob. This is Bill Fogarty."

Moyer knew Fogarty well enough to read his tone of voice; there was business and there was serious business. This was serious. Moyer waited.

"We've got another homicide. Very ugly."

"Do you need us over there?" Moyer asked.

"Bob, I wouldn't ask, but I'm ninety-nine percent sure that this one is tied in with the Flint homicide. It's a different m.o. but Flint and the victim were connected."

"You want Josef?"

"I'd appreciate that, Bob, I really would."

VICE

Jim Finnegan had been on the take for five years. It started when he had worked vice. In those days it was blow-jobs, in the front seat of his patrol car, parked in an alley or on a side street, in plain view of the pedestrian foot traffic on Market. He knew all the "working" girls and all the girls knew Sergeant wrap-your-laughing-gear-around-this Finnegan. Five minutes of good head could keep you from a fifty-dollar fine and a night in the tank.

Finnegan had first encountered professional difficulties when a dental plate containing four teeth, two front and two incisors, was found, during a routine maintenance check, beneath the front seat of his patrol car. Because the sergeant was on sick leave, the dental plate was turned over to his commanding officer. The inlaid rhinestone, in the right front tooth, suggested that the plate did not belong to Sergeant Finnegan, and a quick investigation revealed the owner to be Saline Phipps, a working girl on Jim's beat. Further investigation confirmed that Ms. Phipps preferred to work orally without her denture.

Sergeant Finnegan was busted one week later. Although he claimed the reason that Ms. Phipps was kneeling on the floor of his patrol car, her head not visible from outside the vehicle, was that she was searching for her missing denture, his vice captain did not believe him and, within eight weeks, Officer Finnegan was pounding a beat on North Broad.

His new assignment was like a walk into hell; a big, brash Irishman in a big, black neighborhood. His job anxiety resulted in an eating disorder, and within months, Finnegan's weight ballooned to two-sixty. At six-feet-one-inch, two hundred and sixty pounds was a lot of beef. Plus, he was short on breath; even a one-block chase, pursuing a set of Michael

Jordan air soles carrying a stolen car radio, left Finnegan heaving on the sidewalk.

Horst Nickles hated cops, except the cops he could control. He knew he could control Finnegan the moment the fat man set foot in Animals. From the fingernails, bitten to the cuticles, to the red circles beneath the watery grey eyes, Jim Finnegan looked like a whipped dog.

"I give free membership to all police officers," Nickles had stated.

Six months later, Jim Finnegan weighed two hundred and ten pounds and had lost twelve inches on his waist. He was stronger, faster, and more confident than he had been when he'd played defensive linebacker for St. Bonaventure High. A combination of Cytomel, a thyroid stimulant that increased metabolism and promoted weight loss, dianabol, a good basic, orally ingested anabolic steroid, and weekly shots of testosterone enanthate worked the miracle. Plus a bit of dexedrine, to dampen his appetite, and some intensely supervised one-on-one coaching from the Horse himself.

The steroids had cost Big Jim a little hair on his head, and a few pimples on his ass, but basically he was a new man. He had also increased his earning power by several hundred dollars a week, paid cash in hand, after he'd supervised the delivery of the amphetamines and counterfeit pharmaceuticals to Animals.

Big Jim's real value to Horst Nickles, however, was as a low-level informer; someone on the inside of the Thirty-fifth district, someone with his ear to the ground, able to warn Nickles if things got hot, even warm.

While Johnny Rocka's body was being separated from the tripod with a hack saw, Jim Finnegan was sitting in front of Horst Nickles in the locked office of Animals.

"I don't know this person, he is not one of mine," Nickles said, studying the police drawing.

"You're sure of that?"

Nickles stared into Finnegan's face. "I have never seen him in my life."

"Then, why would a captain from homicide be coming around here?"

"You tell me Jim, that's what I pay you for."

Finnegan met Horst Nickles's eyes; they were two men who knew each other well but would never even come close to being friends. The thirty-six-year-old policeman was tough, but he was afraid of Horst Nickles. Not just physically, but mentally and emotionally, in the same way that a newly commissioned marine remains afraid of his drill sergeant. Nickles would always know the fat, insecure child who lived inside the muscular cop, but Finnegan would never completely understand the German.

"Think, Horst, think," Finnegan said carefully. "Study the picture and think. Does it look anything like anybody on your payroll? Take away the beard, shorten the hair—"

"I don't fucking know the guy," Horst answered slowly. He was becoming agitated.

"All right, all right," Finnegan shrugged, reaching for the drawing.

Nickles pulled the white sheet of paper back from Finnegan's hand.

"I keep this."

The smell of fresh Maxwell House coffee grounds, burning in a frying pan, permeated the atmosphere at Roccoletti's; that and the smoke of several cigars. Along with the Vaseline, they were the tried and true methods of disguising the stink of the dead.

Johnny Roccoletti lay on his side, on a white rubber sheet, the jagged end of the sawn-off tripod extending five inches from his posterior. One man from the mobile crime unit squatted down beside him, carefully encasing Roccoletti's bony left hand in a clear plastic bag, while Josef Tanaka concentrated on the little man's right shoulder joint. Roccoletti's severed arm lay in a clear bag, beside them.

Sharon Gilbey kept a respectful distance from the working men. She continued to stare at Roccoletti's face: the maggots had just hatched and one of the silvery grey creatures had forced its way out from between his painted lips. This was only the second corpse that Sharon Gilbey had been close to. The first had been her mother, dead from a massive coronary at forty-three.

So cold to the touch, cold and hard, like porcelain, Sharon thought, remembering how she had attempted to plant a final kiss on her mother's lips at the viewing, after the embalming. *Like kissing a china doll.* Virginia Gilbey's face had been painted, but not as well as Johnny Roccoletti's. Sharon remembered looking at the mortician, thinking he resembled a combination of the prize fighter, Sonny Liston, and the reverend Martin Luther King, hard but compassionate, with hands the size of shovels. *What could she expect from a man with hands like that?* But Johnny Roccoletti? His face was a work of art.

Fogarty stood behind Josef Tanaka, watching as his friend probed the exposed shoulder joint with a long steel instrument.

"Anything?" Fogarty whispered.

Tanaka pulled the probe out of the dried and atrophied connective tissue and stood up.

"It's definitely a tear, there's no evidence of any cutting, no even surfaces, nothing to indicate a blade may have been used. I'd like forensics to check for traces of metal, even rust, but I'm reasonably certain the arm was ripped from the body."

"Nobody's found anything that looks like a weapon in the house, just the usual kitchen knives, and a hammer in a toolbox in the basement, but nothing else," Fogarty said, looking down at Roccoletti's mangled shoulder. "How 'bout an ax?"

Tanaka shook his head, "An ax would have left a definite pattern of laceration." Then he met Fogarty's eyes, "Come on, Bill, you've seen plenty of that kind of stuff. This is different; this guy's been savaged. The killer must have the strength of an ape."

Tanaka was thinking of Horst Nickles. Fogarty nodded,

reading his mind. Then he recalled Karen Flint's words with regard to her late husband, "However he died, I hope it was painful and slow." He stared, again, at Johnny Roccoletti.

The South Street photographer looked like a mock-up from a horror movie, small and shrivelled, with his grotesquely painted face, the makeup and paint dried to form a parchment death mask. Karen Flint? Fogarty had checked and rechecked on Karen Flint, or Karen Elms, and had come up dry. There seemed to be no connection between Karen Flint and Horst Nickles, or none that he could find. Fogarty's instinct ran ice cold when he thought of Karen Flint. But Horst Nickels? Fogarty got hot flashes when he thought of Horst Nickles.

"C . . . c . . . Captain? Over here, Captain." Dave Roach's voice jarred him from thought. The detective's words were muffled behind a charcoal-filtered mask. The mask was an optional device; Fogarty preferred a nose full of Vaseline, or a good Havana.

"Yeah, Dave, what have you got?"

"There's a tape in the cassette player."

"Take it out and bag it," Fogarty ordered.

Roach had just placed his latex-covered index finger against the eject button when Fogarty changed his mind.

"Press play, Dave. Play the cassette."

Dave Roach hit play and the machine stuttered and stopped.

"It's all played out," Roach explained, pressing rewind.

Fogarty spotted one of the mobile crime officers lift a small shining object from the floor and slip it into an evidence bag.

"What have you got there?"

"It's a tiny pair of scissors, Sir."

"Let me see them," Fogarty said.

The man handed up the evidence bag.

Fogarty walked back to Josef Tanaka.

"I'm almost ready to wrap him and get him down to the morgue," Tanaka said. "There's too much decomposition to tell much more without the postmortem."

"What do you make of these?" Fogarty said, handing Tanaka the bag. "They look like the type of thing a lady would keep in her makeup kit."

Tanaka removed the scissors. They were very small, made of surgical steel and the blades were gently curved. The doctor studied the honed edges, noting the slight discoloration and what, perhaps, was the remnant of flesh up near the joint. He handled them carefully, bending down above Roccoletti's body, lowering the scissors until they were directly above his right eye.

"The curved edge of the blade corresponds exactly with the wound along the upper lid of the eye," Tanaka stated. "It would take a very steady hand to make such an accurate incision; there's no damage to either eyeball."

"Especially if the victim was still alive," the captain added.

Tanaka looked up, "No way I can tell that, Bill, it's too late."

Why do I keep telling myself that Karen Flint has got nothing to do with any of this? Fogarty asked himself.

Tanaka was matching the curve of the scissors to the somewhat deeper incision above Roccoletti's left eye when the music began. The amplifier had been turned to full volume and the opening strains of "Thus Spake Zarasthustra" hit the room like a wave.

"We've got to find the third man on the Flint video; he's either responsible for this or he's the next target," Fogarty shouted to Tanaka, above the swelling music.

SOFTAIL

Rachel Saunders had the afternoon off, so she went shopping for a motorcycle. She remembered the name of the shop, "Riders," and remembered that it was about eleven miles south on Route No. 1.

She felt a little awkward, driving into the parking lot off the main highway, a pregnant woman in a brand-new Mercedes, hardly a biker's old lady. She felt stranger still, dragging her handbag and credit cards through the glass-fronted doors that led to the main showroom. There were two dozen bikes on display, polished and poised like chrome horses with high handlebars, low handlebars, windshields, and no windshields. She began to think she'd made a mistake by coming herself. She couldn't tell one model from the next, it looked like an endless sea of steel.

"Howdy, ma'am, may I help you?"

Rachel looked up from the python-skin cowboy boots, past the faded jeans and suede vest and into a face framed by brown, shoulder-length hair and decorated with a Wild Bill Hickock handlebar moustache.

"I want to buy a motorcycle," she said.

"You'll probably be wanting a sidecar for the papoose," Wild Bill answered, looking down at her belly.

Rachel smiled back, relaxing. "The motorcycle is for my husband; all I know is that I want a Harley."

"These are all Harleys, ma'am, we only sell American iron."

"A Softail," Rachel defined, hitting the bottom line of her two-wheeled knowledge.

"All right, that makes it a little easier. Now are you looking for something used or something new?"

"New." Rachel was so used to being in control in her working life that she suddenly felt like a schoolgirl.

"Okay, if you'll follow me we'll see what we've got," the

salesman said, extending a weathered hand. "My name's Bill."

Now it was Rachel who couldn't resist. "Wild Bill?" she asked, a tease in her voice, accepting his hand.

The moustache arched upward and the salesman laughed.

Fifteen minutes later Rachel and Wild Bill were both studying their reflections in the teardrop-shaped air-cleaner cover of a piece of metal sculpture.

"That's the most beautiful motorcycle I've ever seen," Rachel commented, moving around the machine as if she was assessing a rare oil painting.

"This one's a shop custom, took us about six months to get it all together. Had to wait for bits and pieces to come in from California. Take a look at that tank, see how it flows with the shape of the engine. That's all one piece of metal, Arlen Ness built that tank." Wild Bill's voice took on religious overtones.

Rachel nodded respectfully.

"Sold," she said, without asking the price.

"Yeah, but it's just got that little saddle. Where are you and the papoose gonna sit?" Wild Bill seemed in no hurry to part with the art.

"I don't think the papoose and I are going to be doing much riding," Rachel explained.

Eighteen thousand dollars later and Wild Bill was delivering the bike personally. "If your husband don't like this little sled, we'll take it back, exchange it, anything he wants. But hell, if he don't like it," Bill patted the saddle affectionately, "he must be crazy."

By the time Rachel got back to Rittenhouse Square she was singing along with Patti Scialfa on the car radio, "I am just a humble, I am just a humble, well I am just a humble girl." Bruce Springsteen's wife was actually singing, "I am just a rumble doll," but Rachel rarely paid the kind of attention to song lyrics that enabled an accurate reproduction. Still, when she really felt good, she enjoyed belting out her own renditions as she drove.

There were five messages on her service: three new appointments, one cancelled appointment, and one from Josef, saying that he would be late for dinner.

His birthday was five weeks away. It was impossible to imagine his reaction to the motorcycle. It would probably be somewhere between total shock and sheer euphoria. The euphoria would be counterbalanced by his Japanese side railing against his wife for presenting him with such a burden of *giri,* that old Japanese sense of obligation, a need to repay. Even between husband and wife there was *giri.* Well, she had that one covered, she told herself, rubbing her hand lightly across her swollen belly. She was repaying him for the child inside her.

The telephone began to ring; she was smiling when she picked it up. The voice on the other end was a pained rasp, "Help me, help me, will you help me?"

"My name is J—" A hard finger jabbed the stop button of the cassette recorder, killing her voice.

"Hello. Talk to me. Please, tell me who you are—" Rachel's words flowed from Jack Dunne's telephone. A second later he ripped the wire from the wall and hurled the phone across the kitchen.

"You were weak, Sister, too weak to survive. Too fucking weak!" He shouted as he upturned the kitchen table, then marched to the other side of the room and punched a hole through the door leading to the basement.

ART

Steroids are most effective when used in a logical sequence; the sequence is commonly termed a cycle, the period of time during which the user is on the drugs. A cycle can range anywhere from a three week blitz to a duration of up to sixteen weeks. After a given period of time, in some cases as short as three weeks, the muscle's receptor sites—which form the attachment for the steroid molecule and provide the conduit for the transmission of the "get stronger, get bigger" message to the nucleus of the muscle cell—lose sensitivity and no longer bind with the incoming steroid molecule, in other words, they shut down. At this stage no stack of steroids will produce growth or increase strength. The real art of steroid administration is to develop personalized stacks and cycles which maximize the effects of the drugs.

When Jack Dunne began using steroids he experimented with several types of cycling and many stacks of drugs. Using testosterone cypionate as his base drug, Jack blitzed on various arrays of other chemicals, always changing the combination every three weeks. Still, after twelve months of continual use, Jack required greater doses of his stacking components to get results. Then, with his bodyweight up forty pounds, and his strength proportionately increased, Jack hit a plateau.

He was hypertense, losing the hair on his head, his back and shoulders were covered in acne, and he was not growing. At two hundred and five pounds, he was not big enough and, with a bench press of three hundred and ten pounds, he was not strong enough, not for what he needed to do.

He tried to cleanse his system by stopping the steroids, and lost thirty pounds of bodyweight. His mind deteriorated at a faster pace than his muscles; he lost willpower and confidence, until he trembled at the prospect of his weekly visit to the supermarket. He could not tolerate the proximity of people. Everyone was his enemy, and every enemy was empowered to harm him. He could not close his eyes without "the nightmare," the recurring claustrophobia: cocooned in rotted meat, unable to breath, the stink entering him through every pore of his body. Every room in the house seemed permeated with it, no air freshener was able to mask it, not even the coffee grinds on the stove.

"Up the dose." Wayne Brosky's voice was husky and arrogant. There was no give with Wayne Brosky; you paid your money, took your juice, and got the fuck out of his face. The only reason that he even bothered to offer this pearl of wisdom was that Jack Dunne bought in bulk. Six thousand dollars, cash!

Wayne was a member of Horst Nickles's Aryan Army; he handled the sale of steroids to most of the high schools and all of the power gyms in South Philadelphia. He maintained regular working hours and visited each of "his" three gymnasiums twice a week. Wayne was a tough man to get rid of; once a gym owner got on the circuit, he stayed there, like it or not. One man had had the misfortune of walking into his own gym, after closing hours, to discover nineteen-year-old Wayne fucking his wife, right there on the incline bench, his Sustanon-enhanced performance reflected in a panorama of ceiling-to-floor mirrors. When challenged, Wayne Brosky— jock strap and training pants around his ankles—beat the owner senseless with a sixty-pound dumbbell. A warm-up weight for the skinhead.

Brosky generally investigated the credentials of his prospective clients. The Horse, the only man, aside from Adolf Hitler, that Wayne respected, had warned him about undercover cops. Jack Dunne was an exception. Eyes dilated, limbs quivering and voice trembling, the long hair with the wispy beard could have been a lot of things, an AIDS victim, a junkie, an escapee from the asylum, but he sure as hell wasn't a cop. Plus he had a plastic bag full of hundreds and a question on his lips: "I'm losing everything I gained, what do I do?"

"Up the dose."

Jack recommenced his steroid therapy, building up quickly on the cypionate until he had doubled the 10 cc's a week that he had previously been using. The first result of upping the dose was edema, or water retention, causing Jack's blood pressure to rise at a steady rate and his face to swell, stretching the skin around his cheekbones and eyes. His bodyweight shot back up, initially caused by the water retained in his tissues, and his strength soared, a result of the water added to his muscle and connective fibers. Two hundred and ten pounds of bodyweight, two hundred and twelve. Jack Dunne was on the road again, stacking the cypionate with anadrol and dianobol—a very androgenic, male producing stack— and making a lot of distance between himself and the "nightmare."

He still had it, the claustrophobia, the olfactory hallucinations, but it was no longer controlling his life. He was physically strong and confident, able to look himself in the eyes. The change was as much internal as external. Something was happening inside him, something deep and primitive; he was beginning to sense himself as the "hunter," the predator. He was connecting with the most basic element of his masculinity, the essential quality that made him male: his ability to survive by physical superiority, to be able to run down his prey, rip it to pieces with the strength of his body, then devour it. Making its strength his strength. Jack Dunne was the hunter.

Up the dose.

Eight months into his new program and Jack was tipping the scales at two hundred and eighteen pounds. He had redesigned his lifting routine to include more functional exercises, the movements intended to simulate the rudiments of combat, enabling him to prepare his body for the kill. Gripping strength, punching strength, kneeing and kicking, biting and crushing, everything intended for the battlefield.

Up the dose.

Acne. Headaches. Stomachaches. Extreme aggression. Hypertension. Enlarged heart. Palpitations. Hair loss. Insomnia. Cancer.

Up the fucking dose.

SILICONE

Horst Nickles read about Johnny Roccoletti in the morning paper. By noon of the same day he had locked the door to Animals and assembled the entire Aryan Army. Eighteen men, aged between seventeen and thirty-three, all in varying states of muscular inflation. Horst, attired in a custom-made black and red spandex training suit fitted with two strategically placed silicone-filled bags to create the impression of massive testicles, used the theme music from *Terminator* to propel his march from his office to the flat bench in the far corner of the room. He mounted the bench like a podium, then raised his hand, signalling Randy Dornt to cut the music as he prepared to speak.

"Gentlemen." The room went quiet. "Ve have a problem." Horst Nickles eyed each of his army as if it was one of them who constituted the problem.

"A very major problem," he emphasized, continuing with his eyeball to eyeball intimidation.

There was not a member of Horst's army who weighed less than two hundred and ten pounds, and it gave the big German a great sense of self-worth to witness each of them shift nervously beneath his power-gaze. All except one. Wayne Brosky was not sufficiently ill-at-ease to satisfy the Horse. Nickles made a mental note of Brosky's breach in etiquette before moving on, motioning with his hand for Jim Pinion to step forward. Pinion handed each man an eight-by-ten sheet of paper.

"I vant each of you to study this. Very carefully. It is only an artist's impression, so you must make allowances for error. Have any of you ever seen this man, in the streets, in the gymnasiums, in the food market? Have any of you ever sold product to this man? Think. Think very hard."

Horst Nickles studied each face as each face studied the

photocopied police drawing of Jack Dunne. There were a lot of grunts and a couple of utterances of "no way" and one brief flicker from Wayne Brosky. More a double-take than a flicker, as Brosky looked at the drawing, raised his head once, caught Horst Nickles's eyes, then went immediately back to studying the picture of Jack Dunne.

"Okay. So no one has seen this man?" Nickles asked again, looking directly at Brosky.

Brosky held steady, meeting the German's eyes, and keeping a tight reign on his emotions. He may have respected the Horse, but Wayne Brosky, having recently taken some of his own advice and upped the dose, feared no man, at least, not at this distance. Besides, he had recently tacked another ten percent to his street line of product and purposefully withheld the good news from his supplier. He reckoned he owed the Horse about four grand.

"All right," Horst Nickles continued, moving along the front line with his eyeballs, "I vant each of you to keep your copy of this drawing. For your eyes, only. You show it to no one. No one. Understand?"

The army answered "yes" in unison, Wayne Brosky joining at double volume, relieved to be off the hook.

"If you should see this man, I vant you to find out his name, vhere he comes from, then report to me immediately. That's all. Make no other contact with him. Understand?"

"Yes."

"Ve vill have our regular meeting this Thursday. That is all."

Horst maintained his position on the flat bench, watching his troops file past Dornt and Pinion, through the safety door and into the street.

"Vayne!"

Brosky heard his master's voice; it sounded like "vein." He kept walking.

"Vayne Brosky, I am speaking vith you!" This time there was no mistaking Horst Nickles's tone or intent. The skinhead stopped dead, allowing the remainder of the army to circumnavigate his fifty-two-inch chest and herd out into the comparative security of one of the roughest neighborhoods in Philadelphia. Jim Pinion, Randy Dornt, Wayne Brosky, and the Horse remained in the fifty-foot-square gymnasium.

"Bolt the door and leave us alone," Horst instructed his two flunkies. Pinion and Dornt were gone in seconds, exiting via the rear of Animals. Wayne Brosky felt sick from the overload of adrenaline as he walked to the center of the floor and turned to face his creator.

"Something is going on vith you, Vayne, I can see it in your eyes," Nickles said. "Vhat is it, you know this guy or vhat?"

Brosky was having a difficult time with speech; he wanted to say "no" but the single word would not transmit to his voice box.

Nickles stopped three feet from Brosky and held out his hand, not in the traditional position for a handshake but as a man in a lifeboat might extend his hand to a drowning comrade. The generosity of the gesture was enough to disarm Brosky. He placed his right hand in the hand of the Horse. The skinhead's hand felt cold and insignificant as the German wrapped his thick warm fingers around the nervous flesh.

"You have got the shakes, Vayne, vhat are you on? Clebuterol, are you using Clebuterol? I told you that shit vill cramp your muscles and give you the shakes."

Brosky shook his head; he felt like he was melting from the inside, that his blood and muscles were dissolving and being sucked outward through his pores, absorbed into some all powerful force-field that surrounded the German.

"Vhat's the matter vid you son?" Nickles asked.

Brosky attempted to withdraw his hand, but the Horse held firm, changing his grip so that his thumb was on the underside of Brosky's palm, forcing upward against the skinhead's middle finger.

"Anadrol," Brosky whispered, trying to lay the blame on the new batch of orals that he was popping like M&M's.

"Very bad on the liver," Horst said quietly, reaching forward with his free hand to touch Brosky's chest. "Very androgenic. You got bitch tits?"

Brosky's answer was a scream.

The Horse did not let go; he continued to hold the skinhead's left nipple between his thumb and first finger, squeezing the painfully inflamed gland while Brosky pleaded for him to stop. Horse Nickles knew that underneath the layers of tattoos, vein, and muscle, Wayne Brosky was just another street punk who needed to confess. The bodybuilding, the steroids, all the macho adornments were only the armor plating for an inert weakness. Brosky lacked discipline; he needed to cleanse his conscience.

"You know this man, this man whose picture I give you?" The German squeezed tighter and Brosky's entire left pec began a convulsive spasm.

"Yes!" He bellowed like a bull on the slaughter block.

Nickles released Brosky's nipple while maintaining the lock on his hand, levering the skinhead's middle finger upwards.

"How you know him?"

"I'm not sure it's him. I think it's him. I'm not sure. I might have sold him some product," Brosky answered.

"Vhat is his name?"

"I don't know."

A little more pressure on the finger joint, "Vhy don't you know, Vayne?"

"I never asked him!"

Snap!! Brosky gave a sharp howl as he dropped to his knees, his middle finger collapsing. Horst Nickles stepped closer, altering his grip, using a side thumb lever against Brosky's index finger. The Horse loved interrogations; the experience made him feel very close to the members of his army that he was forced, on occasion, to work on. He likened it to the father and son relationship he never had.

"Vayne, you know that one of the first rules of business is that you know who you are selling to. So how can you now tell me that you do not know this man's name."

"He wasn't a cop," Wayne reasoned.

"How do you know that?"

"He was too fucked up to be a cop."

"Cops are some of the most fucked-up people I know," Nickles countered.

Wayne Brosky was broken inside and out; he started to wimper.

"How many times you sell to this fucked-up guy who vas not a cop?" Nickles continued, levering outward against the finger.

"Two times," the skinhead answered.

"How big a buy?"

Brosky stalled. A little more pressure on the joint.

"Small, very small."

Snap!! Howl!!

"I know vhen you lie to me, Vayne. You know how I know? Because your flesh trembles, the electric pulses inside your body become irregular, like a lie detector. So don't lie to me, Vayne, don't lie."

Brosky looked up into the steel eyes. Nickles now held him by his wrist and little finger and was contemplating whether or not to intensify the pressure. The Horse was an expert on joints, particularly fingers and toes. He'd broken all Jacqueline Dunne's fingers and toes that night at Flint's.

"Twelve grand, he took twelve grand's worth a' product, I skimmed two thousand bucks off the top. I owe you two," Brosky wailed.

Nickles relaxed his grip. "That's a lot of stuff, Vayne, vhat kind of stuff vas it?"

"Cypionate, halotestin, anadrol, di-bol, equipoise," the chemicals flowed.

The Horse's grip relaxed another ten pounds per square inch.

"No Clomid? No HCG?" Nickles asked. Any man using the stack that Brosky had just named would have to be dosing heavily on HCG or the fertility drug Clomid to minimalize the conversion of the androgenic steroids into the female hormone estrogen. Without the counter-balancing agents, the side-effects would be disastrous. Nickles used both HCG and Clomid, and he still had raisins for testicles.

"No. The guy was fucked up," Brosky repeated.

"Vhen is the last time you see this guy?" the Horse asked, loosening his grip again.

Brosky sensed freedom and began to stand.

"Six, maybe seven months ago." Brosky was on his feet now; his broken fingers swollen and numb.

"Well, Vayne, you have lied to me, and stolen from me," Horst said softly, "I should kill you."

Brosky froze.

"You know how easy I could kill you, Vayne," Nickles stepped closer as he spoke. Brosky reached up with his good hand, as if to push him away. The Horse walked through his guard and grabbed Brosky's head, pulling it forward, wrapping his neck from the front, applying pressure with his left forearm against Brosky's carotid artery, cutting off the flow of blood to his brain.

Minutes later, Brosky woke up on the floor, Horst Nickles staring down at him.

"If you can make a man unconscious, you can kill him. It is as simple as that, Vayne. You have just died once for your sins, the second time, maybe you will not vake up."

One of Horst Nickles's silicone testicles had slipped during his exertion and was nestled halfway down the right, inside leg of his spandex pants. It was the first thing that Brosky noticed as his eyes refocused.

"Now I vant you to find this man who is fucked up. I vant you to get me his name and vhere he lives. And I vant the money you owe me. Five thousand dollars."

Nickles's silicone ball slipped another two inches as he leaned forward to drag Brosky to his feet.

MANHATTAN

Bill Fogarty was not a fan of New York City and, even in his family days, before the car accident, when he had taken his wife and daughter up to see the Statue of Liberty and a Broadway musical, he had carried his firearm. It was illegal, an off-duty Philadelphia cop packing his thirty-eight, but it made him feel more comfortable. "Better to be tried by twelve than carried by six," he'd replied whenever anyone asked him about taking his Smith and Wesson to the Big Apple. Today, however, was official business. The city of Philadelphia had paid for his Metroliner ticket and Captain Ron Stakowski, of Manhattan South, was going to meet him at the station and drive him to Karen Elms's home address on East Nineteenth Street.

Two men beaten to death, one of whom was Karen Elms's late husband, the other, at least circumstantially connected to him, was reason enough for Fogarty to make the call to the homicide branch of New York City's police department. Stakowski had taken it from there.

"You guys must all buy your suits off the same rack." A nightclub pimp had once made that comment to Fogarty, sneering at his Brooks Brothers tweed. Two minutes later, Fogarty busted him. He may have been a pimp but he was a perceptive bastard, Fogarty thought, as he spotted Stakowski at the far end of the platform at Penn Station. Beneath a grey overcoat, Stakowski was wearing Fogarty's suit, a Brooks Brothers two-piece pinstripe. Fogarty's was brown, Stakowski's was blue. Ron Stakowski also sported that mark of the city homicide cop, the moustache, full and dyed black, in contrast to his shining domed head. Because of the scar tissue on the left side of his face, Bill Fogarty had never actually managed the moustache; he had tried once, but the damn thing would only grow on the right side, so he'd decided that his scars were distinguishing enough.

"Captain Fogarty?" The blue pinstripe shouted from twenty paces.

Christ, he's spotted the fucking suit, Fogarty thought, extending his hand.

"Ron Stakowski, Manhattan South."

They shook. Stakowski had a firm grip, and a crooked smile. His nose had been broken so many times that he no longer bothered to have it reset. It sat like a potato in the center of his wide-open face. In spite of the damage, Fogarty still figured Stakowski to be ten years younger than himself.

"We appreciate you doing this for us, Captain," Fogarty said as they walked towards the exit.

"No problem, although I gotta say the woman was a pain in the ass, goin' on and on about lawyers and harassment. What the fuck did she have against this guy anyway?"

They pushed through the glass doors and into the crazy energy of New York City, panhandlers and gypsy cabs, a legless amputee bound to a skate board and an obese Chinaman singing opera to a reflection of himself in a shop window. A Manhattan serenade. Stakowski marched on, oblivious, while Fogarty gripped tight to his Samsonite briefcase and rolled his shoulders, adjusting his jacket, comforted by the weight of his Smith and Wesson, and prepared for imminent assault.

"She tried to get him on child abuse, but they never proved anything in court," he answered, climbing into the passenger side of Stakowski's Chrysler.

"Are you guys thinkin' she had a part in whackin' him?" Stakowski asked, turning the ignition on, throwing the car into drive and accelerating in what felt to Fogarty like a single movement.

"I don't think so," Fogarty replied, inadvertently pushing down with his right foot onto a phantom brake pedal as Stakowski outmaneuvered a yellow cab and banged a left off Seventh Avenue, to a chorus of car horns.

Stakowski checked his rearview mirror.

"Pretty rare to find a cab driver who speaks English these days, let alone one who knows his way from here to Central Park. Five of them shot dead last month alone," he commented. "Keeps the immigration problem down."

Karen Elms's residence was a two-storey brownstone on East Nineteenth Street, an expensive house in an expensive neighborhood. Stakowski parked outside, turned off the ignition, pushed back his seat, and stretched his legs.

"She doesn't want me in there. She'll give you thirty minutes, but she doesn't want two cops in her house, that's the deal," he explained.

"I appreciate this," Fogarty repeated, pulling his briefcase from the rear seat of the car as he stepped out onto the pavement.

Karen Elms picked up her security phone on the third buzz. Her voice was already impatient. A minute after Fogarty had identified himself, a tall man in a tailored suit of clothes and a double-thick hair weave answered the door.

"How do you do, Captain Fogarty? I'm Saul Raven, Ms. Elms's attorney."

The hair weave held out his hand, as if it was an offering of peace.

Fogarty stepped into the small entrance hall of the brownstone and then into the main room. It was decorated sparsely but expensively: a single blue and gold silk thread carpet, two chairs and a sofa in matching kilim fabric, and a glass-topped coffee table with wooden lion heads carved at the base of each of its four legs. There were two wall mounted Bose speakers on either side of the oblong room, but no visible television set.

"Would you care to sit down, Captain Fogarty?" Raven said, motioning towards one of the chairs.

Fogarty placed his Samsonite on the floor and sat down.

"May I offer you coffee, or tea?"

"No thank you, Mr. Raven. I'd just as soon speak with Ms. Elms and be on my way."

"This is not going to be distressing to Ms. Elms, is it Captain?"

Fogarty had the distinct impression that he was undergoing some sort of screening process; he had come to interview Karen Flint, or Ms. Elms, not to be vetted by an ambassador from the Hair Club.

"Listen, Mr. Raven, I'm in the middle of a very difficult homicide investigation; I've taken a day out of my schedule to come up here. I've asked for half an hour of your client's time, and I'm not that interested in spending it answering your questions—"

"It's all right, Saul, I'll talk to Captain Fogarty now."

Fogarty recognized the impatience from the entry phone. He turned to see a pencil-thin woman in a dark suit standing in the opening of two French doors. Both Fogarty and Raven stood as Karen Elms entered the room. She was elegant but beat, gaunt in the face with the type of dull blue eyes that, no matter how many times the bags were removed surgically, would always look tired. She wore too much makeup, white, like plaster. Fogarty looked harder as he shook her bony hand and noticed the scars beneath the plaster base. *Bad reconstructive work on the cheekbones, and her nose has been altered.* He took all of this in within the time that their hands touched, then turned away from her and returned to his seat. Between his self-consciousness regarding his own injuries and the good-hearted suggestions from Rachel Saunders as to what she could do to improve them, Bill Fogarty was an expert on reconstructive surgery.

Karen Elms sat down on the sofa, her thigh in contact with Saul Raven.

"I'm doing you a favor, Captain Fogarty, so let's get this over with quickly," she began.

"I will need to ask you a few very personal questions," Fogarty explained.

"I'm not promising that I'll answer them," she replied, inching closer to Raven.

"How familiar are you with Ms. Elms's court case?" the lawyer asked.

"I know that the charges were child abuse and that Dr. Flint was acquitted," Fogarty answered.

"And the case before that?" Raven continued.

Fogarty was not aware of a previous case.

"It took place in Maryland, Captain. John Winston Flint was tried for marital rape. He was acquitted through a legal loophole."

"Lorena Bobbit did the right thing, Captain, believe me," Karen Elms added, referring to the Bobbit trial. It had been all over the national news; Lorena Bobbit had severed her husband's penis with a kitchen knife, then tossed it out of her car window in front of the local 7-Eleven store. Bobbit had been acquitted on grounds of insanity, and Bill Fogarty had not agreed with the verdict.

"Take a good look at my face."

Fogarty looked again at Karen Elms, this time making a thorough inspection of the sharp, slightly irregular cheek-bones, the Michael Jackson nose, the skin that, even beneath the plaster base, appeared stretched and tight. It was an uncomfortable face.

"I've been repaired by one of the finest surgeons in this city. If you take off the makeup, Captain, I don't look as good as you." Her words were cruel but sincere. "John did this to me, with a hot clothes iron."

"That's a terrible thing," Fogarty replied.

"And I had to watch him walk free from a court of law, because his lawyers proved I was an alcoholic, an irresponsible witness. I was drunk on the witness stand."

Fogarty remained silent, studying Karen Elms's eyes. From their previous telephone conversations, he had predetermined her to be a class-A bitch, heartless and self-important. Now he felt nothing but compassion.

"I got a divorce and I got into an A.A. program. A.A.

saved me; it gave me the strength to rebuild what was left of my life." Her mouth twitched nervously as she spoke.

"How about the child abuse charges, how did they come up?" Fogarty asked, his voice was nearly a whisper.

"In the divorce settlement, John was given joint custody of the children. He took his practice and moved to Philadelphia, I came here. Marla and Jane spent weekends and vacations with their father." She stopped and looked hard at Fogarty. "Captain, you've probably interviewed John's ex-patients and I know they've all said he was a marvelous doctor, kind and caring. They said the same thing during the rape trial, but I'm telling you that my ex-husband was two people. He had a side to him that was incredibly sick; he was two separate people."

Fogarty nodded, cleared his throat, and got to the reason for his visit.

"I need to talk to you about that side, Ms. Elms, I know how you feel, believe me, I know how you feel, but I need to talk about it."

Karen Elms tightened her mouth and looked down at the floor.

"I'm going to say something off the record," Fogarty continued, "not as a policeman but as a man. John Winston Flint was beaten to death, slowly and methodically, and from what I know of him so far, he got exactly what he deserved."

Karen Elms looked up.

"I'm having a hard time putting this case together, I'm looking for suspects and I'm looking for motives. I'm certain that John Flint was involved in the rape and torture of a female victim, and I have a strong feeling that the incident is directly related to his own death, but I can't put it together. Not until I identify the network of people he was involved with. Karen, I need your help."

"John Flint abused my children, Captain Fogarty, he did it himself and he allowed his sick friends to do it—"

"Hold on a second," Raven cut in. "Let's get one thing straight." The lawyer looked hard at Fogarty. "Is my client,

Karen Elms, in any way under suspicion regarding this crime?"

"Absolutely not," Fogarty lied.

"And this conversation is one hundred percent off the record?" Raven persisted.

"Yes," Fogarty answered.

"Okay," Saul Raven agreed, holding Fogarty's eyes as he sat back against the sofa.

Fogarty refocused on Karen Elms.

"Which friends did John Flint allow to abuse your children?"

"He had a 'group.' They were into drugs, child pornography, sadomasochism," she answered.

"John Roccoletti?"

"I don't know their names," she answered.

"Horst Nickles?"

"I said, I don't know."

Fogarty changed tack. "What form did the child abuse take?"

"Mainly fondling, no penetration, that's why I couldn't get him. There was no substantiated medical evidence. But I saw pictures, Polaroids, I saw them on John's desk. They were my kids in the pictures."

"Were you able to get your hands on the Polaroids?"

"No. It became my word against his."

"But you did take him to court?"

"I got nowhere. The judge threw it out. I had a child psychiatrist who was willing to testify, but child psychiatrists are easy to pull to pieces. And, aside from me, he was the only one willing to substantiate what was going on. I couldn't put my kids on the stand. I just wasn't willing to do that to them. So it never made trial."

"And John Flint retained his right to see the kids?"

"He retained the right, but he never saw them again, and he never pursued me in court. He knew he got off lucky. Twice."

"Usually, Ms. Elms, the kinds of things you mentioned are fairly compartmentalized. Sadomasochism does not generally spill over to child abuse, or drugs—"

"John was evil. I know, I was married to him. If you knew some of the things my children witnessed."

Fogarty sharpened, sitting straighter in the chair.

"Don't even think about involving them in this, Captain," Raven interjected, "they're both away at school, and they are absolutely off limits."

"Besides," Karen Elms added, "why the hell would I want to help you put away the person who murdered John. I hope he's never caught."

Fogarty lifted his briefcase, placing it on the glass-topped table; he opened it and took out a picture of Horst Nickles. It was a photographic reproduction from the front cover of an out-of-date bodybuilding magazine. It showed the German standing on the rocky ledge of a hillside, flexing both arms and smiling, while the city of Los Angeles nestled like a toy village, many hundred feet below. Fogarty handed the picture to Karen Elms.

"Do you know this man?" Fogarty asked.

She looked at it and nodded her head. "It looks like Mr. Ed."

"Mr. Ed?" Fogarty repeated.

"The talking horse, from that old TV series. It was John's idea of a joke. For the kids. They were always talking about Mr. Ed and how he was daddy's best friend. I don't know what the man's real name was, but I've seen pictures of him before. I remember his long, blond hair." She looked again at the photo. "I think I've even seen a copy of this one."

"The man's name is Horst Nickles," Fogarty stated. He removed the photograph from Karen Elms's hand and placed it down on the table, then lifted one of the Flint crime scene stills from his briefcase, and handed it to Karen Elms.

"Oh, Jesus!" She gasped.

"Could Horst Nickles have done that to your ex-husband?"

Karen Elms looked up, over the photo. "It's possible."

"Please, explain that to me," Fogarty asked.

Karen Elms withdrew against the back of the sofa.

Saul Raven was getting edgy.

"Did something happen between Horst Nickles and John Flint?" Fogarty continued.

Karen Elms squared her shoulders. "Have you got children, Captain?"

Fogarty lowered his eyes and shook his head.

"You'd be amazed at what sticks in a seven-year-old's mind. The idea of someone killing daddy is very traumatic. More traumatic than giving blow-jobs to daddy's friends."

Fogarty straightened.

"The last time I saw John, he'd been beaten up," Karen Elms continued, "one of his eyes was bruised, his mouth was cut, and his thumb . . . he had horrible hands, bulbous fingers and abnormally long thumbs. His right thumb was in a metal tube, like a cast. It must have been broken. The sick bastard was grinning. You see, he enjoyed his injuries."

"How do you know it was Mr. Ed?"

"Because my daughter walked into John's office while it was happening; she thought her father was dying. Saw him strapped into his chair, a leather hood over his head, being beaten up by Mr. Ed. John was screaming. That's what was so confusing to my child. Her father was screaming. For more. It's taken four years in therapy for my daughter to get a night's sleep. She still wets her bed."

Fogarty was thinking of the Flint video, of the initials H.N. which appeared two dozen times in Flint's diary, right up until the day Flint died. He remained solemn, picking up the photograph and returning it to his briefcase.

"Thank you, thank you very much," Fogarty replied. "There's just one more thing." He reached for the print of the police drawing. Laying it down on the table. Saying nothing, waiting for her reaction.

Karen studied the likeness a moment then looked up at Fogarty.

"It's intended to be a likeness of the man who killed your ex-husband," Fogarty explained.

Karen Elms looked back at the picture. "I suppose it could be Mr. Ed." There was no conviction in her tone.

Fogarty cleared his throat and removed the drawing from the table.

"Ms. Elms, you've been very, very helpful. I want you to know that I understand how unpleasant it was to discuss these things, but I also want you to know that this has been a very productive meeting." He took his belongings, placed them in his briefcase, and snapped it shut.

Karen Elms smiled for the first time as she shook Fogarty's hand at the door.

"I'm glad he's dead, Captain."

Ron Stakowski put down the sports page of *U.S.A. Today*, threw the switch to his master lock system, and opened the passenger side door.

"Ya' get anything?" he asked, as the Philadelphia cop slid in beside him.

"I think so."

"So it was worth the trip?"

"Oh yeah, it was worth the trip."

Stakowski started the Chrysler's engine and blasted away.

"You guys gonna be askin' us to bring Ms. Elms in?"

"I doubt it. She hated her husband's guts, that's a fact, but I'm pretty sure she didn't have him murdered."

Stakowski glanced over at the bad side of Fogarty's face and nodded, his eyes locking on the scars before Fogarty turned away. Stakowski wondered what kind of accident had caused the damage, personal or in the line of duty. He knew that Bill Fogarty had taken down a multiple murderer a few years back, Willard something or other, the guy they called the "Mantis"; the New York press had covered it. Bill Fogarty was a kind of folk hero, at least to the cops at Manhattan South. His picture had been in the newspapers, and the Mantis story had made the network news and CNN. Stakowski was dying to ask him if the scars were a result of the case, but he wasn't sure what kind of reaction he'd get, so he kept his mouth shut and drove fast. He felt like he was sitting next to a movie star.

Fogarty knew the New York cop wanted more; he could feel it. He also knew that there were times when you couldn't talk. Talking let the air out of the bubble.

Ten minutes later they were outside Madison Square Garden.

"You can drop me here," Fogarty requested.

Stakowski pulled to the curb and Fogarty got out.

"Thanks Ron, thanks for everything," he said, shaking the New Yorker's hand. It was the only time he'd used Stakowki's first name, and Ron Stakowski felt honored.

"Anytime, Bill," the New York cop replied, watching as Fogarty walked away from the car. It was the first time he'd noticed that Fogarty walked with a slight limp. He tried to cover it, but it was there in his right leg. Another badge of honor. That old fuck's a veteran, Stakowski noted, unconsciously rubbing the permanent lump of dislodged gristle in the upper bridge of his nose, while he prepared a full "Fogarty" report for the boys back at Manhattan South.

The 1:48 Metro rolled and shimmied along the track. Outside the tinted window it was winter in New Jersey, the lawns were brown and the trees were bare. A line of small, shingled houses with wooden fences and covered swimming pools sailed past; the kind of circular vinyl pools that were built around metal frames and stood about four feet above the ground. Every house seemed to have one. The type of thing you put up for your kids, Fogarty thought. A moment later he was thinking about his daughter, Ann. Her birthday was coming up, the twelfth of March. He wouldn't be building her a swimming pool; he'd be putting flowers on her grave. The train rumbled beside a stone retaining wall covered with grafitti. The wall caused the train windows to darken and, for a moment, Bill Fogarty was staring at his own reflection. The rapidly changing light, caused by flickers of cold sun, etched his face with deep lines and shadows. Without the scars, he would have looked old, with them he was a nightmare and, in that moment of self-recognition, Bill Fogarty thought about dying. How merciful it would be to lay down his cross of guilt and sin and discard his ugly flesh. Then, in what therapy had taught him was classic Freudian transference, he took his briefcase from the vacant seat beside him, opened it, and removed the picture of Horst Nickles. He stared down at the German's face. He hated that face.

"I'm coming to get you, motherfucker."

Rachel Saunders could not put the voice out of her mind. "Help me," the two words had gnawed at her all day. There was something in the tone beyond the strange tinny texture— a thorn of familiarity piercing inward against consciousness and memory. She was alone in her office; it was six-thirty and Marge had headed off for a blind date with a philosophy lecturer from Temple. Rachel had loaned her a fake fox fur, so she could not only be sophisticated but politically correct. That was a joke, Marge being p.c.; her nearest concession to p.c. was carrying condoms. "In case I get lucky," she'd said.

Rachel sat at her desk and stared at the telephone, willing it to ring. She was no longer frightened of her caller. The voice on the other end of the line yesterday afternoon had put an end to that. The voice was garbled but the message was clear, "Help me." It had been the only call for a week, so there had been no possibility of a trace. She hadn't mentioned it to Josef. He was preoccupied with linking the remains of his latest homicide victim to John Winston Flint.

"Beaten to death, everything broken, you wouldn't believe the damage," he'd said, "not many men with that kind of strength. It had to be one big, angry man."

"One big, angry man," Rachel repeated Josef's words, continuing to stare at the telephone. She thought of her caller's voice again. "Help me. For Christ sakes will somebody help me. My name is J—" That rasping throatiness, as if the voice was being pushed from the base of the diaphragm, breaking at the top of its range, like a deep falsetto. "One big, angry man."

My name is J— . . . ane, Joan, Rachel began filling in the spaces, *Jean. John. Jack. Was it a man pretending to be a woman?*

She sat straighter in the leather upholstered chair. Now she wanted the phone to ring. Wanted to hear the voice again. A man? Why a man?

Maybe he wants to be a woman. A sex change? "Help me," the voice had said, "help me."

Fogarty walked into the Roundhouse at four-thirty in the afternoon; he was bone tired. The only thing keeping him going was the picture in his briefcase; it had its own momentum. First he checked Millie for messages; there were two calls from Josef Tanaka and one from Diane Genero. She was in New York City, staying at the Carlton. That really killed him. He had been less than a mile from salvation and never known it. I couldn't have seen her anyway, he told himself, I'm in the middle of an investigation. But he would have and he knew it. In fact he wanted to see her badly; she represented everything that his sordid business was not. He took the number of her hotel and suite and stuffed it inside the pocket of his jacket, like a kid saving his chocolate bar for after he'd done his homework. Then, he walked back into homicide, called Dave Roach and Sharon Gilbey from their desks and ushered them into his office.

"Tomorrow we're going to pick up a three-hundred-pound animal by the name of Horst Nickles," he said, opening his briefcase and dropping Nickles's picture on his desk.

"Is he the guy from the tape?" Roach asked.

"Maybe," Fogarty replied, damn sure that he was.

"Are we arresting him, Captain?" Gilbey asked.

Fogarty nodded his head, "That's exactly what we're gonna do."

Dave Roach looked down at the picture, then thought of the man on the Flint video.

"What the hell are we going to d . . . do if he doesn't want to come?"

Fogarty smiled. "We'll just have to think of something, Dave."

Fogarty had already thought of it. It was called a stakeout team, and it came equipped with a pump action Remington and a Mini-14.

After Roach and Gilbey left his office, Fogarty placed a call to the medical building.

"The little guy probably died riding the tripod," Tanaka explained. "All his lower internal organs were ruptured, but it would have taken some time. Plus, his testicles were crushed. John Flint's testicles were crushed, too. In the Flint case I made note of it, but, because he was so badly beaten, I assumed that the crushed testicles were part of the overall beating. Roccoletti wasn't beaten so badly, so I'm wondering if the testicles become significant."

"Are you thinking it's a gay thing?" Fogarty asked. He knew that homosexual homicides were generally the worst of all—crimes of passion with a twist: mutilation, immasculation, ugly stuff.

"I've got a couple of ideas of my own, but Stan Leibowitz would have more," Tanaka suggested.

Leibowitz was a psychiatrist who frequently worked with the police department, sometimes in profiling the personality of a killer, but more often with officers suffering stress disorder following field trauma. He was also the man responsible for putting Rachel Saunders back in working order. Fogarty liked and respected Stan Leibowitz. He had even talked to him once or twice about his own problems.

"It's not a bad idea," Fogarty said, a slight hesitation in his tone, brought on by the results of his trip to New York; Fogarty was fairly certain that he had a picture of the killer sitting right in front of him.

"What's up, Bill?"

"First thing in the morning I'm going to pick up a warrant for Horst Nickles," he answered.

"Why? What happened in New York?"

"Flint's ex-wife linked Flint and Nickles."

"Oh yeah?"

"Yeah, Flint and Nickles had a pretty heavy S&M trip going down. His ex-wife witnessed the results of one of their sessions. That, on top of the amount of drugs that Flint was supplying to H.N., and I'd say we've got a case."

"Is his ex-wife willing to testify?"

"I'll subpoena her if I have to," Fogarty answered.

"I wish I could be there when you pick him up."

"Yeah, Joey, I know."

"So, what do you want to do about Stan Leibowitz?"

"I'd like to hand him the crime stills and hear what he has to say," Fogarty answered.

"I'll put it together," Tanaka promised, then rang off.

Fogarty's next call was to the Carlton, in New York City.

"Suite one hundred and one, please."

After a dozen rings the hotel operator came back on the line.

"I'm sorry, Sir, but your party is not picking up the phone. May I take a message?"

"Yes, please. Say it's Bill Fogarty and that I'll be near my home telephone anytime after seven o'clock this evening. Yes, Fogarty, that's right. Thank you."

Within seconds after putting the phone down, it was ringing again.

"Hello?" A touch of lightness in his tone, hopeful.

"We've got Stan Leibowitz at six-thirty. Could you bring the police photos of both crime scenes?"

"I can do that," Fogarty assured. "Did you tell him we've got a suspect?"

"You think I'd make it that easy for him?" Tanaka replied.

"Good. I'll see you at six-thirty, in Stan's office on Pine."
"I'll be there."

Stan Leibowitz was fifty-two years old. Last year, on his birthday, his mother had presented him with the same pair of jeans that he had worn to hitchhike across America in the mid-sixties. She'd kept them in storage. They were mostly patches, all kinds of patches, from Rainbows to Yin-Yang symbols, sewn on during sojourns from Boston to Haight Ashbury. After the presentation of the jeans, Stan had gone upstairs to his old bedroom in the family's three-bedroom Connecticut house and put them on.

"I hear bell-bottoms are coming back," he'd announced as he reappeared in the dining room.

"Look, still a perfect fit," Nora Leibowitz had crowed to the small gathering, "it's all the exercise he does. Same body that he had at twenty-two."

Considering Leibowitz's twenty years of Aikido, and three times a week in the weight room, his mother was probably correct.

Heal the mind, heal the body, heal the body, heal the mind: that's what Stan Leibowitz was all about. He had studied Yoga and meditation in a vegetarian commune in San Francisco, then learned the practical side of medicine during two tours as a medic in Vietnam. In 1970, Leibowitz resumed his academic career and earned a medical degree from the University of Pennsylvania, going on to specialize in psychiatry. "A throwback to my hippie days; I never could get over Ken Kesey's *One Flew Over the Cuckoo's Nest.*" That was the reason he gave for his predilection for the human mind.

Stan Leibowitz could relate to everyone, from stressed-out combat veterans, to stressed-out police officers, to stressed-out advertising executives from New York. He liked extreme cases.

His office was an eclectic mix of Tibetan Buddhas, Burmese wood carvings, Mexican yarn paintings, and Native American spirit catchers, plus a picture of his wife with his two teenage sons, and a telephone in the shape of a Harley Davidson Full Dresser, a present from a former patient.

"You've got a strange one here," Leibowitz said, comparing a set of stills from the Flint homicide to a set from Roccoletti's. "The positioning of the bodies and the meticulous way in which they've been displayed suggest an 'organized personality,' as if the crime was plotted and premeditated."

Fogarty looked across the desk at the silver-haired psychiatrist. "Displayed." Fogarty had never thought in terms of the bodies being "displayed."

"At the same time," Leibowitz continued, "there's enough anger here, enough frenzy, to suggest a 'disorganized personality,' a loner acting on impulse. The number of blows to the body in the Flint case suggests a frenzy," Leibowitz hesitated, "and here comes the contradiction; the placement of the stockings on the body, presumably postmortem, and the mutilation to the eyes and the administration of facial makeup in the Roccoletti case. They are very 'organized,' very calculated types of acts."

"Calculated for what?" Fogarty asked.

"With regard to the mutilation of the eyes, I would say that the killer wanted his or her victim to be aware of them, probably in order that the victim would witness the killer's power, or dominance."

The same way the woman in the Flint video was forced to witness the dominance of her attackers, same m.o., Fogarty thought.

"It could be some kind of revenge killing. That would explain why it appears both frenzied and premeditated," the psychiatrist suggested.

Revenge for what? Fogarty wondered. He was desperate to read Horst Nickles into everything the psychiatrist said.

"Have you got any doubt that the two crimes were committed by the same person?" Tanaka asked.

"Not much, particularly when you tell me the victims were connected. The biggest link-up is the way the bodies have been displayed," Leibowitz replied. "There's been no attempt to hide them, in fact, just the opposite, they've actually been positioned like storefront mannequins. Probably so the killer could admire his work. The fact that they were not hidden also indicates that he was not particularly concerned with being caught."

"Yeah, but if there was no hard evidence left behind?" Fogarty asked, "no prints, weapons, nothing?"

"That's as much an obsessive-compulsive trait as an attempt at concealment. He's cleaning up after himself, probably an extremely disciplined individual."

Disciplined obsessive. Again Fogarty thought of Horst Nickles.

"I would also say that the killer and the victims knew each other intimately," Leibowitz stated.

Bingo! Again.

"Because of the facial wounding?" Fogarty asked, knowing that when there were knocked out teeth, broken noses, gouged eyes, that the attack was probably personal, and that the perpetrator knew the victim and was very angry.

"Yes."

"And the crushed testicles?" Tanaka asked.

"He hates men," Leibowitz answered, "the wounds to the genitalia are a symbolic taking away of masculine power."

"And the use of the stockings and facial makeup?" Tanaka continued, remembering how Sharon Gilbey had gone on about the artistic quality of the work.

Leibowitz adjusted his reading glasses, then lifted one of the photos from the Roccoletti set and studied it.

"He took a lot of time with this," he said.

"What do you think it means?" Fogarty pushed.

"Maybe the killer didn't believe his victims deserved their masculinity—"

"Keep going, Stan, keep going," Tanaka insisted.

"So he's changing them into women."

Fogarty opened his briefcase, took out the police drawing, and placed it in front of Stan Leibowitz.

"Is this your guy?"

"I think so," Fogarty answered.

Leibowitz examined the drawing, then sat back in his chair, took off his glasses, and rubbed his eyes.

"The two victims were definitely connected?"

"They were involved in a sex crime," Fogarty replied.

"Homosexual?"

"Sadomasochism. The second victim, the photographer, videotaped a number of the sex sessions. Maybe the photographer participated, maybe not."

"All right," Leibowitz said, as if he were surrendering, "the crushed testicles could indicate a demasculinization. Same as the tripod that was forced up the rectum of the second victim. That could be interpreted as a type of rape. Like a prison rape, one male making another subservient."

Leibowitz hesitated, considering, "Maybe the killer has some type of super-male complex."

Fogarty looked across at Tanaka, "Horst Nickles?"

Tanaka nodded.

Stan Leibowitz threw up his hands, "Hey, I told you guys, this is conjecture, off the top of my head—"

The honking horn of the psychiatrist's Harley telephone signalled his next appointment.

Fogarty drove into the parking lot of the Presidential Apartments at eight o'clock. He pulled into his slot, shut off the Chrysler's engine, and sat there thinking. Forensics had run tests on all of Roccoletti's video equipment, and established a probable link between one of the photographer's cameras and the one that shot Flint's home movies. It was an imperfection in the lens, a tiny scratch that created a shadow in the upper-right-hand corner of the tape. Five out of the seven tapes found in Flint's bedroom had the shadow. On top of that there was Roccoletti's choice of music; that was enough to provide the key for Fogarty. He wondered how Quantico was doing with the frame enlargement on the Rolex. He made a mental note to phone McMullon tomorrow and hustle it along.

Tomorrow, he would put Horst Nickles into the backseat of his Chrysler and take him to the Roundhouse, down the ramp, by the cell blocks, and up the rear elevator to homicide. Fogarty was certain that Nickles was the other man in the Flint video. There was not a doubt in his mind. Stan Leibowitz was good, no doubt about it, but the sex-change theory was too far out there. Even Stan had said it was conjecture, and Stan didn't have the facts; he hadn't been to New York, hadn't seen the transcripts. He'd been right about one thing. The victims and the perpetrator all knew each other intimately. About as intimate as you could get. And somewhere, inside that intimacy, was the reason for the crimes. Child abuse, photographs, videos, drugs, death threats. Probable cause? How many fucking probable causes do I need? he asked himself, grabbing his briefcase as he stepped from his car. He glanced across the parking lot; it was the second time that he'd noticed the white Ford cab sitting in front of his building. The first time was when he had pulled in.

He was walking in the direction of his entrance door when the rear driver-side door of the cab opened. He got that funny, nervous feeling, as if whoever was in that cab had something to do with him; he stopped twenty feet away and waited.

"I must say, you have a real way with women." He recognized her voice a moment before he caught sight of Diane Genero's long, stockinged legs emerging from the back of the taxi.

Fogarty stood, speechless.

"Isn't eight weeks notice enough?" She continued to speak as she stood up and closed the door. She was wearing a cashmere coat over a grey Chanel suit and cream blouse. Her raven hair, usually tied back, hung polished and loose.

What the hell was she talking about? Fogarty's mind raced.

"Bookbinders? The Academy of Music?" She hinted.

Suddenly it hit. He faked a smile and ran as quickly as his carbon fiber would allow to the driver's side of the taxi, digging into his pocket, exposing his thirty-eight as he came up with a handful of bills.

Diane Genero glanced down at the holstered weapon and shook her head.

Fogarty grimaced.

"I got to charge for the forty minutes I've been waiting," the driver chimed. Thirty-three dollars later the Ford was pulling out of the parking lot and Fogarty was face-to-face with his salvation.

"Do you know how sorry I am?" he began.

She looked at him and laughed. "You didn't remember, did you?" Her voice expressed disbelief.

"Of course I remembered," he lied, "I've got the tickets upstairs."

Diane Genero glanced at her wristwatch. "I'd say we're cutting it a bit fine, Captain, since the concert starts in forty minutes. Maybe we could just leave out the shrimp cocktail."

Fogarty found her eyes. "All right, I forgot," he confessed.

"I know you did."

Then, he remembered.

"You were coming to New York to look at some fabric for a client in Albuquerque and I asked you to stay over a couple of days, come on down to Philadelphia, and I'd take you out. Now I remember. And I really do have tickets upstairs. Somewhere."

"And it really is too late to use them," Diane Genero concluded.

Fogarty stood, lost for words.

"What do we do now?" she asked.

Fogarty studied her eyes. They were like soft doors. Behind them there was loneliness and there was also nobility. They could see beyond his scars.

"Well, Captain?"

Now he was thinking of his apartment, whether his house cleaner had been in today, whether there was still a layer of dust on the onyx chess set. Were there dirty dishes in the kitchen sink? Had he left his tweed jacket lying on top of the dining room table? Did he really have a choice?

"Do you want to come upstairs?" His voice was stiff, Christ, it sounded like he was arresting her.

"We could spend the evening in the parking lot," she suggested, "turn on the car radio, we'll dance."

Fogarty laughed. Too loud.

"Come on, Bill, it's me, your pen pal from Santa Fe, it's going to be all right." She took his arm and guided him towards the door.

"I'm sorry, I really am sorry. I'm in the middle of an investigation and I don't know what day it is."

The couple from the apartment next door, the Bernsteins, or the Bernsides, Fogarty had never really got their name together, passed them on their way in through the door of the building. Mr. B. nodded politely to Fogarty while Mrs. B. did an entire three-hundred-and-sixty-degree turn, her eyeballs in Panavision, as she once-overed the lady in grey.

"I guess you don't bring a lot of women here?" Diane Genero whispered.

"You're the first," Fogarty answered.

Diane looked at him and realized he meant it. She had a rush of emotion; she always had rushes of emotion with Fogarty, whether it was through the long distance wires or when reading one of his infrequent letters. Something he'd say, or the way he'd phrase a line; he was world weary in many ways but genuinely naive in others. She considered Fogarty a real man and, at forty-four years old, Diane Genero had learned to appreciate endangered species.

Fogarty hesitated when they arrived at the front door of his apartment. He felt like he was entering a crime scene, before the crime had been committed, a mixture of nerves and apprehension. He hadn't even asked her where she was staying or whether she was booked on a metro back to New York.

She wouldn't think about staying here, Fogarty reassured himself, handling his key with the precision of a locksmith. He opened the door and threw the light switch.

CANDLES

There was always something naked about sushi. Particularly by candlelight. Rachel thought it was the way the small, shiny pieces of tuna belly, shrimp, and octopus glistened on their bed of vinegared rice.

Tanaka was slurping. Handling his slender, buckwheat noodles with the dexterity of a master, sucking them from his dish like a vacuum cleaner, using his chopsticks as a ladder, while the noodles climbed from the porcelain to his lips.

"Good, yes? Good?" The Japanese waiter beamed, staring over Tanaka's shoulder and into the disappearing pile of soba.

"*Hai,*" Tanaka answered without breaking rhythm. The waiter smiled, creasing his face into a crescent moon, bowed once to Rachel, and walked quickly back towards the kitchen.

The Zen was Center City's newest restaurant, and Josef and Rachel had been specially invited by Mori Tamura, a friend of Josef's father from Tokyo. Tamura was the man behind the Zen chain, which ran from Atlanta to Boston. "Kind of a Samurai Colonel Sanders," Josef had explained. The restaurant had opened a month ago, and it was already buzzing.

"Do you think we should bring Bill here? To get him out of that Bookbinders habit?" Tanaka asked, at the tail end of a noodle.

Rachel looked at him over a plateful of tempura. She'd vowed to lay off the fried foods until after the child was born, but eggplant, shrimp, and onions, deep-fried in *koromo* batter, were too hard to resist.

"What, after Tokyo? You'll never get Bill Fogarty within a mile of a rice ball," she answered.

Tanaka met her eyes and smiled. She was right. As a result of the "Leopard" case, his friend's impression of Japan had been permanently ruined; Bill would probably choke on a rice ball, and Tanaka couldn't blame him.

"How's he doing with his investigation?" Rachel continued.

Tanaka shook his head, "Tomorrow he's going to bring in that pig from the bodybuilding gym." He kept his voice low, glancing discreetly to his right, then left. Fogarty had entrusted him with official police information and he'd learned a long time ago that you never knew who was listening.

"Your friend?" Rachel asked, quietly. Her tone was subdued for a different reason; she didn't want to arouse Josef's Samurai macho and spoil dinner.

"Yes."

"Did he do it?"

Tanaka glanced around a second time, his back was already to the wall, so he didn't need an over-the-shoulder.

"It sure would be nice and simple that way," he replied.

"You don't think he did, do you?"

Tanaka hesitated. The answer was no, but it was a gut response, flavored slightly by Stan Leibowitz. He shrugged his shoulders. "Bill knows more about it than I do, he's been up to New York, met with the doctor's ex-wife. He's pretty convinced."

Rachel dipped a section of shrimp into her brown sauce and raised it to her lips. She thought a second about mentioning the "help me" phone call, then decided to leave it for another day.

"Not bad with those chopsticks," Tanaka commented, his mind on the German. He had a bad feeling about the arrest, and he couldn't pinpoint the reason.

Rachel held the shrimp in her mouth, considered the fat element in the batter, the sugar in the sauce, and decided it was the best taste she'd had in five months. She swallowed.

"I was trained by a Jap," she said slowly.

"That makes sense," Tanaka replied, getting back to the here and now, "I hear they go crazy for long-legged blondes, you know, that Christie Brinkley type."

"And apparently, some of them have a real thing about

women with big tits," Rachel whispered, squaring her shoulders and puffing her chest forward.

Tanaka stared at nipples through silk and suddenly felt very sexy behind his half bottle of rice wine.

Fogarty was in the shower, Charlie Mingus was playing jazz piano on a slightly scratchy 78, and Diane Genero was sneaking a look into the policeman's refrigerator. Three jars of Paul Newman's All Natural Spicy Spaghetti Sauce, a bottle of Frascati, a head of lettuce, and two tomatoes. She looked above the fridge and saw two bottles of Italian Merlot. Then, hopefully, she opened the door to the cupboard above the stove and searched for some pasta.

Fogarty stepped from the shower, grabbed a white towel, and glanced at his reflection in the medicine cabinet mirror above his sink. *Oh, man,* his heart sank; he walked quickly to the door, checked to make certain it was locked, stepped back to the mirror, wiped some of the steam away from the glass, and looked again. Once, a lifetime ago, he had actually had a good body. He had trained with weights, wrestled in high school, and boxed in the Army. His shoulders were still wide, but so was his waist. He had no belly, but it was thick, giving very little taper between his shoulders and his hips, and his pectoralis muscles had fallen. Beneath the sporadic patches of reddish-blond hair his chest sagged. And then there was his face, sitting like a freshly shaved peach, half rotten, beneath an awning of cornflower hair, gone at the temples and crown. *Another minute of this and I'll stay locked in the bathroom,* he realized, pulling back his shoulders to lift his chest and telling himself that, at least, his body still looked all right in clothes. It was the first time in ten years that he had examined himself as a prospect for . . . for what?

"Wait a second, what the hell are you doing?" he said, meeting his own eyes in the steamy mirror. "You don't think for a second she'd consider it, do you?"

Fogarty and Diane Genero had known each other nearly five years; first through the Mantis case, then through letters and, whenever business brought her to town, the occasional dinner. The issue of sex had never arisen. Fogarty had assumed that Diane Genero was not interested and, as far as he was concerned, that was fine. The tragedy of losing his wife and daughter had left him impaired, psychologically, in the intimate relationship department.

He wrapped the towel around his waist, locker-room style, and listened. The blue piano notes crept from behind the door as Mingus rotated on the outdated turntable; beyond that, the apartment was quiet.

"You all right out there?" he called.

No answer.

He walked to the door, sliding the bolt lock carefully, so as not to let his guest know that he had deemed it necessary to lock himself in. Then he stuck his head out.

"Diane?"

Diane Genero walked from the small kitchen. She carried a box of extra-length Paisano's spaghetti in one hand.

"How old is this stuff, Bill?"

It took him a moment to focus.

"We don't have to go out at all," she continued, walking towards him. He arched back, keeping displayed flesh to a minimum.

"Two, maybe three months," he replied.

"Well, the packaging is airtight. What do you say I try and cook it? A little salad, wine, and we're in business."

"But I was going to take you out. To B—"

"I don't want to go to Bookbinders. Besides you've blown it anyway. By the time we get to the main course it'll be midnight."

Fogarty stood there, head forward and ass forced backwards. "I don't think I've got any dressing—"

"You've got balsamic vinegar, olive oil, and half a jar of honey." Her voice had the ring of authority.

"Do I?" He asked. It must have been the last time that Nellie, the cleaner, had shopped for him. He never knew what she brought in.

"You get dressed. I'll get dinner together."

"Yes, ma'am."

Jack Dunne was doing his usual St. Vitus's dance against the hard mattress of his bed. Beside him on the table, next to his plastic bags of speed and downers, a candle flickered. He had gone to sleep that way—the same way Jacqueline used to, the gentle light relaxing him. Soothing. He had one pillow beneath his head and one on top of it, pulling it down over his eyes with sleeping arms.

It was the blood that woke him, running like water from his nose. It spilled from the rise of his top lip, into his mouth, choking him. He coughed and spit, rolling onto his side, wiping his face with his hands, heaving for oxygen. He pushed himself to his hands and knees, staring down at the pillow, his body like a giant monster, shadowed against the wall. Blood pouring out of him, he turned over, lay back, and pinched his nostrils. He understood what was happening, knew that his blood pressure was dangerously high, that, because of the steroids, his prothrombin time—the time required for blood to clot, usually about ten seconds—had increased to nearly a minute. He could die this way, from a simple nosebleed. He crawled to the edge of the bed and stood, keeping his head back, shaking on leg muscles relaxed by an overload of Valium. Wobbling naked towards the door of his bathroom, he grabbed a towel from the wall rack and then ran back to the bed, pressing the towel to his nose.

Five minutes later he was on his back, and the blood was beginning to clot. He was strangely lucid, staring up at the quivering candlelight against the ceiling. The erratic light made him nervous. He reached out and pinched the flame between his fingers, darkening the room. This was no time for nerves; this was the time to put it together, once and forever. He needed the cunning, the strength, and the aggression. Plenty of aggression. He could feel Jacqueline, as if she were inside him, demanding this one last act. Then she could rest. In peace.

* * *

"Where the hell did you find the candles?" Fogarty's voice had a slight slur.

"Bill, you've asked me that same question three times," Diane answered.

"Right. In the drawer, underneath the . . . sink," he stated, downing the last of the Frascati between *the* and *sink*.

"I don't know how good an idea it was to mix wines," Diane grinned. They had been even until the Frascati, then the captain had jumped ahead by at least half the bottle.

He knew he was drunk, but not drunk enough to tell her exactly how good she looked sitting there in the candlelight. Instead he stared vacantly into her eyes. He needed to say something.

"Whisky."

"What?"

"I've got some Johnnie Walker Red in my gun c . . . case," he stammered. "Christ, I sound like Dave Roach."

"Dave Roach?"

"Some kid downtown. He's working the case with me. First homicide. Nice kid. Stammers a bit when he's nervous. Want some whisky? It's in the gun case." He stopped rambling and looked at her.

"Bill," she anchored him with her voice, low and calm, "if I have any more to drink I'm not going to be able to get back to my hotel."

He stood bolt upright. "Right! Christ, you're right! I'll call you a cab."

He marched towards the phone.

"I don't want to leave yet," she said, stopping him in his tracks.

She stood from the table and walked to him.

"You know, for some reason, you look shorter."

"I took my shoes off," she explained.

She stood very close to him, reached forward, and touched his hand, holding it gently.

He felt something caving in, something inside him. He was

afraid he was going to cry. Still, he allowed her to hold his hand. Mingus had been replaced on the turntable, something less moody, but slow.

"Would you dance with me?" She stepped closer.

He could smell her, sweet like a flower, magnolia. He couldn't dance; he was a big ugly monster. He didn't deserve rhythm, or flowers, or life. He opened his mouth to say no and she placed her head on his shoulder.

"I haven't been with a woman in eleven years." It sounded like a courtroom confession.

She nestled into him, giving him rhythm, and flowers, and life.

"Shut up and dance," she said.

Fogarty woke up at five o'clock in the morning; he was on the sofa, wearing his blue-and-white-striped boxer shorts and covered by a single quilt. He felt good, not at all hungover. He felt very calm, as if everything had slowed down, his entire system: heart, lungs, and brain. He sat up and looked into the dim morning light of the room. It was his room, his apartment; the chess set was still on the mahogany table, the old stereo still in its purpose-built rack against the far wall, the dining table clean and polished. No clutter, no dust. Everything was old, but everything was new. He stood up and walked to the door of his bedroom, half hoping to find her in his bed. Sarah's bed. He pushed the door open and looked into the room. The bed was undisturbed; Diane Genero was gone. Without a trace, without a clue. As if she had never been in the apartment. He walked to the turntable of the stereo, no Charlie Mingus, but in place of a record a square sheet of paper, pressed down over the spindle, with something written on it. He lifted it, held it away from him so that he could make out the writing, half print, half script, done in light pencil: *You're a beautiful dancer.*

Fogarty carried the note to the sofa and sat down, lifting his half-lensed reading glasses from the table beside him. He put on the glasses and reread the note, studying the graceful flow of the writing. He was certain he could detect the smell of flowers, drifting from the paper. He placed the note in his lap, removed his glasses, and leaned back against the sofa. Last night seemed like a dream, but he remembered every detail of the dream. It was the finest dream he'd had in eleven years.

Bill Fogarty was reborn.

It was seven o'clock in the morning. Rachel was in her bra and panties, pulling a blue, light wool suit from her closet, while Tanaka, in his black boxer shorts, was standing over the bathroom sink, shaving. She laid the suit on the side of the bed, and looked into the tiled bathroom. He had his head tilted back, and the shaving gel covered his skin like a square, white beard. He shaved quickly, moving his hand in long, upward strokes, from the base of his throat to his jaw.

"Is that a new razor?" she asked. She knew he had a thing for razors, as soon as a new model was advertised, Tanaka went out and bought it, Track 11, Contour, Swivel Head. He was a collector.

"Guaranteed seven shaves per blade," he answered, mid-stroke.

"Must be the Gillette Samurai?" she teased.

He smiled.

"I got another one of those calls yesterday," she said, almost casually.

"What calls?"

"You know, the stalker."

"Yesterday?"

"Uh huh." she'd felt obligated to tell him, and now she had.

He stopped shaving and turned towards her.

"Why didn't you say anything to me last night?" His voice was edgy.

"I forgot." She sounded lame.

"What?"

"Because we haven't been out in a long time, and I knew it would ruin the evening."

"Ruin the evening?"

"This guy isn't dangerous," she answered, feeling stupid a moment after the words left her mouth. How did she know he wasn't dangerous?

"This guy? Last time it was a she, now it's 'this guy?' "

"He spoke to me."

"Oh yeah? What did he say?"

"Help me. He said, 'help me.' "

Tanaka tightened his lips and shook his head. He felt deceived, cheated.

"He's not dangerous," she continued.

"You know that, do you?" He was heating up.

"Yes. I know that. I've got an instinct for those things."

"Oh, you do . . . . Really?" Tanaka answered between clenched teeth.

"Yes."

"Bullshit."

In Rachel Saunders's professional life, she was the boss. Tanaka may have been right, but she wasn't going to let him talk down to her.

"You want to know the real reason I didn't tell you, you want to know!?" she challenged. Then, without waiting for his answer, "Because you overreact; you're a hysteric." She had both hands by her sides, her hands balled into fists. Her pregnant belly stuck out above the top of her yellow silk panties.

Tanaka stared at her; it was almost funny, but not quite. He laid his razor on the sink, walked forward, and closed the door in her face.

NORTH DIVISION

Commander Reuben Jakes headed the North Division, which included the thirty-fifth district, and covered the area of Philadelphia surrounding Animals. He had a detective division, but no homicide. Homicide was strictly Center City, at the Roundhouse, and Bill Fogarty ran that show.

Jakes had been following the Flint case through the straight Philadelphia newspapers, like any other tax-paying civilian, and through the "white paper," a special police report sent to the commander of each division. He was following the case like a soap opera; it was always interesting when some high flyer came down with a bang like the dead doctor, wearing ladies' stockings with a hood over his head. It was the kind of stuff that made the inside pages of the *National Enquirer*; good, sordid reading, confirming that no one, regardless of income or education, was exempt from the gutter. The gutter was basically what the thirty-fifth district was all about.

Jakes was at his desk, looking out a cracked, dirty window at the most depressing view this side of the cross. Rows of rundown houses, lining rundown streets, lived in by rundown people, whose idea of a good time was grabbing a bus downtown for an afternoon of shoplifting, if they were young enough, and fast enough, and had enough reefer or crack cocaine to make it all seem like a sport. For real recognition, real fame, plus the drugs, there were the drug gangs, which featured a life expectancy of nineteen years. The older folks stayed home and barricaded the doors. It wasn't all like that; there was the Deacon Thomas Rand and his evangelical church choir, always on the recruit for souls to see the light and sing the message. There were also the youth clubs and drug rehab groups, starring ex-addicts and ex-cons, who lectured and offered themselves as examples to the young, pro-

claiming hope, and the possibility of a high school equiv-
alency diploma during incarceration. Or, there was the police
department. Reuben Jakes had grown up on North Broad
and he had, in his twenty-eight-year rise from foot patrolman
to inspector, arrested many of his former friends. Very depressing. That's why he liked to read about the John Winston
Flints; they provided just a bit of equality in a lopsided world.

He was seated at his desk, reading the white paper on the
Roccoletti homicide, when the phone rang. He didn't recognize
the voice on the other end. There was something annoyingly
optimistic about the clear tone, and Jakes didn't know many
optimists.

"Reuben, I need you to do something for me."

Jakes had a thing about people who spoke without first
identifying themselves, as if they were so important that an
introduction was unnecessary.

"I need you to put a guy out front of—"

"Hold on a second," Jakes cut in, "who is this?"

"I'm sorry, Reuben. It's me, Bill Fogarty."

"Jesus, man, you don't sound like you, what's happening,
you win the lottery?"

"Do you know about the Flint case?" Fogarty asked.

"You think I don't read my white paper? Sure I know
about the kinky doctor."

"Well, I'm about to make an arrest."

"Oh yeah?" Jakes sat up straighter in his plastic upholstered
chair.

"I'm coming onto your patch to do it," Fogarty continued.

"What do you need?"

"I need to know when my suspect is in his place of business."

"Go on," Jakes answered, wanting more.

"A big geek by the name of Horst Nickles. He owns a
power gym, called Animals. Do you know who I'm talking
about?"

Jake knew exactly. "I've been trying to get that asshole

closed down for years. Even had somebody undercover in there for a while."

"Oh yeah?" Now Fogarty was interested.

Jakes thought a moment. He still felt guilty about her; the officer had been too young, too inexperienced. It ended ugly.

"I couldn't make it work." Finality in his tone.

"Well, I've got two warrants and a stakeout team, and I'm damn sure going to make it work."

"Tell me what you want out of me," Jakes said.

"A beat cop, preferably white. Nickles has a thing about—"

"I know all about his Aryan Army."

"I need the guy to hang around there today. He can keep a check on Nickles's car, make sure he's in place when we show up, and give us an idea how many people are in the gym. I want it to be nice and clean."

Jakes thought a moment.

"I got a white guy on that beat anyway, you may know him," he answered.

"What's his name?" Fogarty asked.

"Finnegan."

Finnegan. Finnegan. The name had a familiar ring.

"Jim Finnegan. Used to work vice in Center City—"

Fogarty laughed, "He's the poor fuck who got caught with a set of false teeth in the front of his patrol car. The teeth belonged to a hooker."

"That's him." Jakes knew the story.

"Well, don't tell him, but the hooker with the dentures, the one he was getting blow-jobs from; she had a dick. She was a gump."

Jakes laughed. "So, do you want Finnegan, or should I get you somebody else?"

"Finnegan will do just fine."

Horst Nickles was alone in his office. It was Friday, delivery day, but there wasn't going to be a delivery. Not even the "aperitif" from Allentown, although his contact at the testing lab had spoken of a nice group of monkeys that had been flown in from Barbados on Tuesday—"mature males, big heads, two hundred dollars a pop." Nickles had been tempted, but judged it unwise. Not with the Roccoletti murder all over the newspapers. Flint and Roccoletti. He had done a lot of business with both of them; taken gallons of product from Flint and sent dozens of hopeful bodies to be photographed by Roccoletti. The net was closing and he was in the net; he could feel it. Only a matter of time before the homicide cop with half a face and his pet yellow man were back at his door asking questions. He'd stay clean until they went away, until he could find out what was going on. Dornt and Pinion were holding on to the steroid stash, enough to keep business regular for another couple of weeks. Meanwhile, *What's happening?* Nickles asked himself, staring down at Jack Dunne's picture, trying to get a handle on the strange, haunted face. *Something familiar about that face. A customer? An enemy? First Flint, then Roccoletti. Maybe the son of a bitch is coming after me?* Nickles considered. Heavy pounding on his security door broke his concentration. It was the back door. Nobody came to the back door, unless they had a delivery. He stood from his desk, thought a moment of getting his "Streetsweeper," the stainless steel, short barrelled, twelve-gauge shotgun that he kept in his wall closet, then decided against it. If it was the cops, he didn't want to be armed. He walked to the door.

"Yes, I am here!" he shouted, through six inches of wood and intermeshed steel.

"It's me. Finnegan. Open up!" The voice sounded far away, but urgent.

"Go around to the front!" Nickles bellowed. Even in moments of crisis, he enjoyed a military discipline. Front door for members, back for deliveries.

Finnegan pounded several more times and Nickles began the fifteen-second process of unlocking his six security bolts.

"Vhat the hell you vant?" he steamed.

Finnegan looked over his shoulder and then ducked inside Nickles's office.

"There's a warrant out on you."

Nickles had expected it.

"So? My place is clean."

"I'm not talking about a search warrant. I'm telling you they're going to arrest you."

"Vhy?" Nickles demanded, squaring his shoulders and staring down his nose at the man in the blue uniform.

"I don't know, but it's coming from downtown."

Nickles thought of Fogarty. "They are going to arrest me for murder?"

"I don't know," Finnegan repeated.

"Then, vhat do you know?"

"I'm supposed to keep an eye on your premises. They're coming today."

"Vell," Nickles said, standing tall, drawing his shoulders back, "I am not running."

"That's all very good, Horst," Finnegan said slowly, "but it might be a wise idea to call your lawyer, get your story together."

"I did not kill anybody," Nickles announced proudly.

"Fine. That's important," Finnegan explained, "but it's going to go a lot smoother if you're ready."

"I vill vear my black and red training suit," the German answered. He was already thinking of his silicone balls. It would be more dignified to exit in full uniform.

"Horst, fuck the training suit, call your lawyer. I'm telling you that."

Nickles stood silent. He was not used to taking orders, particularly from the weak and insignificant, but he was not dumb, either.

"Vhat time are they coming?"

"I don't know."

"Find out."

"I can't."

The Horse fumed.

"The best I can do is advise them when I think the gym will be least crowded. They don't want a bad scene."

"I vill close at noon. Have them come at one o'clock. After I have lunch."

"Horst, I don't think you understand. This isn't my show; it isn't even the thirty-fifth district's show. This is bigtime. Homicide. I'm just the lookout man."

"One o'clock vould be the best time for me," Horst Nickles stated. He was not nervous; he was innocent.

Finnegan looked up, into the cold, teutonic eyes. *The guy's a maniac, a total fucking maniac*, he thought.

"Horst, I'll see what I can do," the cop said, trying to keep a sincere tone. "In the meantime, please, do yourself a favor, and call your lawyer."

Finally, Finnegan turned and walked out of Animals.

Fogarty and his team actually arrived at 1:25 in the afternoon. It was a full thirty minutes after the Horse had eaten his three-pound container of tuna fish and ten heated egg whites.

Stakeout were the first at the front door, with Fogarty, Roach, Gilbey, and one of Jakes's detectives in formation behind. The mobile crime unit parked behind Fogarty and waited inside their van. Finnegan was assigned to the parking lot, instructed to holler if Nickles attempted a rear getaway. They could easily, at that point, shift position and block his exit from the lot. Fogarty stepped forward and rang the buzzer, fully expecting to have to smash through the heavy door with a sledgehammer. He buzzed a second time.

"I am coming! I am coming!" There was something regal in Nickles's tone of voice. Then, the grinding of metal against stone, as the door began to open.

The stakeout team readied their weapons. Fogarty stepped back. The door opened and Horst Nickles stood, like Superman in red, filling the frame. He looked at the men with their firearms.

"I am very honored, Captain, that you treat me vith such respect." His voice was confident.

Too confident for Fogarty. He read the German his rights, cuffed him, and hustled him off to the backseat of his Chrysler. The stakeout team entered the empty gymnasium, reported it secure, and the mobile unit followed. Horst Nickles watched from the rear window of Fogarty's car. A few minutes later one of the mobile unit officers walked from the door.

"Nothing so far, Sir—no people, no substances—looks like the place was just swept and cleaned."

Fogarty nodded his head, and frowned, then looked back at Horst Nickles. The German was smiling. *Somebody's tipped him off*, he reckoned, glancing at Jim Finnegan.

"Anything else I can do for you, Captain?" Finnegan asked, walking to Fogarty.

"You look good, Jim, lost some weight?"

"A few pounds."

"Working out?"

"A little." Finnegan could feel another bust coming.

"Where?"

"At home, a few push ups, a doorway chinning bar, watching my diet."

Fogarty nodded; he knew it was a lie.

"Well, I want to thank you for telling that asshole in the car that I was coming."

Finnegan straightened. "Captain, I don't understand."

"It could have been a bad scene here, Jim, could have been people inside, drugs, that dickhead could have resisted."

"Captain, I didn't tip anybody off to anything," Finnegan protested.

Fogarty smiled, placing his hand on Finnegan's shoulder. "Right. I'll make sure Reuben Jakes knows."

Myron Schlenk had worked his way up from personal injury claims, chasing behind ambulances, to become a formidable defense attorney. At fifty-two, he was fat, balding, and, having recently beat the city on a tax-fraud charge, in his prime.

"Tell him we're not here yet, so he can just sit on his fat ass and wait," Fogarty instructed, when the news of Schlenk's arrival reached his office, confirming, beyond doubt, that Horst Nickles had been tipped.

"I vant my attorney. I vant my attorney," Nickles had repeated, as Fogarty, Gilbey, and Roach walked him up the back stairs and into homicide. His majestic countenance had all but deserted him by the time he'd been marched into the small, green, interrogation room at the end of the row of desks, each inhabited by a hard-eyed cop.

"Jimmy, will you give me a hand with this?" Fogarty called from the nine-by-eight-foot room. "Mr. Nickles, why don't you take the chair by the table," he continued, guiding the Horse to the stainless-steel chair at the far end of the room. Roach and Gilbey watched from just inside the door.

The interrogation chair was dull and scratched. It looked as if it had been polished with sandpaper in an attempt to remove the sweat stains of its former occupants. A single handcuff was attached to the right armrest, metal welded to metal. The steel restraining chair, coupled with the peeling green paint on the walls and cracked linoleum floor, gave the room a hopeless feel, a place of no return.

"Vhy do I need to sit in this?" Nickles asked, resisting as Fogarty tried to position him.

"It's the way we do things here, Mr. Nickles," Fogarty explained.

"Who you think you are, Gestapo?" Nickles retorted.

"You want me to help him sit down, Captain?" Taylor's deep voice came from outside the door.

Taylor was an African-American, six-feet-four-inches tall and two hundred forty pounds. In his boxing days, before the retina operation that finished his pro career, he'd been the best heavyweight in Joe Frazier's gym, coached by Joe himself.

"You come near me, I'll break your fucking neck," Nickles promised, eyeing the ex-boxer.

Taylor surged forward. Gilbey and Roach stepped in front of him, and Fogarty, pressing with his bodyweight against Nickles's chest, looked desperately and sincerely into the German's eyes. "Please, Mr. Nickles, sit down."

Nickles sat. Fogarty secured the single cuff and removed the set that had been used to bring him in. The whole thing, between Fogarty and Taylor, had been worked out in advance, the good cop and the bad cop. The old tried and true. Fogarty liked to work it with Taylor because of Taylor's size and intimidation value. Not that Nickles was particularly intimidated. He was more confused; but confused was just as valuable. Fogarty shot a look at Roach and Gilbey. They let go of Taylor's arms.

"I vant my lawyer," Nickles repeated for the tenth time. Fogarty would have loved half an hour with the German, without Myron Schlenk present, but it was an impossibility.

"Was it Jim Finnegan who told you we were coming?" Fogarty asked, trying to get Nickles talking.

"Vhere is my lawyer, and vhy is that black bastard blocking the door?"

Taylor stepped forward, glaring down at the Horse. Fogarty turned, standing between them.

"Officer Taylor, you calm down." Fogarty's voice was sharp, authoritative. Then, back to Horst Nickles, it was soft and forgiving. "Mr. Nickles. Where were you on the night of January eighteenth?"

Nickles sat silent.

"January the eighteenth, Mr. Nickles?"

"Fuck you, and fuck your bullshit. Get me my lawyer; I am an American. I have a green card; I demand my rights."

Fogarty turned to Sharon Gilbey. "I believe Mr. Nickles's attorney is already in the lobby of the building. Will you please go down and bring him up here? The elevator might be broken, so it's probably best to use the stairs. Mr. Schlenk is a big man, overweight, so walk him up slowly; we don't want to put a strain on his heart."

Gilbey nodded and left the room.

Fogarty turned back to Nickles.

"You must have known you'd get caught, Horst. Hell, you'd already beaten John Flint up once, strapped him to his chair, put a black leather hood over his head, blackened his eyes, broke his thumb."

Nickles deflated against the steel chair.

"Was it over the drugs he was supplying you, or was it because he had the videotape of you raping and torturing that woman?"

Nickles lowered his head and Fogarty sensed a quick victory.

"Do you want to know something, Horst? No bullshit. I can't blame you. I really can't. John Flint was scum. You want something else? We know all about what he was doing to his own children. Jesus. What kind of man is that? His ex-wife wants to pin a medal on your chest. He was scum. Thank you for killing him."

What happened next was somewhere between an automobile wreck and an explosion. The sound of grating metal, a huge burst of energy, and an ear-splitting war cry. It was followed by chaos, as Horst Nickles lunged from the metal chair, the broken chain and steel cuff still linked to his right wrist, swinging like a scythe. Fogarty flew back against the wall as Jimmy Taylor stepped forward, in time for the chain to slice a four-inch patch of fabric from the shoulder of his jacket. Another inch higher, and it would have been his throat. The ex-boxer got off a right to Nickles's solar plexus, pulling the punch up from the floor, sticking it in, as the German grunted, swallowing the pain, before wrapping both arms around Taylor and beginning to squeeze. Fogarty was in the process of drawing his weapon when Dave Roach leaped on Nickles's back, riding him like a bull, trying for a choke and blocking Fogarty's aim.

Jimmy Stark, who had been seated at his desk, reading the sports page of the *Daily News*, was now on his feet, weapon drawn. He had Nickles covered from the front, Fogarty from the rear; the problem was, they were aiming at a sandwich.

Taylor and Roach were the bread, and Nickles was the filling, stuck in the middle. On top of this, Taylor appeared to be losing consciousness, and Roach was an inch from a concussion, as the German butted backwards with his head.

"Hold it! Stop! That's it!" Fogarty's voice, mixed with Stark's.

"What the hell are you doing to my client! This is assault! Improper procedure! I'll sue this entire department!" The nasal twang of Myron Schlenk joined the avalanche of hysteria.

Sharon Gilbey ran to the warring men and kicked Horst Nickles in the side of the knee, catching the lateral edge of his joint with the hard tip of her shoe. With no effect.

Taylor was just going limp as Schlenk marched forward.

"It's all right Horst, I am here. It's me, Myron Schlenk. Your attorney is present."

Nickles twisted his head to the side.

"Vat took you so long?"

"I've been downstairs for an hour," Schlenk answered.

"Vat should I do?" Nickles grunted between breaths.

"Release the man you are holding," Schlenk instructed.

Horst removed his arms from Taylor and Taylor managed a clean right hand that split Nickles's lip.

"That is assault!" Schlenk screamed.

Fogarty stepped in front of Nickles, his thirty-eight pointed into the German's face. By now, homicide was filling with officers from other departments, attracted by the commotion. Taylor looked like round twelve of the "Thrilla in Manila" and Fogarty was wondering whether anyone had actually ever been shot in the Roundhouse. Not during his tenure, anyway.

"I'm bringing a lawsuit against the Philadelphia Police Department!"

Fogarty had heard Schlenk's threats before. And he knew the hungry attorney would like nothing more than to actually make good on one. It would mean the chance of a fat settlement, a swollen reputation and, above all, an opportunity for the bald head, with its greedy eyes and skin the texture of fried bacon, to get a crack at media exposure. Myron Schlenk on the cover of *Philadelphia* magazine, it was beyond Fogarty's contemplation.

"Yeah, and I'll charge your client with assault on a police officer, I've got plenty of witnesses," Fogarty retaliated, watching Roach drop the five feet from Nickles's neck to the floor, and Gilbey limp backwards. "Now, Mr. Schlenk, why don't you advise your client to cooperate."

Nickles looked at Schlenk, and Schlenk nodded the okay.

The German went into the interrogation room. Schlenk, Roach, and Fogarty followed him through the door. Fogarty stepped forward and used his key to unlock the broken cuff, removing it from Nickles's wrist. He glanced at the chain as he lifted it. Snapped cleanly in two, one of the steel links bent and jagged. Maybe there had been an intrinsic weakness in the steel, maybe not. Fogarty had seen the same chain hold a lot of angry prisoners. If he hadn't seen Nickles break it, he wouldn't have believed it possible. He tossed the cuff onto the table, as if, in fact, the chain snapped on a daily basis. Then, Fogarty turned to Myron Schlenk.

"Your client has been arrested in connection with the murder of Doctor John Winston Flint. The murder took place between the hours of seven P.M. on the eighteenth of January and eight A.M. the morning of the nineteenth."

Myron Schlenk flexed his fat lips and nodded his head.

"Now, Mr. Nickles," Fogarty began again, knowing that with Schlenk present, his suspect was apt to say precious little, "let's begin with your relationship to Doctor John Winston Flint."

Nickles looked at Schlenk, and Schlenk nodded.

"He vas my doctor."

"And did Doctor Flint supply you with steroid drugs?"

Again the glance.

"No."

"That is in direct contradiction to the information I have found in the late doctor's diary, and in his prescription files."

"Vat information?" Nickles demanded.

"Drugs like testosterone, and the amounts prescribed," Fogarty answered.

"Oh yes," Nickles said, as if he was remembering something of little significance, "during a period of ten months, Doctor Flint injected me with testosterone."

"Which is an anoblic steroid."

"It is?" Horst asked, smiling. "I thought it vas a cure for anemia."

Roach was seated, taking notes, the tape recorder was running, and Fogarty was amazed that he was getting this much conversation out of Nickles. In serious cases, when the suspect's lawyer was present, it was more common for the person in the steel chair to say nothing at all. Fogarty mistrusted Nickles's glibness.

"And you were suffering from anemia?"

"Stress related," Nickles confirmed.

"Uh huh," Fogarty answered.

"If you don't mind, Captain, why don't we get to the reason we're all here," Schlenk interjected from the corner. He looked like a poker player with a full hand.

"Right," Fogarty answered. There was a knock on the door and Fogarty used it as a stall, gathering his thoughts, trying to figure a way to get the German to incriminate himself. With Schlenk present he wouldn't get more than a single chance.

Sharon Gilbey was at the door. She looked discouraged. Fogarty kept one eye on Nickles and bent down so she could whisper her message.

"The mobile unit didn't find anything, the gym was clean." Ten words that meant they couldn't even hold Nickles on a secondary charge if the big one fell through. Fogarty whispered something to Gilbey, nodded his head, faked a smile, and walked back towards his suspect like a prizefighter who'd been hurt but was trying not to show it.

"Look, I can cut a deal, get this reduced to accidental manslaughter. I know what you were into, the leather masks, the dog leads, the videos, trading drugs for sex—"

"Hold on a second, officer," Schlenk interrupted.

"I've got this guy," Fogarty bluffed, looking at Nickles. "I've got a witness who'll say you beat Flint up—"

"But you can't place him in Philadelphia on the night of John Flint's death, January the eighteenth," Schlenk smirked, playing his ace.

Fogarty felt like he'd been hit in the solar plexus.

"Or on the nineteenth or twentieth," Schlenk followed through, pulling a stack of papers from his briefcase. He tossed the stack onto the table.

"My client was not in Philadelphia." His voice smacked.

Fogarty was out on his feet. He picked up the three glossy eight-by-ten photographs from the top of the pile. They were pictures of Horst Nickles, holding center stage on a posing platform, both arms raised, fingers pointing skyward, like a conquering hero. In the background, clear as day, an unfurled banner read MR. MIAMI '94, MIAMI BEACH, FLORIDA.

"Taken on the night of the nineteenth, when Mr. Nickles was doing his guest posing routine, before the finals. He had already judged the preliminaries the day before, and the following day, the twentieth, he presented the trophies to the winners, then flew back to Philadelphia."

"I am surprised you did not notice my tan when you came to my gym." Nickles smiled.

"The rest of the papers will validate the dates, times, hotels, and plane schedules," Schlenk added.

Roach stopped writing.

"Now, if you don't mind, Mr. Nickles and I have another engagement," Myron Schlenk concluded, placing his hand on Horst Nickles's shoulder.

Fogarty needed time, just a few more minutes, before he was willing to admit that he was completely dead. He could still feel a pulse, but it was in his forehead, like a migraine.

"Just sit tight, Mr. Nickles," he ordered.

"If you're not going to charge my client—"

"I want to check out these papers," Fogarty said, lifting the stack from the table and walking to the door. "Officer Roach?"

Dave Roach looked up, his face was pale, as if he'd just suffered a bereavement. He respected Fogarty and understood, exactly, what had just happened to him.

"Yes, Sir?"

"Would you watch the suspect while I'm out of the room?"

"Oh, please, spare us the histrionics!" Schlenk exploded.

Fogarty closed the door. He walked straight to Sharon Gilbey's desk; she was just putting down the phone.

"Officer Graves is here now. Ligeya Antonio will take another fifteen minutes," she said.

"Okay. Have her in front of the building, in a patrol car," Fogarty instructed. It was a long shot, but Fogarty didn't have any other shots left. He spread the papers on Gilbey's desk.

"Nickles claims to have been in Miami during the time of Flint's death." He could see her shrink behind the news. "I want you to make a few confirmation calls, airlines, hotels. Just do whatever you've got to do, to use up the time it takes to get the Filipino woman here."

Then Fogarty walked back to the interrogation room, stepped inside, and shut the door.

"A few minutes, gentlemen, that's all it should take." He sounded relaxed and friendly. "I'm sorry, just a formality. Anything I can get you, cup of coffee, shot of testosterone?"

Dave Roach looked over at his captain; he admired Fogarty's tenacity.

Schlenk didn't honor him with an answer, and Nickles was rubbing his wrist, where he'd snapped the cuff. The flesh above the thick bone was red and bruised.

"You wouldn't happen to be considering a personal injury claim?" Fogarty asked.

Nickles kept rubbing, looking at Schlenk.

"I hear, in your prime, you could outrun any ambulance in Philadelphia," Fogarty said to the lawyer.

"You've got a great deal of gall, Mr. Fogarty," Schlenk answered.

"I've also got the feeling that we're not through in here, quite yet."

"How much longer is this going to take?" Nickles asked.

"Are you talking about today, or when I bring you in next week?"

"You are harassing my client," Schlenk protested.

"Shit, I'm sorry. Do you know, Myron, that Mr. Nickles, here, your client, is a very talented man. Have you seen any of his films?"

"And, do you know, Officer, that you are wasting our time?" Schlenk replied.

"Come on, I'm going to have a cup of coffee," Fogarty said, smiling at Nickles. "I hear caffeine's a great fat burner."

Fogarty drank slowly from the cracked mug. Nickles was now concentrating on his split lip, rubbing it with his thumb and glowering at the door that led to Jimmy Taylor. Schlenk was staring angrily into space. A quiet knock and the head games were over.

"It's all done," Sharon Gilbey said, "everything checks out." She handed Fogarty an envelope which contained the papers from Nickles's Miami trip.

"That's fine, Detective, that's just fine," Fogarty said, turning to offer the manilla envelope to Schlenk.

"You can go now, Mr. Nickles."

Roach stepped aside, permitting the self-proclaimed Nazi and his Jewish defender to leave the room.

Nickles eyed Taylor as he walked in front of the policeman's desk. Taylor eyed him back. Schlenk stepped across the floor as if he were avoiding dog shit. When they'd made it to the door, Schlenk turned and looked back at the sea of desks, papers, and faces. "You, and your department, Captain, are a disgrace to this city."

Fogarty let Schlenk's words hang in the air. Then, clearing his throat, he said, "Detective Roach and I will extend the privilege of escorting you and your client to the front of the building."

There was barely room in the elevator for the four men, and the ten-second ride to the ground floor felt like eternity.

"We didn't really need an escort, I've been here before," Schlenk said, as the elevator bumped to a halt and the door squeaked open.

"It's all right, Myron, a man of your stature deserves respect," Fogarty answered, as they walked the hallway to the glass-fronted doors. Through the glass, Fogarty could see the patrol car, with its two passengers in the backseat, sitting across from them, in the parking lot.

By the time they were outside, he had his right hand on the butt of his thirty-eight. All he needed was a wave from the patrol car and he would rearrest Nickles and drag him back upstairs. To hell with Miami. He'd seen elaborate alibis before.

They were close now, maybe thirty feet from the blue and grey, and Fogarty could make out the outline of Ligeya Antonio's face, staring round the shoulder of Roy Graves, the mounted officer from East River Drive. Fogarty concentrated, waiting, as the window began to roll down.

They need a clearer view, he realized, moving to the outside of Nickles, placing him directly across from the car. Fogarty could see the Filipino. She was crossing herself, over and over again, and he could see Graves. Graves was shaking his head. An unmistakable "no."

Myron Schlenk could see it, too. He stopped, turning on Fogarty.

"What's this? Your idea of an identity parade?" Schlenk didn't wait for an answer. "That's the cheapest fucking trick yet."

Fogarty stared into the lawyer's pitted face.

"I'm going to file a complaint against you, Mr. Fogarty. Everything you've done today has gone against proper proce-

dure. Delaying my client's right to council, staging this cir-
cus." He looked at the patrol car, then back to Fogarty. "I've
got friends in the mayor's office, Captain, who will agree,
you are not worthy of being a public servant!"

Fogarty watched, in silence, as Schlenk and Nickles walked
away. "Not worthy." The two words hit him like truth.

TRUTH

Fogarty waved the patrol car carrying his two eyewitnesses away. Then he shrugged off Dave Roach when the young detective tried to stutter a reassurance. After that, he walked back inside the building, heading for the fire stairs.

The passage up was narrow and dimly lit; it may have been the only place in the Roundhouse where he could get a few minutes of privacy. He couldn't take the weight of eyes upon him.

He'd heard once that when the heavyweight, Floyd Paterson, had lost his title, KO'd in a single round in Chicago, that the shamed boxer had put on a false beard and moustache in order to sneak out of the stadium without being noticed. Humiliation was a terrible thing, and Fogarty had just been humiliated in front of his entire department.

He sat down, resting his face in his hands, the concrete steps cold against his backside. He could feel his scars against his right palm, hard and rubbery. This morning, he had resolved to have Rachel Saunders fix them. He'd felt like a new man, and had wanted to look like one, if only for the new woman in his life. "You're a beautiful dancer," he recalled Diane Genero's note, then thought of the "dance" he had just done with Schlenk and Nickles. It was all connected, the good and the bad, the positive and the negative, and he was so used to functioning in the negative that when a spark of fresh energy came his way, he thought he could walk on water. Even Josef had been cautious regarding Horst Nickles, dragging Fogarty along to see Stan Leibowitz. Yet, no matter how many voices had cast doubts, Fogarty had listened to only one, his own. He'd wanted to wrap the case up, get rid of it, and go back to dancing. He lifted his head and stared at the wall, slime green and cracking. He thought of the Flint video; there was still Quantico. A day after he'd shipped the tape, he'd FedExed a picture of Horst Nickles. Maybe they could give him a body match, some distinquishing mark that would appear on both tape and picture, linking them. Then he thought of a bent cop by the name of Jim Finnegan, and started to get angry.

He stood up, adjusted his jacket, and walked back out the fire door, out of the building and into the car park. He climbed into his Chrysler, turned on the ignition, drove from the parking lot and headed north.

The further he drove into the thirty-fifth district, the angrier he got, and the angrier he got the harder he fought to harness it, tucking it right down low in his belly, turning the anger into resolve.

He pulled into the lot marked "visitors," in front of the old, red-brick building, turned off the car and sat a moment, collecting his thoughts. There were two things he needed from Reuben Jakes.

He walked into the building, showed his shield to the officer in the operations room, asking for Commander Jakes. The young cop was still pressing the intercom for Jakes's office when Fogarty headed for the steps to the second floor.

Jakes was waiting in the hallway.

"Hello, Bill."

"Reuben," Fogarty said, shaking the commander's hand. Then, they walked towards Jakes's office.

"Was Finnegan the only guy assigned to keep an eye on Nickles?" Fogarty asked, as the door closed.

"It was his beat, his shift. Yeah, he was the only one."

"And he knew about the warrants?"

"I briefed him this morning. Along with Howes."

Fogarty cocked his head.

"Raymond Howes, the detective who assisted with the arrest," Jakes explained.

"Well, he's black," Fogarty said, "so I doubt very much that he'd be real close to Horst Nickles."

"Trust me. He's not." Jakes agreed, beginning to get Fogarty's drift.

"No. It's fucking Finnegan. We should have dumped him when he worked Center City," Fogarty blurted.

"You did dump him. On me."

"Yeah," Fogarty replied, without humor.

"What did he do?" Jakes asked.

"He tipped Nickles off. Blew my arrest," Fogarty continued.

"Nickles was warned?"

"His place was empty, clean, and his lawyer was waiting at the Roundhouse. You tell me."

Jakes pushed a brown, plastic-upholstered card chair in Fogarty's direction, then walked behind his desk.

"What do you want me to do?" he said.

"I want you to bust Finnegan, kick the son of a bitch right off the force," Fogarty replied.

"I can't bust him without proof."

"Find some proof," Fogarty said.

"Come on, Bill," Jakes hedged.

"Finnegan's bent; he was bent when he worked Center City, he's bent now. It doesn't go away. Reuben, if you want to know about a dirty street cop, where's a good place to start?"

Jakes frowned, nodded his head, and pressed his intercom.

"Ruth, will you have Officer Walker go downstairs and bring me the contents of Sergeant Jim Finnegan's locker. Thank you." The in-house lockers were the property of the police department, and required no warrant for a search.

"How's that?" Jakes asked, looking at Fogarty.

"Good. Now, would you please tell me who you had working undercover in Animals and what happened?"

The question took Jakes by surprise. He sat down at his desk.

"I really do need to know," Fogarty insisted.

"It's history, Bill," Jakes smoothed.

"So's my case against Horst Nickles if I don't find out what the fuck's going on."

"Some low-level drug dealing, that's what's going on," the commander answered.

"So why's he still there?"

"We're working on him."

"How hard?" The anger was escaping.

"Listen," Jake's voice was sharp. "The guy's a dirt bag, but the thirty-fifth is a real dirty place, and the kind of shit that comes out of there is minor."

"Then why did you have somebody inside?"

"To ease the pressure with the white community."

"What was his name?"

Jakes hesitated a moment.

"Come on, Reuben," Fogarty pressed.

"Jacqueline Dunne." He hated to say it.

"A woman?"

"Yes."

"I want to talk to her."

"You can't."

"Why?"

Jakes dropped his eyes. Officer Dunne was the low point of his career. In fact, Jacqueline Dunne could have ruined his career.

"She's no longer a police officer, Bill."

"Where the hell is she?"

"I don't know. After the incident the city settled an amount on her for medical compensation, then gave her a Regulation Thirty-two, a disability pension. That was it. She'll never be hurting for money."

Fogarty sat down in the card-table chair facing Jakes's desk.

"Reuben, you are going to have to talk to me," he kept his voice low, but his intent was clear.

"She got involved with the guy. The German . . . she ended up in a psychiatric unit in Norristown."

"What!?"

"Her involvement with Nickles and her breakdown may or may not have been related."

"Oh, come on, man, you're teasing me. What the fuck happened?"

Jake modulated his voice, keeping it inside the room.

"She was found staggering naked along the boardwalk in Asbury Park, New Jersey. It was five o'clock in the morning and she was drugged, beat up, raped. She was a mess, Bill, a real mess. The cops down there picked her up. It took 'em three days to get her name out of her. Originally, they thought she was a hooker, figured she'd been dumped from a car somewhere, maybe even hit by a car. That's how bad she was."

"So what did you do?"

Jakes shook his head; the memory still hurt. "We brought her back here as a Jane Doe, got her fixed up; we got her body fixed up. Mentally, she was gone."

"So you settled with her family and swept the whole thing under a rug."

"That's not true. The case made the papers, her name was withheld, but it made the papers, and it was in the 'white paper.' "

"Funny, I don't remember it."

"We watered it down, made it a street crime, an off-duty officer mugged, out of state. It was to protect her, Bill."

"When?"

"Just over four years ago."

"And you didn't try to tie it to Nickles?"

"Yeah, we tried. But there was nothing in it. She never talked."

"What do you mean?"

"I'm telling you, Bill, Jacqueline Dunne was a mess. I don't think she knew what'd happened to her; she was a zombie. A blank. We had a shrink look at her; we had her institutionalized, under observation. She got better physically, but she never talked. I mean, talked, period. She just shut down."

"Tell me about her," Fogarty started again, softer.

"She could have been a good one," Jakes began. "She was

smart, ambitious, funny, I liked her, hell, everybody liked Jacqui Dunne."

"Was she married?"

"No."

"Was she involved with anybody?"

"Nobody here, that's for sure. Jacqui was strictly business."

"So how the hell did she get to Animals?"

"She'd been walking a beat for three years, she was bored, and she wanted to go undercover."

"Simple as that, huh?"

"It's never simple as that, is it? She was the right person for the job," Jakes answered.

"Explain that to me."

"About six years ago, we started getting a number of complaints about the sale of steroid drugs. High school teachers, junior high school teachers, parents, church officials. I mean, Jesus, they could accept marijuana, even a run of coke, but needles, man, they didn't want their kids doing needles. Plus, do you know what steroids do to young boys?"

"Not exactly."

"If they start shooting that shit into their backsides before they're fully grown, it accelerates their rate of maturity. Gives 'em a big dick, and a short skeleton. Their bones close at the tips; they end up looking like midgets."

Fogarty nodded.

"It didn't take a rocket scientist to put steroids and Animals together. I mean it was mostly a white thing, white kids selling the drugs to other white kids, and the German is sort of a figurehead in the white community. There were never any problems around his place, no crime—"

"Except he was selling drugs," Fogarty stated.

"Bill, it was a very grey area. Steroid drugs had just been reclassified, made illegal, and they were a specialty item. It was like a minority crime, Bill, not a priority. A white crime."

"And Jacqueline Dunne was white?"

"Yes. And she was tuned into the whole bodybuilding thing, nutrition, weights, she knew her way around a gym."

"So you let her inside Animals."

"It was probably a lot safer than walking a beat in this district." Jakes sounded guilty.

"So, without any experience you let her go undercover with that geek?"

"It didn't seem like a heavy number at the time." Jakes still sounded guilty.

Fogarty looked at him and shook his head. "How could you live with this, Reuben?"

"We've all got to live with stuff, Bill, you know that as well as me." He held Fogarty's eyes.

"Yeah, right," Fogarty answered. He knew.

Jakes's phone was ringing; he picked it up, said, "Bring it in," then told his secretary to hold all calls for fifteen minutes. A fews seconds later there was a knock on the door.

"Okay, Dave," Jakes answered.

Dave Walker entered, nodded to Fogarty and handed Jakes a plastic bag. Jakes placed the bag on his desk.

"Anyway, we got her inside the place," he continued. "Jesus, I'm making it sound like more than it was. We bought her a fucking membership. Used a phony name. She put her occupation down as civil servant, post office employee—"

"It sounds like a loose operation," Fogarty commented.

"It was loose, Bill, it wasn't a priority. I wanted to be able to tell the community that we were on top of it. I mean, I would have loved to have shut down Nickles, but that was more a personal thing. I didn't like what he stood for. I frankly didn't give a shit about whether or not the members of his gym used steroids. I've got guys in this building who've probably used them. It was the kids, and the idea that Nickles was selling to them. If it hadn't been for that I wouldn't have bothered," Jakes hesitated. "Come on, Bill, we've been around the block once or twice. You know what I've got down here. I've got serious drugs, serious dealers—"

Fogarty cocked his head.

"Bill, if you were sitting on top of this shit heap, would

you really care if some Nazi motherfucker was sticking a load of hormone in his ass?"

Fogarty held steady. "So you put an inexperienced cop inside Animals?"

"Don't lay a guilt trip on me. We kept an eye on Jacqueline Dunne, believe me. And she was careful."

"But not careful enough."

"She took it all very seriously. Her first time undercover, you know how it goes. She thought she was onto the biggest bust of the year and, to tell you the truth, it was Jacqueline who made us aware of Nickles's drug network, the Aryan Army, which is the nucleus of his distribution chain. There was a problem, though."

"What was that?"

"Jacqueline got too close to Nickles."

"You mean he was fucking her?"

"I don't know the answer to that."

"Then, what do you mean, too close?"

"You'd only had to take a look at her to know something was going on. I doubt if she could have fit into her street blues after eight weeks down there; she must have put on ten pounds of muscle—"

"She was using the stuff?"

Jakes shrugged. "I don't know for sure. She started getting edgy, aggressive. So I pulled her out. And that's when the problems started. She wouldn't get out, swore to me that she was onto something, close to a bust. It became her personal crusade. She kept going back, training with the guy. What could I do?"

"I don't understand. If you had the information, if you knew the guy was distributing drugs, why didn't you take him?"

"Come on Bill, give me a break, we were in there three times, warrants, mobile unit. You know what we found?"

"Jim Finnegan's jock strap," Fogarty said sarcastically.

Jakes overrode the remark. "Thirty-six pounds of powdered egg whites, about a hundred thousand dessicated liver tablets, ten thousand caffeine pills, multiple vitamins."

"I thought Officer Dunne told you he was dealing."

Jakes looked frustrated.

"Bill, you can't bust a guy for selling liver tablets."

"But how 'bout Officer Dunne. If she was that close to Nickles, and she was certain he was distributing steroid drugs, why didn't she make the arrest herself?"

"First of all, I'd taken her off the case, so there was an ego thing involved. She wanted it to be important, I had other things on my plate. And Jacqui Dunne was smart; I don't think she was interested in a small-time bust—you know, the kind of thing that would have resulted in a slap on the wrist for Nickles, at best, closing down his gym. She was ambitious and, whatever she was doing with the German, the drugs, the training, fucking him, whatever it was, it made her over-confident. The way I saw it afterwards and, believe me, I spent a lot of nights thinking about it, Jacqueline Dunne wanted to get to Nickles's source."

"You don't think he turned her?"

"No. Jacqueline Dunne was a good cop—"

"Who ended up walking naked on the boardwalk in Asbury Park," Fogarty concluded.

Jakes's face fell and he shook his head. "We could never tie it to the German," he repeated.

"Have you got all the files? On Nickles and on Jacqueline Dunne?"

"Of course I've got the files," Jakes answered.

"Can I take a look at them?"

Jakes pressed his intercom, instructing his secretary to bring Jacqueline Dunne's files in from the outer office, then he requested a computer printout on Horst Nickles. While they were waiting, Jakes poured the contents of Finnegan's locker onto his desk. A Gillette razor, a can of shaving gel, two bars of soap, several sticks of deodorant, a new pair of Odor Eater inserts for his shoes, training shoes, three white socks, a T-shirt, sweat pants, four jars of Weider protein pills, and a small grey container, marked DEXAMPHETAMINE SULPHATE BP, 100 TABLETS. Fogarty smiled when Jakes held up the dexies.

"Speed," Fogarty said.

"More like diet pills, and about as deadly as too much coffee," Jakes replied.

"It's a prescription drug, Reuben, and I'm betting that Mr. Finnegan won't have a prescription."

"Probably not."

"You will take care of it for me, won't you?" Fogarty asked.

"One way or another, Jim Finnegan is history."

The files arrived in a grimy, worn manilla folder; it looked as if it had been handled a thousand times. Jakes looked at it as if it were the casket of a close friend.

"I've lost a few cops here, over the years, Bill, but Jacqui Dunne hurt the most. She was special."

Fogarty was about to open the file when the printout on Nickles showed up. It was a good, solid sheet, listing the three searches and seizures of property from his place of business, plus a list of misdemeanors, mostly parking violations. This morning's arrest hadn't made the sheet, yet.

"He's murky, but he keeps sliding by," Jakes said as Fogarty placed the sheet on his desk.

Next, Fogarty opened the manilla envelope.

A picture of Jacqueline Dunne stared him straight in the face.

"She was a good-looking woman," he said.

"High Angel."

"What?"

"High Angel," Jakes repeated. "That's what a couple of the boys around here used to call her."

Fogarty looked at Jakes, puzzled.

"It was because of her blonde hair, her looks, and because of her size. You know *high*, as in tall. Check her physical measurements."

Fogarty ran down the page, past the birth date, and place of birth. "Height/70.5 Inches, Weight/140 lbs."

"We used Angel as her undercover name. Jacqueline Angel."

Fogarty studied the measurements, then looked, again, at the I.D. photo.

"She was built, too. Always exercised. Perfect proportion. That's why she was right for the job; it breaks my heart what—"

Fogarty was flushed in the face, staring into the blue eyes, thinking of the black leather hood and Flint's examination table, shaking his head, saying "Christ, Jesus Christ."

"Bill, are you all right?"

As soon as Wayne Brosky walked down the steps, and through the door to the basement sweathouse, known to its thirty members as Titans, he knew it was going to be his lucky day. The freak was standing by the squat rack, looking nervous, but big enough, and ugly enough, that none of the three men working with the equipment were going to challenge his right to be there. Rick Zabrinsky, the owner, wasn't in his closet-sized office, so Brosky figured the freak had just walked in off the street and stayed. It was the first time Brosky had seen him inside. Their past two transactions had taken place at the bottom of the twelve concrete steps, in the stairwell, outside the door. It was Thursday night, Brosky's night for visiting Titans; he reckoned the freak needed more product.

"Hey man, how's it going?" the skinhead asked, walking forward, extending his left hand, since his right thumb and index finger were temporarily in a splint.

Jack Dunne forced a smile, took the skin's hand and squeezed.

"Okay."

Brosky could see the freak was wired, his pupils were dilated and his skin had the look some people got from too much speed, like it was too tight for his face. Definitely the guy from the police drawing, no doubt about it, Brosky told himself.

Titans was so small that members had to stagger the times they trained, in order to avoid crashing into each other. Even with five of them in the place it felt claustrophobic. There was no locker room or shower.

"Where's Rick?" Brosky asked one of the lumps doing cheat curls in the corner.

The lump hoisted the barbell for a final repetition, lowered it from his chin to his waist, and dropped it to the floor. It landed hard and loud against the thin rubber mat.

"What?" It was against the rules to talk to somebody in the middle of a rep, and the lump was agitated.

Brosky stepped forward, into the man's face. "I said, where's Rick Zabrinsky?"

"Out making a phonecall, phone here's broke." The lump backed off. He knew Brosky by his face and his reputation and, without the 110-pound barbell as a shield, he felt vulnerable.

Brosky turned back to Jack Dunne. "Come on, bro, we'll use the boss's office."

There was barely room for the two of them inside the closet. Brosky sat on top of the old wood desk and Jack Dunne kept his back to the door.

"Whatcha' need?" Brosky asked.

"Some anadrol and some halotestin," Jack answered.

"What kind of quantity?"

Jack reached into his pocket and pulled out a wad of hundred-dollar bills. He handed the bills to Brosky.

Brosky took them and counted the money. "What's your name?"

"Halotestin," Jack answered.

Brosky narrowed his eyes and tightened his lips. "Don't get funny with me."

"Jack Dunne."

"Right, Jack," Brosky relaxed. "Where do you come from, and where do you train?"

Jack Dunne stood silent. Something about his eyes bothered Brosky; there was nothing behind them, no emotion.

It was as if Brosky was staring into small, twin mirrors. The only reflection was his own anger, and that frightened him.

"All right, Jack, here's the story," Brosky explained, looking down at the bills. "I don't have this kind of quantity with me. I can get it, but I ain't got it now. If you tell me where you live, or where you train, I'll bring it to you. If you don't, you can go fuck yourself."

"I'm a friend of the Horse. He said you might be able to help me."

Brosky jumped off the desk and stood face-to-face with Jack Dunne.

"What did you say, man, what did you just say?"

Jack looked down at the top of Brosky's shining head; he could smell garlic, garlic and onions, and rotted meat, sausage. His back was tight against the thin wooden door, and Brosky's breath was all over him. He needed to get away, and quick.

"Number seven, Front Street, I train at home. Number seven. I train in the basement. Home gym. I train alone." His voice was a fast monotone.

This fucker is gone, the skinhead realized, then said, "Okay, okay," backing off, "your name is Jack Dunne, and you live at number seven Front Street?"

"Near I-95," Jack added. He wanted Brosky to know, wanted him to tell Horst Nickles.

"You train at home and you want," he held out the money, "a grand's worth of product."

"Yes, Sir."

"Right. When are you going to be there?" Brosky asked.

"Friday night, eight o'clock. Yes, Sir." He knew it was set, irrevocable. Face-to-face with Horst Nickles, he was sure of it.

Brosky laughed. He couldn't help it. The freak was actually standing at attention in front of him, like a soldier.

"At ease, man, at ease," the skinhead said.

"I want to see the Horse."

"Yeah, I'll bet you do," Brosky answered. He was feeling

better now. In fact, he was feeling fine. "Tomorrow night, eight o'clock, I'll have the stuff with me."

"Bring backup," Jack Dunne ordered, then did an about-face, opened the door of the office, and marched out of Titans.

ANGEL

Fogarty walked into homicide and straight into his office. There was a message waiting, *Robert Burt*, *Quantico*, *Virginia*, and a telephone number. Fogarty got a new rush of energy; he started dialing before he sat down.

"We've just had a result on the first frame of film, the one with the Rolex in it, and we should have either a positive or negative on the match between the body in the photograph and the body in the other frames by five o'clock," the lab technician informed him.

"Please, tell me what you've got, so far." Fogarty was chomping at the bit.

There was hesitation on the other end of the line, a rustling of papers, and then the technician's dry voice, "The date on the Rolex is the twelfth, and the time is ten-o-three."

Fogarty wrote the numbers down.

"Thanks, thanks very much."

"As I said, Captain, we should have the rest for you later this afternoon. The tape is not new, and it was difficult to work with."

"How old would you say it is, the tape?"

"Four, maybe five years, that's a rough guess—it's been played a lot."

It was all coming together, like the pieces of a puzzle, quicker now as the most difficult pieces fell into place. Fogarty was back in the game.

"Mr. Burt, thanks again, I'll talk to you later, this afternoon."

Fogarty put the phone down; it rang as soon as it hit the cradle. He lifted the telephone with one hand, put on his reading glasses, and sifted through Jacqueline Dunne's file with the other.

"Bill?"

"He walked, Josef," Fogarty answered, getting to the last pages, the Asbury Park section, "somebody tipped Horst Nickles to the bust, he was ready for me. The gym was clean, he had his lawyer, an alibi."

"I'm sorry, Bill, I'm very sorry."

"Yeah, it was tough to take, but," he hesitated, looking down, his eyes searching the small print of the photocopied report, "this one ain't over till it's over."

Tanaka waited.

"The lab in Quantico came back with a date and time off the Rolex in the Flint video and," he hesitated, eyes locking on *Date: 9/13/91*, "I've got something sitting on my desk that will blow your mind."

Tanaka could hear the excitment. Bill Fogarty didn't sound like a man who had just been beaten.

"What is it?"

Fogarty was quiet for a few seconds, thinking, *September thirteenth, one day after the date on the Rolex.* He scanned down to the next line, *Time: Approx. 4:30 A.M.* It was a two-hour drive from Philadelphia to Asbury Park, maybe less at that time of night.

"Bill?"

"I know who she is." Fogarty's voice changed; it contained a strange emotion, there was sadness inside it, mixed with uncertainty and anticipation, as if he was talking about someone close, someone he knew well. Someone who had just had a bad accident, and he didn't know how bad.

"The fellas in the thirty-fifth district used to call her High Angel, because she was so tall, so beautiful—"

"Bill, what the hell are you talk—"

"The girl on the Flint tape. I know who she is."

Tanaka went silent.

"Jacqueline Dunne." Fogarty hesitated. "She was a cop."

"A cop?" Tanaka repeated.

"Working undercover, inside Nickles's gym."

Tanaka exhaled. "Is she still alive?" His voice was somber.

"Maybe."

"Where?"

"I don't know."

"How about family. Has she got family?" Tanaka and Fogarty were on the same track.

"Yes, she's got family," Fogarty answered, flicking back to the beginning of the file. "A mother, Betty, a father, Albert, and an older brother, Jack."

"How about one of them, Bill. Her father, or her brother. It makes sense."

"If you take into account the Filipino woman's account of the approximate age of the guy leaving the house, and the mounted officer's report on the guy sitting on the bench at the river, it's more likely the brother," Fogarty answered.

"Have you got Jacqueline Dunne's I.D. picture?"

"Yes."

"Have you matched it to your drawing? Is there anything, a family resemblance?"

"It's a bit of a stretch, but, yes, it could be—"

"Jack Dunne." Tanaka finished Fogarty's sentence as if he was saying, "Case closed."

"I'll locate the mother and father first," Fogarty said, "then, later today, I'm going to get confirmation from Quantico as to whether or not they can match a photograph of Nickles's body with the big guy on the Flint video—"

"Then we'll both hope that Jack Dunne gets to that animal before you do," Tanaka said.

"It starts to make sense, doesn't it?" Fogarty added.

"Perfect sense," Tanaka agreed.

"We'll talk later," Fogarty finished, then put down the phone.

Fogarty was in motion now, the kind of motion that built into a steady inertia, rolling forward. He'd had the inertia before; it never started until the pieces of the puzzle began to fit, but once it started, it wouldn't stop until he closed the case. Food, sleep, loneliness, thoughts of Diane Genero, all lost in the momentum. It was the reason he was a cop; there was no other buzz like it. Nothing. It was complete fulfillment.

He pressed the button to his intercom. "Millie, I want you to get onto information for Lancaster, Pennsylvania, and get me the phone number for Albert Dunne." He spelled the name and gave the address written in the space following the next of kin section on the police I.D. sheet, "Number four, South Willow Street Pike, Southern County."

"Get me any other Dunnes listed in Lancaster, while you're at it," he added, then pressed for an outside line and called information for Norristown.

Once through to the psychiatric unit, after identifying himself, and stressing the urgency of his call, he asked for the current status of their patient, Jacqueline Dunne. There was a long delay before he was transferred to records.

"Are you a family member?" the thin, female voice asked. It was the third time he had been asked the same question.

"I'm sorry, but there must be some confusion, I have already told three of you people that I am a Philadelphia police officer, and that this inquiry is in relation to a homicide investigation."

"Uh huh?" She sounded mistrustful, as if, maybe, one of the patients on the ward had made it to a payphone and was perpetrating a hoax.

"Jacqueline Dunne?" Fogarty repeated.

"Just a moment, please." And the line went dead.

"You fucking idiot," Fogarty cursed into the void, breaking the point of the pencil he was holding against his notebook.

He was about to put the phone down and redial when the line came back to life and a man's voice asked, "Is this Captain Fogarty?"

"It is," Fogarty stated.

"This is David Levitt, I'm the head administrator here."

"Good. Good. And you know what this is about?"

"Jacqueline Dunne," Levitt answered.

"That is correct." Fogarty was actually trying to sound like a cop now, efficient.

"She was released into the custody of her parents on the fifth of April, nineteen ninety-one. She had been with us a little over seven months."

"Could you tell me what condition Ms. Dunne was in?"

"I was not the chief administrator at that time," Levitt replied, "but our records show that she'd been diagnosed as paranoid schizophrenic. She was being treated for outbursts of violence coupled with bouts of acute depression. Her doctors were administering valproic acid—"

"What's that?"

"Valproic acid would have been used to control the episodes of violence," Levitt answered.

"What form did these episodes take?"

"It says here that Ms. Dunne became extremely agitated when in close proximity to male patients; she refused to be touched and would accept no form of physical contact," Levitt replied.

That makes sense, Fogarty thought.

"The valproic acid was used in combination with another medication, Prozac, which was used to control her panic attacks," Levitt continued.

"Panic attacks," Fogarty repeated, scribbling notes with the jagged edge of his broken point.

"That's correct. Ms. Dunne also received a course of electroconvulsive shock therapy, which is used in cases of acute depression."

Electric shock. Fogarty conjured an image of Jacqueline Dunne strapped to a white trolley, with a rubber stopper in her mouth, to prevent her from biting her tongue in half, and electrodes attached to either temple. That, after Flint's examination table.

"What shape was she in when she was released?" he asked.

Levitt ran through his records. "Noncommunicative, but no longer violent."

The report sobered Fogarty. His momentum was still there, but tempered by the reality that he was dealing with the destruction of a human life, a police officer's life.

"Mr. Levitt, would you be kind enough to give me the address and telephone number of Miss Dunne's parents."

He thought he detected hesitation on the other end of the phone.

"Mr. Levitt, there is a reason for this call. I can give you my ORI number, you can telephone the police administration building and verify my identity—"

"I'm sorry, Captain, I'm not doubting you. I'm just trying to find it. Okay, right, here it is."

Fogarty's intercom light had been blinking for the last half-minute of his call to Norristown. He wrote down the phone number, repeated it once to make certain, thanked Levitt, and said good-bye. Then picked up the call from Millie.

"I'm sorry, Bill, there's no listed number for the Old Mill Farm at that address. And no other Dunnes in the area."

"That's all right, I've got it here in front of me."

He dialed, and got a recording stating that the number was not in service. He went through the operator.

"I'm sorry, Sir, that phone shows disconnected."

"And nothing else listed under the name Dunne?"

"I can give you the number for information," the male voice offered.

"This is a police emergency."

"Hold on, I'll connect you to information."

"I don't want information. I've been through information."

"Sir, that line is no longer in operation."

Next, Fogarty called the department of transportation, and ran a computer check on Albert, Betty, and Jack Dunnes' driving licenses. There was a current record of a Betty Dunne at the Old Mill address, but nothing current for Albert or Jack.

"What? Are you trying to tell me they don't drive?" he asked the computer operator.

"Captain Fogarty, what we show on our records is that Albert Dunne did not renew his operator's license as of 1992. It was due for renewal at that time."

"And Jack?"

"We've got a Jack R. Dunne in Johnstown, his license is current."

"Is it a picture license?"

"No. There was an exemption."

"How about a birthdate?"

"February fourteenth, nineteen sixty-three."

"Thirty-one years old," Fogarty said out loud.

"That's right, Sir."

"Let me have Jack Dunne's address, please."

"The license gives his address as twenty-four-twenty-eight Adams Street, Johnstown."

Fogarty wrote down the details, thanked the operator, and got on to Johnstown information. This time there was a number listed and it did ring.

"Hello?" the man's voice on the other end was not much more than a low groan.

"Hello, may I speak to Jack Dunne—"

"Fuck you." *Click*, the line went dead.

Fogarty pressed redial.

Someone picked up the phone and said nothing, waiting.

"Hello?" Fogarty tried.

Still nothing.

"This is an emergency."

Click.

He pressed redial. This time he got the busy signal, and continued to get it for the next five redials.

Fogarty sat and thought. He could call the local police in Johnstown, check the address with them, even have a car go out to 2428. No, that's a bad idea. Tip 'em off and look what happens. I need to get there myself. How far is Johnstown? Maybe 250 miles from here, Lancaster's about midway between here and Johnstown. McMullon will probably authorize a flight. Then he thought of Schlenk's threat to file a formal complaint against him, and wondered if Police Commissioner Dan McMullon would authorize anything other than early retirement. He had another idea. Picking up his notebook, containing Jack R. Dunne's name and operator's license number, Fogarty walked out of his office and into the main room. There were about six people there, at their desks:

Taylor, Gilbey, Roach, and Stark among them. They were trying not to look curious, but they were all looking at him.

"Make sure you put in to get that jacket repaired," Fogarty said, eyeing Jimmy Taylor as he walked towards the far corner of the room.

Taylor smiled.

"Dave, Sharon, don't get bored, I'm about to have something for you."

Fogarty could feel confidence return to the room as he sat down in front of the computer and switched on the screen. He entered the filing program and pressed in "Jack R. Dunne." The computer hummed and clicked, and Fogarty felt as if he was waiting in front of one of the slot machines in Atlantic City. The screen came up blank. Fogarty shut it off, and backed away, trying to lose none of the self-assurance that he'd carried into the room. He was onto something; he could feel it, trembling in his gut. He walked back, through the maze of desks, and into his office. Onto the phone again, to Washington, D.C., the Internal Revenue Service. This time they checked his ORI number, verifying his credentials, before giving him Jack Dunne's social security number and his last place of employment, the Johnstown Elementary School.

"Yes, Mr. Dunne was employed by the Greater Johnstown School District; he worked in our physical education department until June of nineteen ninety-one."

"What were the reasons for his dismissal?"

"He wasn't dismissed; he chose not to renew his contract. Apparently he had personal problems."

"Could you tell me what they were, the personal problems?" Fogarty asked the school registrar.

"I'm sorry. I don't have that information," she replied.

"Have you got any other records of Mr. Dunne, anything that would have a photograph, a medical report."

"Yes, I have his most recent identification photo, and his last health certificate."

"Has it got a height and weight on it?"

"Mr. Dunne was six-feet-one-inch in height and weighed

two hundred and ten pounds. That was in September of nineteen-ninety."

"That's terrific, I can't tell you how much you've helped us. I'm probably going to be up there in the next twenty-four hours, but in the meantime, I'd appreciate it if you would do one more thing. Would you photocopy Mr. Dunne's picture and fax it to me."

"I'm not sure it will fax very well, Captain."

"Just give it a try."

"Okay."

The fax came through fifteen minutes later; it was dark and shadowed but it was hopeful. Jack Dunne's face was wide, and his features were recognizable; they bore the same refined quality as the police drawing. His hair in the photograph was short, but it certainly could have been the same man.

Fogarty sat at his desk, Jacqueline Dunne's police records in front of him, the fax of Jack Dunne's face to the left of the records, and the police drawing of the suspect to the right. The copy of the rap sheet on Horst Nickles was on top of Dunne's police records. He opened his drawer and took out the crime stills of the Flint homicide, then the crime stills from the Roccoletti case. Then, finally, a copy of the Flint videotape. There they were, all present and accounted for, the crimes, the victims, the motives, the perpetrators, all sitting right in front of him. Fogarty looked at the pile of paper, plastic, and celluloid; he got a strange feeling, like an undisciplined clairvoyance, a thousand images and feelings cascading simultaneously, fragmented voices, shouting questions. And the answer? Sitting right there in front of him, buried beneath the questions. He took a fresh pencil from his desk, and laid his yellow, lined pad on top of the pile. Then he started, first drawing the shape of a pyramid on the paper, and was about to place John Winston Flint's name at the top of the pyramid, as if the doctor's death was the culmination of the events preceding it, when his hand stalled. Flint's death, and Roccoletti's, were not the culmination of anything.

They were byproducts of something else, something darker, something with the gravity to suck away human life. His hand moved, as if of its own accord. He drew the figure of a woman at the peak of the pyramid, then scrawled *High Angel* beside it; the figure resembled a star on top of a Christmas tree, beneath it, the tree was empty, barren. *John Winston Flint, Johnny Roccoletti, Horst Nickles*, the *Aryan Army, Karen Elms*: he filled in the names, hanging them like decorations along the black lines of the yellow page, all drawing his attention upwards to the Angel. The tree was incomplete without the Angel. She was the key, the mystery. The single object that gave reason to his hunt; he had to find Jacqueline Dunne.

First, Fogarty put out an all-points-bulletin, attaching Jack Dunne's name to the police drawing that had already been circulated among the seven detective divisions throughout the city. Dunne's size and age already matched the details that accompanied each picture. Then, he organized a surveillance team in case of an attempt on Horst Nickles's life. Sharon Gilbey and a division detective from North Detectives would keep an eye on Animals, and Dave Roach and Jimmy Stark were responsible for Nickles's apartment in Society Hill. The irony of it struck him, he'd rather have been organizing a "hit."

After that, Fogarty telephoned the police administration building in Johnstown, requesting a detective to accompany him to the address given for Jack Dunne, and did the same for the Old Mill Farm in Lancaster. Then, he made a request to police finance for approval on a plane ticket to Johnstown, and money to hire a car. After that, he called Tanaka.

"Josef, I'm going up to Johnstown in the morning, do you want to come?"

"What's happening, Bill?"

"I'm going to find Jacqueline Dunne. I'm going to find her and I'm going to finish this thing once and for all."

"You sound positive."

"I've got that feeling, Josef."

"You know I'd like to be there."

"It's not just your company I'm after, son, I may have to go to a psychiatric hospital in Norristown. It wouldn't hurt my credibility to have a doctor along. You could kind of ask the right questions."

Tanaka smiled. "Let me see what I can do, Bill, I'll talk to Bob Moyer." Diane Genero got through on his private line, a minute after his call to Tanaka.

"Hello, Bill?" Her throaty voice sounded as if it were coming from another dimension. The heavenly planes.

"You back in New York?" he asked.

"Yes, and I miss you."

"I miss you, too." His answer was spontaneous and it made him feel good to say it, touching something inside him that lived beneath layers and layers of protective armor.

"I know you're busy and I shouldn't be phoning you—"

"It's all right."

"Did you make your arrest?"

"Diane, it's been, maybe, the longest day of my life. I made the pinch this afternoon and I blew it. The guy walked; he beat me."

He could feel heaviness down the line.

"But I'm not done with this, not by a mile," he added.

"Well, I'm not going to sit here and waste your time," she said, "you go beat 'em back. I'll be in Santa Fe tomorrow, and I'll be waiting to hear from you. Go get 'em."

He loved the way she'd put it. Like a good corner man to a fighter after a bad round. No fear, no doubt, just go get 'em. It was exactly what he needed. Diane Genero was exactly what he needed.

"I love you, Bill."

He went red in the face and, for a moment, he was conscious of the beating of his heart.

"Okay." He answered as if he was giving his approval. He felt more, so much that it choked him.

"Call me, when you can," she said softly.

"I will," he promised, and put the phone down.

By five-thirty Fogarty had reserved two plane tickets for Johnstown, and arranged with Budget for a rental car at the airport. He hadn't heard officially whether the seven hundred dollars in expenses had been approved but, one way or the other, he was going. By 5:45 he was tempted to phone Quantico and press for news regarding the photographic match. Robert Burt beat him to it.

"Captain Fogarty?"

"Yes."

"It's Burt, in Quantico. I'm sorry it's taken so long, but this one was particularly difficult."

There was something about Burt's tone of voice that rang positive and, as much as Fogarty wanted to jump in and ask the definitive question, he held back.

"First thing we noticed was a configuration of three moles on the skin directly beneath the sternum of the man on the videotape, that and rather large lipoma to the left of his navel."

"Lipoma?"

"A benign tumor, mostly comprised of fat and fibrous tissue," Burt explained, "the photograph you sent us had neither of those things."

Fogarty began to sink.

"It had been retouched, the photo. Which meant we had to trace backwards to the magazine."

Burt's voice was torturing him.

"What we were able to get a hold of was a contact sheet from the photographic session; the magazine had retained it in their files."

"Is it the same man?" Fogarty asked.

"Yes—"

Fogarty closed his eyes, just for a moment, as if a prayer had been answered.

"Not only do the contacts display the same configuration of birthmarks, plus the lipoma," Burt continued, "but they also show a scar that was probably made by an arthroscopic incision in the subject's right shoulder. It's a small crisscrossed scar. We've reexamined the frames from the video and discovered the same scar, in an identical location."

"What are the chances of a coincidence?"

"Probably somewhere beyond the realms of possibility," Burt answered.

"Will it hold up in a court of law?"

"I've acted as expert witness several times, Captain, and I've never been proved incorrect."

"And you'll get that report up to me?"

"I can fax verification of it now, and you'll have the proper report first thing in the morning."

"You're a great man, Mr. Burt, a great man."

"We're happy to have helped you, Captain."

JACK DUNNE

Fogarty looked down from his window as Philadelphia became just another small, grey-green pattern in the mosaic beneath him. Fifteen minutes later the aircraft had reached its cruising altitude of twenty-two-thousand feet. The seat beside him, Tanaka's, was empty.

This morning, at six A.M., there had been a major accident on the expressway. A long distance truck driver, burnt out on speed and caffeine, had slammed through the center barrier and collided head-on with a station wagon, carrying a female driver and four youngsters. Three more cars had piled up behind them. Fire engines, ambulances, tow trucks, the police department's major accident investigation team, they were all there.

The results of major accidents were, generally, a lot worse than homicides. The impact of two vehicles travelling at a combined speed of one hundred miles per hour could tear the human body limb-from-limb. A hit-and-run could leave a pair of shoes and socks standing empty in the middle of the road, while the victim's body was thrown sixty feet. In the case this morning, the truck driver had stepped out of his jackknifed rig, unscathed, while the bodies of the innocent people in the wagon were still being reassembled, in an effort to identify them. Tanaka and the rest of Moyer's crew would have their hands full.

Fogarty was going to miss Josef; they worked well together, Tanaka's mind a perfect counterbalance for Fogarty's. When Fogarty was apt to rush forward, Tanaka would hold back, and where Fogarty would trust instinct, Tanaka was far more pragmatic. They learned from each other, continually. But today, the policeman was on his own, and maybe, as Josef would say, "that's exactly the way it is supposed to be."

By doing his own duty a man reaches perfection, doing the duty of another is full of danger. Was that Dharma, or Karma? Fogarty was trying to remember Josef's explanation of the two, and the difference between them, when the plane hit a rough pocket of air and his cup of orange juice slid from his food tray. He caught it before it landed in his lap, stopping the spill with his napkin, then gulped down the orange juice and tucked the plastic cup into the elasticated top of his seat pocket. The turbulence intensifed and Fogarty leaned his head back and shut his eyes. He hated turbulence because it was beyond his control. He envisioned the wings of the small jet ripping from the body of the plane. Once, on a flight to Cleveland, Fogarty had been seated next to an off-duty Naval pilot, and the man had explained that after a plane was airborne, it was safe. "Hell, you can take the wings and bend them up till they touch at the tip; they still won't snap," the pilot had assured him. "Takeoffs and landings, that's your danger time." Fogarty had felt like a kid, listening to daddy tell him there was no bogey man. Now he tried to remember the pilot's promise as the jetstream dropped thirty feet and bounced hard on its belly, then flew headlong into a hail storm. The seat-belt lights remained on, the air hostesses were asked to sit down and belt up, and the pilot spoke some calming words over the speakers.

Fogarty transferred planes in Pittsburgh, boarding a nineteen-seat propeller-driven J-31, for what seemed like a half-hour spin in a tumble drier. By the time they were on their final approach to land in Johnstown, Fogarty had decided to wrap up the case, retire from the police department, marry Diane Genero, and travel by Greyhound.

He picked up his two-door Toyota at the Budget desk, and asked for a map and directions to the center of town.

Johnstown has a population of just over twenty-eight thousand people, a small town, with a small-town atmosphere. Traffic is thin and the general pace, slow. The biggest single event in the city's history was the Johnstown Flood of 1889, when the Little Conemaugh River burst its dam, turned its streets into a network of canals, and wasted hundreds of lives. There have been two floods since, but nothing as dramatic as the big one.

Fogarty drove down Washington Street, looking for the Penn Traffic Building. "It's a red brick building with white trim around the windows," the girl at the Budget desk had informed him. He saw the lineup of white, Ford patrol cars first, parked along the curb; the red-brick building was to their right.

Inside, a long, thin man with a prominent Adam's apple, and a khaki-colored suit introduced himself as Captain Ed Resillo.

"I understand you've got yourself a homicide," Resillo said, after they had shaken hands.

The moustache fad hadn't made it to Johnstown, and Resillo's thick lips were moist and bare, his nose jutted forward in line with his Adam's apple, and his eyes were brown and predatory.

"That's right," Fogarty replied.

"Well, I've got us a warrant for that house in the Upper End, on Adams."

"That's fast," Fogarty replied.

"I figure if you've come all the way from Philadelphia, it's got to be important. I don't want to take you out to Dunne's place and have him stop us at the door."

"That's assuming he's there," Fogarty answered.

"He's there."

Fogarty looked into the sharp eyes.

"I've had somebody watching the house ever since you phoned."

Fogarty smiled and nodded his head.

"Now, do you want to come up to my office, have a cup of coffee, use the bathroom, you've had a long trip and—"

"I'm fine," Fogarty answered, "the sooner we get going, the happier I'm going to be."

"Right, Adams is only about fifteen minutes from here, I've got a couple of officers waiting to assist, and a backup unit ready if we need it."

"You're very thorough, Captain," Fogarty said.

"I was a homicide detective in Detroit for eight years; I don't like being unprepared."

"I understand," Fogarty answered.

"Looks like a Trinity," Fogarty said as they pulled up in front of 2428 Adams Street.

"A Trinity?"

"That's what we call them in Philadelphia, these little places built with three floors, a couple of small rooms on each floor; 'Trinity,' Father, Son, and Holy Ghost. I don't know how the name got started."

"Right," Resillo answered, driving slowly along the curb, parking just beyond the brick wall that separated Jack Dunne's house from the nearly identical one beside it. He shut off his engine and turned to Fogarty.

"Backup unit's in place," he motioned with his head to the grey Chrysler which sat across the street, "and here come my reinforcements."

A Ford patrol car pulled in from behind, and two uniformed officers stepped out and walked towards them.

Resillo rolled down his window. "It's that little green and white place there, number two thousand four hundred and twenty-eight. There's one rear exit, leading into the parking lot of that liquor store. You fellas slip round back and cover that exit, we'll see if we can get him out the front."

Fogarty watched the two officers walk along the inside of the wall and back, towards the rear of 2428.

"You really think we'll need the posse?" Fogarty asked.

"This guy is one big son of a bitch."

"Oh yeah?"

"That's what they tell me. Probably a bodybuilder."

"That's exactly what I'm looking for," Fogarty answered. "You ready?"

"I'm ready."

They walked quickly up the narrow stone path, to the white painted door. Fogarty had the police drawing in his pocket, the face on the drawing indelibly imprinted in his mind. He'd purposefully not faxed the drawing through to Johnstown. Jack Dunne was his pinch, and locating the whereabouts of Jacqueline was his hidden agenda. He had, however, shown the drawing at the three airports, and got nothing.

Resillo knocked. And again. There was the sound of heavy footsteps; they stopped at the door.

"Who is it?" The voice was deep and gruff.

"Mr. Dunne? Mr. Jack Dunne?" Resillo called through the wood.

"He's not here."

"Would you please open the door?"

"Who the fuck are you?"

"Captain Ed Resillo, Johnstown Police."

The door flew open and a man who looked too big for the small house behind him, lurched forward, knocking Resillo aside and straight-arming Fogarty.

Fogarty fell backwards and dropped to the ground, while managing to catch the cuff of the man's overalls. He held with both hands and was dragged a few steps before the man stumbled. By then, Resillo was shouting, the two uniforms from the back were assisting, and the two-man backup team was blocking the way to the sidewalk. No guns were drawn and, within seconds, the occupant of 2428 was flat on his stomach, his hands cuffed behind.

"This is illegal, fucking police brutality!"

"Get him on his feet," Resillo ordered.

The two beat officers hauled the suspect up.

"It's not him," Fogarty said, eyeing the short dark hair and wide brown eyes.

"Is your name Jack Dunne?" Resillo demanded.

"No."

"Then, where is Jack Dunne?"

"I wish I knew."

"What is your name?"

"Ralph Arnold."

"All right, Mr. Arnold, what are you doing in the home of Mr. Jack Dunne?"

"Wait a second," Arnold said, focusing on Resillo, "what exactly is this all about? Who are you? Do I need a lawyer?"

"My name is Captain Resillo, and I'm investigating a homicide. Now, you tell me, do you need a lawyer?"

Ralph Arnold began to laugh.

"You think that's funny?" Resillo bristled.

"Jesus, I thought you were here cause I didn't show for court last Monday. On the rent thing."

Fogarty was beginning to think of his drive to Lancaster.

"You better explain that to me," Resillo continued.

"I haven't paid rent for nine months, and the property company's got an eviction notice on the place. I was due in court last Friday, and I didn't show up. I thought you were here to grab me for that."

"That's not my department, Sir," Resillo answered, signalling, with his head, for the backup unit to leave.

"Do you think we could all go inside and talk," Fogarty suggested. Resillo dismissed the uniformed officers and he and Fogarty took charge of their prisoner.

"Who got murdered?" Arnold asked, as they led him back to the house. "Is Jack Dunne dead?"

There was something about the downstairs of the house that reminded Fogarty of his own place. A few antiques, a threadbare Kilim carpet, a brass lamp, a Windsor rocking chair. In his case, it had been his wife, Sarah, who provided the style. She loved shopping in the outdoor markets in New Hope; Sarah knew her antiques.

"Is this your stuff?" Fogarty asked.

He could tell by the way Arnold looked at him that he hadn't understood the question.

"The furniture," Fogarty added.

"No, that's all Jack's. Antiques, he liked antiques. I think a lot of it came from his family."

"Did you know his family?"

Arnold looked at Fogarty and shook his head. "Saw a few pictures, never met any of them."

There was a beat-up Chesterfield sofa against the far wall of the room; the springs so far gone that the middle sagged nearly to the floor. Resillo led Arnold to the sofa and sat him down.

"Jack's dog did this," Arnold explained, sinking into the worn fabric, "old sheep dog, always sat here."

"First of all, we're going to need to see some identification," Resillo began.

"My wallet's on the table, with my car keys. Listen, Officer, I'm telling you straight. I sublet this place from Jack Dunne a year ago, I paid the rent for three months, then I lost my job and got into financial trouble."

The photograph on the driver's license testified to Arnold's identity.

"How did you know Jack Dunne?" Fogarty asked.

"From the weight room at the Y.M.C.A.; we both trained there. He mentioned that he had to leave town for a few months and I happened to need a place. I was in the middle of my divorce. Listen, my ex-wife still lives in town, on Washington, you can check what I'm saying—"

"We will. Now, where is Jack Dunne?" Fogarty asked.

"I don't know. He said he was leaving for three months, to take care of his sister; she'd had a car accident. He never came back. I get calls for him, mostly from the landlord, but I never heard from him again. His name's still on the lease."

"Did he leave any personal items, clothes, pictures, anything like that?" Fogarty asked.

"The whole second floor of the house is full of his stuff. Plus the basement; he's got his gym down there, weights and equipment. Tons of it. There must be a thousand bucks worth of food supplements, never opened. Is he dead, did some-body murder Jack Dunne?"

Resillo ignored the question.

"I thought you said you knew him from the Y.M.C.A., what's he got a gym in the basement for?" Resillo asked casually.

"Jack Dunne was a freak."

"Freak?" Fogarty repeated.

"He was a workout junkie, you know, six days a week, two times a day. When he wasn't training at the Y, he was working out in the basement."

"So Jack Dunne's a pretty strong guy?" Fogarty continued.

"When I knew him, he was a monster."

"Was he into steroids?" Fogarty asked.

Arnold hesitated.

"Drugs aren't my territory, Mr. Arnold, but the information I'm asking you for might be relevant to my case."

Arnold met Fogarty's eyes. "Jack may have done some dianabol once, just for a couple of months, but he said it gave him pimples, so he quit."

Fogarty nodded his head.

"How about the stuff in the basement, the food supplements?"

"Nothing, just mail-order crap, vitamins, liver pills, protein powder. Basically, a waste of money."

"Was Jack Dunne violent?" Fogarty asked.

"No."

"You know that for sure?" Resillo followed.

"Yeah, I know that for sure. Jack worked with kids; he was a schoolteacher, a real gentle guy. Aside from training, his hobby was music; he wrote songs and played the guitar, the blues. I figure, somewhere, with his looks, and his body, he thought, maybe one day he'd make it with his music."

Fogarty nodded.

"What happened to Jack?"

"You tell us, Mr. Arnold," Resillo replied.

"Oh, come on, Officer," Arnold replied, "I've been honest with you."

Fogarty believed him. He removed a copy of the police drawing from the inside pocket of his jacket, unfolded it, and handed it to Ralph Arnold.

"Is that what he looks like, now? Long hair and a beard?"

"Is that what who looks like, Ralph?" Fogarty asked.

"Jack Dunne. That is a drawing of Jack, isn't it?"

DEATH

Josef Tanaka was working on the autopsy table nearest the entrance door to the morgue. The table was lit by four strips of fluorescent overhead lights, and six table lamps with large, white reflectors. There were four anglepoise spots set into the workbench, and twin portable spotlights for the purpose of examining body cavities and their contents without having to disturb the shape of the cavity. There was light everywhere. And the hollow feeling of death.

In front of him, on the white-topped table, lay the body of a six-year-old boy, a victim of the early morning crash. Josef stared at the child, pale and naked beneath the harsh lights; he lay on his side, his head tilted backwards, away from Josef. His half-open, brown eyes stared vacantly at the wall. There was not a mark on the boy's body, not a bruise or blemish, but, by the angle of his head, Josef was reasonably certain that whiplash from impact had caused an upper vertebra to sever his spinal cord. Now, it was Josef Tanaka's job to confirm his speculation.

He chose a long, curved scalpel from his instrument tray, placed his hand over the boy's head, holding the body steady, and eyed the area of his first, dividing incision. The body shifted slightly beneath the weight of Tanaka's hand.

What if this was my son? The thought came suddenly. Then, another thought, this time of Rachel.

How can we protect the people we love? At that moment everything seemed fragile. Rachel, his unborn child, Bill, they were all out there, vulnerable, so very vulnerable.

He placed the scalpel back on the tray, and covered the child's body with a green sheet, then walked from the room. Discarding his gown as if it were his flesh, defiled, he dropped it in a bin that contained similar garments. He walked to the stairs leading to the first floor of the medical building; for the moment, he didn't want to think about death. He wanted to think of Rachel, about the life inside her, and he wanted to talk to Bill Fogarty.

He placed a call to the Roundhouse and was told that the captain was somewhere between Johnstown and Lancaster and was contactable on his mobile phone.

Fogarty was driving east, through the small town of Oster-burg. He'd found stacks of photographs and song lyrics in a shoe box in Jack Dunne's closet, along with a crucifix carved from maple wood and covered in dust.

Fogarty had appropriated the shoe box; he wanted the pictures, and the samples of Jack Dunne's handwriting. The box was sitting beside him on the front seat. He looked over; he could read the words that were written on a page torn from a loose-leaf notebook. The writing tilted slightly to the left and the style was a mixture of cursive and script. There were musical notes scrawled on top of the words, Am/Em/Am/G/Am/C/Em. Fogarty assumed they were chord patterns for a guitar. The song was titled, "Angel."

> I remember you from up in heaven, seems like just the
> other day.
> Yes, I remember, you said you was gonna stay
> So, fancy meeting you, way down here,
> Dying to buy your way back into heaven
> Weren't you the angel with the heart of gold?
> You said you'd never fall
> Had to buy, never sold
> Till you heard your heartache call
> Well, fancy meeting you
> down, out on the street
> Dying, to buy your way back into heaven
> We will meet again

We will meet again
When the night is over,
We will meet again.

J.D., Winter, '91

"Angel," Fogarty said the word out loud, wondering if the song was written for Jacqueline. There was something melancholic in the lyrics, something sad and lonely. Something that Fogarty understood.

There were seventy or eighty pictures in the shoe box, pictures of Jacqueline, pictures of Jacqueline and Jack growing up. Then, there were the pictures of Jacqueline in the city blues of a Philadelphia police officer. They were the painful ones for Fogarty; she'd been one of his family, too. He wondered how Jack had learned about what had happened to his sister. Fogarty shook his head, envisioning the Flint video. It would have torn him apart, a big, sensitive guy, religious. It would have driven him crazy . . .

The ringing phone on the seat beside him grabbed his attention. He picked it up, and recognized Tanaka's voice.

"It's Jack Dunne, Joey, I'm ninety percent certain. Jack Dunne is the killer." Even as he said it, he felt a strange guilt. It was difficult for Fogarty to condemn Jack Dunne.

"Any leads on where he might be?" Tanaka asked.

"Philadelphia, somewhere. A Y.M.C.A., a boarding house, we'll pick him up." There was no urgency in his tone.

"Are you okay, Bill? You don't sound right."

"Yeah, I'm okay. It's just that this whole thing is tragic. The only bad guys are the ones getting killed."

"Is there anything I can do this end?"

"Not really. I've got Nickles covered, and I'll put a bulletin out on Jack Dunne. I'm going to make a couple more stops, but I think this one is almost over."

It started to drizzle and Fogarty dropped his speed from sixty to fifty-five, searching with his eyes for the knob that controlled the windshield wipers.

"Joey, it's starting to rain, and I've got some driving to do. I'm going to have to let you go."

"You take care, Bill."

Fogarty placed the phone back on the seat, found the wiper control, turned the blades on, and accelerated. The slapping of the wipers added to the beat of the tires against the joins in the asphalt.

Emotion was not supposed to be a part of Bill Fogarty's job, but now, emotion was all over him.

"Where the hell are you, Jacqueline?" he asked the rain.

JACQUELINE

Genetics" is a term frequently used by bodybuilders; it refers to bone structure. The skeleton is the tree on which the muscles drape; it gives size, proportion, and shape. Without good genetics no amount of training will produce a champion.

Jacqueline Dunne had great genetics. Horst Nickles could tell that from twenty yards away, the distance between his office door and the center of Animals. She was lying on the leg-press machine, and even from the inverted position of her body, long legs pulled back, weight rack balanced on her feet, head down, with a waterfall of golden-blonde hair spilling from the cushioned headrest to the carpeted floor, the German knew she had class. Like a thoroughbred race-horse, there was something special in the lines of her body.

By the time he reached her, Jacqueline was on her sixth repetition; there was six hundred pounds on the weight stack.

"Good, good. Bring your legs back another few inches. Yes, that's right. Vork deep into your gluteus maximus; it vill give you strong, firm hips," Horst encouraged.

Jacqueline looked up and smiled; she had even, white teeth, and deep, blue eyes. Her face was as fine as her body.

"Yes, one more repetition," Nickles soothed.

Jacqueline performed three more repetitions of the exercise, forcing the last two reps. By the time she got off the machine and to her feet, Nickles's erection looked like a tent pole, pushing against his baggy training pants, directly below his wide, leather lifting belt. Above the pole, his waist was narrow and his shoulders heroically wide. His face was chiselled and tanned, his blue eyes piercing, and his recently lightened hair hung like a lion's mane.

"Thanks for the help," she said, happy that after two weeks the Horse had finally noticed her.

She extended her hand. "My name's Jacqui Angel."

Nickles's return handshake was more like a caress.

"Are you serious about your training," he asked, "I mean, really serious?"

"Yes, I am."

He appraised her standing body, trying to keep sex from his thoughts, but failing.

"You know, with a bone structure like yours, the right supplements, and some intense training, you could compete professionally," he said, eyeing the longest muscle of Jacqueline's body, her sartorius, which began at her knee and wound upwards through her thigh to her pelvis. Nickles took a step closer and ran his hand along the back of Jacqueline's arm.

"Flex your triceps," he ordered, doing his best to bring his erection into contact with her body. Jacqueline straightened her arm downwards and twisted her clenched fist outward.

"You've got a nice horseshoe," he responded, noting the formation of the three muscles.

It began then, the svengali and his student.

He tried to fuck her the first time they were alone, practicing a basic posing routine in the full-body mirror on the back wall of the locker room. Jacqueline had turned to place her sweat shirt on a bench. When she turned back, Nickles had lowered his pants.

She stared.

It was only the second erect penis that Jacqueline had ever seen. The first was smaller in overall mass but possessed a single characteristic that the Horse lacked. Testicles. Even his scrotal sack appeared to have withdrawn. Leaving his penis standing like a lone carrot.

She began to giggle. Then, she began to laugh.

A moment later, Horst was tearing apart his own locker room, pulling the big steel cabinets over, punching his fist into the plaster walls, and screaming at the top of his lungs, "Nobody laughs at Horst Nickles! Nobody laughs at the most beautiful man who ever lived!"

It took Jacqueline a week of blistering training under the sadistic eye of the master to patch it up.

Horst Nickles introduced Jacqueline Angel to anabolic steroids during their second month of training, when she had hit a plateau in both strength and development, a "sticking point."

"All right, all right, you've hit the vall. Your body is secreting corticosteroids in response to the intense strain you are putting it under. The effect of these steroids is catabolic; they break down muscle tissue. In other vords, you aren't going to get any stronger or any bigger. There's nothing you can eat and no exercise you can do to get around this," he explained, sitting Jacqueline down on the big leather chair in his office. Horst Nickles wasn't only a giant; he was also brilliant in the field of body chemistry. His own body had been his research lab.

"Except," he continued, opening the drawer of his desk and pulling out a small blue bottle, "by using these."

Jacqueline accepted the bottle, looked at the label, which read DIANABOL—METHANDROSTENOLONE, 5 MG., and knew she was close to hitting a homerun.

"This is a basic oral steroid," Nickles explained. "You take ten mils a day, that's two of those spongy little pills, and you'll grow. In six veeks ve'll combine the di-bol with an injectible medication and you'll grow some more. Are you vith me?" He added an edge to his voice. A challenge.

Jacqueline nodded slowly, meeting his eyes.

He insisted she take the first tablet in front of him. It was a strange feeling; she knew she was breaking the law, but, if she wanted to uphold that same law, she had no choice. She'd heard of undercover narcotics officers using product to confirm their cover; she wasn't alone.

She swallowed the tablet.

In six weeks Jacqueline had put on twelve pounds of bodyweight, a third of it water—the drawback of di-bol was water retention—and her strength had increased by forty percent.

After that, Jacqueline got very close to Horst Nickles; the

kind of close that developed from devoting two hours a day, six days a week, working arm-to-arm, back-to-back with someone, towards the single goal of physical transformation. Nickles was the sculptor, Jacqueline Angel was his piece of clay. She had the genes but Horst Nickles had the know-how and the steroids.

At times she actually admired him, his discipline and dedication and, there were other times, when she found his vanity fascinating, but she never came close to affection. She knew he was dangerous, and that made Horst Nickles the greatest challenge of her short career.

When Commander Reuben Jakes pulled her out of the Animals investigation, Jacqueline felt abandoned. She was left with no purpose or self-worth. She had come a long way, taken risks; she'd seen the drugs, used them. She had earned Nickles's trust. She knew she was close to something bigger than a bunch of kids selling steroids to other kids on the school playground; Nickles had implied it. There were licensed medical doctors involved, a black market drugs network.

Horst Nickles was creating Jacqueline to his own specifications, for his own purpose. After she had won the Miss World, then gone on to take a couple of pro titles, Jacqueline Angel would be worth a fortune in endorsements and seminars. He could build a line of workout clothing around her. Score some very serious, very legitimate money. Start a bodybuilding magazine.

By that time, he'd own her; he'd control everything that went in and out of her body. Every gram of protein and every c.c. of hormone. He'd have her tied up physically, psychologically, and legally.

The "oral," the dianabol, was only the beginning, the starter's course. Enough to show her the potential of his medications.

Injectibles were next.

Always a delicate moment, that first injection. But Horst

felt sure his pupil would accept the needle as readily as she had accepted the oral. He was adamant that she did not learn to inject herself. He wanted that element of control.

"How about that stuff, do I need any of it?" she'd asked, pointing to a 10-c.c. bottle of testosterone cypionate that was lying on his desk.

"That's not for you, that's the stuff I feed the army, very androgenic, very male," Nickles answered, drawing 100 mg. of deca-Durabolin through the rubber stopper of the medical vial and into his twenty-one gauge syringe.

"Okay, drop your pants."

Jacqueline lowered her training pants, as Nickles depressed the plunger of the syringe, flushing enough of the clear fluid to rid the syringe of air bubbles. Then, kneeling beside her, he placed his hand on the upper portion of her left hip.

"Is this going to hurt?"

Nickles answered by driving the one-and-a-half-inch needle deep into her muscle.

"Uh," she exhaled.

"You'll get to love it," Nickles assured, as the warmed, oil-based fluid entered her. He took a long time with the injection; it was like sex to Nickles and he thought he heard her sigh faintly as he withdrew the needle.

"Where do you get this stuff?" Jacqueline asked, raising her pants.

"What?"

"Who's your supplier?" She phrased the question badly and, for a moment, Jacqueline's voice lost its naive, country girl tone.

Nickles stared at her, something dawning in his eyes. Something dark and suspicious.

"Why are you always asking questions?"

Jacqueline backed up until her backside touched the wall of Nickles's office. She could feel the injection sight, burning.

"Just curious, Horst, just curious."

"Well, that's a bad thing to be."

The Horse made a mental note to ask a couple of his

friends on the force, street cops who used a bit of his product from time-to-time, if they had ever heard of a Jacqueline Angel.

It was Jim Finnegan who told him. Jacqueline Angel was, in fact, Jacqueline Dunne, working out of the thirty-fifth district, her first gig, undercover.

"She's lookin' to bust you."

That's when the setup began: the "big buy" from Doctor John Winston Flint, leading Officer Jacqueline Dunne, like a lamb, to the slaughter.

FIRE

Fogarty arrived at the city police headquarters on Chestnut Street, in Lancaster, at three o'clock in the afternoon. He parked in the lot adjoining the building and stepped from the car. The drive had taken him nearly four hours, an hour longer than he had anticipated; his body was stiff, his lower back sore and his bad knee felt as if it was loaded with cut glass. He could have flown, was slightly annoyed with himself that he hadn't, but he'd had no idea how long his business in Johnstown was going to take and didn't want to leave himself waiting at the airport for the scheduled flight. Besides, he wanted to be mobile, still intending a stop at the hospital in Norristown.

He walked into the police building and asked for Captain Richard Knowles, then took a seat on the wood visitor's bench and waited.

Knowles showed up a few minutes later, rounding the corner at the end of the corridor with his greeting hand already in place. He was a medium-sized, nervous-looking man with grey hair and wire-rimmed glasses.

"Captain Fogarty?"

Fogarty stood and accepted the extended hand.

"I'm sorry, Sir, but when you phoned my office this morning, my secretary was unaware that that area of South Willow Street Pike is not within our jurisdiction."

"It's in Lancaster, isn't it?" Fogarty asked.

"It's Southern County," Knowles replied, "that's state police territory."

Knowles read the frustration on Fogarty's face.

"I've looked into it for you, though," Knowles continued, "I have a few friends in the barracks. There is no longer any Old Mill Farm at number four South Willow."

"No Old Mill Farm?" Fogarty repeated slowly.

"The place burned down a little over two years ago; it was a bad fire, people died."

"Who. Who died?" Fogarty sounded grief stricken.

Knowles shook his head; he'd read about it in the papers. Followed the story long enough to know it wasn't arson. He thought the death toll was three, maybe four, immediate family, but he wasn't certain. "The coroner would have the report," he answered.

"Can we go out there; I just want to take a look at it," Fogarty asked. It was as if it was a fresh crime scene, as if he was still going to find a clue, anything that would bring him closer to Jacqueline Dunne.

It was a strange request, but Knowles appreciated that Fogarty was investigating a homicide, that he'd driven a long way. Probably for nothing.

"Sure. Let me make a couple of calls and set it up."

The Pennsylvania state police barracks was located on Route 30, just east of Lancaster.

Richard Knowles did have friends, one of them was Major Simon Tyler. Tyler had gone into the state police directly from the Marine Corps, after his second tour of duty in Vietnam. He was a tough, no-nonsense type of man, and had handled the original investigation on the Old Mill fire, when there was still talk of arson.

They rode together in Tyler's Ford, Fogarty in the passenger seat, Knowles in the back. Fogarty hadn't eaten since Johnstown, and that had been a jelly doughnut and a cup of coffee, courtesy of a white "Dinosaur Doughnuts" bag in the front seat of Resillo's car. The doughnut had tasted like sweetened rubber and the single positive feature of the coffee was that it was hot. On top of that, Fogarty hated to put the sugar-caffeine mix into his system. He knew he'd have a quick rush of energy, then feel depleted. Tanaka had preached to him about the effects of sugar and caffeine on the pancreas. "Releases insulin, then stores the excess sugar as fat." Fogarty had lost seven pounds following the Tanaka principle; he was a convert.

A depleted convert, tired and apprehensive. Worried that it would all end here, his search; that Jacqueline was dead.

The noise coming from the backseat was driving him crazy. Like smacking bubble gum, over and over again. Something mocking and irreverent in the sound. He turned to see Knowles crack another pistachio between his teeth, split the shell, then pull the tiny nut out with his long, twitching fingers.

"Want one?"

"No thanks, I'm on a diet," Fogarty answered.

Knowles gave him a peculiar look, nodded his head, and went back to cracking.

"Walter Brandy ought to be there by the time we arrive," Tyler interjected. Brandy was the county coroner; he'd done the report on the victims at the time of the fire. "There were three bodies, that's about all I can vouch for," Tyler continued. "When a container of oxygen mixes with kerosene, it makes a hell of a mess. The place was like a crematorium; you wait till you see it."

South Willow Street Pike seemed to go on forever, a long, winding road which bisected vast expanses of rolling hills and muddied pastures. Fogarty was a city man, used to people and buildings, cars and noise; it gave him a hollow, lost feeling looking out the window of Tyler's car as dusk began to fall and the twinkling lights of the distant farmhouses beckoned like lonely lanterns. It was hard for him to imagine a city cop coming from a place like this. Hard to place Jacqueline Dunne, with her fine features and statuesque body, walking these empty roads or sitting on the porch of one of the isolated houses. How the hell did she ever get from here to walking a beat on Broad Street? he wondered, as Tyler took a left and drove down a broken macadam driveway, slowing to reduce the effect of the potholes against the suspension of his car.

"There she is, number four, South Willow Street Pike," he said. His voice sounded final.

Ahead of them, silhouetted against the dull-grey after-light of a winter sun, the ruins of Old Mill Farm rose like a skeleton from the burnt earth. Three jagged support beams from the main house's wooden frame, and the stone walls of a single out-building, were all that had survived the inferno.

A red Chevrolet Blazer was parked in front of the skeleton, at the end of the drive.

"That's him," Tyler said, flicking his high beams once as he rolled to a stop in front of the Blazer.

The county coroner looked up from his newspaper; he had the interior light of his truck on, and he was wearing a cloth cap with ear flaps and thick-rimmed glasses. Fogarty could hear the spill of classical music coming from inside the Chevy. Then the music stopped, the interior light went off, and Walter Brandy stepped out to meet them.

Jack Dunne was scared. He knew that something was happening inside him, and he knew it was bad. More than nerves, more than an inflammation of his liver; he felt that he was turning to liquid, that his organs and muscles were in the process of dissolving. He was sweating, his armpits, his hands, his feet, his forehead; the sweat was thick and foul, like a pus running from his pores.

"Why now? Why now, Lord?" he asked his wooden crucifix. "Why have you let me come all this way for this?"

The carved face of Jesus stared back at him.

"Please. Let me finish it."

Jack studied the features of Christ's face. The long, aquiline nose, the wide, forgiving eyes, the high cheekbones, and kind mouth. It was carved from maple wood by their father, Albert; he'd carved two of them, one for each child, to stand beside their beds in the old house. To remind them that Christ had suffered and died for the sins of the world.

"An eye for an eye, a tooth for a tooth. I cannot turn the other cheek, Lord, I cannot forgive. Please give me strength," Jack prayed. A moment later he was twisting in agony, screaming. The muscles in his calves were cramped, contracting in tight, spiralling knots. He reached down to massage them and his biceps went into spasm, then his stomach, forcing air upward in a short, sharp rattle. An involuntary flail of his left arm caused the crucifix to smash against the wall and fragment. Jesus' head landing beside him, like a piece of dead, meaningless wood. Jack was howling, high and shrill, like a woman. His body temperature was 103 degrees and he felt as if he was incinerating, burning up.

"Here's where the fireplace was," Brandy said, shining his flashlight in front of him as he walked the tight line along the charred boundary of wood that had once been the outside wall of Albert Dunne's bedroom. "A spark must have hit the oxygen and whoosh!" He threw up his hands to emphasize the combustion and the beam of the flashlight raked Fogarty's face throwing a glow into the overcast sky. "There was half a chimney here last time I was out, but looks like somebody's come along and stole the bricks," the coroner added.

"You figure one canister of oxygen did all this?" Fogarty asked, looking around.

"There were six or seven canisters of the stuff around, little portable ones. Albert used to use 'em when he drove into town, had a face mask and all. The oxygen itself wouldn't have caused the explosion, but it fed the flames. This place would have gone up like a box of matches; it was always a fire trap, wood frame, wood floors, only half the house had central heating, the other half was heated with log and coal fires, and kerosene. Two kerosene heaters in this room alone, big ones, gallon drums. I'll tell you what I think, as bad as old Al's emphysema got, he still used to suck on that pipe. I knew the guy nearly twenty years, and I can't remember him without his pipe. I think he was smoking at the same time that he had that oxygen running up his nose. Wouldn't suprise me if it was a spark from his pipe that set the fire."

"You found three bodies?"

"No, Sir. Bodies is incorrect. We found three piles of ash."

"But there were three of them?"

"Three for sure. There's a chance there was a fourth, but

it was impossible to tell, more likely the remains of an animal's skeleton."

"And it wasn't arson?"

"No. We had the fire team come out and reconstruct it. They were very thorough, very detailed. It looked, to them, like the old man was in bed, using his Mobilaire, that's an electric oxygen compressor with a headset," Brandy raised his hands to his head, fingers framing his face. "The harness goes around the head and the air tubes run straight up the nose. He probably took the harness off and laid it on the bed with the compressor still pumping. Either an ember from the fire, or, as I said, a spark from his pipe, then whoosh!" The coroner repeated his earlier hand gesture.

"With three people in the room?" Fogarty asked.

"That's where the fire team is really good," Brandy replied.

"Uh huh?" Fogarty said, nodding his head, trying not to appear condescending.

"They reconstruct the situation by the placement of the remains," Brandy went on, "in this case, it seems that Albert Dunne was alone, lying on his bed when the fire started. The two, or possibly three, other inhabitants of the house responded to the smoke, or, maybe, he was calling for help. Their remains were found," he hesitated, walking from the location of the fireplace to the left side of the frame, using the beam of his light to draw the area, "approximately here, as if they were running forward into the room through the opened door. There were two chairs to either side of the door, both old, manufactured before the laws came into effect regarding the treatment of the foam-rubber stuffing; they would have gone up, then the wood wall behind them, causing enough heat for the other cylinders of oxygen to blow, taking out the windows, creating a cross wind, fanning the flames, then the kerosene—"

"The Dunnes had two children," Fogarty said slowly, "Jack and Jacqueline. Were there any theories as to which of the children got caught in the fire?"

"You ever been to a crematorium, Captain?"

"Yes," Fogarty answered.

"You know anything about the way a human body burns?"

"I've seen a few automobile deaths," Fogarty answered.

"First the hair, then the skin, then the fat and the muscles," Brandy lectured, balling his fists, one wrapped around the black casing of his flashlight, and raising his hands in front of his chest, like an old-fashioned prizefighter. "When the heat becomes intense, the muscles coagulate, the hand and arms flex, and the body looks like this; we call it the 'pugilistic attitude.' "

"That's very interesting," Fogarty replied. The county coroner, with his silly hat and flat, pedantic tone, was beginning to annoy him.

"Finally, the bones burn. The heat inside the furnace of a crematorium is about twelve hundred degrees, takes about fifty minutes for a body to turn to ash; heat inside this room would have reached close to that," Walter Brandy emphasized, oblivious to the policeman's impatience.

Tyler and Knowles had been hovering in the background, exchanging bits of local gossip, sharing the pistachios, and waiting for the Philadelphia cop to get through with Brandy so they could find out what was really happening. Knowles looked over when he heard Brandy launch into the crematorium explanation. He'd heard it several times.

"That first rush of flame from the spark, or the ember, fueled by the oxygen from the Mobilaire would have been like a blowtorch," the coroner continued. "It would have taken off Albert Dunne's hair and the first layer of his skin. His wife and whichever of his children responded to the explosion would have rushed in just in time for the chair and sofa to go up, igniting the walls behind them, penning them in. The heat would have been so intense that in under a minute, the bodies would have been burnt to the muscle. All of them in the pugilistic attitude." He raised his fists again. "Then, you got kerosene, like liquid fire—"

"Soaking the bones, like lighter fuel on a barbecue." Knowles filled in the coroner's next line.

"It took the fire department fifty-five minutes to get out here," Brandy went on, shooting a hard glance at Knowles and Tyler. "By then, there was nothing left but ash, a lot of it mixed with the remains of the building. Albert and Betty Dunne were both wearing wedding bands, gold; the gold melted, formed little balls and was lying in their ashes. It wasn't much but it was enough to get a start on identifying them. The kids were another story."

"What about dental records?" Fogarty asked.

"Both Albert and Betty had recent charts with a dentist in Lancaster. Betty had three prostheses, false teeth on a metal bridge, and Albert had a set of lower dentures and a metal bridge up top," Brandy said, eyeing Fogarty to make sure he wasn't losing him, "which simplified the process of identification because the bridging alloy doesn't melt till a little bit over thirteen hundred degrees. The postmortem radiographs matched the antemortem records. As for the other remains, there were no dental charts on either of the Dunne children either here or in Johnstown. Didn't matter anyway, since there was no other bridgework found."

"And the fourth skeleton?" Fogarty asked. Somewhere inside, he knew that Jacqueline was dead.

"Impossible to tell, most likely, though, it was the remains of an animal, probably a dog. I think they had a dog. The pile of ash didn't weigh enough to be human."

Fogarty felt a wave of sorrow; he turned his face away from the coroner, away from his beam of artificial light, looking out past the scarecrow of the Old Mill and onto the darkened fields overgrown with weeds.

"A tragic family." Walter Brandy's voice rang hollow in the night.

BETRAYAL

Horst Nickles had mulled it over for most of the night and half the day. "Jack Dunne." As soon as Brosky told him the name, it had made sense. His initial reaction had been to go to Myron Schlenk, push for an immunity deal with the police: Jack Dunne in exchange for his own freedom. But when he thought it over, he knew it wouldn't work. No way the half-faced homicide cop was going to let him walk away.

Jacqueline Dunne: she had been punished for betraying him. They thought they had killed her, but he'd heard from his sources that she'd survived. Too fucked up to talk, and probably too fucked up for anyone to believe, but alive. They'd sweated for a few months, but then it all died away. And now it was back, right in his face.

Jack Dunne: Nickles would have to take care of him, and he'd have to do it carefully. No sending in the army, no hiring an outside hit; the fewer people who knew about Jack Dunne, the safer it was for Horst Nickles. Wayne Brosky could be the sacrifice; a lot of drug deals went sour and, sometimes, when they went sour, people got hurt. Even dead.

He pressed the button on the intercom that connected him with the main gym.

"Yes," Randy Dornt answered.

"Send Vayne in to see me."

Brosky had been in the gym all morning, working out to kill his nerves, squatting with six hundred pounds for reps of tens, pumping his quads until he waddled like a cripple between the squat racks and the stacks of weights that he loaded onto the Olympic bar. He knew he was halfway back into the Horse's good graces, but a lot of bad stuff could happen between halfway and home.

Dornt put down the phone and walked over to the squat

rack. Whatever was going on between Brosky and Nickles was nothing to do with him. He wanted to keep it that way.

"Boss wants to see you in his office," Dornt said.

Brosky rose from his ninth rep, levered the bar onto the racks, then bent to remove the elasticated supports that he wore on his knees whenever he worked this heavy. He stuffed the wraps into the hip pocket of his training pants as he wobbled towards the door of Nickles's office; as if maybe seeing him wobble would cause the Horse to look more benignly upon him.

"Vayne, come in." A certain friendliness in the tone, and Brosky felt his legs steady.

"Close the door, son."

Brosky shut the door and the lock automatically engaged. Nickles was half facing him, seated on his desk, holding something in his hands. Brosky couldn't see what it was.

"You did good bringing me the man's name and his address. You redeemed yourself and, in this life, redemption is all ve've got."

"Thank you, Sir," Brosky answered, still unable to see what Nickles was holding.

"Tonight ve vill go together to this man's house."

Brosky felt a tinge of nerves.

"What are we going to do when we get there?" he asked.

"You leave that to me; that is my department." The friendliness in Nickles's tone turned a darker shade.

Brosky's unease turned to fear. He felt like he was caught in quicksand, sinking, and thought for the first time about going to the law. With what he knew about Horst Nickles he could get him put away. Then, what about the rest of the Army? There was no escape.

Nickles turned to face him; he was smiling, with the hypothalamus fluid from the cracked animal's skull running like grey yolk from the side of his mouth. Brosky felt his stomach contract and began to heave up, then covered his mouth with his good hand.

"Vayne, come here," Nickles ordered.

Brosky kept his hand in place and walked forward, as Nickles extended the head.

"Good for you after training. Raw glandular fluid, nothing like it."

Brosky stared at the offering. It took his eyes a few seconds to focus on the face of the dead monkey, its round eyes, like brown stones, staring at him. The animal's dark fur formed a widow's peak against the yellowed skin of its low forehead, and the ears stuck out from the side of its head in disproportion to the small, flattened nose. The animal's mouth was closed, pink, its upturned lips frozen in a sad, frightened line. The face looked human.

"Take it, Vayne."

Brosky's hands trembled as he held them forward, accepting the head.

"Suck it from the crack in the skull. Go ahead Vayne, be a man."

Brosky looked into Nickles's eyes, searching for one glimmer that would allow him a place of retreat, one fissure in the steel.

"Suck it," Nickles growled.

Brosky lifted the head to his lips; he could feel the cold, thin skull beneath his fingers, smell the musky odor, stale and hollow, like rotting teeth. He closed his eyes, centering his mouth above the crevice beneath the matted fur. He pretended to suck. Nickles watched intently, sliding from the edge of his desk, standing close.

"Tilt the fucking thing backwards Vayne, push your tongue inside it, suck the juice." His voice hardened as he lifted the monkey's head, forcing it against Brosky's lips, pushing so hard that it hurt his neck.

"I can't hear your sucking, Vayne."

Brosky could feel it now, running thick and ugly down his throat. The taste came a moment later, like a sour, curdled milk. He began to vomit and, still, Nickles forced the head against his mouth until he dropped choking to the floor.

"I vill leave you vith your friend," Nickles said, looking first at Brosky, then at the monkey's head which lay beside him.

Brosky watched as Nickles walked to the door leading to the gym. Nickles turned, and looked once more at Brosky. "I feel like vorking out. Vhen you are man enough, you join me."

Brosky dropped his eyes to the floor, listening as the door clicked shut.

Jack Dunne is lying on Jacqueline's bed; he has a dull pain behind his ribs, about four inches to the right of his solar plexus. He knows exactly what is causing the pain; his liver is inflamed. He's been sucking halotestin all morning and dropping anadrol, and his liver is protesting its job of absorbing the poison. He doesn't care about the pain, only the possibility that if it becomes too intense, it may inhibit his ability to perform. But he won't let that happen, won't let pain or anything clse stand in his way. He tells himself that over and over again as he smells her perfume, hears her voice, thinks her thoughts.

He plans to remain like this, resting, for another half-hour; then he'll get up and eat: bananas, pears, and grapes. High in fruit sugar. No protein today, pure fructose, the type of high-level carbohydrate that the body expends when it exerts at maximum potential—like twelve rounds of boxing or one two-minute burst of killing.

Last night he cleared his basement, stacking his weights beneath the stairs and removing his heavy bag from its hook. Then he swept the floor, finally getting on his hands and knees to scrub the cold concrete, using soap and water to remove the dried and caked blood that had dripped from his nose and the knuckles of his hands. After the soap and water he used Lysol to disinfect the entire area, including the walls and steps leading from the kitchen down. The place smelled like a hospital when he finished. And it was clean, as clean as the examination room of the doctor's office.

* * *

Fogarty looked hard at the burly black nurse in his white overalls; his name was Frank Pierson and he was seated next to him on one of the wood benches that lined the wall of the locked adult psychiatric ward of the Norristown State Hospital. Pierson had a round face with huge, doleful eyes and charcoal-colored hair peppered with grey, cut close to his head.

"Jacqui was like a wounded animal, a great, wounded animal," he said. "She was with us for three months."

"And, after that?"

As they spoke patients drifted by, women in carpet slippers, robes, and nightgowns. Aged between eighteen and seventy, each appeared lost, travelling the linoleum-floored corridor without direction, eyes looking down, their movements slow and dreamlike.

"Her family signed for her release," Pierson answered, looking up at the passersby. "She was too beautiful to be in here. Too fine for this. Jacqui wasn't sick; she was wounded, deep inside; do you understand what I'm trying to say?"

"I think so," Fogarty replied. The place was already getting to him, the occasional screams, the strange peals of laughter like disembodied bursts of sound, and the ghostlike walkers wandering the fluorescent corridor.

"It's the futility of it, Captain, the lack of reason, of purpose. Locking Jacqui in here was like caging a wild animal. After a while, the glow started to go from her eyes, her hair lost its luster, everything got kind of dull."

Fogarty followed Pierson's eyes and saw a woman standing outside the open door of one of the rooms. She was tiny, her face skeletal, her hair so white and thin that it seemed translucent, and her body frail and hunched. Her feet were bare and her toenails were long like the talons of a wild bird. She stared vacantly at the floor. Standing still, as still as a statue.

"Now what's that all about? Is that any kind of life?"

Fogarty stayed quiet. He had that feeling again, that same

wistful feeling, the one he had in Lancaster when Simon
Tyler was driving him down those long, empty roads towards
the remains of the Old Mill. He was trying to imagine Jacqueline Dunne wandering those lonely roads or these hopeless
corridors.

"Which room did she have?"

"Come on, I'll show you," Pierson replied, standing.

They walked the twenty feet to room 305. The door was
open and Fogarty looked inside. A single bed was positioned
along the light-green wall, the floor was the same grey-white
linoleum as the corridor, and there was a folding card-table
chair next to the bed.

"Sorry, Ruthie, just showing a visitor around," Pierson said
to the figure in the bed, her body covered by a thin wool
blanket and her face obscured by a pillow. The figure appeared to be barely breathing.

"I'll be back later to give you a bath," Pierson promised.

"Uh." A muffled voice from beneath the pillow.

The room was less than eight feet long and maybe six feet
across.

Smaller than a prison cell, Fogarty thought.

"Jacqui spent most of her time in that room, sitting in that
folding chair, staring at the wall. I used to go in and talk to
her, read to her. Sometimes, I'd take my cassette recorder
in and play her music. She liked that, the music. That's when
she'd smile. And man, when she smiled she lit this whole
place up."

"What kind of music?" Fogarty asked, curious.

"At first I'd play her the stuff I thought she'd like. Rock
and roll, country, you know, white music. That didn't do a
lot for Jacqui; then one day, I brought in an old John Lee
Hooker tape, good old blues. She liked that; that made her
smile all right."

"I think her brother played the blues guitar," Fogarty said.

"He was good, too." Pierson added.

"You knew Jack Dunne?"

"He came here a few times to visit his sister. Brought his

guitar and played for her. Half the ward was standing at the door listening to him. He had a sweet voice and he could play that guitar, slide and everything. Quieted the whole place down when he was here; might as well have been singing lullabys."

Fogarty reached into his inside pocket and pulled out the artist's drawing.

"This is rough, but do you think it could be Jack Dunne?"

Pierson took the drawing and the two men walked back to the bench and sat down.

"Could be. His hair wasn't so long and he didn't have a beard, but the eyes, there's something about the eyes. Has he committed a crime?"

Fogarty looked at the slippered feet that were shuffling by him, then up into another blank face. He thought of Jacqueline Dunne and of the bastards who'd put her here.

"No," he answered.

"Has something happened to him?"

Fogarty thought about the fire at the Old Mill, about Brandy's words, "a tragic family." He looked at Pierson.

"We're not sure, maybe."

From somewhere, inside one of forty rooms that lined the long corridor, a radio was playing, Roy Orbison's voice echoed, "Only the lonely, know the reason that I cry—"

"Now there's a sweet voice," Fogarty said, attempting to break the spell of gloom.

Pierson nodded and smiled.

"Did you have much interaction with her brother, Jack Dunne?" Fogarty asked.

"I talked to him, watched him work with Jacqui; he was real good."

"Work with Jacqui?"

"Oh yeah, the guy was a physical-education teacher, gentle, but big as a house. He used to get her up, out of bed, off that metal chair; he used to get her exercising. Push ups, lunges, resistance kind of stuff; he'd make her push against him, pull against his arms. He was real smart with the way he handled her. Real easy."

"But I've heard she could be violent," Fogarty said.

"Jacqui Dunne was an angel. Unless you tried to touch her. I'm talking about laying a hand on her shoulder; then she'd half kill you. And she was dangerous cause she was big, and she could move. The best thing you could do when she was acting up was call for help; it'd take three of us to push her back into her room, strip her down, take away anything she could use to hurt herself with, then lock the door."

Fogarty nodded. It was an ugly image.

"Her brother could touch her, though. He could pick her up, hug her, kiss her. She trusted him."

"Did he talk to her?"

"Sure, he talked to her."

"Did you ever hear their conversations?"

"Just little bits and pieces, it sounded like family stuff."

"Nothing about why she was here?"

"I don't know, Captain, but they did talk. They talked for hours."

Fogarty nodded. It was making more sense all the time, the little pieces of the puzzle were coming together. Adding up to "motive," for Jack Dunne.

"How about her parents, did you meet them?" he asked.

"I only met her mother; I think her dad was sick, but her mother and her brother came to take her away. That's the last I ever saw or heard of Jacqui Dunne." There was sadness in Pierson's tone, and Fogarty didn't have the heart to tell him that Jacqueline Dunne was almost certainly dead.

RUINED

Rachel Saunders had been working for eight hours. This was her second emergency of the day.

While Josef dissected the dead, Rachel patched up the living.

Her patient was twenty-six years old, blonde and pretty. At least she had been pretty, until the car accident that crushed her cheekbone against the steering wheel of her outdated automobile.

"Don't worry, I can fix that for you, good as new," Rachel assured her in the anesthesia room prior to surgery. She could read the fear behind the swelling, in the woman's eyes. Rachel had seen it many times before.

"Scars, will I have scars?"

"No, the CAT scan says you have what we call a 'blow-out fracture' over the orbit of your left eye. I'll do all the work from the inside, nothing will show," Rachel answered, indicating with her head for the anesthesiologist to begin the induction to the general anesthetic.

"I don't want to get knocked out; I'm scared of getting knocked out," the woman whimpered as the doctor lifted her left hand to insert the butterfly needle for the I.V. feed.

"Relax," Rachel answered, placing her palm lightly against the woman's shoulder, "you'll just float away on a cloud. When you wake up, you'll be perfect again."

"I'll never be perfect again. I'm ruined."

Rachel heard the woman's words as she pushed through the windowed doors that led to the operating room.

"I'm ruined." She'd heard the exact words before. Once, years ago, in the same place. On that occasion the injuries had been far worse, and they had been caused by a human hand.

Jane Doe: Rachel had never learned the woman's real

name. Her mind and memory had been shattered with her body.

Rachel had spent hours, between reconstructive procedures sitting beside Jane Doe's bed, talking. Jane Doe loved to hear Rachel's voice and had asked her name a hundred times.

"Rachel, Rachel Saunders," the doctor had replied patiently.

"Rachel Saunders." She'd repeated it like a prayer.

Horst Nickles was still in the gym. He had a particular way of moving when he was there, different from his street strut which was more a march than a walk; his gym walk was like a lion on the prowl. He took the distance between the Smith machine and the squat racks in quick, measured strides, head shifting rapidly from side-to-side, eyes alive, alert. He moved in circles around the periphery of the mirrored room, hands loose at his sides, aware of everything and everyone simultaneously. He usually came out of his office once every hour, circled the perimeter twice and returned to his quarters. Every now and then, if he felt particularly benevolent, he would stare at a member and grunt, "Big arms," or, "Get big," or, "Up the dose." Today after summoning Wayne Brosky to his office, Nickles had emerged alone, and remained. Dornt and Pinion shot nervous glances at him as he prowled, and both wondered what had happened to Brosky.

Now the Horse had stopped his patrol of the perimeter and was standing by the leg-press machine in the far corner of the room, arms folded across his chest, back to the machine, staring at Jim Pinion. Pinion tried to ignore the stare for the first few seconds, but gradually the steel eyes weighed him down. Finally, he walked towards the Horse.

"You want me, boss?"

"Peroxide." Nickles said the single word, leaving a question mark in Pinion's eyes.

"You got peroxide in the first-aid kit?" Nickles turned his proclamation into a question.

"I think so." Pinion answered.

"Get it."

Pinion nodded, turned, and walked into the locker room. Opening the first-aid cabinet, he found the brown bottle of hydrogen peroxide. The bottle had never been opened. He carried it back to Nickles.

"Good," Nickles said, taking the bottle, twisting off the cap, and sniffing the liquid, "still strong. Hey Jim, you vant to look like me?"

"I'd love to look like you," Pinion answered. He meant it.

"Well, we start vid your hair," Nickles replied, handing the bottle back.

"You take this, soak your hair with it, then let it dry underneath the sunbed. After you finish come out and see me."

Pinion's hair was very thin and very brittle. The idea of soaking it in hydrogen peroxide and drying it under the high-intensity bulbs of the sunbed was not appealing.

"You got a problem?" Nickles asked.

"I don't want to go bald, boss," Pinion answered meekly.

"Do I look bald?" Nickles challenged.

"No."

"Vell, I been lightening my hair for ten years. Vhat you think of that?"

Pinion looked stunned.

"Jim," Nickles continued, stepping closer, which brought the top of Pinion's head about even with Nickles's sternum, "you vant to look like me, or not?"

"Yeah, sure," Pinion spoke directly into the German's chest.

"Then take the peroxide and do vhat I fucking tell you."

Pinion nodded, turned, and walked back to the locker room.

BLUES

At first, Jack had tried to alter Jacqueline's police uniform; he'd opened up the seams of the arms and legs, then forced the trousers of the uniform up over his calves and thighs, until the fabric stretched and ripped along his backside. The blouse coat was an impossibility; not with his nineteen-inch biceps and his enormous chest and shoulders.

It had taken three shops to find a uniform that came close to fitting, and a five-hundred-dollar deposit, on top of the fifty-dollar rental fee, to hire it without credit cards or proper identification. It was several inches too long in the legs and sleeves and five inches too big in the waist, but Jack fixed that himself, then sewed on his regulation buttons and pinned his merit commendation in place. He wanted to go outside in his new blues, to walk the city streets, but he fought the urge.

The uniform is cleaned, pressed, and laying purposefully on Jacqueline's bed. The closet door is open and Jack is standing, studying himself in the mirror. His hair has been cropped short and he has shaved his face. Still, he doesn't look right, something is wrong with his skin color: he's ashen yellow and the whites of his eyes are the color of ripe lemons. His head aches and his heart is racing. *Your liver's gone, you're dying*, a voice inside his head tells him. He tries not to listen but the voice is persistent. He hardens his body, flexing the ridges of pectoralis muscle that line his chest above his rib-cage. Spreads his latissimus dorsal and the muscles of his back open like wings. He looks impenetrable, except for his color and the voice inside his head: *You're a dead man, Jack Dunne. A dead man.* It's true; he knows it. Somewhere he knows it but he can't let it touch him, not here, not now, not in Jacqueline's bedroom, and not tonight.

He needed the methadrine like a transparent cement to hold his exhausted body together. He snorted two thick lines of the stimulant, then injected 10 c.c.'s of testosterone in his upper gluteus before swallowing the last of his anadrol. He's fully charged, but he's not "right."

"Proper prior planning and preparation prevent poor performance." An instructor made them learn the "Seven-P Principle" during a special close-quarter combat course.

"Proper prior planning and preparation prevent poor performance," he recites the words over and over again, until finally, his mind clears and he focuses on their meaning.

He bends and lifts his athletic supporter from his drawer of underclothes. The supporter has a purpose-built guard which fits into a pocket at the front of the elasticated fabric; the fiberglass guard is meant to prevent injuries to the testicles. Jack fixes the guard in place, locks the snaps that keep the pocket shut, then steps into the strap and pulls it up over his thighs and hips, adjusting the protective cup so that it completely covers his private parts.

HANDS

Sharon Gilbey and Raymond Howes were parked in an unmarked Chrysler, on a side street which intersected with North Broad, giving them a clear view of Animals. They'd been there since eleven A.M., jotting notes as to who came in and who went out, and making voice notations in a portable cassette recorder. They took turns reading the newspaper or strolling to the corner deli for sandwiches and soft drinks; Diet Pepsi for Gilbey, Gatorade for Howes.

"Got used to drinking this sugar water when I played college football," he'd announced after finishing his first quart-sized bottle.

Now it was early evening and time for caffeine; they were drinking their coffee from pint-sized paper cups, talking and laughing like old friends. By three o'clock they had discovered that they'd both grown up in the same area of the city, down along Cobbs Creek Parkway where the terraced houses, made of stone and wood, are large and well-maintained, look out onto the trees and grass of the park, across the busy road that connects West Philadelphia with Interstate 95 and the Philadelphia Airport.

Howes and Gilbey had gone to the same schools, but Howes, being seven years older, had never noticed Sharon Gilbey. Now he was married, with two sons and a working wife, and he was noticing her in a big way. She was wearing a brown leather motorcycle jacket, with a white T-shirt underneath, blue jeans, white socks, and Adidas running shoes. Every time she left the car, Howes got a good view of her ass, stretching her jeans below her jacket. It was a nice ass, rounded and not too prominent; a lot of black women had "pucker asses," as Howes termed them, the hips jutting out over the back of the thigh. Gilbey's ass didn't pucker, but it wasn't flat either, and Howes wondered what type of underwear she had on. Her running shoes were practical in case there was some action, but that didn't necessarily mean she was wearing those high-topped cottons that looked liked men's jockey shorts. Howes preferred to think of her in very fine, silk bikinis, maybe yellow or pale blue, the kind you could just about see through. And her tits? He hadn't wanted to be too obvious, but when he'd leaned across the front seat to return his empty coffee cup to the cardboard carry box, he'd managed to brush against her chest. There was definitely something there, not big, but not flat either.

"You seeing anyone?"

His question seemed to come straight out of the blue, but it was the question that Sharon Gilbey had been waiting for; she'd felt it coming for the past hour, and now it was there in the open. She looked at him. He was a good guy and he was an attractive man, lean and muscular, with short, slightly receding hair and smooth, coffee-colored skin. Some kind of Afro-Jamaican mix, she'd figured. He had a great smile, white and self-assured, and his hands were beautiful, medium-sized, well-proportioned, his fingernails clean and even. Sharon Gilbey was a "hands" person. She had checked out Raymond Howes's hands the first time he'd offered her a cup of coffee. She'd wondered what it would be like to be touched by his hands. The first time they had relaxed enough to laugh, she'd met his eyes and saw the spark, like a white flash inside the brown. The spark was life. Some people had no spark, Raymond Howes did and, at that moment, she'd wondered what it would be like to make love with him. Embarrassed and vulnerable, she'd looked down, away from his face. Back down to his beautiful hands, to the third finger of his left hand; the gold wedding ring also had a spark, a life, and it did not belong to Sharon Gilbey. He was taken. And that was that.

"You know, like have you got someone serious?" Howes continued, his voice suddenly hushed, barely audible above the Chrysler's fan, which blew a dry heat up from below the seat.

She was looking at him, wondering how to say what she needed to say without hurting his feelings. She wanted to let him know that he was attractive to her, but that was as far as she would allow it to go. She turned from his eyes to collect her thoughts, and spotted the headlights.

"I am seeing someone," she answered, straightening. "I'm seeing Horst Nickles driving out of his parking lot."

Howes looked from Gilbey to the wired compound with the chain-linked security gate, about one-hundred yards from the front of the Chrysler. The gate was open and the German's Mercedes was turning left. Howes could see Nickles at the wheel. Gilbey was already marking the time in her notebook.

"You want me to stay with him?" Howes asked, turning the key in the Chrylser's ignition.

"That's what we're here for," Gilbey answered.

Bill Fogarty was on the turnpike thirty miles from Philadelphia. His body was sore from driving and his eyes hurt every time he caught the glare from the headlights on the opposite side of the highway, but his mind was lucid. He was thinking about Jack Dunne, wondering where Jack was right now, what he was thinking, and what he would do next. As a policeman, Fogarty knew he was going to have to stop Jack Dunne. As a man, Fogarty didn't want to hurt him. Jack Dunne had been hurt enough.

DECEPTION

Horst Nickles was flat on his back looking up into the eyes of Wayne Brosky. A six-foot-long bar, rounded and three and a half inches in diameter, separated the air between them. The overhead lights of the gymnasium reflected against its knurled steel. There were three iron plates on either side of the bar, each of them weighed one hundred pounds.

"The plates plus the bar, how much they veigh?" Nickles asked. He knew exactly how much they weighed; he just wanted to hear Brosky say it.

"Six hundred and forty-five pounds," Brosky replied. He had counted it up when he'd loaded the weights onto the bar, and had never, personally, seen anyone perform a flat bench press with as much.

"I feel very strong tonight," Nickles said. "How do you feel?"

Brosky thought of the empty monkey's head that lay on Nickles's desk. He had poured the thick fluid down the sink in the small bathroom next to the refrigerator before venturing out into the gymnasium.

"Good," Brosky answered.

"Raw glandular fluid, I tell you the truth, there is nothing like it."

Brosky smiled and nodded his head.

"You didn't pour it down the sink, did you Vayne?"

"No. No way," Brosky answered, breaking eye contact.

Nickles's laugh sounded like a low grunt, then he took a deep breath and concentrated on the Olympic barbell, placing his palms against the knurled gripping section of the steel, about two feet apart. Again, he locked eyes with Brosky.

"Okay," the Horse signalled, wrapping his hands around the bar.

Brosky placed his hands inside Nickles's, gripped, and

heaved upward, while the German pushed from below. The weight shifted from the racks until the bar, bending slightly at either end, was extended at arm's length above Nickles's head. Brosky let go with his hands and stepped back as Nickles inhaled, lowering the weight to his chest, touching his T-shirt half-an-inch above his nipples. Then with a loud exhalation, he shoved the barbell up, locking his elbows at the top of the lift.

"Jesus Christ," Brosky whispered, as Nickles lowered the weight for a second repetition, touching his chest before he pushed upward. He locked out and smiled up at Brosky.

"You think I can make three?"

"Go for it," Brosky responded in his best *Rocky* voice. It sounded phony in the empty gymnasium.

Nickles lowered the weight a third time, touched and shoved upward. He stalled midway, his right arm pushing past his left, throwing the weight out of balance. The right-sided plates began to slip along the bar.

Brosky was the spotter; his job was to make sure the man beneath the weight didn't get stuck, to step in and assist, to rescue. A heavy weight could easily fall backwards and crush the chest, or roll onto the throat and rupture the windpipe. Horst Nickles was in a potentially fatal position. His arms had begun to tremble and he was staring wide-eyed at Brosky.

"Take it!" Nickles said, between clenched teeth.

Brosky stepped forward, bent over the barbell, and hesitated. He had the power. For once, he had the power.

"Take it!"

Brosky placed both hands on top of the bar and allowed his palms to settle, restoring the balance but adding weight. Nickles struggled beneath him as the bar dropped another inch.

Right now, I could kill him, Brosky realized. He looked down and the Horse was smiling.

"Your choice," Nickles whispered. The combination of his smile and his words tilted the balance. Even in the face of death the Horse was omnipotent.

"You okay?" Brosky said, helping to lift the weight. And Nickles knew that Wayne Brosky was his.

"Let go, Vayne," Nickles said, "I show you somethink."

Brosky released his grip and Nickles forced the barbell up, then performed one more unassisted repetition before levering it onto the rack. Standing, he faced Brosky.

"Life is a matter of trust, Vayne. Today I test you. Tonight, I trust you. I trust you with my life."

Nickles placed his arm around Wayne's shoulders and guided him back to his office, unlocked the door to his closet, and took out the "Streetsweeper." He handed the shotgun to Brosky.

"Now, ve take your car and go visit Jack Dunne."

Gilbey and Howes followed the Mercedes west onto the expressway. They were right behind it and they could see Nickles adjusting his rearview mirror.

It began to drizzle.

"You think he knows we're here?" Howes asked, flicking on his wipers.

"The captain said it didn't matter, as long as we know where he is."

The Mercedes rolled onto the expressway like a Nazi war tank, the *Terminator* cassette playing so loud that the speakers crackled. Jim Pinion, with five 5 mg. tablets of dexedrine pumping his heart in tune with the synthesized base guitar, gripped the wood steering wheel with both hands, arms straight like a racing driver. He was in his own action movie; he was the star outrunning the bad guys. Glaring defiantly into into his rearview mirror, he could see two people in the car behind him, their heads but not their faces.

"Come on motherfuckers! A little closer!" he yelled, reaching up to tilt the mirror down, enough to spill some of the glare from their headlights. He was concentrating hard, his eyes searching the antique, silvered glass for the shadowed details that would give identity to his pursuers. Clearer now, behind the slapping wiper blades, he could see two black faces.

"Niggers!" he shouted.

The thought of a superior man being hunted by members of an inferior race incensed him.

"Fuckin' jungle bunnies!" His voice was a decibel louder than the music.

He concentrated harder on the mirror. A man and a woman? Is one of them jungle bunnies a woman? I ain't running from no woman. He shifted position against the cushions trying to get a better view, and was distracted by a flash of red. Dead ahead. The brake lights of a stalled Ford van. He jammed his foot down but his leg was too short to get the brake pedal all the way to the floor. The van's New York state license plate loomed in front of him, rushing forward in perspective. He could hear his tires screeching. Then saw the van's rusted tailgates, held together by an iron chain, half open, like the jaws of a shark, raindrops glistening like drool against its metal edges. A moment later, everything turned upside down—

"Stop!" Gilbey shouted. "We're going to hit him!"

By 6:55 P.M. the rain had stopped, and Wayne Brosky drove his blue, eighty-nine Plymouth along Front Street; he slowed down when he got to the red-brick house.

"Looks derelict," he commented.

"Take the next street and park," Nickles ordered.

Jack Dunne watched from behind the curtained windows of Jacqueline's bedroom. He saw the skinhead at the wheel of the Plymouth and recognized his passenger. *Call it in, get backup. Don't try and take these guys on your own. Don't be a hero. Cemeteries are full of heros. Be careful out there.* He quelled the voices in his head and ran downstairs, methadrine and adrenaline masking the pain inside his body, his heart ramming blood through his leaking organs. He got to the kitchen. The cassette player was on the table, the tape inside. *Hours of work, hours of preparation. For this one bust. This is the big one. You're nervous, your heart's pounding, your adrenaline's up. You're scared. Scared shitless. That's normal.*

"Control yourself, Officer Dunne," Jack said.

"Yes, Sir. I am in control," he answered.

"I'm scared," Brosky admitted.

"I am not asking you to kill anybody, Vayne," Nickles repeated for the fourth time, "I am asking you to get inside the house and take charge of this guy."

"I'm scared shitless," Brosky repeated.

"The difference between a coward and a hero is not fear, Vayne, it is the control of that fear. You think I have never been frightened?"

Brosky looked at Nickles in the dim light spilling through the Plymouth's windows from the steetlamps. The German's body occupied most of the front seat. His eyes seemed to glow with a light of their own, a superhuman vitality. Brosky could not imagine fear in those eyes.

"Come with me?" Brosky asked.

Nickles reached across and placed his dry, steady hand on Brosky's forearm.

"Control yourself," he whispered.

"Why can't you come with me?" Brosky was pushing it now.

Nickles looked at him, trying to keep his contempt from surfacing. Brosky was a weakling; he'd be easy to kill and Jack Dunne would be a necessary pleasure. But he had to get them inside the house, together, to do it. Two shots from the Streetsweeper, one to the femoral artery on the upper inside of Jack Dunne's thigh, a blast that would probably take off most of his leg and both testicles, and one, point blank, to Wayne Brosky's head, the spread of pellets from the twelve gauge enough to remove it from his shoulders. Then he, the Horse, would place two gloved hands on Jack Dunne, preventing him from getting to a phone or the street, and explain to him, in vivid detail, everything they had done to his sister, while Jack Dunne bled to death. Another drug deal gone bad.

"This guy knows me, Vayne," Nickles replied softly, squeezing the skinhead's forearm like a reassuring lover. "If he sees me it will get messy. I vill vait for you. You get inside, take control, then I vill come and do vat must be done."

"Which is what?"

"I trust you, Vayne, now you must trust me," Nickles answered, smiling, waiting.

Brosky felt more alone than he ever had in his life. He thought of his mother, Irene. She'd be at home now, in her second-floor walkup apartment on Forty-fifth Street, cooking sausage. The smell of it would be winding down the wooden steps, all the way to the sidewalk. She'd be waiting for him to stop by after his workout. "Sixty grams of protein in a pound of this stuff," he'd say. He liked to tell her how many grams of protein everything contained. It made him feel smart and it made Irene laugh. Brosky's father was dead and dealing paid for his mother's apartment. I'm all she's got, there was tragedy in Brosky's thought.

"Go over it for me once more, boss, tell me what I do when I get inside?" he asked slowly.

Josef Tanaka had finished for the day. His work area was clean and he'd left the window above his table open to clear the smell of antiseptic spray from the room. The floor, surrounding the table, had been mopped with a solution of soap, carbolic acid, and hot water. Everything possible was done to remove the smell of death.

The children affected him the most. Three had come in today; three too many.

Now, he sat on the sofa of their living room. He was alone in the apartment, wondering where Rachel was and what her day had been like. He knew that at least three of the living victims of the expressway accident had been ambulanced to the emergency ward of Jefferson Hospital. He also knew that Rachel would be exhausted, as exhausted as he was, but probably not as depressed. Her work would have, at least, been positive. Reassembly, as opposed to disassembly. He considered cooking dinner for both of them, having it ready when she walked in the door. Maybe some chicken, rice, and salad, a bottle of wine. The bottle of wine appealed to him more than the idea of the food. Besides, being pregnant, Rachel had an unpredictable appetite. She may not want chicken.

Josef got up, walked to the kitchen, and pulled a bottle of Chilean Cabernet Sauvignon down from the rack above the refrigerator. He uncorked it and poured a glass, then returned to the sofa. Picking up the remote, he switched on the television in time for the local news, sipping the wine as the picture came into focus.

"In a day of tragedy, the Schuylkill Expressway has claimed another victim," the female commentator shouted over the sound of a helicopter's rotar, as the craft descended for an aerial view. "A single, yet-to-be-identified man was the driver of this Mercedes-Benz sedan, which was involved in a rear-end collision on the westbound lane just minutes ago. At this moment we are not sure if the driver of the car is dead—"

Tanaka jumped to his feet and stared at the television. He thought he recognized the Mercedes. It was upside-down, its roof crushed flat against the highway, the area surrounding it cordoned off; there were fire engines, police cars, and an ambulance in attendance. The helicopter dropped for a closer look and Tanaka saw a man being carried on a stretcher, his white-blond hair spilling from the sides of the wool blanket that obscured his face.

"Horst Nickles!" Tanaka couldn't believe it, but the proof was on the screen.

ARREST

Brosky walked slowly from his Plymouth; he was wearing a long, black-leather coat, and rubber-soled, high-laced combat boots. The wind was whistling, cold off the river, and Brosky kept his collar tight to his throat. His walk was stiff, caused by the Streetsweeper held in a downward position against the left inside lining of his thick leather coat. His shooting hand went straight through the cutout pocket, gripping the stock of the weapon, while his finger rested nervously on the trigger. He carried an impact-proof aluminum case in his right hand, his fourth and last fingers gripping the handle. Inside, the case contained fifty preloaded syringes of Sustanon 250, ten multiple-use vials of testosterone enanthate, five hundred tabs of halotestin in foil wrap, half-a-dozen bottles of syntex anadrol, a condom containing an ounce of uncut cocaine, and five thousand dollars in used bills. Nickles had included the cocaine and the money to add credibility to his drug-deal-gone-wrong scenerio.

Brosky's assignment was to gain access to Jack Dunne's house, secure the premises, which included holding Jack Dunne at gunpoint, then signal Nickles by way of leaving the front door ajar so that the he could gain access. The Horse had promised to take it from there. In fact he'd told Brosky he could "go home and eat those stinking sausages vid your mother. I vill attend to business."

Brosky walked the final stretch of unlit pavement to the front steps of Jack Dunne's house. He was thinking of his mother's overheated apartment on Forty-fifth, with its K-Mart furniture and pink-papered walls; it seemed like the safest place in the world.

He reached the three stone steps and looked up at the door. The house was quiet. Maybe no one was inside, maybe he would knock and no one would answer. Then he could go back to his car and drive away. Or he could drop the gun and the drug case, and sprint. To where? The Horse knew his mother's address. He had nowhere to hide. Control yourself. He took the first two steps, stopped, and listened. Nothing but the sound of wind, merging with the rumble of traffic from Delaware Avenue. Control yourself. But I've never fired a fucking gun in my life. Control yourself. Fuck it. He got a firmer grip on the Streetsweeper, took the final step, placed the drug case down, unbuttoned his coat, enabling him to swing the gun barrel upwards, and knocked on the door.

"The door's open!" Jack shouted. Then, he pressed the play button on his cassette recorder and walked from the back door of the house.

Brosky recognized the freak's voice, husky and broken like an adolescent's voice, somewhere between child and man. He gripped the old, cast-iron knob and turned; a sliver of dim light cut the cracked, stone step, pointing a way inwards.

"I'm in the kitchen!" Again the freak's voice, trying to sound friendly, but somehow mechanical, concealing nerves.

Brosky pushed inwards; the light came from a room at the end of the shallow corridor. He put one foot inside, then the other, testing the water.

By now, Officer Dunne was in the narrow passageway between the Trinity and the building next door, moving quietly.

"All right, I'm inside!" Brosky called.

"Close the door and come into the kitchen." The voice was more controlled now, less broken, but there was something wrong with it.

"Close the door and come into the kitchen," the voice repeated, exactly five seconds after its initial command.

Officer Dunne stood in the shadow of the building; he could see the suspect in the door of the house, back facing the street, his taped, right hand gripping a container, his left arm tight to his side.

"Walk straight ahead," the voice ordered.

It's a recording, Brosky realized, lifting the Streetsweeper clear of his long coat, pointing it directly in front of him.

The suspect is armed, Officer Dunne noted.

No way I'm walking into a trap, Nickles or no Nickles, Brosky thought, taking a step backwards, his heel on the door stop.

"Mr. Wayne Brosky." Officer Dunne's voice caught him from behind. Brosky spun, his gun lowered to clear the door frame, as the big cop jumped from the sidewalk to the top step, bringing his side-handled baton down in a close falling arc, connecting with the top of Brosky's elbow joint. The Streetsweeper clattered to the ground.

"You are under arrest for the possession and distribution of steroid and narcotic drugs."

Brosky lunged forward trying to push the policeman aside; the wood baton smacked him again, above his eyes, dropping him unconscious.

"You have the right to remain silent."

Nickles checked his wristwatch; it was ten past seven. Brosky had been gone twelve minutes. He slipped the Rolex, a gift from John Flint, from his wrist. There was no sense in breaking the Oyster on Jack Dunne's head. He stepped from the car, closed the door, and stood up straight.

His wide, rubber soles were sure against the pavement; his eyes were open, ears tuned, and nose sniffing the damp air. There was no sound of struggle, no distant wail of sirens, no feel or smell of disturbance. It was a strange phenomenom, one that he had first encountered while working the club doors in North Beach; violence transmitted like radiowaves, giving texture to the atmosphere. Nothing here, all was calm. He walked briskly to the corner and rounded it, both arms swinging in counter time to his long strides. Decked out in his heavy, hooded tracksuit, training shoes, and thin, suede gloves, Horst Nickles could have been out for a cardiovascular exercise walk.

* * *

It was dark in the basement and cramped beneath the stairs, but Wayne Brosky was alive and grateful for it. He was lying on his side, his hands cuffed behind his back and his mouth bound shut with surgical tape. Tied in such a way that if he tried to straighten his legs, the rope tightened on his throat. But he was alive and praying for Horst Nickles to arrive: To save him. Whatever Horst Nickles was, however bad, however dangerous, the cop was worse. He was insane.

Nickles marched by the front door of the Trinity, glanced up, and kept walking. The door was open, not ajar as they had agreed, but wide open. There was a strong wind blowing up from the river, howling down the corridor of houses and buildings. Probably the wind that blew the door open, Nickles reasoned, dropping his head, face to the sidewalk, keeping the sharp gusts from his eyes. He thought of Wayne Brosky. The kid had been shaky enough before he'd left the car for the house, and now he was inside with a shotgun pointed at Dunne, pissing in his pants, waiting to be told he could go home to his mother. Nickles did an about-face and walked back towards the Trinity. He felt no danger coming from the house.

Officer Dunne is on patrol, looking for his suspect; he spots him, approximately fifty yards away, walking north towards the Trinity. He recognizes the man, Horst Nickles. He knows that he is violent and extremely dangerous. Horst Nickles is wanted for murder, for the murder of Jacqueline Dunne.

Officer Dunne is cradling the Streetsweeper in his hands; it is not an authorized police weapon, but his thirty-eight standard-issue piece is no longer a part of his uniform. He remains in the shadows as he narrows the gap between them, stopping occasionally, wary that Nickles will sense his presence.

Horst Nickles walked to the front steps of the Trinity, stopping to look up, then down, the empty sidewalk before mounting the steps. He stood in the opened door. Inside, a yellow light cast a glow against the faded wallpaper and dark, wooden floor. He was on the verge of calling for Brosky but instinct silenced him. He was not armed. He had planned it that way, in case of a fuck-up. Let Brosky be found with the weapon; Nickles was clean. He remained very still outside the opened door listening like a hunter listens, tuned to the slightest sound.

The footsteps came from behind him, light and quick. He spun in time to see the gun rise, its wide barrel pointed at his head. At first he did not recognize the weapon as his own, or the uniformed policeman aiming it.

"Vhat the fuck—"

"Mr. Horst Nickles, you are under arrest for the murder of police officer Jacqueline Dunne."

There was something wrong Nickles realized. Something crazy about the cop, his eyes, his voice.

"You must be mistaken," he said calmly, inching forward.

Officer Dunne leveled the Streetsweeper and took a step closer, blocking his suspect's escape route.

"Please step inside the house, Sir," Officer Dunne ordered.

"Why?"

"Because I fucking said so!" Officer Dunne shouted and, for a moment, his voice broke.

Horst Nickles stared at the policeman, trying to place him. It was his eyes; they were the same wild eyes that the police artist had captured in the drawing of Jack Dunne, but it was more than the man's eyes—

"Turn around and walk into the house," Officer Dunne repeated his command. He did not want to kill Nickles here on the sidewalk, but if there was no alternative he was prepared to do it. He tightened his finger on the trigger.

"All right, I do as you say," Nickles said, sensing his captor's resolve. "Vhere is my friend, you kill my friend?"

Officer Dunne did not answer, the fewer words the better. He followed the German inside the house, locking the door behind them.

"Against the wall, spread your legs, extend your arms, palms flat against the wall, that's correct."

Nickles had been a world-class wrestler, a discipline that required a blind man's sensitivity with regard to the human body, and the close physical contact between bodies. He had learned to feel weakness and vulnerability, to sense it through flesh, like reading braille. Any shift in balance or position, and he could turn defeat to victory. He felt the cop's hand on him now, strong fingers running down the inside of his thigh towards his training shoe, searching for weapons. Nickles knew exactly where the policeman was in relation to himself, exactly how the cop's body was bent forward, one hand on the Streetsweeper, pointing the gun up beneath his armpit, the other hand patting him down. Knew that the cop was squatting, his hips forced backwards to facilitate the bend of his body, rendering him off balance. Nickles decided to wait until the hand started down his other leg before he made his move. One explosive turn and he could reverse their positions. Another shift and he could be behind the cop choking him to death. He relaxed.

"Please remain in the position," Officer Dunne ordered, stepping back, placing the Streetsweeper in his left hand in order to pat his suspect's right side. He moved close to Nickles, forcing the barrel of the gun up beneath the German's left armpit as he ran his right hand down the corresponding side of the giant's body, searching for anything that could be used offensively, even a set of car keys, anything hard or sharp. He squatted, finger light against the shotgun's trigger, right hand on Nickles's inside thigh—moving lower down along the inside ankle, feeling the outline of thick, high socks through the cotton pants, then the tops of soft, leather shoes.

Nickles willed every grain of tension from his muscles, half closing his eyes; he felt the hand against him, the barrel of the gun an easy fit beneath his arm. He concentrated, waiting for any slight hesitation, any awkwardness in balance, any weakness.

Then suddenly, the hand was gone, and the gun removed from his armpit.

"Lower your hands, down behind your back," the police-man ordered.

Nickles complied, feeling the steel cuffs grip tight to his wrists. He was starting to worry now, the cop was good, very well trained.

"Take one step back from the wall, turn to your right, and walk straight ahead," the cop continued.

"I don't understand vhat is happening?"

"One step back, turn and walk," Officer Dunne repeated.

"Vhat are you playing at?" Nickles asked. He wasn't budging.

Officer Dunne pulled back his right foot as if he was kicking a football, and sent the metal tip of his shoe into the soft zone between Nickles's legs.

The German howled, dropping to his knees, his torso half turning as he landed, fury overcoming caution, "I kill you—"

The butt of the Streetsweeper ended his threat and re-moved his two perfect front teeth.

"Stand up, turn to your right, and walk towards the light."

Nickles stood, turned, and, trailing a flow of blood from his mouth, walked the fifteen feet to the door of Jack Dunne's basement. Inside, to the top of the steps.

"Keep going," Officer Dunne commanded, lifting the tape recorder from the kitchen table.

Nickles balked and Officer Dunne kicked him again—this time in the coccyx—so hard that Horst Nickles fell headlong down the ten wooden steps.

Brosky heard the thud, the groans, the muttering in Ger-man, and knew that the Horse had not arrived to rescue him.

Officer Dunne followed, holding the Streetsweeper with one hand, the butt pressed into the side of his stomach.

"Stand up," he ordered.

"I cannot stand, I am paralyzed," Nickles replied.

"Stand up or I will blow off one of your legs. I mean it."

Nickles stood.

"Walk over to the bench in the center of the room."

Nickles looked at the bench beneath the bare bulb of the overhead light. It was a standard flat bench, the type used for bench pressing, but this one had been modified. Each of the four support legs had been screwed to the concrete floor and there were chains with padlocks attached to them. Restraints. Beside the bench there was a low table covered with a white cloth, a tool box on top of the cloth. He could see the gleam of steel from inside the sectioned compartments of the box. The gleam came from the blade of a small woodworking saw. Next to the saw, lay a pair of gardening clippers.

"Move!"

Nickles walked to the center of the room and turned. He saw Wayne Brosky, hog-tied and jammed beneath the stairs, staring at him through terrified eyes. Pathetically. The sight of Brosky's weakness infuriated him.

"Vat is the meaning of this?" Nickles demanded.

"You have been arrested for the rape and murder of Jacqueline Dunne. You have been sentenced to emasculation."

"Vat?"

"I'm gonna cut your fucking dick off!"

The thought flashed red through Nickles's mind. He supressed its horror and held on to the crazy man's eyes. There was more than anger inside them; there was pain. He breathed in and exhaled slowly, fighting for self control.

"Your name is Jack Dunne and you are not a cop," Horst Nickles pronounced each word clearly. "You are vanted for murder. If you release me I vill give you money and help you to escape. That, I promise."

Officer Dunne levelled the shotgun at Nickles's head, and pressed the play button on the recorder. The music began, a vast orchestral wave, too big for the recorder's small, single speaker. He had neglected to lower the volume control after luring Brosky inside the house, and his recording of "Thus Spake Zarathustra" was distorted beyond recognition.

Nickles remained standing, eyes locked to the eyes of the freak, waiting for an answer.

"My name is Jacqueline Dunne. Jacqueline Dunne!" a recorded voice screamed above the music, but the words were indecipherable.

"Vat is that?! Is that supposed to mean something?!" Nickles shouted; he was gaining confidence.

"That is the name of your victim!" Officer Dunne responded. It had started again, the pain in his gut, his stomach was in spasm.

"You are guilty of torture and rape." As the words left his mouth the claustrophobia began, the stink of garbage filling his nostrils, the spasm spreading from his stomach to his arms. Trembling. Difficult to hold the gun. Then, the memory of fear. A fear beyond reprieve. No hope of rescue or salvation. The memory exploded, a ball of fire, and the fear flew forward on the lips of the flame. Fear. All over him. Soaking his bones.

"Lie down on the bench!" Officer Dunne ordered, his voice desperate. The next stomach spasm caused him to crunch forward, the shotgun thrusting in line with his body, aiming at the floor.

The German moved to the side, away from the gun, and stole a step forward.

Reality was breaking up inside Jack Dunne's mind. Splintering into a million pieces. She was coming back to life, inside him. Her fear was becoming his fear. Her terror, his terror. He found the volume lever with his thumb and pulled it down, bringing her words into focus.

"My name is Jacqueline Dunne."

CRIME SCENE

"There's a body in the basement, Sir," the young cop said, trembling, as Dave Roach walked through the door of the Trinity.

"You haven't touched anything, have you?" Roach asked, keeping his voice calm. He was nervous, too, but determined not to show it.

"Nothing, Sir."

"Have you checked the rest of the house?" A little stutter. Still in control.

"The body doesn't have a head."

Roach nodded, as if he was used to bodies without heads.

"The rest of the house?"

"No god damned head, just a body, no head. I was all alone down there with the thing," the young, uniformed man repeated.

Roach placed his right hand on the kid's shoulder, "Sounds like a n . . . nightmare, I'm sorry."

The young cop nodded.

"Have you looked anywhere else?"

"The rest of the house is empty."

Roach turned and, for the first time since they'd been inside, acknowledged Jimmy Stark. He and Stark had just finished their surveillance shift when the probable homicide call had come.

Roach motioned with his head and Stark walked towards the stairs leading to the second floor. He placed a hand above his weapon, unsnapped the holster strap, then proceded up.

"All right," Roach said, redirecting his attention to the uniformed officer, "now before the ambulance gets here, before the mobile crime unit arrives, and before this place is crawling with people asking questions, I want you to tell me exactly what happened. As clear as you remember it."

The cop looked down.

"What's your name, Officer?" Roach asked, starting to make notes. He'd already checked the man's I.D. badge; it read "R. Benjamin," but he needed to get the guy talking.

"Roger Benjamin."

"Well Roger, we've only got a few minutes so let's see if we can get your story right."

It was a strange feeling for Roach to be on the experienced side of an investigation. The last two weeks had changed him, made him grow up.

"I didn't do anything wrong." There was guilt inside the policeman's tone.

"Tell me what happened."

Roger Benjamin straightened and looked into Roach's eyes. "I heard a muffled gunshot—"

"Where were you?"

"Walking my beat, maybe fifty yards away. I heard the shot, but I couldn't tell exactly where it had come from. Like I said, it was muffled. So I walked straight ahead, towards the approximate location," he hesitated, "then I heard screaming so I ran towards the house—"

"Detective?" Stark's voice interrupted them.

Roach turned, "Not now."

Stark stood on the stairs and waited.

"These two guys came flying out the door; they landed on the pavement. They were biting, gouging—"

"What did you do?"

"I tried to separate them, but I couldn't."

"Did you draw your weapon?"

"Yes."

"And they didn't respond?"

Benjamin looked down and shook his head, "I don't even think they were aware of me."

"Be more explicit, Officer." Roach was taking notes.

Benjamin kept his head down and lowered his voice, "They were on the ground, the big guy on top. And all the time the man on the bottom was kicking; he had both legs out to his sides, kicking inwards with his heels, into the big guy's kidneys. From the position they were in; it almost looked like they were fucking."

"Keep going," Roach said.

"When I bent down to try and separate them, I could see that the big guy had wrapped his arms around the smaller man's neck; he was choking the life out of him. The more he choked the less the smaller man kicked, until—"

"Until what?"

"Until the man getting choked buried his teeth into the side of the big guy's neck and started biting. Blood was coming out the sides of his mouth, everywhere. It was all over the sidewalk. The big man was going white in the face—"

"Hold on a second," Roach said, turning to Stark. "Would you go outside and make sure nobody walks in the blood on the sidewalk. Secure it till the mobile unit gets here."

Stark didn't enjoy being treated like a uniform; he hesitated long enough to get his message across.

"I'm sorry, Jim, it's just until I get Officer Benjamin's statement," Roach apologized.

Stark nodded. "Then, I've got something upstairs I think you should see," he said, as he walked past.

Roach held Stark's eyes.

"Some photographs," Stark explained.

Roach nodded, then returned to Benjamin.

"All right, so you've got two men fighting, one of them is biting the other on the neck. It's a life-threatening situation, so what did you do?"

Benjamin finally looked up, his eyes clearing. "I ordered them to quit. I pointed my weapon at the biter's head, pushing the barrel against his ear, shouting at him."

"He didn't repond to a loaded thirty-eight?"

"That's correct."

"I find that hard to believe," Roach said.

"This guy was crazy, his eyes were like glass; he had to be on drugs, out of his mind," Benjamin lowered his voice, less defensive, "the plain truth, Detective, is that I was scared.

I've never been in a situation like that before. What was I supposed to do, shoot both of them?"

"Where did they go?" Roach asked, looking out towards the street.

"Gone."

"Gone?"

"The big guy got to his feet, took the biter's head in his hands, and ripped it away from his neck. There was plenty of blood but the German guy kept moving—"

"What did you say?"

"The German just staggered away. The other guy lay on the ground, either hurt or exhausted, or both."

"German?"

"He was shouting in German. I studied German in college; it was German."

"You say the guy was big. Was he big like a bodybuilder?"

"Yes," Benjamin answered.

"Did he have long, blond hair?"

"Yes."

"Where did he go, which direction?" Roach asked, suddenly intense.

"I lost him, Sir."

"Come on, you've got a weapon, you've got a phone, you can't have lost him."

"He ignored my command to stop and surrender. He pushed me aside and kept walking. He got into a car," Benjamin said, handing Roach a slip of paper with a number on it. "A blue Plymouth, that's the plate. The car was parked, heading west on Catherine Street; he started it and drove off."

Roach snapped the sheet of paper from the cop's hand.

"Why the fuck didn't you shoot him?"

Benjamin held steady, "It was the first time I've ever drawn my weapon. I couldn't shoot him; he was unarmed and injured and I thought, maybe, he didn't speak English—"

"And maybe, if you didn't kill him, he'd turn around and snap your neck?"

"Are you speaking from experience, Sir?" Benjamin asked. He kept his tone sincere but the words had bite. He'd had enough. Roach wasn't a lot older than he and Benjamin had been honest; he didn't deserve to be humiliated.

Roach simmered then let the challenge go, "So what happened n . . . next?"

"When I got back to the front of the house, the smaller man had disapeared. I thought maybe he'd gone back inside. I searched for him. That's when I found the body in the basement."

"That's it?"

"Yes."

Roach thought for a moment. "Now I want you to go outside, secure the premises, and ask Detective Stark to come back in here with me."

The patrolman walked to the door and turned, "Detective?"

Roach already had his hand set out and was dialing homicide. He looked at the young face.

"Did I fuck up?" the patrolman asked.

"No, you did okay," Roach said, and continued to dial.

Bill Fogarty dropped off the rental car at the Adam's Mark Hotel, which was a five-minute walk from his apartment. He could hear his mobile phone ringing from inside his briefcase as he walked through his front door. He had the phone in his hand by the fourth ring.

"You're god-damned right I want to be there," he said to the homicide lieutenant who relayed Roach's call. "I'm on my way."

Half an hour later, Bill Fogarty arrived at the crime scene. Roach met him on the sidewalk.

"We've got a b . . . ody in the basement, Sir, an unidentified, male Caucasian. Head blown clean from his shoulders. Brains splattered all over the wall, bits and pieces of the skull everywhere, D . . . d—" Roach hesitated, inhaled and blew out quickly. "Doctor Tanaka is on his way over and the mobile unit has started inside the house."

Fogarty looked at the cordoned area on the pavement. A photographer was taking pictures of the blood spills.

"There was a fight, there, on the sidewalk. Two men, one of them fits the description of Horst Nickles—"

Fogarty nodded. "And the other?"

"Big, but not as big as Nickles. Short, light-colored hair, crazy, staring eyes—"

"Brown or blue?"

"The officer was v . . . vague about the details; there was no overhead light."

"Could it have been Jack Dunne?"

Roach hesitated.

"The guy in the police drawing?"

"I don't know."

Fogarty didn't look satisfied.

"There are two types of blood on the pavement," Roach continued. "The blood that corresponds with the man fitting Nickles's description trails right around to Catherine Street, where the man got into a blue Plymouth and drove west."

"How about the other blood?"

"There's a trail leading south, away from the house."

Fogarty looked in the direction that Roach was pointing.

"Call 'Canine'; get me a couple of tracker dogs."

"Yes, Sir."

"And, there's this," Roach added.

Fogarty took the small, framed picture from Roach's hand. It was a head and shoulders shot, and Fogarty could see that the woman was wearing a police uniform. Then, the crime scene photographer's flash illuminated Jacqueline Dunne's smile.

Rachel Saunders was driving home. She was listening to disc five of a collection of classical CDs. The track was Ravel's "Pavane for a Dead Princess." Often, after emergency surgery, the weight of the classical music was the only thing that could lift her thoughts. She worried about the welfare of the people whose lives she touched. About grafts that wouldn't take, about limbs that would require reamputation because the patient's body had rejected them. The anxiety was short-lived, but it was intense. Rachel often went step-by-step over her procedures as if there was something she had neglected to do, something she had overlooked. Usually a good night's sleep cured her, but her classical collection always helped during the drive home.

"I'm ruined." Her last patient's voice repeated in her mind.

"No. You're going to perfect." And she was. The eye socket and cheekbone had lifted back into perfect realignment.

Ravel's music came to an end and the opening swell of Tchaikovsky's "Marche Slave" began as Rachel entered the one-way system, two blocks from her home. She was beginning to relax.

It was dark and the streets were deserted, with the exception of a solitary figure, seated, back pressed against the black-iron fence that surrounded the grass and pedestrian foot-paths of Rittenhouse Square. Rachel paid little attention to the figure, other than to note that it appeared to be a man and that the man stood up as she rounded the last corner before the entrance to the underground car park.

She turned off the CD player and drove slowly down the ramp, then into the enclosed area, stopping to locate her I.D. card, slipping it through the security lock. The gates opened and she drove inside the large, multicar garage.

She didn't see him until she had locked her car and turned towards the elevator door. By then, the man from the street was a hundred feet from her, lurching forward, one arm hanging limp to his side, the other extended towards her.

Rachel ran; she got to the door of the elevator and jabbed at the button. The door remained shut; she could hear the machinery grinding and clanking. The elevator was in use. She turned. The man was thirty feet away, coming forward.

Don't panic. Don't panic, she told herself, searching her purse for the small cylinder.

"Stop! Right there! Stop!" shouting as she lifted the Chemical Mace, aiming it. Her voice echoing loud in the concrete cavern.

"Stop!" as Jack Dunne stumbled and fell. Pitching forward onto his face, ten feet in front of Rachel Saunders.

CAPTURE

Horst Nickles knew enough to stay away from hospitals. With his injuries, particularly the distinct impression of human teeth outlining the blackened, swollen skin on the downside of his neck, the first thing the medical staff would do was report him to the police.

Instead he drove back to Animals. There, locked inside his office, he used a few grams of cocaine, administered directly to the wound to numb the pain, then went to work with a needle and thread. His patch-up job was crude but it stopped most of the bleeding. He couldn't afford to worry about tetanus. Then, with his freshly stitched neck wrapped in Wayne Brosky's knee-support tape, he studied himself in the mirror. His face was so swollen that his eyes were on the verge of closing, and his broken front teeth looked like jagged fangs behind puffy, bloodied lips. His shrunken testicles were too sore to touch and his kidneys throbbed. He limped from the mirror to the toilet and passed as much blood as water. He was in trouble, inside and out; he needed a safe place, a good doctor, and time to heal.

Mexico, Tijuana. He had contacts there. If only he could get across the border. Nickles considered driving; he could make Brownsville in three days, cross there, then head west to T.J., but he knew he wouldn't last the journey and, by now, the cops would have an all-points out on Wayne Brosky's car. He had no idea where Pinion had taken the Mercedes. "Get out of town, spend the night in a hotel, and bring it back in the morning," he'd ordered, and Horst Nickles knew he didn't have until morning to hang around. He needed to move now, grab the first flight to Florida, or Atlanta, change planes and fly south. His wallet, containing his credit cards and a small amount of money, was in the pocket of his corduroy trousers hanging in the locker room, but the people he knew in Mexico were not big on plastic. I need cash and I need my passport. Both were in the wall safe inside his apartment. He walked back to his office, forcing himself not to limp, picked up his phone and punched the memory button for Randy Dornt. With the lisp caused by his newly vented mouth, it took him a full minute to convince Dornt of his identity.

"I can't just go breaking into your apartment, boss," Dornt protested.

"Okay, okay, come here first, I give you the keys, but be quick."

Dornt arrived ten minutes later; he was wearing thermal socks, high cavalry boots, and a long leather overcoat buttoned high to the neck, protecting him from the icy wind.

"Jesus Christ, boss, what happened?"

Nickles ignored the concern and shoved his keys at him.

"The safe is in the closet in the bedroom, behind the shoe rack. I have written the combination, here," he lisped, pressing a piece of paper into Dornt's hand. Dornt looked down at the six-figure number, then again into Nickles's eyes. They were nearly buried behind the ripening lids.

"Vat are you staring at?" the Horse challenged.

"Nothing," Dornt said, looking away.

"You go now, get all the money in the safe and my passport. You know vat a passport looks like?"

"Yeah."

"Then you meet me at the United terminal at the airport. You know how to get to the Philadelphia Airport?"

"I can get there."

"Then, vat are you waiting for."

Nickles called a cab, changed his clothes, then found a pair of dark glasses to hide the damage to his eyes. He locked Animals and waited on the corner, tossing his used and bloodied clothing into a public trash bin.

The taxi, with Nickles in the backseat, pulled away less than thirty seconds before Bill Fogarty and Dave Roach arrived. They jumped out of the Chrysler and ran to the door of the gym. A stakeout team slid to a halt behind the Chrysler, and another car brought a backup unit with a sledgehammer.

"Get it open!" Fogarty shouted.

The steel safety door took a dozen swings; the inside door only three.

"No alarm; he's either in here or he's been in here," Fogarty said, allowing stake out to lead the way into the building. The floor in front of the mirror had a spill of blood that led to Nickles's office.

The ride to the airport took twenty minutes and the sixteen-dollar fare left the Horse with forty-five cents in his pocket.

He walked into the United terminal, checked the wall monitors, and spotted the last outgoing flight to Atlanta: 9:05. He looked at his Oyster; Randy Dornt had one hour and sixteen minutes to make it. *No problem*, Nickles assured himself, joining the small line in front of the ticket desk. The ticketing agent balked when she saw him.

"I am a boxer, I loose the fight," he explained, handing over his American Express card. The woman smiled apologetically.

"I have a window seat available or would you prefer an aisle?"

"I like to look out the vindow," Nickles replied, returning her smile.

She stared briefly at the serrated stumps that had once been front teeth.

"The flight is showing 'on time' and will be boarding at eight-forty-five at gate Twelve-D," she said, processing his card then handing him the receipt.

He signed and she placed his ticket and boarding card on the counter.

"Have you any luggage?"

"No."

"Have a nice flight, Mr. Nickles. I'll tell my husband I met you; he's a boxing fan."

Nickles forced another pumpkin grin, took the ticket, and

walked away. He wanted to go directly to the departure gate but he was afraid Dornt would miss him, so he went to the front of the terminal and sat down in one of the hard-backed chairs. Twenty minutes passed. Nickles checked every face that walked by, his own so swollen and discolored that only the children returned his glances. "He looks like a Halloween man," he heard a small girl giggle.

Another twenty minutes and he had to urinate. He didn't want to risk being in the men's room when Dornt walked in, so he crossed his legs and remained seated. Finally, a metal voice over the Tannoys announced his flight. He stood, stuffed his right hand in his pocket to stop the trickle and wobbled towards Departures.

Dornt would have to meet him in Atlanta with his passport. Until then he'd get a hotel room on Peachtree Street and lie under an ice pack. He walked slowly along the corridor towards the gate. A bearded man, dragging a suitcase on wheels, edged by and brushed lightly against Nickles's left side. The contact sent an electic current through his kidneys; the man turned to apologize and Nickles cursed him in German. By the time he arrived at 12D he'd pissed in his trousers, and the single thought in his mind was a safe room, a locked door, and a bed.

They were boarding, so he hobbled straight for the small line of people. There were five in front of him, then four, then three, then he heard the voice.

"Mr. Nickles, would you please step out of line and place your hands on top of your head."

The big black policeman looked even blacker through the dark lenses of Nickles's shades.

"Do it now, Sir," Jimmy Taylor insisted, taking Nickles by the arm and forcefully guiding him towards Bill Fogarty and Dave Roach, who waited beside the United desk.

Jack Dunne was asleep, floating on a mix of morphine and nembutol. All physical pain was dead and, in his drug-induced slumber, Jack Dunne was also dying, layers of personality breaking away as Jacqueline's soul eased through the wreckage like a snake through its discarded skin. Back to a time before the fire, before the rape, before the stink of garbage and the touch of rubber fingers. Floating. Floating on waves of music, guitar chords, rising and falling from major to minor, lilting changes, like a blue mist, then the voice, that sweet, soul voice: We will meet again, we will meet again, when the night is over, we will meet again.

An hour earlier, he had been stretchered from Rachel's Mercedes, through the side door of the Bryn Mawr Reconstructive Center wearing nothing but a torn shirt, trousers, and a single shoe. The clothes were similar to those of a police officer, but Rachel Saunders was familiar with the police uniform and had reckoned this man more likely to be a night watchman or some type of security guard.

"Help me. Help me. Rachel Saunders, please help me," he had called from the concrete floor of the garage. At first it was only his voice she had recognized. "Help me, help me," as much by the rhythm of the words, as by their tone. It was the voice of her unidentified caller. Then, his face, battered and swollen, but familiar. The last time she'd seen him, he'd worn a wispy beard, and his blond hair was shoulder length, but his eyes; she had not forgotten his eyes. The same eyes that had stared at her through the dim light of a late afternoon, in the parking lot on Pine and Fifth. Those frightened, animal eyes.

However, it was not until Jack Dunne was sedated, not until she had examined him thoroughly, that Dr. Saunders knew the whole truth.

Horst Nickles sat on the chair in the small holding cell in the basement of the police administration building.

"I vant a doctor. I am not an animal, you cannot treat me like an animal. I demand you get me a doctor!"

Bill Fogarty did not answer. He simply stood in silence, studying the hulking man inside the cage with a mixture of anger, disgust, and curiosity. He had no pity for Horst Nickles.

"A doctor! You hear vat I say?"

Fogarty allowed his lips to rise slightly at the outside corners of his mouth, not quite a smile, but enough to give his face the expression of satisfaction.

"Vat you are doing is illegal. You cannot deprive me of medical attention. You are committing a crime." There was still an unmistakable arrogance in the German's tone.

Fogarty nodded his head slowly, then stepped up to the steel bars. Pushing his face between them, he whispered, "Why did you kill Wayne Brosky?"

"Fuck you! I am bleeding to death inside my body. I demand you get me a doctor! I vill sue the city!"

"I mean, Wayne Brosky worked for you, he was loyal, not like that little shit who told us where you were. What's his name? Dornt? Randy Dornt? Jesus, he turned you over fast when it came down to saving his own ass. I mean, I can see killing him, but why Wayne Brosky?"

"I am an in . . . no . . . cent man, this is po . . . lice persecution."

"Wayne's mother was very unhappy with the way her son looked; I mean, Horst, you left her kid without his head. In order to do that with a twelve gauge you had to hold the muzzle about two feet in front of his face. God, that's a terrible way to treat an employee. And now, Irene—did you know that was Wayne's mother's name?"

Nickles stared silently, but he was listening.

"Irene. Irene Brosky. She's out to get you. Even if I let you go we'd have to give you police protection. Irene Brosky's a tough lady. Why the hell did you kill her son?"

"I did not kill him. The other guy killed him. Jack Dunne killed Vayne."

"Oh come on, Horst, you can do better than that. There was nobody else there. Just you, Brosky, a pile of drugs, and a shotgun. Oh, wait a second, now it's starting to make sense.

The handcuffs, the rope, the marks on Brosky's wrists and his neck. You had him tied up, didn't you? Same kind of thing you used to get up to with John Flint, the S&M stuff. The stuff on the videotapes. You and Brosky were gay. This was a lover's quarrel."

Nickles stood up from the cot and Fogarty stepped back from the cell.

"It was Jack Dunne," Nickles said, walking forward to grip the bars.

For a moment, Fogarty wondered if the German was strong enough to bend the steel. He looked too big for the small rectangular room and, even wounded, his energy seemed enough to explode the concrete and metal.

"Oh really? Then where the hell is this Jack Dunne now?" Fogarty asked.

"I need a doctor," Nickles stated.

"Do you realize, Horst, that nobody knows where the hell you are. Nobody, but me and the other two guys who brought you in here. And Horst, those two guys hate your guts. They'd like to hear that you dropped dead. Plus, they're going to laugh their asses off when I tell them that you're queer. A big, gay muscle man. A screaming queen."

Nickles tightened his lips and aimed a heartful of hate into the cop's eyes.

"What the hell did Wayne Brosky do to make you kill him?" Fogarty asked, raising his voice.

The German released his grip on the bars and crossed his arms in front of his chest. "No more head games, Captain Fogarty. Get me a doc . . . tor. After that, I vant my lawyer." His voice was quiet and final. Afterwards, Horst Nickles turned his back on the policeman and took four steps to the opposite side of the cell. He stood silent, staring at the cracked, yellowed wall.

"All right, Horst, all right, I'll get you a doctor," Fogarty acquiesced.

DOCTOR

Mr. Nickles?" Fogarty's voice was respectful, "the doctor is here to see you, Sir."

Nickles mumbled something in German, then turned, a conquering arrogance in his expression. The arrogance melted quickly, "Vat! Vat kind of trick you pulling?!"

"Dr. Tanaka has very kindly agreed to take a look at your injuries," Fogarty answered.

"Doctor? The yellow man is a doctor?"

"Yes," the policeman replied.

"I vant a vhite doctor."

Tanaka stood quietly, hands at his sides, looking in at the man inside the cell. Nickles met his eyes and, for a moment, Tanaka felt the challenge return. He stepped forward, anger rising, as if preparing an attack. Then, as quickly, he got a handle on his emotions. Horst Nickles was just another piece of meat on the butcher's block. To be viewed objectively, assessed. Tanaka stopped a foot in front of the bars of the cell and peered inwards.

The damage to Nickles's face appeared superficial, but there was blood leaking from the elasticated wrap around his throat and, by the way he was gripping his side, palm pressing inward, Tanaka wondered what shape his kidneys were in.

"Does your urine contain a great deal of blood?" he asked, his voice void of emotion.

Nickles found his eyes again, and held, "Yes, I am pissing blood."

"Maybe one of your kidneys has been torn from its connective tissue," Tanaka suggested. "Do you understand what that means?"

"Don't talk down to me, yellow man, I know about the human body. Probably better than you."

Tanaka held it together, calm. "Then, you'll understand that if a kidney has become detached, or if one, or both of them, have ruptured, the poisons that they excrete in your urine will be flooding your system."

"Vhy do you think I vant a doctor?"

"Are you breathing easily?" Tanaka asked, moving a step closer.

"Vat?"

"Can you inhale deeply?"

"You talking about my ribs?" Nickles replied. "You think it's my twelfth rib; you think my rib has punctured my kidney?"

"It's a possibility," Tanaka replied.

"My ribs are painful. I have a sharp pain in my lower abdomen," Nickles said, hobbling closer to the bars, sizing up Tanaka, his strength, his size. He was thinking now, clearer than he had been thinking since they'd tossed him in the cell.

"And the wound to your throat?"

"He bit me," Nickles answered.

"Looks like he may have hit your external jugular," Tanaka observed.

Nickles softened his eyes and nodded his head, "Maybe you should come in and take a look?"

Tanaka considered, his senses heightening.

"I am not well," Nickles conceded, his voice relaxing as he backed up and sat down on the cot.

Tanaka felt his own nerves, warning him of danger. Fogarty was uncomfortable, too; he was about to call upstairs for Jimmy Taylor, when Dave Roach entered through the main door.

Fogarty met him half way up the narrow corridor.

"We g . . . g . . . got him, Captain," Roach tried to keep his voice down but he was excited and his words carried. "The mobile unit found a pair of suede gloves with Nickles's fingerprints inside them, right outside his gym in a trash can. All his clothes were in there, too, covered in blood. There's residue from the shotgun blast on the outside of the leather gloves. The gun had only been fired once, so Nickles was the shooter. We got him."

Nickles had heard enough to know the score. With or without Myron Schlenk, he was headed for murder one. He lowered his head and bit his tongue, so hard that the tip tore free.

"That's good news, Detective," Fogarty replied, keeping his voice down, containing his satisfaction, "how about the tracker dogs? Anything yet?"

Roach shook his head. "They got him as far as Broad Street, but there was a burst water main and the street was flooded; the dogs couldn't pick up the scent on the other side."

Fogarty nodded his head. "Right. Now, Dave, I want you to go upstairs and send Jimmy Taylor down here."

Nickles raised his head and swallowed the severed tip of his tongue. He held his lips tight, allowing his mouth to fill with blood, watching as Fogarty walked towards him. The policeman was barely stifling a smile as he nodded to Tanaka.

"Mr. Nickles?"

Nickles met Fogarty's eyes, tried to speak. Blood flowed from his mouth. He gasped for breath and pitched forward onto the concrete. He struggled to his hands and knees, shook convulsively, and fell to his side.

Fogarty hesitated, suspicious.

"I can't breathe!" Nickles gasped, a shower of blood spraying the wall.

A second spray of blood and Fogarty was in motion. Running forward, thinking, *Don't die on me now, not now!* He wanted more from Horst Nickles; he wanted a way back to Jacqueline Dunne. Needed to know what had happened on the night of the video. He wanted the German bastard to tell it, to relive it, to suffer for it. He opened the lock as Nickles turned onto his back, his legs locking out.

"Can't breathe."

"Let me have him, Bill, a rib may have punctured his diaphragm," Tanaka said, moving forward.

Fogarty stepped aside and Tanaka squatted down over the German, cautious of their proximity. He stared into Nickles' eyes. The pupils were dilated, indicating adrenaline secretion, probably caused by extreme pain.

"I'm going to need an ambulance," Tanaka stated, reaching out to touch the area of Nickles's chest, above his lower ribs.

Nickles convulsed, and his stomach locked, his muscles like steel girders, stretching the blood- and sweat-soaked fabric of his denim shirt.

"Hurry up! He's going into paralysis!" Tanaka shouted.

Fogarty turned towards the door of the cell as Tanaka bent forward to prop up the German's head. Their faces were inches apart when the German spat, sending blood and saliva into Tanaka's eyes. Another twist of his body and Nickles was behind him, his arms wrapped firm round Tanaka's throat, forearm pressing inward against his windpipe. Nickles stood with Tanaka in his grip, using him as a shield from Fogarty's drawn thirty-eight.

"You shoot, you kill the yellow man," Nickles said, shifting his grip from a strangle to a break, so that his right palm cupped Tanaka's chin while his left hand levered against the back of his head. "I twist, I kill him. Either way, his blood is on your hands."

In the first few seconds of his capture, Tanaka's reaction was neither fear, nor anger. It was humiliation. He had allowed himself to be tricked by an enemy, taken unaware, without *zanshin,* the mental alertness of a master. Endangering his own life and the life of his friend. And for that moment, he believed he deserved death. Accepted it. That brief surrender caused him to relax and, as he did, he felt the German's arms wrapping and tightening, adjusting, as if their bodies were locked in some primal communication.

"I don't know what you think you're doing," Fogarty said, pulling the edge off his voice while keeping his weapon trained on the two men. "You can't get out of here, it's impossible."

"Vat is the difference between killing one man and killing two men?" Nickles asked, bending at the knees to tuck his head directly behind Tanaka's, adding torque to his leverage.

"Horst. As far as I'm concerned, you're going to get medical attention and your going to get your lawyer. He's on his way now. If he gets here and we've got a situation," Fogarty stayed smooth, motioning towards Tanaka, "there's not going to be a hell of a lot we can do."

"Don't talk bullshit," Nickles countered, "I hear vat your man says; I hear about the gloves, the clothes. Don't talk bullshit."

Fogarty and Tanaka were making eye contact, and Tanaka's eyes said shoot.

"Everything okay in here?" Taylor's voice broke Fogarty's concentration. He saw the black man from the corner of his eye.

"Not exactly," Fogarty answered, "why don't you come in and close the door." The last thing Fogarty wanted was twenty armed cops gathered outside, to add an audience to the drama. The quieter he could keep it the more controlled it would remain.

Taylor entered the room, closed the door behind him, and stood next to the captain.

"This is a bad situation for all of us, Mr. Nickles," Fogarty said. "As it stands now, there's no way it can end without you dead."

"The yellow man dies first," Nickles responded, again changing his hold, dropping his forearm to the front of Tanaka's throat, augmenting the lock by pulling inward against his wrist with his free hand. "If I squeeze fast I break his vindpipe and he vill drown in his own blood." Then, sliding his forearm clockwise, he positioned the bicep of his other arm above Tanaka's carotid artery. He handled Josef like a toy doll, playing with him. "If I squeeze slow I shut off the oxygen to his brain. Maybe he lives, but he von't be the same."

Tanaka's body was relaxed to the point of appearing limp, but his eyes were alive. He was concentrating, aware of every point of contact between his body and the German's, every shift of balance.

Nickles changed grips again, from a choke to a neck break, constantly angling his body away from the policeman's weapon.

"What will it take to end this?" Fogarty asked.

"My credit cards, my passport, a car to take me to the airport, then a plane to take me to Brazil," Nickles answered.

"That's crazy and it's impossible," Fogarty replied.

"Then ve all stay right here."

"For how long, Horst? Till you can't stay awake any longer, till you die from internal bleeding? So far, this incident has been contained within this room. You release the doctor and we'll go back to where we were before it started. You'll get medical attention, you'll get Myron Schlenk, and you'll get a trial. This way you get nothing but dead."

"I tell you vat I do," Nickles answered, relaxing his grip. "I put this man to sleep for you; I show you how easy it is for me to kill him. I put him to sleep this one time. Between vhen he goes to sleep and vhen he comes to, I vant you to think about how to get me out of here. You tell me vat you can do for me; you put yourself in my place. Vat would you ask for? You tell me how to get out of my situation. But, Captain Fogarty," Nickles said, "once the yellow man goes out, he has only a matter of seconds before his brain is permanently fucked. He never valk the same; he never talk the same. You understand?"

"Don't be crazy," Fogarty warned.

"You better think fast, and think clear, no bullshit," Nickles threatened, shifting his position in a preparation for the choke, "because next time I kill him."

Tanaka felt the slack in Nickles's arms and twisted his head to the right, towards the German's clenched fist, grabbing a final breath. Then, lifting his foot, he stamped down hard, toes pulled back; the heel of his shoe scraping across Nickles right shin, cutting, like a knife, into his instep. Tanaka felt the bone snap as he lifted his pelvis, clenching the muscles of his hips, contracting them to create space and striking distance. Then, he thrust back, his hard buttocks exploding into Nickles's groin, causing shock and pain, forcing the German's head forward in time with Tanaka's reverse head-butt. The strike flattened the cartilage and bone of Nickles's nose, and gave Tanaka space to pivot within his arms.

"Stand clear, Josef, stand clear!" Fogarty shouted.

Tanaka heard the voice, but it was just noise. He was moving so quickly that his actions were a blur to the two men watching from outside the cage.

To Tanaka, it was a vacuum, a hollow space in which years of combat training triggered reactions so fast that, later, he had only flash memories of his encounter: the body shifts, the twisting of his hips, the punches, the strikes.

"You're gonna kill him Josef!"

Another elbow to the lower ribs and Horst Nickles dropped to his knees.

"Back off, Josef, back off!" Fogarty ordered, as Jimmy Taylor wrapped his arms around him.

"Easy, Josef, easy," Taylor said softly.

"Okay, son, okay," Fogarty soothed.

Tanaka relaxed, and the black man dropped his arms. Fogarty stepped back as the German pitched forward, his head smacking against the concrete floor. He groaned like a dying beast.

"Nice one, Josef," Fogarty said, as if his friend had just bagged a six-point buck.

"Mr. Nickles?" Tanaka's voice returned to a peaceful quiet as he regained control.

The German groaned again.

"As a doctor, Sir, I would say that your lower ribs are

definitely broken and that the twelfth has, now, almost certainly punctured you diaphragm. You are going to need emergency treatment. In a hospital."

"Help me," Nickles croaked.

"Have you been using any deca-durabolin?"

Fogarty and Taylor exchanged glances.

"Yes," Nickles managed.

"You have to consider, Mr. Nickles," Tanaka continued, "that deca-durabolin prevents the blood from clotting properly. Whatever internal bleeding you have will be intensified by the reaction of the steroid. In other words, Mr. Nickles," Tanaka's voice hardened, "you are currently in the process of bleeding to death."

"Hospital. I need a hospital."

"Mr. Nickels, did you kill Wayne Brosky?" Fogarty asked. He had no compassion for the German. None, at all.

"I don't vant to die like an animal in this cage."

"Did you kill Wayne Brosky?"

Nickles looked up at the policeman.

"It was an accident," he answered, "I vas struggling for the gun; it vent off."

"I don't believe you," Fogarty replied.

Nickles stared into the blue-grey eyes, shadowed on one side by the terrible scars.

"No lies, no games, Mr. Nickles," Fogarty said.

Nickles lowered his eyes, recalling his struggle with Jack Dunne. Once he'd tackled him, it had taken only seconds to disarm him before beating him senseless with the butt of the gun. Then, he'd freed Brosky, tearing the tape from his mouth, dragging him to his feet. He'd been eighteen, maybe twenty-inches from him, when he levelled the shotgun, pointing the barrel at Brosky's nose, ensuring that the spread of pellets would be concentrated. "No, please boss, no," Brosky had pleaded. Crying. The tears made it easier. The blast had shaken the plaster walls of the basement. Rousing Jack Dunne. Before Nickles could turn and get off the second shot, Dunne was on him, fighting like a wild animal, wrenching the Streetsweeper from his hands, biting, gouging, screaming. High, shrill screams, devil screams. There had been something unnatural in Dunne's strength, his rage. Nickles had panicked, tried to escape up the stairs, but Jack Dunne had clung on to him, out of the house, into the street.

"Did you kill Wayne Brosky?" Fogarty repeated.

"Yes, but it was an accident."

"I see . . . and, Jack Dunne. What about Jack Dunne?"

"I never saw Jack Dunne before last night. He tried to kill me. I don't know vhy."

"You knew his sister, didn't you?"

Nickles shook his head.

"No lies, no games, Horst. You are dying. Right here in this cold, little room. You are dying."

Nickles looked up.

"Tell me about Jacqueline Dunne," Fogarty continued.

"She was a cop."

"Yeah, she was a cop. Now, she's dead."

"That's not down to me." Nickles's voice was softer now, his vitality ebbing.

"I think it is," Fogarty answered.

"I did not kill her," Nickles replied.

"You tried to kill her, though, didn't you, Horst?"

"She vanted to send me to prison."

"You raped, beat, and tortured her?"

Nickles looked at Tanaka. "I can feel blood in my underpants."

Tanaka bent down and pressed inward above Nickles's lower ribs. The German winced. His face was white and sweat dripped from his forehead.

"Better get an ambulance, Captain," Tanaka said. He reckoned Nickles could survive for hours, bleeding slowly, but he was playing along, adding urgency to the situation.

Fogarty ignored Tanaka's request.

"What happened after you raped Jacqueline Dunne. How did she wind up in New Jersey."

Nickles continued to look at Tanaka, his eyes begging for mercy. Tanaka turned away.

"Answer me," Fogarty insisted.

Nickles bowed his head and spoke to the floor.

"Ve put her in the trunk of a car. Jim Pinion dropped her someplace near the shore. In a garbage dump. He told us she was dead."

"I see." Fogarty's voice was ice cold.

Nickles looked up. "Dr. Tanaka, I need help."

"I've done all I can," Tanaka answered.

"Wayne Brosky?" Fogarty continued.

"I told you."

"You told me it was an accident. I don't believe you."

"All right. It vas not an accident."

"And you'll sign a statement to that effect?"

"Yes."

"And, waive your right to an attorney?"

"Fuck you, yes."

"Good, let's get a statement of confession ready for Mr. Nickles to sign," Fogarty answered, then, turning back to the German, "before the ambulance takes him to intensive care. Jesus, I hope they can save you. At least some of you."

It was Tuesday. Four days had passed since Rachel Saunders had taken Dunne to the private hospital, seven miles west of City Line Avenue, outside of Philadelphia and beyond the jurisdiction of the Philadelphia police department. The center was owned by a consortium of doctors, and Rachel was a major investor; she'd charged the single room to her own account, along with the endocrinoligist, the intraveneous food drip, and the life-support system that kept her patient alive during the first forty-eight hours. Rachel was way out on a limb and she knew it, risking her career, even criminal charges.

The center's new patient set hospital records on two blood tests, the LDH, and the SGOT. The LDH measured cell destruction within the body, and the SGOT measured specific cell destruction within the liver. The normal range on the LDH was between 100 to 125; Jack Dunne's was 1,000. Against a normal of 50 to 100 on the SGOT, Dunne recorded 900.

"It's a miracle this one's still alive," Richard Schwab, the endocrinologist, said to Rachel as they watched the monitors bleep in time with the slowly beating heart of the unconscious figure in the metal-framed bed. "The liver cysts have stabilized and begun to shrink. If it wasn't for that, well?"

Rachel met the doctor's eyes. It was a strange sensation; for once, she was the person in doubt, silently asking for information, yearning for reassurance. The way that so many had looked into her eyes. She understood that Schwab would be cautious, unwilling to build her hopes. It was the same way she had been on so many occasions.

"There's been such trauma to the organs, that until I can get a few more tests done it's impossible to judge the extent of internal damage. With regard to the liver, I'm not certain how much of the organ is actually intact."

Rachel felt her eyes well with tears and turned away. She was thinking of another room, in another hospital. Years ago. A beautiful young woman who had endured rape and torture, whose nose had been shattered, whose cheekbones had been crushed. Rachel had been able to repair the physical damage, but the internal damage, the ruination of the mind, the heart, and the soul? Who could repair a human soul?

"I mean," Schwab continued, sensitive to her sorrow, "I've handled one or two similar cases; there's a lot that can be done, but," he glanced again at the bed, "this is the most extreme."

"Yes, I understand," Rachel said softly. She, too, had been close to destruction, once, and a part of her would remain, forever, tainted. In that way, she and the person in the bed were bound, closer than flesh and blood. And for that reason, Rachel would shield and protect for as long as she could. She owed.

Rachel cleared her throat and looked at Schwab, guessing

his age at fifty, and then only because his hair was grey and gone at the crown. His face was square and there was a sureness to him. His wrists and hands, extending from the cuffs of his tailored suit, looked strong and able. Rachel had read several of his articles in the *New England Journal of Medicine*. His last one, "Steroid Abuse Among College Athletes," had impressed her, enough to ask for him by name at the medical center.

"I'll fix everything I can," he said.

"I know," Rachel answered, then walked closer to the bed. Schwab watched as she placed her hand against the bearded cheek.

"There's a nurse on duty, right outside the door," Schwab whispered before he walked from the room.

The patient can feel the warmth of Rachel Saunder's hand. In a world where there has been no love, no trust, and no, nonviolent physical contact, the warmth is a strange, alien sensation. Like water on an arid wasteland.

Rachel looks down and sees the tears form, glistening beneath the lids of the closed eyes. The tears begin to fall.

"We've been to every hospital in Philadephia, Sir, every emergency ward, checked out every John Doe, and we've got nothing that matches the description of Jack Dunne, nothing that resembles his picture," Sharon Gilbey said. She stood beside Dave Roach, directly in front of Bill Fogarty's desk.

"Nothing in the D.O.A.s either, Sir," Roach added.

Fogarty sat back against his chair. He looked from Roach to Gilbey, wondering why, somehow, they didn't look like kids to him anymore.

"How about a private practice? Maybe he had a friend who was a doctor. Maybe he went there," he suggested.

Roach opened his notebook. Inside was an alphabetized list of every certified doctor in Philadelphia. There were 2,243 names on the list.

"I've been through this once; b . . . broken it down into

surgeons, G.P.s, specialists, checked out any of them that I thought was a possibility, by telephone, in person, and I've come up dry."

"Camden, maybe he got across the bridge into Camden," Fogarty thought out loud. The entire Jack Dunne investigation had been a *maybe* for the past four days.

"But, Sir, the dogs tracked him going west," Roach said, quietly.

"Well, maybe the dogs got it wrong. Maybe he doubled back, maybe he got a ride."

"We haven't done the private practices over there, Sir, but I did fax pictures and descriptions to the hospitals; they've come back negative," Gilbey covered.

"Yeah, I know, I know," Fogarty said, regaining his patience. "But if this guy was hurt as bad as Nickles swears he hurt him, he would have needed some kind of medical attention."

Roach looked at Fogarty and nodded his head.

"Dave, Sharon, I want you to go back out there, go to all the hospitals again. Talk to everybody who was on duty that night and the following morning: Ambulance drivers, interns, hell, talk to cab drivers, bus drivers, people in the street, somebody's got to know something. Let's do it one more time."

The patient's body weight dropped from 220 pounds to 190 pounds within the first five days. With kidneys functioning at twenty-five percent, the poisons circulating through the system caused the blond hair to turn a silver-grey. Muscles, once pumped and hard, hung like ruptured inner tubes, and the few hours in which there was sufficient energy for consciousness were spent in uncontrollable sobbing. Not only flesh and muscle were dissolving without the stimulation of the drugs and exercise, but the testosterone-induced armor plating that had housed and supported the personality of Jack Dunne was evaporating, leaving a residue of fear and self-hatred.

Sleep was torment; there was fire and death. Often there were animals in the dreams, deer and fox, running across fields, through bushes and trees, to a highway, dark and lonely. Running from the heat and flames of the burning farmhouse.

Waking to find Rachel Saunders, looking down, repeating a name—Jacqueline—a name that was shrouded in blood-colored memories.

J. DOE

It had been eight days since J. Doe's admission to the hospital in Bryn Mawr. Eight days that Rachel Saunders had kept their secret.

She and Josef were sitting together on the sofa, each with a glass of wine. The local six o'clock news was on, and the story of Horst Nickles and his Animals gymnasium was the feature. Drug rings, pornography, murder; it was a televised tabloid. Tanaka watched, always surprised at the difference between fact and fabrication. According to the reporter, Nickles had been a Mr. Universe, and Wayne Brosky, a promising college student. The story claimed that the "steroid syndicate," operated by Nickles, was "nationwide," and netted profits of four million dollars a year. The Philadelphia police department was reported as heading the crackdown on the entire organization.

Tanaka was wondering which city official had fed the misinformation to the television journalists, when the altered Horst Nickles's police drawing of Jack Dunne appeared on the screen. Dunne's hair was short and he was shaven, but his eyes were unmistakable.

"In connection with the Wayne Brosky murder investigation, the police are searching for this man. His name is Jack Dunne. He is six-feet-one-inch in height and approximately two hundred and twenty pounds. Muscular, with—"

Click. The television screen went black.

Tanaka turned as Rachel laid the remote on the table.

"I know where he is," she said quietly.

"Who?"

"Jack Dunne. I know where he is," she repeated.

Josef stared at her, "What do you mean, you know where Jack Dunne is?"

"I need a month, Josef, you've got to promise me a month.

No police, no Bill Fogarty. If you'll do that, I'll tell you. I'll tell you everything."

J. Doe walked on the eleventh day.

"Bodyweight's down to one-sixty," Schwab whispered, as the gowned figure stepped towards them like a tentative infant. "The kidneys are working more efficiently, and we've got a near normal blood pressure."

J. Doe stumbled, and Rachel and Schwab rushed forward, gripping the soft body and guiding it back to the bed.

"I want to start with the heat treatment next week," Schwab said, looking at Rachel. "I think there will be just enough physical strength by then to withstand it."

The heat treatment was the reason that Rachel Saunders had requested Richard Schwab; he was the first doctor on the East Coast of America to test and verify the results of a detox program that had been pioneered in Australia. The treatment remained controversial, because it was a natural cure, based on exercise and sweat. An hour of intense physical activity, preferably running, followed by five hours in a 180-degree sauna. J. Doe's treatment would begin with fifteen minutes of assisted walking, followed by half-an-hour in the sauna, progressing from there. Hopefully, it would drain from the fat cells the toxins created by the incapacitation of the liver and kidneys, and flush them through the pores of the body. Otherwise, the poisons would crystallize and remain for life. Schwab had used the heat treatment on two Villanova University football players, and documented significant results.

"Rachel?" The voice was still low and hoarse, but it was changing; there was no aggression inside the tone, less torment.

Rachel walked to the side of the bed.

"I look like hell, don't I?"

"You're getting better," Rachel answered.

"I saw myself in the mirror this morning," then, the voice stalled and broke, "that can't be me. Can't be me."

"You're safe now, safe," Rachel reassured.

Safe? Safe from the demons that waited on the other side of consciousness, safe from the rubber fingers and the flames that invaded sleep? Where was Jack? Jack had been the protector, and Jack was gone.

"They're all gone," Rachel said, "dead or locked up, nobody is going to hurt you again. Ever."

Nineteen days. Nearly three weeks. An eternity when the last piece of the puzzle won't fit into place, when it seemed to have disappeared from the face of the earth.

Jack Dunne got away clean, that's the way I wanted it, Bill Fogarty told himself for the hundredth time, I didn't want to put Jack Dunne inside. I got Nickles, and Nickles will do life, and that's good enough.

But it wasn't good enough. If it had been good enough Fogarty would have closed the case, taken Gilbey and Roach off the streets, stopped sifting through the clothing and pictures from the Trinity. The place had been like a training camp, exercise equipment, drugs, syringes, and food supplements. Except for the room on the second floor; that had been a shrine to Jacqueline Dunne.

Fogarty continued to phone his contacts in Johnstown and Lancaster; and he continued to study the copy of the four-year-old police report that sat, open, on his desk. He kept staring at the picture of Jacqueline Dunne, rereading the details of her case, as if there was something he had missed, sitting there, in front of him.

It was six-thirty in the afternoon, Friday, the 25th of March, and it was Josef Tanaka's birthday.

Mentally, Fogarty was trying to shut down for the weekend, attempting to turn off his frustration, but it continued to seep into his consciousness, like a leaky tap, dripping anxiety. He picked up the J. Dunne file and placed it inside his top drawer, then closed the drawer, locking it, as if that would stop the leak.

Finally, he swivelled around in his chair and looked from his window, out above the commuter traffic, into the cold, clear sky. More to my life than one unsolved case, he told himself, thinking suddenly of next weekend, and Diane Genero. She was coming to town, planning to spend the weekend at his apartment. And tonight? Tonight was Josef's birthday dinner, just the three of them, like family. When he'd asked Rachel what he could give Josef, she'd told him about the Harley and suggested any of the number of accessories that went with the new bike. He'd picked up a black, leather-covered open-faced helmet, then added a set of police-issue riding gloves. They were still in the plastic Center City Cycles bag, and he wondered if he could get to Tanaka's apartment early enough to have Rachel wrap them. He was feeling better by the time he lifted the phone to dial her office. It was then that Dave Roach walked through the door of homicide and headed straight for him.

"G . . . ot something, Captain, I think I got something."

Fogarty placed the phone down.

Roach was holding a plastic evidence bag in his hand.

"What is it, Dave?"

Roach laid the bag on Fogarty's desk.

Fogarty could see the shoe inside the bag. It was a black shoe.

"Size eight, Captain, small for a guy that size, but the blood type matches—"

"Slow down, Detective, slow down."

"It belonged to Jack Dunne," Roach stated.

Fogarty nodded and removed the shoe from the bag. "Where did you get it?"

"You know Marty the Hat?"

Everybody who'd ever walked a beat knew Marty the Hat. Marty was a street person. Had been for as long as Fogarty could remember. His name, *the Hat* was derived from the red-plastic colander that he wore tied to his head. He pushed a shopping cart which carried all his earthly belongings and, rain or shine, Marty lived outdoors. It was only when he camped in front of the more exclusive Center City residences that the police were notified.

"Sure, I know Marty."

"I was talking to him, in connection with Jack Dunne, and I spotted the shoe in his cart. It just caught my eye, looked like a cop's shoe, and it looked like it had blood on it. Marty says he picked it up from the sidewalk in front of Rittenhouse Square," Roach continued, as Fogarty examined the leather shoe, with its thick, rubber sole. "I had forensics check it, the blood type matches the blood at the crime scene, and the footprints found at the scene match the shoe."

"You sure it was Rittenhouse Square?" Fogarty asked, warming up.

"There were three registered complaints about Marty being there that night," Roach answered. "He's still living in that area, and he says he remembers where everything in his cart comes from. Calls them his 'travelling parts'."

"Did he see anything?"

"Nope. Just the shoe. Makes sense, though. Jack Dunne was tracked going west. Rittenhouse Square is west of Broad," Roach said, hesitating, "Doctor Tanaka lives around there, doesn't he?"

Fogarty looked up into Roach's eyes. There was no insinuation.

"Yes, Josef and his wife live right on the square," Fogarty answered, as something clicked in his mind. "Good work, Dave, really good," he continued, smoothing it over, "let me hold on to the shoe. I've got a couple of ideas. You stay out there, keep talking to people."

Fogarty waited for Roach to leave his office before he unlocked his top drawer and removed the police file on Jacqueline Dunne. He turned quickly to the last page of the file, scanning downwards until he found the section that contained an account of Detective Dunne's personal injuries. "Multiple wounding to head and face," was written in longhand in the column adjacent to "required rhinoplasty and other reconstructive surgical procedures." Fogarty had read the same words before, many times, without attaching particular significance to them. After all, he had seen the videotape of Officer Dunne's beating; the few scrawled sentences were a sham when compared to the visual evidence. Now, he had a hunch. It was a far shot, and he didn't like the implications, but he couldn't deny it. He picked up his phone and asked to be connected to Reuben Jakes.

"Reuben, it's Bill Fogarty. Listen Reuben, I need you to tell me something. I've got it down in the Jacqueline Dunne file that she had some reconstructive surgery to her face. No doctor's name is given in the report. I need to know who did the work. It's real important to me. Reuben, do you remember who it was?"

Fogarty arrived at Tanaka's apartment building at eight o'clock. He was carrying the bag containing the helmet and gloves. He took the elevator to the second floor, walked to Tanaka's door, and hesitated.

FE/MALE

It was a woman doctor. Jacqui wouldn't let a man near her. It had to be a woman, Jakes had replied after a few seconds of thought. Cinders, or Sanders. Something like that. I think she worked out of University Hospital.

Fogarty had thanked him and put the phone down before Jakes could even ask why? And now, Bill Fogarty was moments away. From what? Arresting Rachel Saunders on a conspiracy charge? Or Josef? Was Josef involved? He'd hardly spoken with Josef in the last two weeks. Had Tanaka been avoiding him?

Fogarty wanted to turn and walk away. Except for Diane Genero, Rachel and Josef were the only true friends he had. And now he was contemplating their arrest.

He rang the entry buzzer. He heard footsteps on the other side of the door, and asked himself, *How am I going to do this?*

The door opened.

"Bill!" Rachel beamed, her smile dispelling his paranoia.

Josef was a step behind her.

"Happy birthday, kid!" Fogarty said, extending the bag containing the helmet and gloves.

"Thanks, Bill," Tanaka replied, smiling as he accepted the gift. Then, "Champagne? I'll get you some champagne." And Tanaka was gone, walking towards the kitchen.

He didn't meet my eyes. Couldn't look me in the eyes. Fogarty's paranoia returned.

Dinner was a mixture of Japanese and American cuisine. Soft noodles and tempura for Tanaka, marinated slices of chicken, steak, and fresh green salad for Rachel and Fogarty. Rachel had never been a fan of soba, noodles made from buckwheat flower, and she knew that Fogarty was a steak and potatoes man from way back. Tonight, however, she'd omitted the potatoes in deference to his new diet.

"You look good, Bill, you've lost more weight," Tanaka commented, pouring the last of a bottle of Merlot into Fogarty's glass.

"I thought you said I shouldn't drink wine with dinner. Isn't the sugar going to make me store body fat?" Fogarty asked. It was his third glass and he was feeling it. Relaxed.

"It's my birthday, Bill, you can swing a little," Tanaka answered.

"You haven't even seen Josef's new bike. It's a work of art," Rachel added.

"If I could get it inside the elevator, I'd keep it in the living room," Tanaka added.

Fogarty laughed, looking across the table at Josef. Tanaka's face was laughing, but not his eyes. Fogarty held them a moment.

"Come on, let's go down and see the bike," Josef said, pushing away from the table.

"We haven't had the cake yet," Rachel protested.

"I've got to show Bill the bike," Tanaka insisted. He was already walking towards the door, as if he needed to get out of the room.

Rachel was suddenly serious and Fogarty caught the glance between them. "Come on, Joey, sit down," she said.

Tanaka returned to the table. The mood of joviality had popped like a bubble.

"How's the case going, Bill?" he asked.

"Jack Dunne?" Fogarty noticed that the name added to the sobriety of the room.

"Yes."

"Well, it's funny you asked, cause today we had a break."

"What kind of break?" Rachel enquired. She was on her feet, walking towards the kitchen.

"One of my detectives came up with one of Jack Dunne's shoes. It should give us some idea which direction he took after the homicide on Front Street."

"Where?" Rachel asked, placing the chocolate layer cake in the center of the table.

Fogarty looked at the cake.

"There's no sugar in it," Rachel commented, making a stab for levity.

"Where?" Josef repeated.

He had them now, and he knew it. Something was going on. They were his best friends and they were holding back. It was still a hunch, but it was getting stronger. Fogarty waited, studying Josef.

"Right out in front of your place," he answered.

Suddenly the room was quiet, and Fogarty felt a mixture of apprehension and anger. He turned towards Rachel.

"About four years ago there was an incident involving an undercover policewoman. She was badly beaten up. Needed a lot of cosmetic repair. You might remember her. Her name was Jacqueline Dunne."

The silence deepened.

Fogarty kept his eyes on Rachel.

"You know where Jack Dunne is, don't you?" Playing his hunch. Laying it flat on the table. Risking everything. And for a moment, Fogarty feared that he had lost.

"We were going to tell you, Bill. I swear to God, we were going to tell you," Tanaka said, softly.

"We couldn't, not yet." Rachel sounded close to tears.

It was, to Fogarty, as if the last people he would ever trust had died in front of him. Josef and Rachel had been his family, his friends. He would have given his life for Josef and Rachel. And now, they had become strangers.

"How could you do this to me?"

"I was protecting you, Bill," Tanaka replied. "I didn't want to put you in the position we were in. Didn't want to compromise you. I couldn't."

Fogarty was confused.

"Come on, Bill, come on," Rachel said, reaching across to touch his arm, guiding him up from the table.

* * *

The elevator bumped to a halt at the garage level of the building. Rachel, Fogarty, and Tanaka stepped out, turning to the right. The black and chrome Harley Davidson Softail shimmered beneath the fluorescent overhead lighting.

They walked past the bike and got into Rachel's Mercedes. Rachel drove, with Josef beside her, and Fogarty in the backseat. They went west out of the city, onto the expressway, continuing to the City Line Avenue exit. Fogarty looked up at the Presidential Apartment Building; he could see the window of his place, the old air conditioner, grey and rusted. They drove past, continuing out, towards the suburbs.

The Bryn Mawr Center for Reconstructive Surgery was a large, two-storey complex directly off Lancaster Pike.

The parking lot was half empty. Rachel pulled into a space marked RESERVED, shut off the engine, then turned and looked back at Fogarty.

"I'm sorry, Bill, but no matter how carefully you would have handled this, there would have been police guards, doctors, physical examinations, psychological tests and, probably, somebody would have leaked it to the media. It would have destroyed a human being. I couldn't be responsible for that."

Fogarty met her eyes and nodded his head, then followed Josef out of the passenger side of the car. Their footsteps echoed against the red-brick walls of the building.

The receptionist looked up from her switchboard as they entered the building. Rachel walked to her and spoke quietly.

"Yes, certainly," the receptionist answered, "you know where the room is, don't you?"

Rachel nodded and motioned the two men forward. Leading them down a long corridor and to the door of room 21A. There, she turned towards them.

"Please, let me go in first. I'll only be a minute, just a minute."

Tanaka looked at Fogarty as if to acknowledge that the policeman was in charge.

"Go ahead," Fogarty answered.

Rachel opened the door and walked into the room, closing it quickly behind her.

Fogarty was nervous. He reached back over his right hip and unfastened the safety snap to his holster.

"You're not going to need that, Bill," Tanaka whispered.

Fogarty removed his hand from his weapon as Rachel opened the door to 21A. She stood aside as they entered. The lights were dim and he could only make out the outline of a figure in the bed.

Rachel stood to his side; her eyes begged for understanding.

"Bill, I want you to meet Jacqueline Dunne."

The name stunned him. He walked forward as far as the night table, looking down at the figure's face. It was porcelain smooth, the skin a fresh pink, cleansed pure from the hours in the sauna. The eyes were pale blue; the same eyes that had stared at Fogarty a thousand times from photographs. Now they were real, in front of him.

Jacqueline Dunne pushed herself up against her pillow. She weighed 145 pounds and her small, rounded breasts pressed outward against the cotton hospital gown; the glow from the overhead light created a halo around her silvered hair.

High Angel. It was the only thing Fogarty could think of.

Finally, he managed to speak. "Jack Dunne. I'm looking for Jack Dunne."

Jacqueline stared at the policeman as if she was using him as an anchor, as if speech had been removed from her reality, and maybe, this one time, she had something to hold onto, something solid and sure. There was a painful hesitation as she breathed in, then out, clearing her throat, all the time clinging to Fogarty's eyes.

"Jack isn't here." Her voice was low and hoarse.

Fogarty's mind was racing. There was something about

Jacqueline Dunne's voice, something wrong, and, her face; he studied her face. Her features appeared distorted, as if they had been enlarged, the jaw made more square, the nose more wide. Wide, like in the police drawing. He tried to imagine Jacqueline Dunne with long, blonde hair.

He bent down closer, stopping only when she withdrew, pushing back from him, her shoulders tight against the wall. He could see the shadow of beard beneath the flush of her skin. And suddenly, Fogarty knew. Didn't understand *how*, or *why*, but, he knew.

Jacqueline cleared her throat. "My brother died in a fire; there was nothing I could do to save him. Jack Dunne is dead." It had taken hours of psychotherapy for Jacqueline to say those words and, even as she did, fear overcame her. She was alone. No one to protect her. Terror. She fell forward, clutching her pillow, pulling it to her body, curling around it. Heaving giant breaths, sobbing.

Rachel ran to the bed and took the trembling woman in her arms, cradling her. "It's all right, Jacqueline, it's all right, you're safe now, safe."

Tanaka looked at Fogarty and whispered, "Let's go outside."

They stood in the empty corridor, beyond the closed door.

"I've only known for a week, Bill. It's been the hardest thing I've ever lived with; I was going to tell you. We'd both agreed to tell you. It was just that Rachel wanted more time to contain some of the damage. She figured if she could get the physical effects of the drugs under control then a lot of the mental symptoms would fade. Rachel was afraid for her. Afraid that if she was forced to speak to a lot of people, to answer questions, to go through any kind of physical examination, that it would finish her completely; she'd be ruined," Tanaka hesitated, placing his hand on Fogarty's shoulder. "We didn't have any doubts about you, Bill, you've got to believe that. We just didn't want to put you in that position, as a police officer."

"What position do you think I'm in now, Josef?"

"Bill, I'm sorry."

Fogarty looked at the closed door. "So that's my suspect. That's my killer."

Tanaka shook his head.

Fogarty met his eyes.

"The person inside that room is Jacqueline Dunne. She's not a killer; she's a victim."

"She committed the crimes," Fogarty replied.

"What happened to her, physically, is termed *viralization*. The deep voice, the body hair, the thickening of the skin, the enlargement of the facial bones, the sexual organ—"

"I don't follow you?"

"Her clitoris has increased to about ten times its normal size; it resembles a small penis. Physically and emotionally, Jacqueline Dunne was in the process of becoming a man."

"Jesus."

"The physical changes are irreversible, permanent."

Fogarty lowered his eyes and shook his head.

"It's her mind that we need to save," Tanaka continued, "Jacqueline Dunne had already been diagnosed as paranoid schizophrenic when she began using the drugs. She'd lost her family in a fire. They'd been taking care of her till then, her mother, father, and brother. But it was her brother, Jack, who was the strongest influence. He had her confidence; he gave her strength, looked after her. So, when her mind broke, when she needed to escape the trauma of what had happened to her, and what had happened to Jack, her protector; she became him, Jack Dunne. Nickles was the key; he'd taught her how to use the steroids, and the more male hormone she pumped into herself the further from Jacqueline, and Jacqueline's pain, she was able to go. She developed a man's physical strength, size, aggression."

"How the hell will I take her to trial?"

"The best you'd do is get her committed to an institution for the criminally insane," Tanaka answered.

Fogarty looked up.

"What's my alternative? You were at those crime scenes; you saw what she did."

"I also saw the Flint tape. I saw what they did, too."

"I'm a police officer, Josef," Fogarty stated.

"So you're going to get her locked up in some state institution? Where they can control what's left of her with more drugs. Strap her to a bed—"

The door opened, interrupting them.

"She's asleep," Rachel said quietly.

Fogarty looked at Tanaka, then walked past Rachel, into Jacqueline's room. He closed the door behind him.

Fogarty walked to the woman in the bed, memories of crime scenes and videotapes spiralling. Ugly, gnarled memories, of rape and torture. He remembered how he felt when he'd first watched the Flint tape. His own anger, his own desire for revenge.

He stopped at the bed.

Jacqueline was lying on her back, her head against the pillow. In sleep, with her features relaxed and her breathing slowed, she looked more like the picture from her police I.D., more like the photographs that had been recovered from the Trinity, when she had been Officer Jacqueline Dunne, from North Division. The young woman they'd nicknamed High Angel.

Fogarty remained like that a minute, looking down, studying her face, watching her breathe. "Why did this happen to you, Jacqui? Why?" he asked, reaching out, laying his hand softly against her cheek.

It was as he touched her that she opened her eyes, creating a vertigo between them, pulling Fogarty down, into the pale blue.

"I've seen some bad times, too, lost my family, got my scars," the words fell from his mouth, "but it gets better. Trust me, Jacqui, it's going to get a whole lot better."

He thought he saw a smile on her lips but he wasn't certain. He just knew, by the look in her eyes, that she was not afraid of him, and that made all the difference.

"You've got friends here, Jacqui, friends. We look after our own."

Fogarty bent down and kissed Jacqueline Dunne lightly on the forehead. Then he turned and walked from the room.

Rachel and Josef were on the other side of the door. Neither of them spoke.

"I'm going to close the investigation," Fogarty said.

"I don't understand," Rachel replied.

Fogarty looked from Rachel to Josef, then back to Rachel. "The suspect in my investigation was a male, Caucasian, named Jack Dunne. Jack Dunne is dead. My case is closed."

EPILOGUE

Jacqueline Dunne remains at the Waterford Institute in Big Sur, California. The Institute is privately owned and was founded by Rand Waterford, a longtime friend and associate of Stan Leibowitz. Jacqueline has undergone electrolysis to remove her facial and body hair, and undergone intensive megavitamin therapy to rejuvenate her damaged organs. Mentally, she is responding well to intensive psychotherapy, and a release date has been tentatively scheduled for 1998.